Praise for A. J. Matthew's debut thriller

The White Room

"A suspense thriller with a dash of the supernatural . . .
builds to an exciting and satisfying conclusion."
—*Cemetery Dance*

And praise for

Looking Glass

"This gut-wrenching story offers a supernatural twist that
lies in waiting like a coiled stinger . . . extraordinarily ef-
fective. The climax is first-rate. This is [A. J. Matthews]
at the top of his game." —*Cemetery Dance*

"What an incredible book! *Looking Glass* is like no other
you've read. You won't be disappointed."
—BookReviewCafe.com

UNBROKEN

A. J. MATTHEWS

BERKLEY BOOKS, NEW YORK

THE BERKLEY PUBLISHING GROUP
Published by the Penguin Group
Penguin Group (USA) Inc.
375 Hudson Street, New York, New York 10014, USA
Penguin Group (Canada), 90 Eglinton Avenue East, Suite 700, Toronto, Ontario M4P 2Y3, Canada
(a division of Pearson Penguin Canada Inc.)
Penguin Books Ltd., 80 Strand, London WC2R 0RL, England
Penguin Group Ireland, 25 St. Stephen's Green, Dublin 2, Ireland (a division of Penguin Books Ltd.)
Penguin Group (Australia), 250 Camberwell Road, Camberwell, Victoria 3124, Australia
(a division of Pearson Australia Group Pty. Ltd.)
Penguin Books India Pvt. Ltd., 11 Community Centre, Panchsheel Park, New Delhi—110 017, India
Penguin Group (NZ), 67 Apollo Drive, Mairangi Bay, Auckland 1311, New Zealand
(a division of Pearson New Zealand Ltd.)
Penguin Books (South Africa) (Pty.) Ltd., 24 Sturdee Avenue, Rosebank, Johannesburg 2196,
South Africa

Penguin Books Ltd., Registered Offices: 80 Strand, London WC2R 0RL, England

UNBROKEN

A Berkley Book / published by arrangement with the author

PRINTING HISTORY
Berkley edition / April 2007

Copyright © 2007 by Rick Hautala.
Cover illustration by Cliff Nielsen.
Cover design by Annette Fiore.
Interior text design by Laura K. Corless.

ISBN: 978-0-425-21480-0

BERKLEY®
Berkley Books are published by The Berkley Publishing Group,
a division of Penguin Group (USA) Inc.,
375 Hudson Street, New York, New York 10014.
BERKLEY is a registered trademark of Penguin Group (USA) Inc.
The "B" design is a trademark belonging to Penguin Group (USA) Inc.

PRINTED IN THE UNITED STATES OF AMERICA

10 9 8 7 6 5 4 3 2 1

*To Christopher Golden,
who noodges and prods
and keeps this old scrivener working,
even when he'd prefer not to.*

All of my life I've been afraid
Something's gotta change
And I don't know what
But it's got to be right now
Blessed by the stars above
You'll be alone and awake when they find you

Satellite Lot, 'Long Lost Love'
From their CD *Second Summer*

❧

Since we cannot change reality,
let us change
the eyes which see reality.

Nikos Kazantzakis,
Report to Greco

CHAPTER 1

Frozen Lightning

~1~

"Where'd you go last night?"

Kiera Davis jumped when her husband asked her that question, but she didn't answer him right away. Her first thought was, *I could ask you the same question,* but she was slumped at the kitchen table, her shoulders hunched forward as she cradled her head with both hands. Her thumbs supported her chin, while her fingertips pressed with steady pressure against her forehead and temples. Her long, red hair fell forward in a cascade that fringed the limits of her vision with a rich, ruby glow.

Faint echoes of the migraine she'd had last night shot hot, bright sparks of electricity through her temples when she turned her head, ever so slightly, and looked up at Nate. He was standing in the doorway that led down a short hallway to the front foyer. He was barefoot and wearing a dark blue golf shirt and faded, tattered jeans. His thinning brown hair was still wet from his morning shower. Kiera noticed that it needed a trim.

"I was here . . . at home," she said, noticing the constriction in her throat that pitched her voice just a little higher than usual. She'd hoped she wouldn't have to remind Nate about the headache she'd suffered all night, but it took too much effort even to say that much. She was worried that, if she made even the slightest movement, the migraine would come roaring back full force.

"That's funny . . . I could have sworn I saw you driving downtown when I was heading home last night."

"What time was that?"

"Round one o'clock."

Kiera squinted, praying the pain wouldn't come back.

"I think I was still on the couch around that time . . . with an ice pack on my head."

"Hmm . . . It sure looked like your car."

Kiera sighed, not daring to shake her head, but she said, "Chances are I'm not the only person in town with a dark blue Volvo." She didn't like how snappy she sounded, but she couldn't help herself.

"I could have sworn it was you."

Nate moved over to the counter and poured a cup of coffee. After adding milk and sugar—leaving the carton of milk on the counter like he always did—he came over to sit down in his usual chair at the kitchen table.

"So, did you have fun last night with your poker buddies?" Kiera asked after a long silence.

She was trying not to wonder if that's where he *really* had been, but she was in too much pain and too tired to go there now. The pain was still hovering behind her eyes, threatening to break loose any second. She had a sharp mental image of a huge, opaque curtain with something horrible lurking behind it, just waiting to slash through it.

"Always do," Nate said as he took a slurping sip from

his coffee and leaned back in his chair, hooking his thumb through one of his belt loops as he gazed outside.

Kiera watched him without moving her head or eyes any more than she had to. Her peripheral vision was still vibrating with splinters of white light, and the edges of her sight kept breaking up like poor reception on a television. When neither of them was talking, she could hear a low humming sound, just at the edge of hearing. It wavered up and down with a steady throb that she was convinced any second now would rise in intensity and bring the migraine back full force.

"You win last night?" Kiera was mildly surprised that speaking didn't make things any worse. At least not yet.

"Winning's not the point," Nate said after another noisy sip of coffee. "It's just fun to get together, have a few beers, shoot the shit, and relax."

Kiera sniffed with laughter, trying not to remember how many times she suspected he *hadn't* been playing poker at all, but today, she could smell the cigar smoke that still clung to him.

"How much did you lose?"

The silence that followed made the humming in her head all the louder. She flinched when a sudden pulse behind her left eye sent a flash of white light across her vision. For a frozen instant, the light hovered like the piercing eye of a searchlight. Then it slowly dissolved into a wavering line, looking like a bolt of lightning frozen on film.

Kiera moaned softly as she pressed her fingers harder against her forehead and temples as if trying to contain the inevitable explosion that would follow. She half expected to hear a deep, grumbling roll of thunder. When she shifted her eyes to one side, the jagged streak of white light shifted, too, cutting her vision in half. Looking at Nate, the frozen white streak split him down the middle.

"You okay?" Nate asked, shifting in his chair and looking at her earnestly.

Does he really care? Kiera wondered, but not daring to speak or move her head even a little, she whispered, "Not really."

"Those migraines . . . They're bastards, huh?"

She nodded, but even the slightest motion made the pain worse. A thick, salty taste clogged the back of her throat, almost gagging her. She closed her eyes, but the white line remained, shifting back and forth as her eyes twitched involuntarily.

"Yeah. Another migraine," she whispered. "Or the same one I had yesterday. I don't think it ever really went away."

"What can I do for you?" Nate asked. As solicitous as he sounded, Kiera found herself getting irritated at him for taking so long to realize how bad she felt.

"I already took something," she said in a raw whisper.

When the white line across her vision drifted to the left, her eyes shifted with it, following it. Waves of vertigo swept over her, and she leaned forward, pressing her elbows hard against the table, desperate to orient herself. She could almost imagine that her eyes were revolving inside her head, spinning around in complete circles as she tried to follow the shifting line of frozen white lightning. The edges of the light were beginning to dissolve into thick, grainy blotches that flickered with a deep, violet glow. The feeling of tumbling head over heels grew so strong that Kiera braced herself, afraid she would cry out.

Why is this happening to me? she wanted to scream, but her rising panic choked her because of the memory that came back to her as she stared into the flickering white light.

Last night . . . when the migraine had started . . . it wasn't just a headache . . . she had *seen* something . . .

Most of her adult life, Kiera had suffered from migraines, but they were usually relatively mild. They certainly were nothing like the ones she'd been having for the last couple of weeks, since around the first of August during the worst of the summer heat. She had always ascribed them to tension or maybe a minor sinus problem. Lord knew she had enough tension in her life, but they usually centered just above her left eyebrow and always went away if she took some over-the-counter pain reliever and took a short nap.

But not lately. And the one last night had been the worst yet. It almost brought tears to her eyes, remembering how much she had suffered. And Nate out playing poker with his buddies—or wherever he was—didn't help, either. She tried to choke down the bitterness and sense of betrayal she felt, but she couldn't stop thinking, *He should have been here to help. Even if there was nothing he could do, he just should have* been *here with me.*

But the sad truth was, she felt as though he had never been there for her, no matter how different what had happened last night was.

Kiera closed her eyes and concentrated, forgetting all about Nate as she tried to recall what had happened yesterday. It was late in the afternoon, a little after four o'clock, when the migraine slammed into her like a freight train. She had just come back from shopping at the Maine Mall with her friends, Joanie and Marsha. She'd been about to take a quick shower before supper when the blinding pain had lanced through her forehead so hard she cried out, crumpled up, and covered her face with both hands.

Thinking about it now made her worry it would come back again, but she had to try to think this through. Why now, all of a sudden, were her headaches worse? It couldn't be just because of . . .

"No," she whispered, pursing her lips.

She knew she was missing or forgetting something. With her eyes closed, she shifted her eyes back and forth, staring at the wall of darkness before her. It was all too easy to imagine that the darkness didn't stop at her closed eyelids, that it had dimension and depth.

And what was it? What did I see?

As the jagged streak of frozen white lightning drifted across her vision, Kiera tightened the muscles in her arms and legs to keep them from trembling. The white line brightened and then dimmed in time with her hammering eyes to track it.

She wasn't sure exactly when, but at some point she realized the light had changed. It had happened so subtly she didn't realize it for a long time, but she was aware of . . . something—a dark mass—between her and the light. Because the light was drifting slowly to the left, the object also moved whenever she shifted her eyes, so she could never look at it directly. She stopped moving her eyes and looked to one side, trying to see the object from the corner of her eye. The shape was less distinct, but she realized it was a human silhouette.

Her heart skipped a beat and started racing, and her breath caught in her throat. Sweat broke out across her forehead, and a tightening choking sensation wrapped cold fingers around her throat. She wanted to look directly at whatever this was, but she knew it would dissolve the instant she shifted her eyes, so she kept staring straight ahead, concentrating and willing it to come into focus.

The shape was blurred, but it certainly *looked* like a person. It was so hazy against the blinding glare of the frozen lightning she wasn't even sure if the person—if that's really what it was!—was facing her or turned away. She made a tiny sound in the back of her throat but stopped herself before she spoke out loud.

The figure shifted to one side, almost lost in the glaring brilliance, but a chill ran up her back when she realized it was subtly moving toward her. She watched with steadily mounting horror as the shape resolved more clearly. As it got closer, it raised one hand as though reaching out to grab her. Kiera stared at the hand that was coming closer . . . ever closer to her, its fingers curled like a hawk's talons.

That's what I saw last night, only I didn't have my eyes closed!

It was in the house!

What she was seeing now mixed with the memory of what she had seen last night. She couldn't breathe as the figure glided steadily closer, its outstretched hand grasping at her, clawing as though it wanted to catch hold of her and drag her into that burning, white light.

Kiera moaned softly and involuntarily raised her right hand, but she had no idea if it was to protect herself or to take hold of the hand reaching out to her. Her chest ached from holding her breath so long, and the cry building up inside her was close to bursting out of her as a scream.

A sudden pressure on her shoulder made her squeal. Jerking back, she lashed out with her hand, which made a loud *smack* when it contacted with something solid.

"Ahh! . . . Jesus!"

Her eyes were still closed, and it took her a moment to recognize Nate's voice. She opened her eyes just enough to see him standing beside her, but he was shying away from her and rubbing his arm on the biceps.

"What the *hell*?"

After another heartbeat or two, her confusion started to clear. Kiera was stunned as she looked at her husband.

"What's the matter with you?"

She wasn't sure she believed the wounded look on his face. She couldn't move. She just sat there, blinking her eyes in confusion. A faint flash of light shot across her vision, but it dissolved instantly and—thankfully—wasn't followed by any corresponding pain in her head.

"I . . . You startled me," she said, conscious of how lame she sounded. "I wasn't expecting you to . . ."

Nate looked at her, a forced smile twisting one corner of his mouth. He kept a safe distance between them, looking at her like she was a snake that would strike without warning.

"Did you even hear what I said?" he asked.

Kiera looked at him, totally confused, and shook her head. She was waiting for the migraine to come roaring back, but—for now, anyway—it didn't.

"No . . . What'd you say?"

"I said I was going over to the high school. I want to make sure everything's ready for when school starts next week."

Kiera stared at him, taking a long time to process what he'd just said. Then she nodded and said, "Yeah. Okay."

"You gonna be okay, with the headaches and all?"

Kiera winced as she massaged her left eyebrow. It struck her as a little sad how no matter what Nate said or did, it seemed terribly inadequate. She glanced at him and found herself wondering—again—just how far apart they had drifted. After more than twenty years of marriage and one child—their daughter Trista, who was seventeen and going to graduate next June—they seemed like separate planets that orbited around each other but never came into contact. Maybe they had always been like that.

"Trista still in bed?" Nate asked.

"What do you think? Does any teenager get up before noon . . . especially at the end of summer vacation?"

"Well, if you need anything from the store or whatever, maybe she can get it for you . . . or call my cell." When he hesitated and looked at her, Kiera thought for a moment she caught a trace of genuine concern in his eyes. "You sure you'll be all right?"

"I'm sure. I'm going to take it easy this morning. I'm playing tennis with Jon and Liz this afternoon. Alex Burdette is going to join us for doubles."

"At the high school courts?" Nate asked.

Kiera thought she caught a look of momentary anxiety in his eyes before he smiled.

"We always play there," she said.

His question struck her as odd, and she wondered if there was something he wasn't telling her, but she let it drop. If she started in with him now, they'd end up arguing and ruin the day for both of them. Maybe he didn't like the idea of her playing tennis with Alex . . . or maybe it was Jon, who she had dated years ago, back in high school.

As if he has any right to be jealous, she thought. *Is that it? . . . Does he think I'm not going to be playing tennis at all? . . . Does he think I'm having an affair with Alex or Jon?*

That struck her as rather ironic because, for all his faults, Nate never struck her as the suspicious type. She was about to mention it but decided not to.

Let him have his little suspicions, she thought. *It might do us some good for him not to take me so much for granted.*

"What time's your game?" Nate asked.

Now that she was looking for it, Kiera was positive she caught a hint of suspicion in his tone. What was he going to do, skulk around and spy on her? Maybe he could see the tennis courts from his classroom window. What if he set up a telescope in his room to watch her, to make sure that's what she was doing?

Kiera found that amusing. Their relationship certainly wasn't the best thing going, but cheating was the farthest thing from *her* mind, even with Jon O'Keefe. They had dated in high school, but that had been so long ago it seemed like another life. If she was ever going to have an affair, overweight, balding, married Jon O'Keefe was low on the list.

No, if she needed anything, it was just a little more attention from her husband. It struck her as more than a little sad how out of touch they had grown over the years, and how both of them seemed to accept it as the natural course of events.

Or maybe it had always been that way, and something— something was building up inside her now that was just making her see it.

"I guess I'm off then," Nate said, leaning forward and giving her a perfunctory kiss on the cheek. It still seemed like he was holding back on her, as though he didn't quite trust her. "I'll keep my cell on, so call me if you need anything."

"Yeah. Sure thing," Kiera said, twisting in her seat and watching as he grabbed his car keys from the counter, patted his back pocket to make sure he had his wallet, and went out the door into the garage.

The garage door rattled up, and she cringed, her teeth on edge when his car started up. Thankfully, the migraine didn't return. Nate's tires made a high-pitched chirping sound on the cement floor as he backed out into the driveway perhaps a little too fast. Kiera stayed where she was, staring at the closed door and listening as the garage door rattled back down. The sound masked the receding sound of Nate's car as he pulled out onto the street. Only once the house was quiet again . . . quiet except for the low humming of the refrigerator . . . did a thought occur to Kiera.

What if Nate's acting so strange . . . not because he thinks I'm having an affair . . . but because he is?

They had dealt with that issue a few years ago, and she had thought . . . had hoped they had worked it all out, but as she got up to clear the kitchen table, Kiera told herself she had to be vigilant and watch for any signs that things might be getting bad again.

~2~

The *thwock* and *ping* of the tennis ball as it bounced off the asphalt and strings of tennis racquets echoed in the little hollow where the town had built the high school's four tennis courts. Even this late in the day, the afternoon was hot and humid. A bank of thunderheads as dark as ripe plums lined the western horizon. Kiera hoped it would rain later to break the sticky heat. Even before they'd finished warming up, she was dripping with sweat, but it felt good not to have any lingering traces of the migraine.

Today, she and Jon were partners, pitted against Jon's wife Liz and Alex Burdette, the local pharmacist and another friend of theirs from high school days. After two sets, Kiera and Jon were ahead two to nothing, but Kiera knew she wasn't playing her best game, not with the worry that, at any second, her migraine might come roaring back.

She couldn't help but notice how comfortable she felt playing partners with Jon. They hadn't seen each other and had barely stayed in touch by letter or telephone over the years, but she had been happy when he and Liz, whom he met and married while in college in Boston, moved back to Stratford after living in Denver for the last twenty years. The reasons for Jon's return to Maine were sad. His father, Sam, had died, and Jon, being an only child, had come back home to help his aging mother, who died less than six months after his return. Still, after more than twenty-five years—ever since high school graduation, really—Kiera felt a connection with Jon that she didn't feel with any of her other friends.

Of course, the secret she and Jon shared bound them in ways much deeper than most friendships, but they never spoke about it, even though it seemed—at least to Kiera—always to be hovering between them like a dark, dangerous storm cloud. It was something she could honestly say she thought about every day for the past twenty-five years, and she knew she would carry it around with her until the day she died.

It was Kiera's serve, but even though they had been playing only a short time, she felt absolutely exhausted as she positioned her feet on the baseline and gripped her racquet. She bounced the ball a few times at her feet, but before she took her first serve, she had to step back from the line.

"Can we take a little break?" Her voice sounded thin, shaky. "I don't know about you guys, but this heat is killing me."

Everyone agreed to a break, so they walked over to the shaded side of the court. It didn't help much with the humidity, but at least it was shade. Kiera let out a sigh as she sat down on the asphalt and fished a bottle of Gatorade from her pack. Her hands felt almost too weak to unscrew the top, but she finally managed. Leaning her head back, she took a huge gulp, gasping as the cool liquid dropped like a sledgehammer into her stomach.

Jon, who was standing close beside her, toweled his face. Other than the three times a week they played tennis, he didn't get outside much. His face was flushed and red, and his thinning hair, which was going white above his ears, was plastered in thin strands against his forehead.

"You feeling all right?" he asked Kiera before leaning his head back and taking a noisy gulp from his Poland Spring water bottle. His wife was standing a little to one side and seemed more interested in adjusting the strings on her racquet than in anything Jon or Kiera might have to say. Alex had walked up the hill to his car to have a smoke.

Kiera squinted and looked up at him. Seeing him silhouetted against the hazy sky reminded her of the figure she had seen this morning and last night . . . the figure of someone reaching out to her from the slash of frozen white lightning.

"Yeah . . ." she said, swallowing hard. "I'm okay." She wiped her face on the sleeve of her tennis shirt and forced a smile. "It's just . . . the heat's got me down."

"Can't say as I blame you," Jon said. "It was hot in Denver, too, but I don't remember the humidity ever being this bad." He pinched his damp shirt on the shoulder and pulled it away from his skin. "Not like this."

"It's global warming," Liz piped in, but she said it with such a neutral tone Kiera couldn't tell if she was supposed to take her seriously or not. Liz was a few years younger than she and Jon, and Kiera didn't always get her sense of humor.

"Global warming's got nothing to do with a few exceptionally hot days," Jon said, sounding a bit perturbed as he glanced at his wife. "Global warming has to do with the average world temperature, which doesn't vary all that much but is rising—"

"I know what global warming is," Liz said. "I was making a joke."

"Well sor-*ry*," Jon said, rolling his eyes when he turned his back on Liz and looked at Kiera.

For her part, Kiera didn't want to get between them. From the time Jon moved back home, Kiera had picked up a not-so-hidden tension between him and his wife. Maybe it was that way in all relationships; she just had never noticed it before. But she couldn't help but wonder if it had anything to do with Jon seeing her after so many years.

The bottom line was, she didn't care.

As much as she enjoyed being around Jon again and doing things like playing tennis or going to a movie, she didn't feel anything like the old spark she'd once had for him. There was almost nothing of the young man she'd known and dated back in high school in this overweight, balding real estate agent. He was like a new person. And she couldn't help but wonder if the young girl she felt she still was in so many ways was just as lost to him.

"You know," Kiera said, changing the subject, even though she didn't think global warming warranted any kind of argument, "when it's really hot like this, we should play after dark and use the floodlights."

"Not a bad idea," Jon said.

"What's this about playing after dark?" Alex said, smiling wickedly as he opened the door to the court and walked over to them. "I'm always up for a game after dark."

Kiera groaned at Alex's feeble attempt at innuendo, and Jon gave him a not-so-light punch on the arm.

"Oh, good," Alex said, rubbing his upper arm. "Hurt my right arm so my game will be off . . ."

"Your game's off whenever we play," Jon said. "Whenever you're on my team with doubles, I feel like I'm playing with three women."

Kiera couldn't tell if he was joking or not, but it seemed as though Alex was getting a little mad.

"Hey, I got your doubles right here," Alex said as he grabbed his crotch and shook his hand. "Any day you wanna go one-on-one, buddy, I'll beat your sorry ass in straight sets."

"Your mouth is writing checks your ass can't cash," Jon said. He still had a good-humored lilt in his voice, but Kiera sensed there was more to this just below the surface. She wondered why she was always looking for deeper meaning in things people said. Jon and Alex always acted like this in high school, so maybe it was just the way guys—at least *these* guys—related. To her, it didn't sound like very much fun, though, and it never had.

"Enough, already," Liz said, her upper lip curling with undisguised disgust. "If you *boys* are done with your *macho* bullshit, can we play some tennis?"

Kiera caught the look Alex flashed at Jon that all but said: *Sorry you married such a bitch,* but everyone tossed their drink bottles and towels aside, grabbed their racquets, and trotted back onto the court.

Even on her first serve, though, Kiera knew she didn't have her game back. As she bounced the ball a few times and adjusted her grip, she felt a little off-balance and paused to take a deep breath. When she looked at Alex, who was waiting in the far court to receive her serve, a rim of darkness at the edges of her vision started to close in like a stage curtain, collapsing shut. She squinted and shook her head, unnerved to see that the outline of Alex's body was hazy, indistinct.

Jon, waiting at the net for the serve, seemed to catch her hesitation and glanced at her over his shoulder. A frown of concern wrinkled his forehead. His eyes, Kiera thought, glowed with an unusual brightness, giving her the impression they were filled with some internal light.

Kiera sucked in a breath, concentrating as she bounced the tennis ball a few more times and then tossed it above her head. She cocked her arm back, twisted slightly, and then swung at the ball when it was at its peak. Her racquet whistled through the air, the strings vibrating and creating a deep thrumming that momentarily took her focus off the ball. As she brought her swing down, she missed the ball entirely, and it bounced off the top of her head. At the end of her swing, she let go of the racquet, and it flew from her hand, clattering as it skittered across the asphalt.

For a split second, Kiera just stood there, hunched over and looking down at her feet. The bright green asphalt glowed and vibrated with frightening intensity. She had the disorienting impression she had actually sunk ankle-deep into the hot asphalt. A tiny whimper escaped her as her vision dimmed.

"Jesus, Kiera. Are you all right?" Jon called out as he dashed over to her. His voice echoed in her ears with a muffled thud. As he came forward, he extended his arms to catch her before she fell. Kiera braced herself and shook her head.

"Yeah . . . I just—" She shivered as she wiped her face on her shirtsleeve. "I just feel . . . I dunno . . ."

Jon was a few feet away from her, close enough so she could see beads of sweat on his face and smell the soap and aftershave he had used.

"If the heat's really getting to you, we don't have to play, you know."

Kiera looked from him to Liz and Alex, who were standing on the other side of the net. They both had funny expressions, like they had no idea what to say or do.

"I'll be all right," Kiera said, trying to shake the feeling off and wishing she could muster more strength in her voice.

Jon regarded her steadily for another few seconds and then went to retrieve her racquet. He inspected it before handing it back to her. Kiera saw scuff marks on the hand-grip, but she held it tightly as she fished another tennis ball from her pocket.

"Maybe we'll keep it to one set today," she said weakly as she went back to the line and got ready to serve. She was praying she could get control of herself, but she was concerned about what had happened to her vision. The darkness closing in from the edges and the sudden intensity of Alex's figure when she had looked at him were truly frightening. She feared her migraine was coming back, but she told herself just to keep playing. It would be all right.

Just go with the flow . . . Relax . . . Take it easy . . . This is supposed to be fun, she told herself, but she had a lump in her throat when she tossed the ball up and swatted at it with her racquet.

The impact sent a mild electric jolt up her arm to her shoulder, and she smiled with satisfaction when she carried through on the serve and watched the ball hit inside the service court and then shoot like a bullet past Alex before he even had time to set his swing.

"Ace! Way to go!" Jon said, turning around and smiling at her.

"I thought you'd ease up on your second serve," Alex said, smiling and shaking his head at his error.

"Technically, that was my first serve," Kiera said, trying

to get into the spirit of things, but she still felt odd. "I didn't make contact with that first one."

"Technically," Alex muttered as he moved in toward the net, and Liz stepped back to receive the next serve.

Kiera realized she'd been holding her breath and let it out slowly as she stepped up to the line and prepared to serve again. She had a ritual of bouncing the ball three or four times while spinning her racquet in her hand. When she had first started playing tennis, her coach had cautioned her not to do that, but it was a habit she found impossible to break.

In the far court, Liz bounced up and down on her toes as she waited for the serve. Just as Kiera tossed the ball into the air, Liz set her feet and crouched, leaning forward.

Kiera's serve was another solid one. It sprang off the strings of her racquet in a near perfect line and hit inside the centerline, but Liz was ready for it, and she gave the ball a firm return. Jon, at the net, darted for it and, with a light touch, dropped it only a few feet away from the net for the point.

"Pure luck," Liz said with a derisive snort as she approached the net, and Alex got set to receive.

"Pure skill's more like it," Jon said, smirking.

"Thirty love," Kiera said, not wanting them to get started again. She bounced the ball at her feet and spun her racquet to get a grip. When she was ready, she delivered another solid serve. As she watched Alex go for it, she was thinking how peculiar it was that, after that brief episode of whatever had just happened, she seemed to be fine. Whatever it was, it seemed to be gone now.

She watched as Alex, ready this time, made a solid return. The bright green ball made a *thunk* sound as it skipped off the court. Jon swung at it and missed completely, but

Kiera, honed and ready, planted her feet, cocked her racquet back, ready to swing, but she suddenly froze. In an instant, it was as if everything had stopped. An odd sepia-toned light suffused the court, and she had a brief impression that everything around her was trapped in amber.

Everything, that is, except the tennis ball.

It hummed as it flew through the air, getting steadily larger in her vision until it looked like a cannonball coming straight at her. She cringed and tried to swing her racquet or get out of the way, but her body wouldn't move. The racquet suddenly felt too heavy to hold. If she could have moved her fingers, she would have dropped it.

The tennis ball loomed in front of her with frightening intensity. At the very last instant, Kiera squealed as she turned her head to one side and ducked. The ball made a loud *thwack* when it smacked her in the side of the head just above her left ear. A brilliant flash of light exploded across her vision and was replaced an instant later by a shower of white sparks that corkscrewed into the sky like a display of fireworks. A loud sizzling sound filled her head, and everything around her disappeared into a blinding glare as her knees crumpled, and she went down, hard.

~3~

The next thing Kiera remembered, she was listening to voices. At first, they didn't make much sense.

". . . just standing there . . ."

". . . never even saw it coming . . ."

". . . lucky it didn't kill her . . ."

She was floating in a warm, comfortable darkness, and the voices were pulling her out of it, but she liked it here . . . wherever "here" was. There was no pain. No panic.

No worries. She thought she remembered something weird happening to her vision, that she had been seeing things with an odd intensity that made the edges of things vibrate, but down here in the darkness, there was none of that. Everything was warm . . . and dark . . . and soothing.

I don't want to go back, she thought or—maybe—said out loud. It didn't matter. Nothing mattered. She concentrated on staying right where she was and not allowing herself to be drawn back by the voices that were still speaking in excited tones around her.

She finally realized she was lying on something hard, so she knew she wasn't home in bed or in a hospital or anything. Besides, if she was home in bed, what were all these people doing in her house, talking about her like she wasn't even there?

". . . call nine one one . . ."

". . . should give her a few minutes . . ."

". . . something to drink . . ."

No! Don't do this to me! she wanted to cry out. Maybe she did say it out loud. She honestly couldn't tell. But she felt safe here, and she realized that for a long time, now, she hadn't really felt safe. Things in her life seemed always to be crushing down on her . . . things she didn't want to think about . . . things she didn't want to remember . . . things that made her feel threatened . . . but down here . . . in the darkness . . . she felt none of those things.

What's there to feel threatened about? she asked herself. *My life is just fine . . . Isn't it?*

But even as she asked herself that, she knew she was kidding herself. She didn't believe her own lie because she *did* feel threatened every day of her life . . . threatened and guilty. The worse part of it was, she couldn't talk to anyone about it . . . Not her husband or her friends or her daughter. There was *no one* she could talk to about how she felt.

How could she when she wasn't even sure herself?

But it didn't matter now . . . not down here . . . in the darkness . . .

". . . even know what you're doing . . ."

". . . have any better ideas . . ."

With each passing moment, Kiera became increasingly aware of the hard surface she was lying on. She let out a low moan—at least she thought she did—as she rolled her head from side to side. Something like pebbles or grit crunched against the back of her head. The sound echoed inside her skull and set her teeth on edge. As the voices grew louder—it sounded like a woman and two men—she realized they were talking about her.

"I've never seen anything like it."

"That return must have been going a hundred miles an hour."

"Don't flatter yourself. It wasn't *that* good. She just wasn't paying attention."

Kiera let out another moan, and this one, she was sure, was audible, because one of the men said, "Hey. She's coming around."

"See?" the other man said. "I told you she'd be all right."

Kiera thought she should recognize the voices, but she still couldn't place them.

"Jesus, Kiera," someone said and—finally—she recognized Jon O'Keefe's voice. "You gave us quite a scare there."

Kiera tried to open her eyes to see where she was, but she was afraid of what would happen if she did. Even now, a long streak of vibrating white light shifted across her vision like a wind-driven cloud, flickering with a dangerous internal lighting.

No . . . Please, she thought, trying to will the pain and rising panic away. She felt her elbows and back grind against the hard, gritty surface that was hot against her back. For an instant, she imagined she was lying on a large skillet.

Out of the frying pan and into the fire.

For some vague reason, that thought disturbed her. She knew it was just a cliché, but it had come from someplace deep inside her, and it filled her with inexplicable nervousness.

"Open your eyes, Kiera, and look at me. Can you do that?"

". . . Jon . . . ?" Kiera finally said. She licked her lips, feeling how dry they were even though she remembered—or thought she remembered—having a drink recently.

A drink of what?

Someone—probably Jon—raised her head and cradled it so it wasn't on that hot, flat surface. Then someone—probably still Jon—started rubbing her forehead with a moist towel. The sensation was amazing, but it also brought her closer to consciousness, and with that came the first real jab of pain that pierced her head like a hot spike just above her left eye. The strand of hazy white light intensified like the afterimage of a photographer's flash, making her wince.

"Damn! Did I hurt you?"

Kiera wanted to say *no*, but the pain behind her left eye was gathering strength like water building up behind a dam that was crumbling away. She knew she couldn't hold it back much longer.

"I have a . . . wicked . . . headache," she whispered so softly she wasn't sure anyone heard her.

She started to raise her left hand to her forehead, but the

effort proved to be too much, so she let it flop back onto the hard surface. Only then did she remember that she had been playing tennis with Jon, Liz, and Alex. She must have fainted and was now flat out on the tennis court.

"Sorry about that return," someone—it must be Alex—said. "I, uhh, didn't mean to . . . I thought you were ready."

"Yeah," Kiera whispered as she licked her lips again. "I thought I was ready, too, but I—"

She caught herself before she said anything more. She had no idea what she might have said while she was out of it, and she wanted to be careful now about anything she revealed. These people—especially Jon—were her friends, but she had to be careful. She had secrets to protect. Jon would understand, but Liz and Alex certainly wouldn't.

"You caught it on the side of the head," Jon said. "I'd really like it if you'd open your eyes."

Kiera concentrated as hard as she could, still not quite daring to do that, but she knew she had to if only so her friends would know she was all right. She wanted to get off the court and into the shade. After taking a deep breath and holding it, she slowly raised her eyelids.

The sky was a piercingly bright blue backdrop to the three indistinct blurs that loomed above her. The dark silhouettes shifted in and out of focus because a jagged diagonal line of white light cut them in half. But it was what she saw *inside* that beam of light that made Kiera react. As the indistinct outline of a figure rose in a slow motion, Kiera tried to track it, but it seemed to move closer and recede at the same time, darting back and forth across her vision with every twitch of her eyes.

"You're not really focusing, here, Kiera," Jon said.

"My head hurts something fierce," Kiera whispered, again so softly she doubted they heard her.

"I still think we should call nine one one," Liz said, her voice tight with worry.

"I'll get my cell," Alex said, but before one of the silhouettes moved away—Kiera couldn't distinguish which one was Alex—she cried out, "No!"

As much as her head hurt, she didn't want to go to the hospital. She knew this was more than a migraine. It had to do with something that had happened a long time ago . . . something that had been eating away at her all of her adult life.

Forcing her eyes to focus, she looked up at Jon's face. For a moment, she imagined him as much younger. He was a teenager again, and he was tending to her after she had gotten hurt on another night long ago.

"I've been having really bad headaches ever since yesterday," she said.

"Well, getting hit on the side of the head probably doesn't help." Jon smiled weakly.

Kiera struggled to sit up but couldn't do it without Jon's help. Supporting her under the arms, he got her to her feet and then guided her toward the shaded area of the court. She knew she couldn't have gotten there unassisted, and she leaned her weight against him.

"Just give me a little time," she said weakly. "I'll be all right."

Her vision was clearing gradually, but the bolt of white light that cut across it was still there, twitching and wavering whenever she shifted her eyes. And the blurry figure inside the light was also still there. Whenever she concentrated on trying to see it more clearly, it faded away; but whenever she looked past it or tried to ignore it, it suddenly loomed in close. At times, it seemed as though the figure— and Kiera had no doubt it was a person—was reaching out to her. She couldn't tell if it was a threatening or an imploring gesture, but she shrank away from it.

Moving slowly, not wanting to jolt her head and make the migraine any worse, she finally got to the fence and, with Jon's help, sat down, leaning back against the chain-link fence. Her breath hissed out in a long, low sigh as she closed her eyes, but when that made the white line all the more intense, she quickly opened them again.

"Have you been having headaches a lot lately?" Jon asked. He was so close his breath was warm against her skin. Kiera thought for a moment he was about to kiss her, and she had another quick flash of when they had dated back in high school.

"It's nothing . . . really," she said, but she knew she wasn't convincing anyone, even herself.

"Look," Jon said, "I'll drive you home in your car. Liz can follow in ours."

"No. I can drive," Kiera said. She looked at Jon but couldn't focus long on his face because the white line still wavered in front of her eyes.

"The hell you will," Jon said. His face was still close to hers, and now she struggled against the sudden impulse to lean forward and kiss him.

What's going on here? . . . What am I thinking?

She knew she didn't have any romantic feelings for Jon. Not anymore. What they had back in high school was long over. They were just friends now. Nothing more.

"I insist," Jon said, and by his tone of voice, she knew he meant it.

Liz stepped forward and handed Kiera a water bottle, which she tipped back and sipped from with a nod of thanks. The water felt unbelievable as it washed down her throat, but it didn't come close to touching the throb of pain behind her left eye. She imagined the pain was like a hungry tiger, tensed and ready to strike without warning.

"You up to walking?" Jon asked.

"I told you. I'm fine," Kiera said, but when she tried to get up, she found she couldn't. Letting out a low moan, she sagged back against the fence and would have fallen if Jon hadn't caught her.

"Yeah. You're doing just great," he said, holding her in an awkward embrace that struck her as more intimate than necessary. She glanced over at Liz, wondering if she noticed it, too, or if this was all just her imagination.

Her legs felt as stiff and brittle as sticks as she allowed Jon to lead her slowly down to her car. She fished her car keys from her handbag and handed them to him, surprised and more than a little frightened that she couldn't see them when she looked right at them because of the white line across her sight. There was no way she would have been able to drive.

Am I going blind? she wondered as a shiver raced up her back. *Or am I having a stroke or something?*

Jon unlocked the passenger's door and helped her into the car. It amazed Kiera how much effort it took just to lift her legs and swing them around. As Jon went around to the driver's side, she sighed and, closing her eyes, leaned back against the car seat. Without even looking at what she was doing, she snapped on her seat belt.

She was grateful the pain hadn't come back full force, but she was still worried that the white light was just a prelude, that the pain was about to strike at any second. Jon sat down and adjusted the seat and rearview mirror. Then he looked at her and smiled. Kiera couldn't see his face clearly, but she smiled back and nodded.

"You know," he said, "this is all because of how you live."

Kiera winced and shook her head.

"Please, Jon. I don't want to get into that now."

Jon started up the car but was still looking at her.

"You've got to stop punishing yourself."

The rumbling sound of the engine made Kiera wince and grit her teeth. She braced herself, squeezing the door handle so tightly her fingers were going numb. Once again, unbidden, the memory of what had happened back in high school came rushing back to her. Maybe it was simply because this was the first time since high school she had been a passenger while Jon was driving. She made a soft whimpering sound in the back of her throat, wishing the memory would go away.

Before shifting into gear, Jon said, "Are you sure you don't want to swing by the hospital? You've really got me worried."

Kiera reached out with her left hand and touched him gently on the forearm. Memories and fears were so mingled inside her that she couldn't tell what she was feeling as tears filled her eyes.

"Remember that night—?" she said, her voice so low it was barely audible above the sound of the car's engine.

Jon looked at her and said, "That's what I'm talking about." For a moment, the unnaturally bright gleam in his eyes pierced the line of white light, shooting at her like laser fire. "You gotta let that go, but if you can't, I don't want you to talk about it. *Ever!*" The anger in his voice frightened her, making her flinch as if he'd just slapped her.

"I hurt my head," she said, raising her hand and rubbing her left temple. "Remember? That night, I banged my head on the dashboard."

The dark silhouette centered in the glare of the white light suddenly leaped forward. For an instant, Kiera thought it was Jon as hands reached out to grab her. She whimpered and shied away, pressing herself against the car door.

"I *mean* it!" Jon said so emphatically Kiera thought he actually might slap her to make her shut up.

"But I—"

She hated to hear the weakness in her voice, and for a moment she thought the figure was reaching out to her with a sense of desperation . . . of need.

"Don't you think, after all this time, we should talk about it?"

Looking over his shoulder, Jon snapped the gearshift into reverse and stepped on the gas. He backed up so fast Kiera wasn't ready for it, and the motion snapped her head forward. There was an instant of blinding pain, but it quickly subsided.

"There's nothing to talk about," Jon said evenly. "You can't let this thing eat at you all the time like this." His features were set in grim, hard lines as he looked ahead at the road and started driving. "You have to forget all about it, because if you start thinking about it too much . . . We . . . You'd just be jumping out of the frying pan and into the fire."

Kiera started at the exact words she had thought only a short while ago. She turned and stared out the side window as he pulled onto the street and drove away. When they passed the high school, Kiera wondered if Nate was still in his classroom, getting ready for the first day of school next week. Even if he was, though, she thought he might just as well be on the moon for all she was concerned.

Something was seriously wrong with her, she knew, but right now, all she wanted to do was get home and lie down.

She had to get rid of this headache. Closing her eyes, she leaned her head against the headrest, and all the while, the indistinct figure behind her eyelids reached out to her. The problem was, she still couldn't decide if this person wanted to help her or hurt her, but she was sure she knew who it was.

CHAPTER 2

Last Gasp

~1~

"Oh boy," Kiera whispered when she and Jon crested the hill in front of her house, and she saw the battered black Mustang parked in front of the garage.

"What is it?" Jon glanced at her just before he pulled into the driveway and stopped beside the parked car without seeming even to notice it.

How would he know what that rusted, old Mustang means to me?

During the drive home, Kiera had her head back and her eyes closed. The white light—at least a trace of it—still weaved and danced in front of her eyes, but it was fading gradually, leaving behind a dull pain centered behind her left eye.

She made fleeting eye contact with Jon, knowing that her worry and tension were obvious. She debated telling him what was upsetting her but decided not to. He was worried enough about her as it was. No sense dumping more of her crap onto him.

"You want me to come in with you? Make sure you're

all right?" Jon leaned close to her, and for a second, Kiera thought he was going to kiss her.

"No," she said, shaking her head slightly, but even that bit of movement made her wince. She was reaching for the door handle when Jon shifted closer and took hold of her wrist.

"Hang on a sec," he said, turning so he was facing her, his mouth close to her face. Once again, Kiera had the impression he was going to kiss her, but he released her hand and straightened up. "Let me get the door for you."

Before Kiera could say anything, he got out of the car and came around to her side. His back was turned to the house, and just as he was opening the door for her, the side door opened, and Trista stepped outside. Although Trista's hair wasn't as vibrantly red as her mother's, it glowed with auburn highlights in the sun. Two steps behind her was the owner of the battered black Mustang—Robbie Townsend.

Robbie was a tall, lanky twenty-four-year-old who had served a few stints in the county jail for traffic violations and drug possession. He blinked in the sunlight, like he wasn't quite used to seeing it. His skin looked unnaturally pale, especially so close to the end of summer. Greasy strands of long, dark hair hung down to his shoulders, and his bare forearms, thick and muscular, were covered with tattoos. Just looking at him made Kiera's flesh crawl.

When Jon heard them behind him, he paused and looked at them over his shoulder. He smiled when he saw Trista, but Kiera saw him tense when he noticed Robbie. Leaning down to help her out of the car, Jon whispered into her ear, "Okay, now I know what upset you."

"Don't get me started," Kiera whispered as she shook her head.

"Oh. Hey, Mom," Trista said, smiling as though absolutely nothing was wrong, even though Kiera and Nate had told her *hundreds* of times that they didn't want anyone in the house—especially Robbie—when they weren't home.

Robbie eyed Kiera and Jon with a cold, reptilian deadness in his eyes. Kiera assumed they'd just smoked some weed and hoped—but doubted—that's *all* they'd been doing.

"How many times do I—" she began, but she cut herself short, not wanting to get into it with both Jon and Robbie right there.

Trista regarded her mother with a bemused expression and, although she had no reason to feel guilty, Kiera felt funny having Jon drop her off at the house like this. Before anyone said anything else, Liz pulled to a stop at the top of the driveway and tooted the horn.

"We're gonna go get something to eat," Trista said as she and Robbie got into the Mustang. "See yah." She slammed the car door, cutting off anything her mother might have to say to her.

Robbie started up his car, and the sound of the Mustang's blown-out muffler made Kiera wince. If she'd had the energy, she would have done something to stop Trista from leaving, but the pain behind her eyes was throbbing stronger now. Tiny white dots of light zigzagged like fireflies across her vision. The car exhaust smelled like burning rubber, which made Kiera's stomach churn.

"Be right with yah," Jon yelled, waving to Liz, who was waiting in the car. When he took Kiera's left arm to support her, he leaned close and whispered, "She can be such a bitch at times."

"Who, Liz or Trista?" Kiera asked, but she paid scant attention to him as she watched Robbie back his car around. Behind the closed car window, his pale face looked corpselike. In spite of the humid weather, Kiera shivered as she watched them drive away.

"That kid's not your favorite person, I take it," Jon said.

Liz gave the horn another quick blast.

"He's not a kid," Kiera said. "He's seven years older than she is, and he's a—"

"A loser, far as I can see."

Kiera shivered again as she stared down the road. The Mustang was long out of sight.

"The kind of person you wouldn't want to meet in a dark alley, that's for sure," Jon added.

"From what I know, he can't hold a steady job. He lives in an apartment on Grant Street with some other reprobates." Kiera turned to Jon. "What's a grown man want with a teenager like Trista other than to take advantage of her?"

Jon shrugged and, pursing his lips, nodded his understanding. "Yeah, but—you've got to put your foot down. Once you let them walk all over you . . ."

"Easy for you to say," Kiera said. "You and Liz never had any kids."

As soon as the words were out of her mouth, she regretted them. She didn't know why Jon and Liz never had children. They hadn't really talked about it since he came back to Stratford. It may have been a conscious decision to stay childless, or it may have been something biological, something they couldn't help. She hoped she hadn't hit a raw nerve without realizing it.

"I'm sorry. I didn't mean—"

"Forget about it. No problem. Liz and I decided early on that we didn't want kids." Jon shot a quick glance at his wife's car on the street. "Liz's folks . . ." He blinked and looked up at the sky for a moment before continuing, "Let's just say they weren't the best role models on the planet. Being the oldest, she pretty much raised her brother. Even before we got married, she made it perfectly clear that she wanted no part of raising any more children."

Kiera sighed and said, "The way things are today? I can't say as I blame you. Trista's all we got, and believe me, she's *more* than enough."

As she said this, she glanced at the door leading into the garage. Robbie hadn't closed it when he left, and she assumed it had been carelessness on his part, not that he had left it open as a courtesy because she was home. She was sure Trista had told him all about how much her parents—especially she—complained about him.

The door loomed open on the sunlit wall, a dark rectangle that promised escape from the heat outside and safety within, but Kiera couldn't bring herself to move. The muscles in her legs felt too loose. She was afraid she'd crumple to the ground if she took even a single step forward. A sudden surge of fear filled her, but she had no idea what she was afraid of. Thick sourness churned in her stomach, and the pain inside her head expanded until it filled her skull with a pulsing throb that kept time with her pulse.

There's nothing to be afraid of, she told herself, but she was far from convinced. She glanced at Liz's car, sensing her increasing impatience and wishing she could tell Jon she was fine, that she could take care of herself from here, but tendrils of fear spread inside her like a fast-growing vine. The edges of her vision spun with darkness that threatened to close down on her any second.

Just get inside the house . . . Take some Tylenol . . . Lie down and rest, she told herself, but she still couldn't move. She took a breath, but her lungs didn't seem to fill up. As the air whistled in her throat, she pictured that her lungs were riddled with pinprick holes through which the air leaked. Fighting the rush of fear, she looked desperately at Jon. His face distorted and loomed closer with cartoon craziness.

"Let's just get you settled inside, okay?" he said. His voice was distorted and wavered, dragging so badly she almost couldn't make out what he said, but she nodded in agreement and let him take her by the arm. She leaned against him, but when he put his arm around her and held her tightly, she found it all the more difficult to breathe.

She was afraid she was going to pass out, but—somehow—they made it into the house. Jon directed her through the kitchen and down the short hallway to the living room. By the time he eased her onto the couch, the room was spinning. He placed one of the throw pillows under her head. She could barely focus as she looked up at him, but she could see the genuine worry in his expression.

"Promise me one thing," he said. His words didn't seem to match they way his mouth moved.

Kiera forced a smile as the pain in her head spiked.

"What's that?" she asked, hearing her voice as if it was someone else, speaking in the next room.

"Call your doctor and make an appointment." When Jon touched her forehead, his fingers were cool against her skin. She wondered if Nate would be this gentle and understanding with her if he was here, and for just an instant, she imagined she and Jon were married.

It could have been that way, she thought as she gazed at his warm, caring expression. *We might not have broken up . . . We might still be together . . . if it hadn't been for—*

"Do you think . . ." she said. Her voice sounded sludgy, and she paused to lick her lips, unsure if he could hear, much less understand her.

"Think what?" Jon asked, bringing his face so close his warm breath washed over her skin. The moment was frighteningly intimate.

"Do you think this"—she tapped her forehead gently—"has anything to do with what happened to Billy?"

Jon's expression instantly froze. Kiera had the terrifying impression time had actually stopped as they stared into each other's eyes. Then, very slowly, Jon's face shifted from sympathetic and caring to cold and harsh. The blood drained from his cheeks, making his lips look blue, as a cold glint of anger flashed in his eyes. In an instant, it was gone, but it had terrified Kiera.

"Don't say that. Don't even *think* it," he whispered.

"But I—"

"Look, Kiera. What's done is done. No matter what we think about it, there's not a damned thing you or I or anyone else can do about it."

"But I've been—"

"It's over, and we're going to forget about it. Right? You've got to stop punishing yourself so much."

"Yeah, but I—" Kiera's voice cut off as she took a shuddering breath and struggled to clear her head, but heated pressure was building up inside her. "The night of the accident. Don't you remember? I hit my head on the dashboard really hard." Her fingers felt cold and clammy as she gingerly touched the skin above her left eyebrow. "What if I got some brain damage or something . . . something that hasn't healed? What if that's why I'm having these headaches?"

Jon rolled his eyes and looked up at the ceiling as he shook his head like he was dealing with a difficult child, but his expression was grim when he looked at her again.

"I'm just a real estate agent, not a doctor, so I wouldn't

know. If you're really worried about it, then definitely you should see a doctor. I'll make the appointment for you if you want."

"No," Kiera said, rolling her head from side to side even though that small motion sent waves of pain through her head. "Don't worry. I'll do it. Right now, all I want to do is sleep and try to get this pain to go away."

Jon got up slowly from the couch and started backing out of the room. The whole time, he maintained steady eye contact with her. His sympathetic smile had returned, and Kiera was left wondering if she had imagined the flash of anger she had seen moments before. She sighed and closed her eyes, settling her head into the pillow.

"Who's your doctor?" Jon asked. He was in the doorway, but his voice seemed to be coming from so far away it echoed.

With her eyes still closed, Kiera spoke so softly she thought she might only have thought it. "Dr. Schwartz."

"On Upper Main?" Jon sounded so distant now his voice could have been one of her thoughts.

". . . Don't worry . . . I'll call tomorrow . . . I promise . . ."

And then she drifted down into the darkness behind her eyes and was asleep.

~2~

"You know what it looks like? It looks like a door that's open, and this bright light is shining inside it so bright I can't see anything else."

Nate sat on the edge of the couch, one hand resting on the mound of her hips as he touched the side of her face.

"You don't have a fever. Is the pain gone?"

It surprised Kiera that he looked genuinely concerned for her. She winced when she raised her hand to her forehead and touched the spot above her left eyebrow. Even when she applied some pressure, all she felt was a dull numbness. She couldn't believe her head had hurt so much just a few hours ago.

"Now, yeah, but I can't tell you how scary it was . . . especially the visual part. The streak of light was . . . it happens just before the pain. Then . . . *my God*, it hits me like a freight train."

"Did you call the doctor?"

Kiera shook her head, surprised that it didn't hurt to move.

"Tomorrow."

She hiked herself up on the couch, blinking as she looked around. She noticed for the first time that the living room lights were on, and the view outside the windows was black. "What time is it, anyway?"

Nate stretched out his arm and glanced at his wristwatch. "A little after ten."

"You're kidding."

Kiera sat up but couldn't stand because Nate was in the way. "I've been sleeping for—" She did a quick mental calculation. "—more than four hours?"

"Looks that way." Nate shrugged. "What time did you get home from tennis?"

"I'm not sure. Jon drove me. It must have been four, maybe four thirty."

She closed her eyes and rubbed them vigorously, still trying to fathom how she could have been out of it that long. The time had just disappeared. Her stomach rumbled, reminding her that she had missed supper, but she was still nauseous and didn't feel at all hungry.

"Ten o'clock," she murmured, shaking her head in disbelief. Then another thought struck her. She narrowed her eyes and looked at her husband. "Where were you?"

"Huh?" Nate said, not making eye contact with her.

"Are you just getting home? You can't tell me you were at the school this late." She cocked her head to one side and looked at him, her vision going double for a moment. "What were you doing out until ten o'clock?"

"I called and left a message. I went out for a few beers with Doug and Travis." As if he could read her suspicions on her face, Nate pointed toward the kitchen. "Play the message if you don't believe me."

Kiera waved him off, trying to convince herself that she was being foolish to doubt him, but she'd had her suspicions over the years, enough to mistrust him at least a little.

"I'm not really hungry. I think I'll take another dose of Tylenol and go to bed. I want to keep the headaches at bay if I can."

"Can't say as I blame you."

Nate moved back so she could get off the couch. As she trudged up the stairs, Kiera knew he was right behind her, and she wondered why the first thing that popped into her head was that he was having an affair. This wasn't the first time she'd had her doubts about his fidelity.

When she walked into their bathroom and opened the medicine cabinet to get the Tylenol, she wondered if maybe she thought that because earlier today, when Jon had been so solicitous to her, she'd had the fleeting impression that he was coming on to her . . .

Or maybe she still carried a spark for him.

No! . . . That's ridiculous! she told herself as she ran the water until it was cold and filled a paper cup to wash down the Tylenol.

She and Nate weren't perfectly happy together, but what couple was?

How could anyone who had been together for more than twenty years still feel the same level of passion?

It was perfectly normal for the initial rush of infatuation to fade. What bothered Kiera was realizing how long and gradual the erosion had been. Everyday things like jobs and money worries and children and life's other myriad pressures had eroded the romance, but if she was honest with herself, she had to admit that she had always felt a certain distance between her and Nate, and over the years, she had a sneaky feeling that he had not always been honest with her.

It's just the way life goes, she told herself as she stared at her reflection. It was okay to think about the might have beens, the ways things could have been but never would be because of choices she'd made.

This was the life she had chosen, and no matter how guilty she might feel about things she had done—and not done—no matter how much she might suspect Nate was cheating on her, she had to be content with her life, because it was just the way it had turned out.

"You 'bout done in there?" Nate called from the bedroom. "I can use Trista's bathroom if you're gonna be a while."

Kiera realized she'd been leaning against the sink and staring at her reflection in the mirror, almost hypnotized by the pale, glazed look in her eyes. She shook her head to clear it. The faucet was still running cold water, and because the drain was a little clogged, the water had risen and almost overflowed.

"I'll be right out," she called back, even though she hadn't washed her face or brushed her teeth. She could do that once Nate was done. She turned the faucet off and walked back into the bedroom, moving slowly, her shoulders hunched with tension.

"Head still hurt?" Nate asked.

"Not really," she replied. "I was just . . . thinking . . ."

"'Bout what?" Nate asked, but before she answered him, he walked into the bathroom and closed the door. She listened to the tinkling sound as he urinated, knowing without having to check later that he hadn't bothered to raise the toilet seat. It was all so predictable.

"Nothing . . ."

She undressed quickly and tucked into bed before Nate came out of the bathroom. By then, she was too tired to get up and brush her teeth, so she waited until he turned off the light and then rolled over onto her right side, away from him. Staring into the darkness, she prayed that sleep would come . . .

~3~

. . . But it didn't.

The seconds and minutes dragged slowly by as she lay in bed with her eyes wide open. Soon enough, her eyes began to adjust to the ambient light. She stared at the hazy outlines of their bedroom furniture—the walls—the open window. Still, especially at the edge of her vision, she caught glimpses of dark shapes that shifted against the darkness in the room . . . shapes that didn't look like they belonged there. She tried to convince herself these were just tricks of the eye, but every now and then, she was sure she saw someone moving silently around in the darkened bedroom.

It hadn't taken long for Nate to fall asleep. The slow,

steady sound of his breathing filled the bedroom. Whenever he started snoring loud enough to bother her, she nudged him with her elbow . . . just enough so he'd roll over and stop snoring at least for a little while.

But Nate's snoring was nothing compared to the worries that haunted her. Her nap on the couch had ruined any chance for sleep. There wasn't even a hint of pain in her head now, but she knew it was still there, lurking just below the surface like a hungry shark . . . circling patiently . . . waiting to strike.

What worried her most was wondering what caused these attacks. She had a tendency to think the worst, so her first thought was that it had to be a brain tumor and, of course, it had to be the worst kind of tumor possible . . . malignant and inoperable.

Why else would she be seeing flashing lights?

The tumor was probably so big it was pressing against her optic nerve or the back of her left eye, causing the flashes of light and pain. She knew enough biology to know that the brain didn't have any pain receptors, so who could tell how big the thing inside her head might be? She wouldn't even know it was there until it started to affect other parts of her . . . like her eyesight.

A cold, sinking feeling of impending doom swept over her, chilling her in spite of the warm summer night. She shifted her gaze to the windows and watched as the lacy curtains billowed in and out with the gentle breeze. The fluttering motion, especially when she saw it from the corner of her eye, almost convinced her a ghost was lurking in the darkness, and as much as she tried not to, she couldn't help but think back to that night so long ago . . .

It *had* been an accident. She was sure of that. Still, her friend Billy Carroll had died that night. She hadn't caused his death in any way. She still believed that, but what made it worse was knowing she hadn't done anything about it, not before or after. She had been there when Billy died, and she hadn't reported it to the police like she knew she should have. She had told Jon they had to report it, even if it was anonymously, but they hadn't.

Instead, she had gone along with what Jon had said and done. They didn't leave Billy where he had died for someone else to find him. They had done something much worse, and she had lived with the guilt ever since.

What if that's why this is happening? she thought as rushes of panic boiled up inside her.

What if Billy's ghost has come back? . . . What if he's haunting me because I was there when he died?

On a rational level, she knew none of this made any sense.

Why would it be happening now, after more than twenty-five years?

But Kiera thought she knew the answer to that.

It was because Jon had moved back to Stratford.

Maybe it's not me, she thought, trying to push away these irrational thoughts. *If it's really Billy's ghost, maybe he's come back because Jon's back . . . They're the ones who are connected . . . not me . . . because Jon—*

She didn't finish the thought. She couldn't. She had tried to broach the subject with Jon earlier today, and he had dismissed it outright, telling her to forget all about it and not to worry.

But she couldn't stop worrying as she lay there in the darkness, listening to her husband's steady breathing as he slept . . . the soft sighing of the wind outside . . . and the light rasping of the curtains as they scuffed against the windowsill.

She couldn't stop remembering that horrible night, and she cringed whenever she recalled the figure she had seen inside the line of white light that streaked across her vision. The figure was silhouetted against a bright glare of light—*like headlights*—and if it was at all real, it had to be the ghost of Billy Carroll, come back to haunt both her and Jon because of what they had done . . .

And what they *hadn't* done.

Kiera whimpered softly and covered her mouth with one hand to stifle the scream that was building up inside her. Cold sweat broke out across her skin and ran in small, tickling streams down both sides of her neck. It wasn't just because the night was humid. The wind, wafting through the open windows, blew across her face like the gentle touch of unseen hands, and all too easily she could imagine the hands touching her were skeletal hands . . . insubstantial hands that were moldering with rot as they materialized like vapors and reached out of the darkness to touch her . . . to clench her throat . . . to drive pain into her head . . . to choke off her life . . .

With a sudden roaring gasp, Kiera bolted upright in bed, her hands covering her chest as she looked, wide-eyed, around the room. Nate was awake in an instant.

"Jesus! What is it?" he cried out.

His weight shifted on the bed as he fumbled for the light switch. When he knocked something onto the floor, he swore softly under his breath.

"Don't turn on the lights!" she cried out, covering her eyes, afraid the sudden blast of light would trigger another migraine.

"Christ! Are you all right?" Nate sounded calmer now. His hand slapped the bed as he reached out for her. When he touched her side, instead of finding it reassuring, she shrank away from him.

"I'm fine . . . I . . . I must have been dreaming . . ."

It was a lie. There was no way she had fallen asleep, but she wasn't about to tell him what she had been thinking. She wasn't sure she could recapture her train of thought, and she definitely didn't want to. An unsettled feeling churned her stomach as a sour taste filled the back of her throat. She thought she might throw up.

"Must've been a doozy," Nate said softly.

He ran his hand up her side to her shoulder, but his touch wasn't at all reassuring. Kiera shied away from him, sighing as she wiped her face with her forearm. The sweat on her forehead felt like a thin coating of oil. Her pulse was rushing so fast in her ears it throbbed in her neck and wrists.

"Wanna tell me about it?" Nate asked as he settled back down in the bed. His hand still rested lightly on her arm, patting her.

"I can't really remember," she said, cringing at the lie. The problem was, she could remember all too well what she'd been thinking, and even now, the idea that the ghost of Billy Carroll was in the room—unseen and unheard as it watched them—terrified her. And she knew—if Billy was in the room with them—he knew she was lying.

And I'm living a lie, she thought, twisting inside with guilt.

"Want a glass of water?" Nate asked.

Kiera shook her head and whispered, "No, I'll be all right. I just . . ."

Moving slowly, she lay back down in bed and took a long, slow breath, hoping to calm herself. The darkness of the room pressed down on her like a heavy blanket. She still felt as though she couldn't get any air deep enough into her lungs. Spinning spots of white light trailed across her vision, hissing softly in the darkness.

"You sure?" Nate asked, sounding sleepy now.

"Yeah . . . I'm sure," Kiera said, but as she lay on her side, her back to her husband, her eyes were wide open as she stared into the throbbing darkness.

I know you're there, Billy . . . she thought, shivering as she hugged herself. She felt terribly alone as tears spilled from her eyes and ran in warm tracks down her face before soaking into her pillow.

I know you've come back to torment me because of what we did . . .

-–4-–

That thought was still echoing in her mind the next morning when, unable to sleep, she got out of bed earlier than usual—around five thirty—and went downstairs. It felt good to be alone. The sun was just starting to come up, and the house was filled with a dense, peaceful quiet. She cringed whenever she broke the silence. Even her bare feet scuffing on the linoleum or the sounds she made as she filled the coffee carafe with water and started making coffee set her on edge. While the coffee was brewing, she sat at the kitchen table and tried to sort out what had been on her mind last night.

Her clearest thought—what she really wanted to believe—was that she had been so worn out after everything that had happened yesterday that she had overreacted. Lying in bed unable to sleep and worrying about having a brain tumor or losing her mind—or that the ghost of Billy Carroll was haunting her—seemed slightly ridiculous now.

The coffeepot steamed and snapped as hot water trickled through the grounds. Kiera sighed and, leaning forward, rubbed her face with the flats of her hands, trying to decide if she really would follow through and make an appointment with her doctor today.

It didn't seem worth the bother now.

She wanted to convince herself that she had overreacted, but the memory of that frozen band of white light and the silhouette inside it came back, filling her with an uneasy feeling. Resting both elbows on the table, she glanced at the wall phone. She could see the little red cross that designated the speed dial number for Dr. Schwartz's office.

It was too early to call now. All she'd get would be his answering service, and she knew, no matter *what* she felt or thought about what had happened—what *was* happening—this wasn't an emergency. She was determined to have her coffee, make breakfast for her and Nate, and see how she felt later.

Nate would sleep late today. He was taking advantage of the last few days of summer vacation before the school year started. And Trista wouldn't show up until noon—if then. She sighed as she got up from the table and set about preparing breakfast for herself.

The day was already warm, even this early in the morning. The thunderstorm that had threatened had never materialized to break the humidity. Once her breakfast was ready—toast with blueberry jam, coffee, and orange juice—Kiera walked out onto the back deck and sat down at the metal picnic table after wiping the dew off the chair. The sun looked like a huge orange ball through the morning haze, lighting the dew that sprinkled the lawn and making it sparkle. Twisting shreds of mist rose like smoke from the woods behind the house. The sound of birdsong filled the woods, almost loud enough to be irritating instead of soothing.

Kiera raised her cup of coffee to her mouth and blew on the steam. She knew what she was doing wasn't healthy. Marsha, her best friend who'd had her own battles with alcohol and was now in recovery, had told her this was called "taking inventory." It wasn't healthy for her just to sit here, stewing about what was or could be wrong with her. She should be active and do something about it.

Maybe Jon and Liz or Alex would want to have an early game of tennis to make up for breaking off the game early yesterday.

As much as she liked the idea, she simply didn't have the motivation to do that or anything else. It was so much easier just to sit here and space out as the sunlight angled across the yard and drove back the darkness and damp of night.

But as she sat there staring off into the woods, she realized she had been focused on something . . . a shape in the foliage that didn't look quite right.

A shiver uncoiled up her back as she slowly lowered her coffee cup to the table and leaned forward. Her eyes were wide as she strained to make out what she was looking at.

Was there really a person in the woods?

There was no wind, not even the hint of a breeze, so the leaves and branches were perfectly still. Even the loud chatter of birdsong seemed to have died down as though the birds had fled the immediate area. The sun was higher now, but the gauzy shadows under the trees appeared all the darker, like splashes of ink.

Kiera shivered in spite of the warm day and the coffee she'd drunk. As she stared at the woods, trying to see if what she was seeing was real or just a trick of the eye, she experienced a curious sensation. Her eyes widened as she tried to pierce the shadows, but another feeling slowly took hold of her. She had the odd feeling that—somehow—*she* was crouching in the woods, watching herself on the deck.

This strange feeling of duality grew stronger, sweeping over her in fast, intense rushes. The sharp contrast of light and shadow, of sunlit greens and shaded brown and black deeper in the woods was vibrating with frightening intensity. Kiera let out a frightened whimper as she sat poised, waiting for the streak of white light to slash across her vision. Thankfully, it didn't come . . .

Not yet, anyway.

The light was a precursor of pain, so if she didn't see the light, maybe she wouldn't get a migraine today.

Why is this happening *to me?* she wanted to scream as the feeling of dissociation got steadily stronger.

It was easy to imagine that she was out there in the woods, crouching on hands and knees on the damp soil, clinging to the shadows as she watched this . . . this *stranger* sitting on her back deck.

She inhaled sharply and smelled the rich, damp aroma of rotting vegetation. Her shoulders tensed, and when she clenched her hands into fists, she could almost feel the squishy, black mulch of the forest floor ooze between her fingers. She shivered as the cool, damp touch of shadows from the branches rippled like water across her back, and she felt her knees pressing into the soft, yielding soil . . .

No! . . . Stop it! . . . Stop it now, she told herself, but the dense, humid air felt too thick to breathe. It muffled her voice as a dense heaviness pressed down on her. For an instant, she felt as though she was drifting helplessly underwater, being sucked down into dark, unknown depths. Her eyes were wide open and staring as she looked at the stretch of lawn between her and the woods. The air was roiling with heavy, gray clots, even though she knew there was no breeze.

Frantic desperation rose up inside her, but she just sat there paralyzed, with no idea what to do. She wanted to get up and run just to do *something* to dispel this panicky feeling but, at the same time, she was riveted to her seat, her body frozen with fear. She wished she could clear her throat and call out to Nate. The bedroom window was open. He should hear her. But she couldn't make the tiniest sound. She didn't dare even to try to form a word because she was afraid of what might come out.

Would it be a cry for help or a scream?

Kiera knew, no matter what sound she tried to make, when she opened her mouth nothing would come out except—maybe—one faint, final gasp.

You're having a panic attack, she told herself, surprised by such a clear, rational thought in the midst of such mounting fear. *That's all it is. Just relax. It will pass.*

But the feeling was more than that.

She tore her gaze away from the woods and looked down at her hands, which were clasped tightly in her lap. The intensity of her sight scared her even more. Every vein and tendon shifted beneath her skin at the slightest twitch. Every hair on the back of her hands, every skin pore, every wrinkle and blemish stood out with near psychedelic brilliance. The feeling of dissociation got so strong she knew she had to cry out or get up from her chair and *do* something if only to keep moving.

Worst of all, she was convinced, now, that she was being watched, but she couldn't distinguish if she was sitting on her deck being watched by someone in the woods, or if—somehow—she was lurking in the woods, watching someone else—or herself—on the deck.

Slowly, she got to her feet. Her knee knocked the underside of table hard enough to spill her coffee. The cup hit the deck floor, rolled away, and fell off the deck onto the lawn. She heard it hit with a dull thump.

Her shoulders were hunched, and her hands were clenched as she turned her head from side to side, trying to get her bearings. The sense of unreality was too much. Waves of vertigo swept over her. She staggered and would have fallen if she hadn't caught hold of the deck railing and gripped it tightly. Glancing down at her hand supporting her, she was surprised and terrified to see how thin and fragile it appeared.

Like a skeleton's hand, she thought as her panic spiked even higher.

The instant she turned and started back to the house, her legs gave out and she dropped to the deck. Hard. It happened so fast she was barely aware she was falling until the impact jolted her, making her teeth clack together so hard she nipped the tip of her tongue. The metallic taste of blood flooded her mouth as her vision darkened.

At least there's no white lightning, she thought, and she almost laughed out loud before hawking up some saliva and spitting. The spit was flecked with blood, but she didn't connect that it was *her* blood. Her pulse thumped in her ears, making her vision jump with every beat.

She was on her hands and knees, but she didn't have the strength to get back up. It felt like it was happening to someone else. Her joints and muscles were as loose as a stack of old clothes. She was aware of the solidity of the deck planking, but she felt like she was on a boat that was pitching wildly from side to side. The swells of vertigo kept coming faster and faster, lifting her up and then dropping her down . . .

Up and down . . .

Still on her hands and knees, she scrambled toward the door, but when she looked at it, her vision telescoped, and it looked impossibly far away. She'd never get there. When she looked down at her hands again, she had the terrifying thought that they—or the deck—were too insubstantial to hold her up much longer. Either the deck or she was going to disappear, and she would plunge down into . . .

Nothing.

" . . . *Nate* . . ."

That single word, almost unrecognizable, came from somewhere deep inside her, but her voice was as light as the whisper of an extinguished candle flame. Her stomach was churning, and she knew she was going to vomit. The feeling that she was being watched hadn't gone away, but even if someone was watching her from the woods, it didn't matter. Her only thought was that she had to get back into the house where she'd be safe.

The pressure crushing down on her became intolerable. Her arms and legs buckled. As she crawled, her hands and knees thudded when they hit the wooden deck, but she had no sense of motion. Everything around her—the deck, the house, the yard—was spinning crazily, and she was the still point, the unmovable axis.

She might have been closer to the door, but no matter how hard she tried, safety kept slipping away from her. The metal frame and screen door towered above her, expanding and bulging outward as though pressure inside the house was building and about to explode outward. She shied away from it but still struggled toward it.

A loud humming sound filled her ears. She hadn't noticed when it had started. It seemed as though it had always been there, humming below her awareness, and only now was she consciously aware of it. Once she knew it was there, it filled her head like the maddened buzzing of a bee-hive. It blocked out every other sound.

Where are the birds? she wondered. *Why can't I hear the birds singing?*

It was a mundane thought that struck her as pathetic, al-most funny, because she realized and accepted that she might be dying. She must be having a stroke . . . or else the tumor inside her head had exploded . . . Whatever it was, she knew she was dying. Her senses were closing down, shutting off, and she was falling into a dark, backward spin. The only other time she had felt like this was when she had given birth to Trista seventeen years ago. The birth had been long and hard, and toward the end, she remembered her senses had narrowed down until all she had left was a single pinpoint of concentration to get that baby out of her.

Why is this happening to me? . . . I don't want to die!

Her panic was so strong now it blotted out everything else. She couldn't even remember what she had been trying to do. When she looked up and saw the screen door in front of her, she no longer remembered that she was trying to get to it. The heaviness pressing her down was too much to bear. Her elbows buckled, and with a long-drawn-out groan, she collapsed face-first onto the deck. Darkness surged over her as she finally gave up the struggle. She spread her arms out wide across the deck floor as if to embrace the darkness that was pulling her down like a powerful undertow she couldn't possibly resist.

And then, as she plunged into the darkness, the last thing she heard was a voice whispering to her. It, too, faded away before she could make sense of what it had said.

~5~

Am I dead?

That was Kiera's first thought as she regained consciousness. She had no idea where she was, but she didn't dare to move. Keeping her eyes closed, she stared into a well of impenetrable darkness.

Finally, when she tried to open her eyes, it was a long time before she realized where she was. She recognized the deck floor and the side of the house, but the angle was strange. The left side of her face was mashed flat against the deck, the rough wood sticking to her skin.

She took a tiny breath, amazed to feel her chest expand as clean, fresh air filled her lungs. She felt dizzy and closed her eyes for a moment before opening them again.

Finally, she realized she was lying facedown on the deck, her head cocked to one side, her arms and legs splayed. The sun was higher in the sky. Its warmth beat down on her back. She felt compelled to roll over and sit up, but she didn't have the strength. Every muscle in her body felt as limp as old rope.

What the hell happened to me? she wondered, but her memory was a complete blank.

The last thing she remembered was walking out onto the deck to eat breakfast. That seemed like a long time ago and, judging by the angle of the sun, it had been.

Did I fall down and bang my head?

She raised her hand and touched her forehead, but she didn't feel any bumps or dried blood.

So what the hell . . . ?

She had to get up off the deck. She didn't have anything planned for the day, but her mind was so fogged she might be forgetting something important.

Something's seriously wrong with me . . .

She knew that much. No one wakes up facedown on the deck without *something* being seriously wrong, but her memory was a blank. Groaning from the effort, she shifted around and somehow managed to get onto her hands and knees, but that was all. It would take too much to stand up, and she couldn't stay like this for long. Every ounce of strength had drained from her, and a cold, hollow sourness filled her stomach.

She knew she should ease herself back down onto the deck and gather her strength, but—somehow—she found the reserves to stagger to her feet. The effort was almost too much. At first, she just stood there, her feet planted wide, her head spinning as she took a few slow, even breaths. The morning air was thick with humidity. She glanced at the picnic table and saw her plate with a piece of toast on it, but that was all.

Where's my coffee? she wondered.

In spite of the pain, she rotated her wrist and looked at her watch, surprised to see that it was a little after eight o'clock. It felt so much later. She had a vague memory that something weird had happened, but she couldn't remember what it was.

Even though it hurt like hell to move, she managed to get to the screen door and slide it open. When she stepped into the kitchen, she was surprised how cool it was inside the house. The sound of blood rushing in her ears made an audible whooshing sound she found distracting. Her vision—especially at the edges—kept clouding over and shifting out of focus.

Taking short, jerky steps that made her feel like an old woman, Kiera walked over to the wall phone and picked up the receiver as if she had the clear purpose of making a call. Shaking her head to clear it, she watched with dispassionate detachment as she pressed the number on the speed dial marked with a red cross. Only when the phone started beeping as it dialed the numbers did she realize what she was doing.

"Good morning," said a voice that was entirely too chipper this early in the morning. "Dr. Schwartz's office. This is Cheryl."

"Yes. Hi, Cheryl," Kiera said, amazed that she could speak at all. He throat was parched. "I need to see Dr. Schwartz today."

CHAPTER 3

Afterimage

~1~

"I'm not sure I could ever do this, even when I was young."

Kiera looked down at her feet and then back at Dr. Schwartz, who was standing off to one side. He had her medical chart in one hand and his arms folded across his chest. The rounded bulge of his paunch stuck out beneath his arms. A smile twitched the corners of his mouth.

"Give it a try," he said. "I'm not asking for an Olympic-level performance here."

Kiera nodded and placed the heel of her right foot in front of the toes of her left. She extended her arms to keep her balance as her weight shifted forward. With a little adjustment, she caught her balance and, leaning forward, brought her left foot around so the heel was in front of the right foot.

"How far do I have to go?" she asked, not daring to look up, afraid to break her concentration.

"Not far. Just down the street to the Dunkin' Donuts. I'd like an iced mocha latte and two glazed donuts."

"This isn't as easy as you'd think," Kiera said, shooting him a mock-angry glance. She tried not to laugh at his wisecrack, but she and Dr. Schwartz had the kind of doctor-patient relationship where they could joke back and forth with each other. Usually, this put Kiera at ease, but today she wasn't nearly as relaxed as she normally was— not after what had happened on the deck this morning.

"You're doing just fine," Dr. Schwartz said. "A few more steps, and you're done."

Kiera had to wave her arms a little to keep her balance. She wondered how well she would have done on this test if she hadn't been so worried about what was happening to her. Once she got the hang of it, she kept walking heel to toe, heel to toe until she reached the wall.

"Can I stop now?"

"Sure," Dr. Schwartz said. "Now, without repositioning your feet, I want you to jump into the air, turn around one hundred and eighty degrees, and then walk back to the exam table on tiptoes."

For a second, she thought he was serious. Kiera gave him a concerned look over her shoulder and then broke into a smile.

"You're a regular laugh riot, you know that?"

"I missed my calling as a stand-up comedian."

Kiera walked back to the examination table and sat down. For the last thirty minutes or so, Dr. Schwartz had been putting her through the paces, asking her all sorts of questions and checking her visual and hearing acuity, reflexes, and sense of smell. She was still feeling a little light-headed.

"You did just fine," Dr. Schwartz said. "Your sense of smell seems a bit diminished, but that's normal with age. You're—" He glanced at her chart. "Forty-six?"

Kiera nodded and said, "Stop reminding me."

Dr. Schwartz paused for a moment and looked at her like he had something he didn't really want to say. Finally, he cleared his throat and added, "But to be honest, I don't like the visual problems you've been experiencing."

"Believe me, they're terrifying."

Just thinking about what she'd gone through the last few days made her fearful that the streak of light was going to return. It seemed always to be hovering just out of sight, waiting to strike without warning. She cringed, poised and waiting to see it now.

"Seeing flashing lights or that 'lightning streak,' as you called it, is a classic precursor to a migraine. You say the headaches usually follow within fifteen minutes to half an hour?"

"Yeah. I think so." Kiera bit her lower lip. "This all started happening just over the last few days, so I'm not really sure I can see a pattern yet." She chuckled. "I'm not sure I want to."

"But you absolutely have had no symptoms like this before? No headaches that didn't go away? Dizziness? Vertigo?"

"Not really." Kiera shook her head.

"You ever suffer any head injuries? Bang your head?"

"Nothing I can remember other than the tennis ball whacking me on the side of the head yesterday. But that was after the migraines started."

Dr. Schwartz frowned as he opened her medical records and scanned them briefly.

"How about when you were younger? Any instances of head trauma or injury?"

Kiera swallowed hard before he finished the question, and she wondered if Dr. Schwartz caught her reaction. The blood rushed from her face as a chill spider-walked up her spine.

Should I tell him about it?

"Ever fall out of a tree or off a bicycle when you were a kid?"

She regarded him with a blank stare and was struck by something odd. As he spoke, Dr. Schwartz's lips seemed to move out of synch with his voice. It was like watching a poorly dubbed foreign movie. The feathery rushing sound in her head suddenly got louder until she could feel her pulse throbbing in her neck and wrists. It was so loud it almost blocked out what Dr. Schwartz was saying. She rubbed her hands together, feeling the slick, oily sheen of sweat.

"No, I . . . Not that I recall." She scrunched her eyes as though trying to remember, but she was certain Dr. Schwartz detected the lie in her voice. He could see it in her eyes.

"Tell me, what does the expression 'a stitch in time saves nine' mean?"

Kiera cocked her head back and looked at him, confused for a moment by this sudden shift in conversation.

"What?"

"What does that expression mean?"

" 'A stitch in time saves nine' . . . It means if you . . . if you take care of something before it's a big problem, it won't become a bigger problem and need more work and attention to fix."

"Good . . . good. And who is president?"

"Of the U.S.? . . . Dick Cheney."

It was Dr. Schwartz's turn to be taken aback for a moment, but then he smiled and said, "I didn't vote for him, either. How about your appetite? Have you been eating normally?"

In answer, Kiera cupped the small bulge of her belly and shook it. "A little *too* normally, I'm afraid."

"And your bowels have been normal?"

Kiera nodded.

"How about sleep? Are you sleeping through the night?"

"Up until last night, yes. I mean . . . you know, the usual things that bother me when I'm trying to get to sleep."

" 'Usual things'? . . . Like what?"

Dr. Schwartz was leaning against the desk next to the examination table with his legs crossed. Kiera wondered why the examination had changed from physical to mental. She took a deep breath and dropped her shoulders, trying to relax.

"Bills . . . money . . . and—you know, problems with Trista and—"

"And?"

Kiera shrugged. She and Dr. Schwartz had no secrets, but it was still difficult to admit.

"And with Nate."

"You mean you still think he might be fooling around?"

Kiera shrugged and shook her head, feeling really uncomfortable.

"How about with Trista? *Problem* problems, or just the typical teenage stuff?"

"What's 'typical' about teenagers?"

"Good point."

"I just don't like the guy she's seeing."

Kiera looked at Dr. Schwartz and told herself to relax. He was more than a doctor. He was a friend. She could—and had—told him just about everything.

Everything except about the night Billy Carroll died, and I hurt my head so bad I thought I had a concussion.

"She's been dating an older man, and I'm—Nate and I aren't so keen on him."

"Anyone I know?"

"Robbie Townsend," Kiera said, and she had to look away because of the rush of embarrassment she felt. Dr. Schwartz looked suddenly serious and nodded his understanding.

"Between you and me? I agree Townsend wouldn't be my first choice for a son-in-law, but teenagers have to rebel. Deep down, Trista's a good kid. She'll get past it."

"I just hope it's before she—you know, does something stupid."

"You've talked to her about birth control and STDs?"

"Of course," Kiera said.

"Anything else bothering you?"

Once again, Dr. Schwartz changed the subject so fast Kiera found it disconcerting.

"No . . . I—It's just . . . I'm really worried about what's been going on with me. I . . . Okay, I'll admit it. I spent a little too much time on the Internet checking out medical symptoms, and I—"

"And you have immediately jumped to worst-case scenario. You think this is a brain tumor, cancerous, no doubt, or something equally horrible."

Embarrassed, Kiera was silent for a moment. Then she nodded.

"Well," Dr. Schwartz said, "to tell you the truth, I'm also a little concerned."

His words were like a splash of ice water in the face. Kiera had been hoping he would say everything looked perfectly normal, and she would just have to medicate her migraines.

"In most cases," Dr. Schwartz continued, "symptoms like you've described are all migraine-related with no organic cause. We can treat the headaches with a prescription drug if they get severe."

"Believe me. They're severe." Kiera unconsciously raised her hand to her forehead and massaged the spot above her left eye.

"There is some indication something may be pressing against the back of your retina or optic nerve."

Oh, no, Kiera thought, finding she suddenly couldn't take a deep enough breath.

"I want to make sure you understand," Dr. Schwartz continued, "this is *very* inconclusive. I'll give you a prescription to deal with the migraines if they come back and, to be honest, with menopause coming on, we might want to start thinking about hormone therapy. That might help with the migraines, but—"

He hesitated, and in that moment of hesitation, Kiera experienced another frigid rush of panic. Her pulse thumped loudly in her ears as a dark wave swept across her vision.

"And . . . ?" she said, her throat constricting.

"What I'd like to do is schedule you for a CAT scan."

"A CAT scan . . ." she echoed.

"Just so we can get a clearer picture what—if anything—is going on in that crazy little head of yours."

Kiera bristled, thinking he was patronizing her, but all she could say was, "You mean . . . like a tumor?"

"Please, Kiera. Don't make any more out of this than is necessary. I think it's best to err on the side of caution. That's all."

"Yeah, but—" Kiera heard her voice as if it was coming from far away. "So when do you want to do it?"

"Sooner rather than later."

"So this could be really serious?" The blood in her veins seemed to have turned to water, and she was afraid she was going to cry. As far as she was concerned, he had just handed her a death sentence.

"Are you listening to me?" Dr. Schwartz asked, leaning closer to get her attention. "At this point, my guess is it's nothing serious. But that's just a guess. I want to do the CAT scan as a precaution, and I want to do it soon so we can settle your mind about it. Honestly? I'd say there's a ninety-nine percent chance nothing's there. But I don't like leaving *anything*—even that one percent—to chance."

"So when should I schedule it?" Kiera was all too aware of the tremor in her voice. She got off the examination table but had to lean against it for support.

"See Cheryl on the way out. She'll call the hospital and schedule it before you leave."

Dr. Schwartz walked over to Kiera and smiled as he placed his hand on her shoulder. The touch was supposed to be reassuring, but Kiera shrank away from it.

"There is . . . well, one more thing I should tell you," she said in a shaky voice.

Dr. Schwartz's left eyebrow shot up, and he looked at her with curious intensity. Before she spoke, Kiera took a deep breath that whistled in her nose. The room seemed to be pitching gently from side to side.

"When you asked about head injuries . . . When I was in high school, I was in a car accident and banged my head." Again, she unconsciously raised her hand to the spot above her left eye and massaged it. "This was before seat belt laws. It hurt pretty badly. I think it might have been a concussion."

"Did you see your family doctor about it and get medical treatment?"

Biting her lower lip, Kiera shook her head. The motion sent a splinter of pain shooting behind her left eye, making her wince.

"No. It was—" She shrugged and smiled weakly. "My boyfriend and I didn't want to get into trouble, so we didn't report it."

"Was anyone else injured?"

No one except Billy . . . who died, Kiera thought, but there was no way she could say that out loud.

"No. We weren't going very fast, and Jon O'Keefe—he was my boyfriend at the time—hit the brakes a little too hard. I was thrown forward and smacked my head on the dashboard."

She finally realized she was rubbing the spot above her left eyebrow and noticed that, even with that slight pressure, she was wincing. Dr. Schwartz seemed to catch her reaction.

"Do you have a migraine coming on now?" he asked, his voice low with concern.

Kiera closed her eyes and stared into the swelling darkness behind her eyelids. Dark red and blue afterimages swirled before her eyes, but—so far, anyway—there was no hint of the white lightning. But in the darkness of her closed eyes, she saw something else . . . something that froze her. It emerged from the swirling colors, blurry and out of focus, but it left her with the clear impression that she was looking at the distorted shape of a person.

"Kiera?" Dr. Schwartz said.

His voice echoed, sounding farther away than it should have; but no matter how much Kiera felt compelled to open her eyes and look at him, if only for reassurance, she was enthralled by the hazy silhouette that emerged from the light behind her closed eyes.

"No, I . . . I'm just . . ." She motioned with her hand for him to be silent. "Give me a second."

The vision gradually resolved, seeming to both advance and retreat at the same time. It was an indistinct splotch with a pulsating red and violet glow behind it. Like looking at objects in the dark, it seemed clearest when she focused her attention to one side or the other, like looking out the corner of her eye. Only then did the figure look real, almost three-dimensional as it raised its arms out to her.

Kiera was aware that Dr. Schwartz was in the room with her, but her attention was focused on the figure. She thought she recognized it, but it was still hazy enough so she couldn't be sure. She really couldn't tell if it was a man or a woman.

She cleared her throat and started to speak, all too aware of how fragile her voice would sound.

"You know how when you close your eyes and press on them, you see colors and images?"

"Yes."

"It's like that now . . . I see . . . It's like there's this pressure on the back of my eyeball that's making me see things."

"Like what?" Dr. Schwartz asked, his voice low and steady but sounding oh so faraway.

"Lights . . . shifting globs of lights that are moving toward me . . . and flashes of—"

She cut herself short and opened her eyes when she realized the light behind the figure had suddenly brightened and was morphing into a jagged white beam.

"Oh no . . . Oh *no*," she whispered as she looked around the office, startled by the dazzling brilliance of everything.

"What is it?" Dr. Schwartz asked.

He clasped her shoulder, but even his touch seemed strangely distant. A rush of pins and needles tingled her hands and feet. Her chest ached when she took a breath, and the air in her lungs felt stale, as if she'd been holding it too long. The antiseptic-smelling air of the exam room seemed dense with humidity. The dizziness she'd experienced earlier came back even stronger, and she whimpered as she leaned back against the examination table.

"I don't know if . . . I . . . I'm . . . this rush of panic just came over me," she said in a rasping voice.

"Does your head hurt now?"

Kiera did a quick inventory and realized that, in spite of her nervousness, her head didn't ache. Hazy afterimages of light still darted like shadows everywhere she looked, but they were fading.

"Let me give you some Imitrex for the migraines," Dr. Schwartz said, "and I'd suggest you go home and take it easy for the rest of the day. Have a nap out on the deck in the sun. You're wound way too tight. Do you drink a lot of coffee?"

Kiera shrugged. "I don't think so . . . Just a cup in the morning."

Dr. Schwartz nodded. "These could also be caffeine-related panic attacks. You might want to cut coffee out for a while. See what happens. You'd be surprised at the reaction some people have to caffeine."

When he stopped talking, Kiera realized he was staring at her with an intensity she had never seen before. She knew he was worried about her but didn't want to say too much because of how fragile she was right now.

"Are you okay to drive? I can call Nate if you'd like."

Kiera shook her head no as she picked up her purse from the examination table.

"Does Nate even know you're here? Have you told him about what's going on?"

Kiera didn't say a word, and she knew her silence condemned her.

"I'd strongly recommend that you talk to him about this," Dr. Schwartz said.

"I have my cell if I need help." Kiera patted her purse. "I'll be fine."

Even as she said it, she knew Dr. Schwartz wasn't convinced, but she couldn't let herself fall apart like this in front of him. She was determined to get the CAT scan without telling Nate about it, and everything would be fine. She wanted to believe that she didn't want Nate to worry, but she knew otherwise.

"I'll have Cheryl set up the appointment for the CAT scan and give you a call later today," Dr. Schwartz said. "You go home and take it easy. When migraines first come on, they can be scary if you don't know what's happening."

"Yeah . . . Thanks," Kiera said. Her voice still sounded too feeble, but there was nothing she could do but take her purse and leave. Even after she'd made it out to the car, though, a single thought lingered in the back of her mind.

What if what I'm seeing isn't *just a trick of the eye? . . . What if it's* real?

As she started up her car and pulled out of the parking lot onto Main Street, she had no doubt that what she had seen was the ghost of Billy Carroll.

There was no other explanation.

She remembered the famous statement by Sherlock Holmes, about how when you have eliminated the impossible, whatever remains, however improbable, must be the truth.

She remembered that night out on River Road all too clearly. She had lived with the memory of that night ever since it had happened. In some way, if she was honest with herself, she had to admit that living with that lie had ruined her life. And now that Jon was back in town, the memory was coming back even stronger to torment her.

Even without closing her eyes, she could see Billy standing there in front of Jon's car, his hands raised in a silent, angry gesture as he shouted something she couldn't hear over the roaring sound of the engine. She still remembered how Billy's face had been illuminated by the glare of the headlights—like frozen lightning—and she could imagine that image was burned so strongly into her retina and mind that it would never go away.

Never!

～2～

A not-so-subtle gloom had settled over Kiera by the time she got home. It was a past three o'clock when she pulled into the driveway and hit the button on the garage door opener. She was absolutely wrung out and more than a little scared. The loud rattling of the garage door as it slowly rose hurt her head. When she pulled into her parking spot in the garage, she realized Nate's Subaru wasn't there.

"Good," she whispered, and then immediately felt guilty.

If she was going to be honest with herself, she had to admit that—right now—she didn't want to see him or anyone else. She hadn't told him about her appointment today because she had almost convinced herself she didn't want him to worry. She knew it was really because she wanted to deal with this alone. She didn't want him involved. A dark cloud of mortality was pressing down on her, and she couldn't admit to anyone—even him—how frightened she was.

On the drive home, she wondered if what she was experiencing might not be physical after all. Was that denial, or—as crazy as it seemed—was there a chance something supernatural might be happening?

Was the ghost of Billy Carroll haunting her?

She couldn't shake the feeling that it had everything to do with what had happened on out River Road that night back when she was in high school.

At the time, she had barely been able to look at, much less save, any of the newspaper articles about Billy Carroll's disappearance, but she had always wondered why his body had never been found. The real tragedy was Billy's parents. His mother and father had never gotten an answer about what had happened to their son.

How can anyone overcome the loss of a child?

All Billy's parents knew was their son had disappeared. Until the day she died, Billy's mother had insisted her son had run away and was still alive somewhere, and that he would come back to her . . . eventually. Billy's father had taken to drinking heavily after his son disappeared. He lost his job with the town highway department, and he ended his life by hanging himself in the family garage a few months after his wife died.

But Kiera knew perfectly well what had happened to Billy. She also knew that it was much too late to tell anyone what had happened. Jon was right. It was a terrible secret they shared, and they would carry it to their graves.

But we weren't the only ones out there . . . Billy was, too . . .

As she sat there in her car, parked in the garage with the engine still running, that thought twisted inside her like a live snake. Her hands on the steering wheel were slick with sweat, and her pulse squeezed her throat like unseen fingers. A thin haze of exhaust filled the garage with a blue tinge.

What if someone else saw what happened? . . . What if someone else knows? . . . And what if they're using it now to scare me after all these years?

That thought paralyzed Kiera.

It made perfect sense.

Kiera cringed, unable to stop the feeling that she was being watched. She shifted around in the car seat and looked out the open garage door. The sunlight dazzled her sight and made her head hurt as she looked around the yard. She didn't notice anything unusual, but that didn't mean something threatening her wasn't there.

"Come on . . . Just calm down," she cautioned herself.

She wanted to do what Dr. Schwartz had suggested, but right now she couldn't muster the strength to turn off the car, much less get out. The sense of unseen danger all around her was so imminent she didn't dare to move.

Is it possible? . . . Could someone else have been hiding in the brush or on the opposite side of the river and seen what we did to Billy?

As frightening as that thought was, it didn't explain everything that had been going on. It certainly didn't explain the sudden onset of migraines or how she could be seeing things.

No, she told herself, biting her lower lip and shaking her head. *It* has *to be something else . . .*

She jumped when the door leading into the house opened a crack, and Trista peeked out with a perplexed expression. Kiera realized the car was still running and quickly turned it off. Her hand was trembling as she opened the car door and got out.

"Hey," Kiera said, concerned about the expression on Trista's face. She winced when she slammed the car door shut a little too hard. "Everything okay?"

Her first thought was that Robbie had come over to the house while she was gone and maybe was still in the house. Trista was panicking, wondering how she was going to get him out without her mother seeing him. But Robbie's Mustang wasn't in the driveway, so he probably wasn't here . . . unless a friend had dropped him off or they had hidden his car down the road.

"Sure," Trista said. "Just wondering what you're doing out here."

Kiera shrugged, trying to appear nonchalant as she started toward the door. The smell of exhaust was thick in the garage.

Trista stepped back from the door to let her in. Once she was inside, Kiera looked around, still expecting to see Robbie, but he was nowhere in sight. She let her breath out as she hung her keys on the hook by the door, put her purse on the kitchen table, and walked over to the refrigerator.

"Anything you want to talk about?" Kiera asked. She could hear the edge in her voice and wished it wasn't there, but she couldn't help herself. She was still upset about what she was going through, and dealing with Trista right now was the last thing she wanted to do.

Trista shrugged and shook her head no, but the worried look was still there in her furrowed brow. Maybe Robbie was hiding upstairs in her bedroom.

Kiera opened the refrigerator and took out a bottle of diet Pepsi, then got a glass from the cupboard.

"Want some?" she asked, holding up the bottle. It made a little explosive sound when she loosened the cap.

Again, Trista silently shook her head no. Usually at this

point, she would have left, gone upstairs to her bedroom or down to the family room. It pained Kiera that she and her daughter didn't talk anymore, certainly not the way they used to when Trista was young. Kiera pegged it right around the time Trista started junior high. She didn't care for some of the kids Trista started hanging out with, and it had only gotten worse through high school. Whenever or whatever it was, they had lost the closeness they'd once had. Now that Trista was almost eighteen, about to start her senior year in high school, they had so little interaction it was pathetic . . . nothing beyond superficial, day-to-day things.

"Something's bothering you. I can tell," Kiera said.

After a moment's hesitation, Trista cleared her throat and nodded toward the door that led out into the garage.

"I heard you drive in a while ago, but you just sat out there in the car for quite a while with the engine running. What were you doing, trying to kill yourself?"

"Don't be ridiculous, I was—" Kiera said, but she left the thought unfinished and busied herself with getting ice cubes from the freezer and then pouring herself a glass of soda.

Trista shrugged and stared at her mother until Kiera started to feel uncomfortable.

"You have any plans for tonight?" she asked as she walked over to the sliding glass door and put her hand on the handle. But she didn't open it. She didn't like the tension she saw in Trista, but she didn't have the energy to try to drag it out of her . . . not if Trista wasn't willing to talk, too.

"I'm gonna sit out on the deck and relax a bit before starting supper. You're welcome to join me."

Trista shrugged again and said, "Naw. I got stuff to do."

Kiera was positive that "stuff" included meeting up with Robbie later tonight—unless it was smuggling him out of the house now, but she was too drained to get into it.

"Do you know where Dad is?" Kiera asked.

"Nope," Trista said. "Probably still at school, getting his crap organized."

"Crap . . ." Kiera echoed, nodding, but for some reason, she had a flash of doubt and thought her husband might be doing something else. She and Trista looked at each other in silence for a moment until Kiera couldn't take it any longer and turned away.

"Well," she said as she slid open the glass door and the screen door. "I'll be outside if you need me."

"'Kay."

Kiera didn't like that she felt a measure of relief when she stepped out onto the deck and slid the screen door shut behind her. The ice cubes in her drink clinked like rattling dice, and as she set the glass down on the plastic table next to a recliner, it almost slipped out of her hand because of the moisture that had beaded up on the glass. She sighed as she sat down in one of the chairs in the shade. Leaning her head back, she closed her eyes.

From inside the house, she heard the sudden chirping ring of Trista's cell phone and then the thumping sound of feet on the stairs as she ran upstairs to her bedroom.

Kiera hated that there was such a division between her and her daughter, but no matter what she tried, she had no idea what to do about it. She knew it was as much her fault as Trista's. Maybe more. She was the adult. But sometimes Trista seemed to go out of her way to provoke her when she wasn't simply ignoring her.

Kiera wished things weren't so awkward between them. It seemed as though they never spoke honestly and openly to each other anymore. Either they were arguing or else—worse—they dealt with each other with frosty indifference. There wasn't one incident she could pinpoint as *the* moment when things went bad between them. They were just rotten.

And Nate certainly wasn't any help. He got along just fine with Trista, which only made Kiera out to be the bad guy. As far as Kiera was concerned, Nate let Trista get away with entirely too much, and they were going to pay for it, sooner or later.

As she rolled these and other thoughts around in her mind, Kiera closed her eyes and was staring, hypnotized, into the thin, red haze of daylight that lit her closed eyelids. Splotches of color swelled and faded, pulsing and drifting like amoeba under a microscope. Without looking, she felt around until she found her glass and picked it up. When she took a sip of soda, she reveled as the cold, fizzy liquid exploded on her tongue. The wind sighed through the trees that bordered the yard, and Kiera realized that for some time she had been listening to a faint voice that was whispering to her.

Startled, she jumped and opened her eyes, looking all around. The sudden brightness brought tears to her eyes, but the instant she opened her eyes, the voice—if it had ever been there—cut off.

Kiera tensed as she turned and looked at the house, half expecting to see Trista standing in the doorway, watching her. Maybe that's what she heard, Trista talking on the phone in her room. Other than the wind and a few birds singing, the afternoon was perfectly quiet. Not even the distant drone of a neighbor's lawn mower or the sound of a car passing by on the street broke the silence. The air was heavy and still, and it settled around her like a blanket.

As she looked at the backyard, the unnerving feeling that someone was still out there in the woods, watching her, was still there.

Is that who was talking to me? she wondered, but she knew that thought was irrational.

Why would someone be out there spying on her . . . and then start talking to her?

She wished she could remember what they had been saying, but the voice was like a dream that slipped away the instant she awoke. She was left with a vague, uneasy feeling of something just out of reach. She had no idea if the voice had even been making sense, but it didn't matter. It was gone now.

The medication Dr. Schwartz had given her was still in her purse. She wondered if a migraine was coming on and thought it might be a good idea to take something preemptively, but she wasn't convinced this was a migraine. There hadn't been any flash of light. There wasn't even a hint of pain above her left eye.

"Okay, so I'm having auditory hallucinations," she whispered, her voice low but still loud enough to make her cringe.

The feeling that someone was watching her hadn't gone away, but she ignored it. Her hand was shaking as she raised her glass to her mouth and took another sip of soda. The soda was already flat and warm, and she wondered how long she had been out here, drifting between wakefulness and sleep while listening to a voice that wasn't there.

Sourness filled her stomach, and she thought she might throw up. During the exam, Dr. Schwartz had told her that nausea might also presage a migraine. Maybe that's what was happening now.

Or is it just the power of suggestion?

Even as the memory of it faded away like sand sifting between her fingers, the voice had seemed so real she had simply accepted it . . . until she thought about it.

And it had been telling her something . . . something important, she was sure . . . but no matter how hard she tried, she couldn't dredge up the memory other than a vague impression of a woman's voice.

"Is anyone out there?" she called out suddenly, surprising herself by the strength of her voice.

A faint echo rebounded from the woods, but other than the birdsong, that was all.

Shifting forward in her chair, she got ready to stand up, even though she wasn't confident that she had the strength. Her body was completely wrung out, like she had just finished a four-mile run. She was scared, and the feeling that somewhere close by someone unseen was watching her was getting steadily stronger. Pressure filled her head, and she found it almost impossible to swallow or breathe.

"I'm going out for a bit."

Trista's voice, coming suddenly from inside the house, startled Kiera, making her jump and knock over her glass of soda. The glass hit the deck and shattered. Dark soda bubbled as it washed across the deck and splattered between the planks to the ground below.

Kiera sighed and turned quickly to her daughter, who was standing in the doorway. The screen obscured her like a wall of smoke that made her look insubstantial. Forcing herself to use a milder voice, she asked, "Where you going?"

"Just out," Trista said, and without another word, she turned and left, disappearing like a ghost that had never really been there.

"Who are you going with?" Kiera shouted. "When will you be back? We're having supper as soon as your father gets home."

But Trista was already gone, slamming the door shut behind her.

"All right, then," Kiera whispered to herself. "See yah later."

Warm tears filled her eyes and ran down her face as she knelt down to pick up the shards of broken glass from the deck.

~3~

"I can't believe you didn't tell me about this."

Nate's face was twisted with anger as he paced back and forth at the foot of the bed. It was another warm night, a little past eleven. Kiera was lying outside the covers, wearing only a thin nightgown. The fan was rattling in the window, making the curtains billow.

"I already told you why. I didn't want you to worry."

"Yeah . . . Sure . . . Okay . . . So it's okay for me to worry *now*? Is that what you're saying?"

"Don't you think you're overreacting just a tad?" Kiera spoke with a calmness she didn't really feel. She was just as frightened—if not more so—about what was happening to her. After all, this was her *life* that was in jeopardy.

Nate stopped pacing, turned, and looked at her. His dark eyes glistened in the dim bedroom light. His face looked paler than it should this time of year, but he didn't get out and exercise much. The lines in his face, especially around his mouth, stood out in sharp relief.

"Dr. Schwartz says it's nothing to worry about. He said there's a ninety-nine percent chance it's nothing."

"There's always that one percent," Nate said, raising his forefinger and pointing at her.

"Thanks. You know, I really don't want to talk about this right now." It took effort for Kiera to keep her voice steady. "The truth is, I'm a lot more worried about what's going on with Trista than with what's happening to me."

She glanced at the alarm clock on her bedside table and saw how late it was.

"She left the house around four o'clock with *him*, and she hasn't called."

"You call her?"

"I tried. I'm just worried. Robbie drove away so fast he laid a patch of rubber on the road in front of the house."

Nate sniffed. "Trista's fine. I see teenagers all day at school. She's not half as bad as she could be."

"Well *they* aren't my daughter," Kiera said as a sharp pain lanced the left side of her head. She winced, waiting for the pain to intensify, but it quickly faded. "I swear to God," she muttered, "sometimes I wish we'd never had her."

She hadn't meant to say that out loud, but it was out of her mouth before she could stop it. She looked at Nate, who was staring at her, his face pale.

"At least you finally admitted the truth," he said softly. "But why not go the whole distance? Why not say you wish we had never gotten married, too? If that's how you feel . . ."

"No," Kiera said, but her voice choked off before she could say more. Her face flushed, and her body tensed, as she waited for another migraine to kick in behind her left eye. "I never said that."

"Come on. You don't have to," Nate said. "You make it so frigging obvious every day, especially lately, that you'd just as soon not be with me."

"I do *not*," Kiera said, but she cringed because she couldn't add anything like, *because I love you.* "Did it ever occur to you that I might be a little bit frightened about what's going on?"

"What, with Trista or with me?"

"With my head!" She pressed the flat of her hand against her forehead and winced. "These headaches! You have no idea . . ." Tears welled in her eyes, but she wiped them away before they could fall. "You have no clue how much they hurt and how . . . how scared I am."

Nate seemed to deflate in an instant. His shoulders slumped, and his eyes were downcast as he walked over and sat down on her side of the bed near her. He took hold of her hand and squeezed it, but Kiera noticed how cold and clammy his touch was.

Is he really *that afraid our relationship is going down the tubes, or is this just an act?*

She blinked as she stared up at the ceiling, then shifted to look at her husband's face. The bedside light under-lit his features with a harsh glow. She wished she could see some trace of genuine tenderness and warmth in his face, but his face was a mask.

What am I really afraid of?

"Don't you get it?" Nate said. "That's why I was so up-set when you didn't tell me about it. I wanted to—I *want* to be there for you, but I can't if you don't let me."

"I know . . . I know," Kiera said, looking down to avoid his steady gaze. "It's just that . . . this is really scary."

"I know. So what's next?"

He took a breath and leaned away from her, and all Kiera could think was, *Isn't this when you should hold me?* She slipped her hand away from his and wiped her eyes.

"I have to have a CAT scan in two weeks."

"And what if the headaches get worse between now and then?"

"Then I'll deal with them."

She shuddered when she realized she was trying to convince herself as much as her husband that everything was going to be all right. Still, she had never felt so alone, so abandoned before. When she looked at Nate, even with him sitting so close, she felt there was a chasm between them, and she couldn't help but wonder how—and if—they could ever bridge it.

Something had been lost, or maybe it had never been there in the first place. Maybe Nate was right, and she did regret that they had ever gotten married. And now, she wasn't even sure if she had the energy or the desire to find out what it was, much less try to get it back.

"Look, I really need to get some sleep," she said, "but there's no way I can until—"

Before she could finish, a door downstairs opened and shut. The sound carried through the quiet house. Seconds later, footsteps, moving stealthily, came up the stairs.

"Trista? That you?" Nate called out.

After a moment's hesitation, a reply came.

"Uhh . . . yeah."

"We're awake," Kiera said, noticing the edge in her voice. Trista didn't answer.

From the sound of her voice, Kiera knew Trista was standing outside her bedroom door, no doubt anxious to get into her room and shut the door.

Something else has been lost here, too, Kiera thought as a heavy sourness settled in her stomach.

"So where were you?" Kiera called out.

Again, Trista didn't answer. The only sound was that of her bedroom door opening and shutting.

Kiera looked at Nate. It was his turn, now, to have trouble maintaining eye contact.

"Are you going to talk to her, ask her where she's been?" Kiera asked.

Nate just sat there on the edge of the bed, looking back and forth between Kiera and the door.

"She's fine," he finally said. "I think the best thing for us would be to get off her case all the time." He paused, and neither of them spoke as they glared at each other. "Okay, so you don't like Robbie. Did it ever occur to you that giving her so much crap all the time might only be driving her to him?"

Kiera had no idea what to say about that, but she practically leaped off the bed and strode down the hall to Trista's room. She clenched her fist and pounded on the door.

"Open up," she said, her voice hard with command.

After several seconds, she heard footsteps approach the door. The lock clicked, and the door opened a crack. Trista peered out at her.

"You want to tell me where you've been?"

"Not really," Trista said. "It's none of your business."

"Oh yes it is, young lady." Kiera put her hand on the door and pushed it open, making Trista back up. She stood there looking at her mother, her hands clasped against her chest.

"I want to know where you were and who you were with."

In a flash, Trista's expression changed from timid to furious. Her eyes widened, and her face flushed.

"As if you don't already know!" she yelled, so loudly, Kiera was taken aback.

"What—? What are you talking about?"

"You don't think we saw you?"

Totally confused, all Kiera could do was stand there and shake her head and say, "Saw me? Where?"

"In your fucking car!" Trista shouted, her voice shrill to the point of breaking. "You were following us."

"I . . . I was not. I was right here all evening."

Trista wrinkled her nose and snorted. "Like hell. You think I wouldn't recognize you? Jesus, how fucking stupid are you?"

"You watch your language, young lady."

Trista's face contorted with rage as tears filled her eyes and ran down her cheeks.

"Just leave me alone! Let me live my life the way I want to! I don't need you following me around and spying on me!"

"But I wasn't . . ." Kiera was conflicted. She felt impelled to go to her daughter and talk to her, try to figure out what she was talking about and calm her down, but at the same time she was frighteningly aware of just how distant they were.

"I never left the house tonight," she said, but Trista snorted again.

"I don't want to talk," she said, pointing out the door. "Just get out and leave me alone."

Convinced there was nothing she could do or say—at least not now—Kiera stood there for a few seconds longer; then she turned and left, closing the door softly behind her so Trista wouldn't slam it shut.

As she walked down the hall to her bedroom, she could hear loud banging sounds from Trista's room as she threw things around. Consumed with a sense of overwhelming defeat, she slipped into bed without a word, turned out the light, and just lay there with her back to Nate as she stared into the darkness.

"You wanna talk about it?" Nate asked after a minute or two.

"I need to sleep right now," Kiera said tightly. She squeezed her eyes so tightly shut tears ran from them as she waited . . . waited for the first throb of pain to begin. Hopefully, she'd be sound asleep before another migraine came.

CHAPTER 4

Reflections

~1~

The next two weeks passed without incident. Although Kiera never got another full-blown migraine in that time, it seemed as though one was always looming like a thunderstorm on the horizon, ready to strike without warning.

Nothing had changed between her and Nate, and things were even worse between her and Trista. There was still an icy distance between her and both her husband and daughter, and she couldn't help but wonder how much of it was real and how much was just her. More times than she cared to admit to herself, especially late at night as she tossed and turned, unable to fall asleep, she found herself wondering how different her life would have been if she had never married Nate and had never had Trista. She spent much of her days feeling nostalgic about the years that had passed, and she couldn't help but wonder if this was because she was feeling her own mortality or if most, maybe all, of what she was feeling was real.

The morning of her CAT scan was tougher than she

thought it would be. Because they were going to be examining her head, the doctor had told her she probably wouldn't have to drink a contrast solution, which was used for digestive and circulation scans to help get a clearer picture of the internal organs. As a safety precaution, though, a nurse from the hospital called the night before and instructed her not to eat or drink anything after midnight.

Nate insisted that he go to the hospital with her. Kiera wasn't sure she even wanted him to be there. She still wanted to deal with it on her own. Alone. She actually enjoyed the feeling of independence, but she realized there was no way she would convince him not to come.

It was just as well, she finally decided, because she knew she'd be in no condition to drive after the exam . . . especially if they found anything.

And *that's* what was bothering her most. These other problems could wait until she was through with the tests.

Through the last two weeks, researching on the Internet, she had become even more convinced a tumor was growing in her head. Dr. Schwartz told her there were no nerves in the brain, so she wouldn't have been able to feel anything, but she was aware of a cold pressure building up inside her head and centered behind her left eye. Schwartz assured her that, after the exam, the doctor would give her a quick analysis, and she was mentally preparing herself for the worst-case scenario . . . inoperable cancer.

"You 'bout ready?" Nate called from the foot of the stairs.

Kiera had just finished applying her makeup and was ready to go, but Nate's impatience irritated her.

Why is he hurrying me like this?

How come he can eat and drink anything he wants to, and I can't? . . . Not even a cup of coffee?

"Just a sec," she shouted back.

Trista was still asleep, but Kiera didn't care if they woke her up with their yelling. It'd be nice if she bothered to get up and at least wish her mother good luck today, but like everyone else these days, Kiera hadn't talked to her about what was going on.

Staring into the mirror, she gave her thick, red hair another few quick strokes with the brush, then turned to leave. As she did, though, she saw something that made her catch her breath and freeze. Just as she was turning away from the mirror, in the corner of her eye, she caught a glimpse of her reflection. The odd thing was, it didn't turn when she turned. For an instant, her reflection appeared to be frozen in the glass, unmoving as it stared back at her.

A wave of chills slid up Kiera's back when she turned to look at the mirror. She held her breath and stared at her reflection, moving her head from side to side. The reflection appeared perfectly normal now, and she wanted to believe it had just been a trick of the eye. She raised her hand and brushed her hair away from her face. Her reflection did exactly what she did—as it should—but even now, as she moved, a smear of gauzy purple light followed her movements.

"What the . . . ?" she whispered. She brought her face close to the mirror. Her breath made two small fog rings on the glass when she exhaled.

Blinking her eyes a few times, she tried to re-create the visual effect, but once again, everything appeared normal. She turned away and then looked back quickly at the mirror, expecting to see another strange visual effect, but nothing happened.

"All right," she whispered. "Just calm down."

Her face and neck were slick with sweat, and her pulse was racing. When she wet a washcloth with cool water and blotted the back of her neck, a shiver ran through her. Again, when she wasn't thinking about it, when she glanced down at the sink, she had the impression her reflection in the mirror didn't move in time with her. Looking quickly back at her face, she stared into her eyes, which were wide with fear.

"Don't mess with me, okay?" she whispered as she raised her hand to her left eyebrow and rubbed it gently.

"Kiera?"

Kiera jumped, startled. Nate was standing in the doorway, but she'd been so involved looking into the mirror, she hadn't heard him come upstairs. The light from the bedroom lit him from behind, making his features indistinct.

"You okay?" he asked as he took a step forward.

Suddenly embarrassed and feeling foolish, Kiera nodded and somehow managed to say, "Yeah . . . I'm fine."

Nate stretched his left arm out and tapped his wristwatch. "If you're supposed to be there by seven o'clock, we'd better get going."

The morning had a slight chill, a presage that autumn was on its way, so Kiera grabbed a sweater before going downstairs. Nate was a few steps behind her and went out into the garage first to open the car door for her.

"Thanks," she said as she sat down and snapped on her seat belt. Nate didn't reply as he walked around the car and got in on the driver's side. He gave her a tight smile but still said nothing. He pressed the garage door controller, and as the garage door rumbled up, he started the car and backed out into the driveway.

They barely spoke during the drive from Stratford to Maine Medical Center in Portland. Kiera couldn't stop thinking about how nervous and worried she was, but she didn't feel comfortable talking about it to Nate. She stared blankly at the road ahead or out the side window, watching the familiar landscape flash by, but not really noticing anything.

"All right," Nate muttered as he pulled up to the ticket booth in the hospital parking lot. He took the ticket, tucked it under the visor, and drove around the lot looking for an empty slot.

"Didn't think there'd be so many people here this early," he said, glancing at her, but Kiera still had the impression he was talking to himself, not her.

They found an empty place and parked. Kiera opened the door for herself and stepped out while Nate got out and shut his door. When he activated the automatic door lock, the sudden chirp startled her and made her jump.

The chill in the air and what she was about to face made her shiver when she looked up at the imposing multistoried brick front of the hospital. The size of the place had always intimidated her; but as she looked at it now, she couldn't help but think a death sentence was waiting for her inside. Nate walked over to her, took hold of her hand, and squeezed it.

"Don't worry. You're gonna be fine," he said, but she wondered if he meant it. As they crossed the street and walked through the wide revolving doors of the hospital's front entrance, Kiera wished she could believe him.

After getting directions from a Middle Eastern woman at the front information desk, they took the elevator up to the third floor. They wandered around a while until they found the exam room where she was supposed to report.

"Well," Kiera said as she tried to swallow the dry lump in her throat. "Here goes."

~~2~~

"Your blood pressure's a bit elevated, but that's to be expected."

The nurse giving Kiera her preliminary examination before the CAT scan was young and rather plain. Kiera was so nervous she forgot the woman's name as soon as she told her, and she was so close, Kiera couldn't read the name badge on her hospital shirt. The nurse asked a series of questions—if Kiera was pregnant, if she was allergic to any medications, if she had recently had any head or heart surgery, if she had any metal objects implanted in her body, and if she wore permanent eyeliner.

"How's your appetite been?"

"Fine."

"And you've been sleeping well?"

Kiera almost said *sure,* but she stopped herself. She *hadn't* been sleeping well at all. For the past two weeks, she'd had trouble falling asleep and staying asleep. And night after night, the anxiety dreams were much more vivid than usual. In the morning, she could never remember many of the details, but they left her feeling unsettled throughout the day.

"All right, then," the nurse said, but Kiera was certain Nurse What's-Her-Name didn't believe her. After a few more routine questions, she asked Kiera to step behind a screen and change into a hospital gown, removing all of her jewelry and any other metal objects that might interfere with the scan.

Wearing the hospital gown made Kiera feel self-conscious and vulnerable. Maybe that was the point. What was going to happen to her was definitely out of her control.

She got even more nervous when the technician—a young man with long, sandy hair and bright blue eyes—entered the room and introduced himself simply as Paul. He was friendly enough, but he was all business as he directed her to lie down on her back on the examination table. The large white donut-shaped metal ring at the head of the table intimidated Kiera, and she felt an impulse to get up and run out of there.

"Looks like something out of *Star Wars*," Kiera said with a nervous laugh.

Paul barely reacted and, for an instant, she wished Nate was here with her instead of in the waiting room across the corridor.

Moving stiffly and feeling clumsier than usual, Kiera climbed up onto the table and shifted around so she was lying on her back. Paul helped her get into position so her head was resting comfortably on the U-shaped, padded headrest.

"Comfortable?" he asked.

"Nothing but," Kiera said with a weak smile. She folded her hands across her chest, but Paul asked her to place them at her sides. The examination table was almost too narrow for her to do that comfortably, and Kiera wondered how long she could hold this position without getting antsy. Probably less than one minute.

"Would you like some music while we do this?" Paul asked.

"No. I think I'll be fine," Kiera said, but she didn't feel at all confident when she looked at the arc of bright white machinery that encircled her.

"I'd recommend it," Paul said. "How about something classical just to soothe you?"

"Sure . . . fine. Whatever you say."

"If at any time during the procedure you start to feel uncomfortable or claustrophobic, there's a microphone close by, so don't hesitate to speak up. 'Kay?"

Kiera nodded, although the headrest restricted her movement. The table hummed as Paul moved her into position. When he shifted her a little too far forward, a bright beam of light at the top of the arc stabbed her eyes. She panicked, thinking the sudden brightness would trigger a migraine, but she blinked away the afterimage and told herself to take a breath and stay calm.

Yeah, like I'm cool and calm . . . Just relax and go with it . . . It's entirely out of your hands now.

She felt like a slab of meat and, knowing there was nothing she could do about it, she closed her eyes and settled down, praying for it to be over.

Paul left the room and entered the observation booth. "All right, Mrs. Davis." His amplified voice sounded loud and tinny through the speaker next to her head. "Just relax. Try not to move. It'll all be done before you know it."

With her eyes closed, Kiera lost any sense of time as the table started to shift forward, moving inch by inch. It made faint clicking sounds, and the scanner whirred and clicked with no discernable pattern as it moved all around her, getting different angles. Although she told herself it was just her imagination, she was sure she could feel the heat of the light and X-rays burning into her.

"How you doing in there?" Paul's amplified voice asked.

"Fine," Kiera replied, but the truth was, she was starting to feel a bit claustrophobic. She wished Paul hadn't mentioned it and struggled to keep her eyes closed and take shallow, even breaths, but her panic was getting stronger by the second. Even with the classical music playing softly, the sound of the machinery was loud enough almost to drown it out. Gears and cogs clicked and whirred as the table kept moving her slowly farther into the metallic cylinder. She was disoriented and was convinced the table was tipping her headfirst into the machine. Her throat was dry, but she was cautious not to move too much. She barely swallowed.

The sound of the machinery got increasingly louder, especially whenever there was a pause or low passage in the music. Kiera tried to convince herself she was someplace else, and after a while she drifted into an unusual mental state. She felt completely dissociated from her body, even when Paul asked her again how she was doing, and she replied that everything was just fine.

At some point, she realized that, even with her eyes closed, she was having an odd visual experience. It was almost as if—somehow—she was outside of her body, floating up near the ceiling and looking down at herself, lying immobile on the table.

Am I dying . . . or already dead?

She tensed when she recalled the illusion she'd had this morning, that her reflection in the mirror didn't move when she did.

It's like that now.

A rush of panic swept through her, making her body tingle . . . especially her hands and feet. Her eyes remained closed, but she had the distinct impression that she could see right through her eyelids. The thought occurred to her that it didn't matter if her eyes were open or closed. In fact, it didn't matter if she was awake or asleep or even if she was alive or dead . . . she would be seeing the same thing. Amazed, she stared into a dark, swirling vortex behind her eyelids. It was filled with subtly shifting lights and shadows that left blurry afterimages on her retina.

"Still doing all right?"

Paul's voice seemed to be coming from an impossible distance. Kiera was so lost in the whirring sounds of the machinery and the jerky motion of the table that she didn't know if she responded to him. She was adrift in a world of gauzy white light and shifting smudges of shadows.

"Yeah . . . I'm all right," she either said or thought. Somehow, it didn't seem to matter.

"That's good," came the faraway reply.

Kiera tried not to react when she realized this had been a woman's voice, not Paul's.

Did he leave? . . . Is someone else taking his place?

She experienced a feeling of abandonment but told herself it didn't matter.

Nothing matters anymore.

Still, something about the voice had a familiar resonance that she couldn't quite place. She was still distantly aware of the table, sliding forward inch by inch, but she also had a sensation of floating . . . of falling.

How much longer can this go on?

She still wasn't sure if she spoke out loud or simply thought it.

"How much longer?" said the woman's voice. *"What are you talking about? It's been going on all your life."*

Kiera tried to respond. Her mind was a total blank as she struggled to figure out where and when she had heard that voice before. It sounded so familiar. Even though it was oddly distorted, it reminded her of her own voice and how foreign it sounded when she heard a recording of it.

I mean this exam . . . How much longer will this exam be going on?

"It will never end . . . It's been going on ever since you were born," the woman said. *"You just didn't know it."*

Kiera didn't miss the edge of threat in the woman's voice.

Can I stop it now? . . . Can we be done now?

"It's totally out of your hands. It's out of my hands, too," the woman said. *"I don't know what's changed, but something has. Something's shifted, and there's nothing you or I can do about it."*

As much as I want to find out what's wrong with me, I'm also really scared . . . I'm afraid I might . . . die . . . I don't want to die.

"Neither do I," said the unseen woman. *"I don't even know why I'm here."*

You're helping the doctor, aren't you? You're a technician who's helping Paul.

"Who's Paul?" the woman said. *"I don't have any idea how I got here. I'm not even sure where* here *is."*

As soon as the woman said that, a jolt of fear as strong as an electric shock hit Kiera. She willed her body to move but couldn't. She was paralyzed. There was no way she could move. The thought that she might already be dead filled her with terror and despair. She imagined the white ring of the scanner expanding all around her until it became a swirling white tunnel of light that pulled her in.

But I don't want to die! Kiera said or thought as a feeling of immense sadness and loss swelled inside her. She struggled to open her eyes—*if they aren't already open!*—but the whirling vortex of light and shadow surrounded her and held her down. Then, ever so slowly, a face resolved above her. At first, the light behind it made it impossible for her to see who it was, but she was certain it was a woman. A nimbus of light surrounded her head like a halo as the woman leaned over her.

Am I dead? . . . Are you an angel?

Kiera was amazed that she could think, much less speak through her panic.

"Far from it," the voice said, and Kiera realized she was looking at the woman she had been speaking to.

The figure hovered above her, a solid, dark blotch against the glaring light. Her hair shimmered like a bright red halo, and her eyes glowed as if they had their own internal light. Gradually, the woman's features resolved. Her face was perfectly expressionless; her skin had a ghostly pale radiance. Her eyes—as green as Kiera's—widened with anticipation—or fear—as she looked down at Kiera.

"How many times do I have to tell you?" the woman said. *"I have no idea what's going on, either."*

Kiera noticed that the woman's lips moved out of synch with her voice, but what she said filled the weirdly lit void like the rush of a storm wind.

Kiera had the urge to reach up and touch the woman's face, but her arms were frozen. She wanted to cry out for help. Maybe Paul was close by and would make this stop.

Who are you? . . . What are you doing here?

At the edge of hearing, Kiera became aware of a high-pitched whirring sound punctuated by a series of soft, irregular clicks. Her body was still moving forward, and she felt like she was falling backward. When she looked up, the face above her resolved more clearly, and she realized she was looking at herself. It was like gazing into a mirror, only the reflection—like the one that had unnerved her this morning—moved independently of her.

Tears filled Kiera's eyes, blurring her vision and turning everything into a dull, gauzy haze. Emotions she couldn't even begin to identify welled up inside of her. She wanted to cry . . . and scream . . . and laugh. She wanted to close her eyes, if they weren't already closed, so she could get away from this vision of herself before her, but somehow she knew this vision would never fade away.

Are you . . . me? she asked, hearing the quaver in her voice.

"What'd you say?" a man's voice said. It took Kiera a second or two to realize Paul had spoken to her. She licked her lips and swallowed dryly, terribly aware of not having had anything to eat or drink in a very long time. It seemed like it had been days or weeks since she had felt liquid flowing down her parched throat. She couldn't quite believe she had spoken loud enough for Paul or anyone else to hear her.

"We're just about done. How you holding up?"

This was definitely Paul's voice. Kiera blinked her eyes and looked around to see if the face—her face!—was still looming above her, but it was gone. All that remained was a hazy afterimage that floated before her eyes like a puff of smoke that was rapidly dissipating.

Reality came back in slow, steady waves that lapped over her like a gentle tide. The confusion and fear she had experienced was rapidly fading. Even though stark memories of what she had seen and heard were seared into her brain, already they were slipping away like half-remembered fragments of dreams. No matter how hard she tried to hang on to them, they were slipping away.

"I was . . . I saw . . ." she said, but her voice choked off, and she remained silent as she waited for the slow, inexorable movement of the examination table to stop. The machinery was still whining, louder now. Afraid of what she might see, she didn't dare open her eyes.

"Just about done . . . All right. *Fini.* You can open your eyes now."

Paul's voice was clearer than it had ever been, and Kiera found it reassuring, but she still hesitated to open her eyes.

What if that woman—the one who looked like me—is still here?

The thought gradually lost some of its terror. It slowly ebbed away, leaving her with a terrible feeling of utter loss and sadness. She wished she could be someplace else as she waited for the machinery to finally stop making its clicking and buzzing noises. Then, after sucking in a deep breath and holding it for a moment, she opened her eyes . . .

. . . and found herself looking up at the ceiling. Down by her feet, she could see the circular opening of the CAT scan, looking like a wide metallic mouth that had just disgorged her.

"Don't move. You'll probably feel a little disoriented, after lying so still for so long. Let me help you off the table."

Feeling absolutely drained, Kiera did as she was told. Her muscles didn't feel strong enough to support her, but with Paul's help, she sat up and swung her feet over the edge of the table to the floor.

"You did great," Paul said, smiling at her. She no longer felt self-conscious about sitting there in a skimpy hospital gown. She was just glad the ordeal was over.

"When do I get the results?" Her voice was shaky and sounded more like the voice of the woman she had imagined while she was inside the scanner than her own. She wanted to believe she *had* imagined it. There was no way anyone could have been inside there with her.

"We'll do a preliminary reading while you get dressed, and I'm sure the doctor will want to meet with you to review them."

Kiera wanted to ask if *he* had noticed anything unusual while the procedure was going on, but she decided not to. She also wanted to ask him if it was common for people to hallucinate or daydream while they were inside the scanner, but she decided to let it drop, too. The sound and her nervousness had contributed to make her imagine that woman. That was all. She was mostly anxious about what the results would show.

~3~

"I have to be honest with you," said Dr. Martindale, the neurosurgeon in charge of Kiera's case. After studying the CAT scan on the light board, he, Nate, and Kiera were seated in one of the small, cluttered offices. "I don't like what I'm seeing. There is definitely something on your prefrontal lobe that doesn't belong there."

Kiera was stunned. She sat there, staring at him, barely able to think above the heavy thud of her pulse in her ears. Slowly, she took a breath and let it out as she slumped back in the chair.

So that's it . . . Her vision kept shifting in and out of focus as cold tingling sensations rushed across her body. *I got the death sentence I've been dreading . . . It's for real.*

"Judging by where the growth is located and how small it is, I'd say we were damned lucky to find it now rather than later."

"So it's operable?" Nate asked, shooting a concerned glance at Kiera.

"Absolutely," Dr. Martindale said. "But first, we have to figure out what it is. For that, we'll need to do a biopsy."

"A biopsy," Kiera echoed.

For the next ten minutes or so, Dr. Martindale explained

the biopsy procedure in great detail. Not much of it stuck with Kiera, who was still too stunned by the news. All she could think was—*This is it . . . I'm going to die . . .*

But one thing kept coming through. Dr. Martindale told her a number of times that, although the diagnosis was serious, it was by no means terminal. There was a better than average chance the growth was benign, and even if it wasn't, they had most likely caught it early enough so it hadn't metastasized.

"It's no wonder you've been having visual symptoms. The growth appears to be pressing against your left optic nerve. You said you'd been experiencing flashes of light, is that right?"

Kiera had to force herself to pay attention. She shook her head and looked back and forth between the doctor and her husband, fighting the disorienting feeling that she had to be imagining all of this. It couldn't be happening to *her*!

Why the hell is Nate looking so worried? . . . He isn't the one who has to face this . . . He might even welcome this.

"Lights . . . ?" she said distantly. "Umm, yeah. Yes . . . I've been seeing flashing lights and . . . and sometimes dark shapes that look like . . ."

She let her voice drift away. She had been about to tell them about the figure she had seen during the CAT scan, but she realized it had started long before this, when she had seen a person's silhouette in the streak of frozen white lightning.

But this couldn't have been the same person. She was convinced the one she had seen before had been Billy Carroll.

"I . . . I don't know," she finished lamely. Out of habit, she started massaging her left eyebrow. She couldn't help but think both the doctor and her husband were aware that she was hiding *something* from them.

"It's no surprise," Dr. Martindale said. "The optic nerve connects directly to the brain, so any pressure on it could produce the light patterns you described. When you were a kid, did you ever close your eyes and press against your eyelids until you saw shapes and flashes of light?"

Kiera nodded, barely registering what he was saying.

"It's pretty much the same thing."

"Is this what's causing the migraines, too?" Kiera asked, struggling to pull her attention back into the room.

"It could be," Dr. Martindale replied. "We'll know more once we get in there and have a look at what's going on."

"Have a look," Kiera said, shuddering at the thought of someone operating on her brain. Nate reached out and took her hand, giving it a firm squeeze, but she didn't feel the least bit reassured. Her hand was cold and lifeless in his grip, and she couldn't stop thinking about how she might prefer to face this ordeal on her own.

"So . . . ummm, when will we do this biopsy?" she asked.

"As soon as possible," Dr. Martindale said. "Like I said, we're lucky we caught it so early. Even if it is serious, which I doubt, we can take care of it now."

"I just . . . I can't believe there's a tumor in my brain." Kiera slowly shook her head from side to side. She was tense, waiting for a stab of pain, but nothing happened.

"Let me reiterate," Dr. Martindale said, leaning forward. "The prognosis is *very* positive. I'd like to get you in for the biopsy tomorrow morning, if that will work for you."

Kiera glanced at Nate, then at the doctor and nodded.

"Sure . . . Whatever's best."

"Good," Dr. Martindale said. He stood up and rubbed

his hands together. "I'll schedule it and have someone give you a call at home to confirm."

Kiera wasn't sure if her legs were strong enough to support her as she stood up. She placed both hands on the desk to steady herself and noticed that Nate didn't reach out to help her.

"I know it sounds like empty advice," Dr. Martindale said, "but please—don't worry. You're in good hands here."

Kiera nodded before starting for the door, but even with Nate at her side, she didn't feel the least bit reassured. Her only thought was that she should be satisfied; she had gotten the death sentence she had been expecting all along.

~4~

It was late in the afternoon, and daylight was rapidly fading, bringing a chill with it. Blue shadows from the trees striped the backyard, and Nate still wasn't home. He'd told her he'd be at school, but Kiera was beginning to have her doubts. She didn't remember him needing this much prep time last year or the year before. Plus, he wasn't answering his cell. Those two things alone were enough to make her wonder if he might be off somewhere doing something else.

Like what? she wondered. *Is he off somewhere getting drunk with his friends, drowning his misery and complaining about me . . . or is he having a fling with someone, maybe one of the female teachers?*

As much as it hurt, she had to admit because of the way their marriage had been going—especially lately—it wouldn't be all that surprising if he *was* having an affair. When she was honest with herself, she had to admit that for most of their marriage, neither one of them seemed truly satisfied. She knew she certainly wasn't. But it bothered her that now, when she really needed some loving support, she wasn't getting it from either her husband or daughter.

She felt so alone . . . so isolated, and ever since the visit to the hospital this morning, she'd been feeling restless. With the telephone in hand, she paced back and forth, from the deck to the kitchen to the living room and then out to the deck again.

She needed to talk to *someone*, but she had no idea who to call. Both of her parents had died within a year of each other more than six years ago, so she couldn't very well talk to them. Her brother Mike lived in Oregon, where he taught phys ed at a community college, but because he was five years younger than her, they had never been very close. She had plenty of friends she could call or even drop by to visit—Joanie or Marsha or Jon and Liz—but she wasn't sure she wanted to tell anyone about what was happening.

Not yet, anyway.

Where would she start? If she got started on how worried she was about the tumor in her head, it wouldn't be long before she spilled it all and confessed that she was worried . . . no, not worried; she was all but convinced Nate was sleeping around. He'd done it in the past. She knew the signs. It's just that now, feeling so vulnerable, she wasn't sure she was seeing clearly. The tumor was just her most recent crisis. She didn't want to unload her crap on any of her friends.

She had to face this on her own.

Besides, like Dr. Martindale had told her, he had to do more tests before they really knew how serious this was. Why get anyone else worried?

"It may not even be serious at all," she whispered as she stared at the long, thin shadows that reached across the lawn. Still, like in the hospital, she couldn't stop thinking she'd been handed a death sentence. She'd deal with this, then she'd figure out what to do about her marriage.

"If I survive," she whispered. "And if I don't . . . then I won't have to worry about anything . . . I'll be dead."

No matter how hard she tried to remain positive, though, she felt as though she—or at least an important piece of her—had already died. In a way, it was like she had known all along that she wouldn't live past middle age. She had known it all her life—or at least ever since that night Billy died.

"Jesus, stop *thinking* like that!" she shouted, but the nervousness gnawing at her insides just wouldn't let up.

She walked back into the kitchen and looked around, desperate to find something to do . . . *anything* to keep herself busy; but the dishes and laundry were done, and there was no cleaning to do unless she wanted to tackle cleaning the stove, and she didn't have *that* much energy. She had already tried reading and watching TV, but her mind kept sifting through what had happened this morning . . . especially that woman she had seen inside the scanner who looked like her.

She was positive she had imagined that. The CAT scan machine was much too narrow. *She* could barely fit into it. In fact, she was surprised she hadn't felt more claustrophobic. There was no *way* anyone else could have been in there with her.

Before she left the exam room, she had checked the scanner to see if there were any chrome or reflective surfaces that might have mirrored her face. She was sure there had to be something inside the machine that had given her a distorted image of herself. She hadn't seen anything, but that didn't mean it wasn't there.

"No, it's all in your head . . . all in your head," she whispered as she walked into the living room and looked around. Her grip on the phone was slick with sweat, and she was going to replace it on its base, but she squeezed it as she turned and walked back out onto the deck. The sun was below the horizon, and the blue shadows on the lawn had deepened. If she stared into the woods for any length of time, she was convinced she could see figures shifting about in the deepest shadows.

"*Stop* it! . . . Please . . . Stop it!"

She clenched the phone in her fist and shook it, and then let out a startled yelp when it suddenly rang. For a moment long enough for the phone to ring a second time, she just stood there staring at it like she had no idea what it was or what to do with it. Then, on the third ring, she flicked the switch and put it to her ear.

"Hello?"

For a heartbeat or two there was only silence on the other end of the line . . . a silence so complete she wondered if she had imagined hearing the phone ring. If that was the case, though, she should hear a dial tone, and there was nothing—only silence on the other end of the line.

"Who . . . who is it?" she asked, a note of rising desperation twisting her voice.

She was holding the phone so tightly her hand began to ache. Her own breathing was the only sound in the earpiece, but then, very faintly, whoever was on the other end of the line took a slow, shuddering breath.

"I'm hanging up now. Don't call again," she said, but before she took the phone away from her ear, a voice said, *"Don't."*

"Who is this?"

Kiera's eyes darted around the backyard. She was convinced more than ever that out there in the gathering gloom, someone was watching her.

"Where is he?" the voice at the other end of the line asked.

"What are you talking about? What do you want?" Kiera said. "Who are you?"

"A friend," the voice said with a rasp.

Kiera thought it was a woman, but the voice was so low and distorted, almost lost in the faint static, she wasn't sure.

"Tell me what you want, or else I'm hanging up," Kiera said nervously.

"Where is he?"

The voice modulated oddly, and Kiera assumed the caller had a bad cell connection.

"Who?" Kiera asked, but even as she said the word, she was sure the person meant Nate. Whoever this was, she was playing coy, hinting at the reason Nate wasn't home because he was having an affair.

"Billy," the voice said through a wash of distortion. *"Where's Billy?"*

Kiera's throat closed off with an audible click. Without thinking, she said, "I'm sorry. You have the wrong number. There's no—"

"Billy Carroll . . . What did you do to him?" the voice whispered.

Panic raced like electricity up and down Kiera's back. She was still staring at the backyard. The shadows under the trees suddenly deepened as if someone had thrown a light switch. The sky above the trees was a deep, rich violet that throbbed in time with her pulse.

"I don't . . ."

But that was all she could say before her throat closed off as if fingers wrapped around her neck like steel springs and began to squeeze.

Kiera staggered and almost fell. A tingling sensation rushed through her, making her body feel lifeless and numb. Her hand opened involuntarily, and the phone dropped to the deck, clattering on the floorboards so loud it sounded like a sudden clap of thunder.

"Tell me . . . Where's Billy Carroll?"

The voice was so faint Kiera thought it had to be inside her head. How could this be happening?

"I . . . I don't know," Kiera said as she started backing away from the phone. "I *really* don't know."

"Oh, but I think you do . . . I know you do."

She kept backing up until she bumped into the side of the house, hitting the wall hard enough to throw her head back and bang it against the siding. The sudden jolt shot pinpricks of light across her vision like a shower of sparks that sizzled and sputtered as they swirled around her. Somehow, though, she remained on her feet and realized she was staring at the phone she had dropped. In the gathering gloom, it was a faint cream-colored blob on the deck.

"You know perfectly well where he is," the voice said, buzzing and faint, *"but you'd better not tell anyone else."*

The phone was far enough away so Kiera wasn't positive that's what the person had said, but it didn't matter. The voice screaming inside her head was all too clear.

"It was an accident." Her voice was a raw whisper that grated in the gathering darkness. "I swear to God it was an accident!"

A sudden blast of bright light broke across the backyard. Though her panic and confusion, Kiera realized a car was pulling into the driveway. It had to be either Nate or Trista.

Come on, she told herself. *Pull it together,* but rushes of fear were still playing up and down her back. She doubted that she could move, much less put on a happy face as if everything was all right.

What just happened? she kept asking herself.

Moving stiffly, she walked back to the phone, looking at it like it was a rattlesnake curled up and ready to strike. When the door from the garage opened and slammed shut, she sucked in a quick breath, bent down, and picked up the phone. It was cool, almost cold in her hand.

"Hello . . . ? Hey! Where are you . . . ?" Nate called out.

"Out on the deck," Kiera replied.

She wasn't sure her voice was strong enough to carry, but the screen door slid open, and Nate stepped out onto the deck. He looked at her with a confused expression and asked, "You all right?"

"Sure," Kiera replied shakily, but she knew she didn't sound at all convincing.

"You on the phone?" Nate indicated the phone in her hand.

"Uh—no. No. Just finished."

"Who you talking to?" he asked, but Kiera didn't answer him. For several seconds, neither one of them said anything. They just looked at each other. Kiera was almost overwhelmed by the feeling that she was looking at a total stranger.

"You hear back from the hospital?" Nate asked.

Kiera was relieved he had broken the silence, but she was still almost overwhelmed by the tension inside her. She held the phone out and looked at it like she had no idea what it was or what she was supposed to do with it.

"The message machine was blinking," Nate said. "I thought maybe they called, and you missed it."

Kiera shook her head. "No. I've been here the whole time. Just trying to unwind."

"Can't say as I blame you," Nate said as he walked over and put a hand on her upper arm. "It's been a tough day." He leaned forward and kissed her lightly on the cheek. Kiera couldn't help but notice how perfunctory it was, but she didn't say anything. She narrowed her eyes and looked at him, convinced all the more that her suspicions must be true. But even if he had been out with another woman, now wasn't the time to confront him about it.

"I'll check the messages. Maybe it was important." Nate turned away quickly, but not before she caught a brief look of . . . what—?

Was that worry or guilt or maybe panic in his eyes?

Kiera nodded but didn't follow him back into the house. The light came on in the kitchen, spilling a warm, buttery glow onto the deck. Turning so the light was behind her, she looked out at the woods again. They were shrouded in darkness now, but she was still convinced someone was out there, watching her. A shivery feeling tickled the back of her neck, but still she didn't go into the house, even when she heard the message machine inside beep and the message begin to play. The volume was too low for her to make out what the caller was saying. It sounded like a man's voice. All Kiera could think of was the distorted voice she'd heard, asking if she knew where Billy Carroll was.

"Did you hear that?" Nate called out from the kitchen.

"No," Kiera said.

She still didn't move. The feeling of being watched pinned her where she stood. It was almost as if the person watching her shifted from one side to the other so he was always behind her, no matter which way she looked.

"It was the hospital. Dr. Martindale says he can't do the

procedure until the day after tomorrow. He's scheduled you for Thursday at seven o'clock."

Nate's shadow suddenly filled the doorway before he stepped out onto the porch. Kiera didn't know why she was feeling so vulnerable, but the tingling sensation rushing up her back was getting steadily stronger.

"Oh, man. That's the first day of school." Nate shook his head, and after a slight pause said, "But don't worry. I'll get a sub. We don't do much the first day, anyway. And it's not like I don't know the students."

The cold clenching in Kiera's stomach got worse as she considered which prospect seemed least appealing—*not* having Nate there with her or *having* him come with her.

"Crap," she muttered.

"I know. It really sucks."

Nate walked over to her and gave her a hug, but Kiera noticed again how fleeting it was, as if he was doing it out of obligation, not real affection.

"Were you taking a shower or something so you didn't hear it?" Nate asked. "I called, too, but didn't leave a message."

Kiera wondered if that was a convenient lie. She bit down on her lower lip to keep from letting out the scream that was building up inside her.

"I was out here most of the afternoon and evening," she said.

Nate frowned. "Well, Martindale wants you to call his office in the morning to confirm. He left his number. It's on the caller ID."

As soon as he said that, Kiera jumped as though startled. *Of course,* she thought. *The caller ID.*

She raised her hand holding the phone and pressed the

backward arrow button to get the number for the last call. Her heart skipped a beat when she looked at the small, illuminated screen and saw the name *Martindale* and his office number. She pressed the arrow again, but the next call that had come in was from Jon, who—according to the time on the caller ID—had called the house a little after noon. Apparently he hadn't left a message, but Kiera assumed he was calling because she hadn't made it to tennis the day before. The call before that had been a little after eight o'clock that morning, from *Townsend*. That hadn't been long after she and Nate had left for the hospital. Kiera flashed with anger, thinking about what Trista and her boyfriend might have done while she was at the hospital.

But there was no number identifying the call she'd just had before Nate got home . . . from school, if that's where he really had been, and there was no indication he'd called, either.

How can there be no number? she wondered. Even if the caller blocked the ID, there should have been a message reading *Blocked Call* or *Private Number.*

But there was nothing.

"You all right?" Nate asked. "You look a little shaky."

The light from the kitchen window lit him from behind, so she couldn't see his expression. What she imagined was bad enough. But with the light shining directly onto her, she knew Nate could see the worry and doubt she was feeling.

"Sorry I'm so late. You eat supper yet?" Nate asked.

Kiera wasn't sure if she was angry or relieved that he didn't even try to pry out of her what was bothering her. She sighed and let her shoulders droop, and even though she still convinced someone was close by, watching her every move, she told herself to ignore it.

"I hope you're all right with sandwiches," she said tiredly as she walked into the kitchen and replaced the phone. "I'm not really up for cooking anything."

"How 'bout we go out to eat?" Nate asked, but Kiera shook her head.

"I'm too tired," she said. "Sandwiches will have to do."

CHAPTER 5

Going Down

~1~

"Can't sleep, huh?"

Kiera jumped and spun around in her chair to see Nate standing in the doorway that led into the family room. The glow of the computer screen—the only light in the room—illuminated his face with a soft blue light that made him look almost ghostly.

"You scared me." Kiera took a quick breath and listened to the blood rushing in her ears. "I didn't hear you come down the stairs. What time is it, anyway? Is Trista home yet?"

Nate shook his head as he took a few steps closer. "I didn't hear her come in, but I don't know."

Kiera glanced at the clock at the bottom of the computer screen. "It's almost one o'clock."

"You want me to check her room?" Nate asked.

Biting her lower lip, Kiera shook her head.

"What do you want me to do then?" Nate had an edge in his voice as he gave her a helpless shrug. "Try calling her cell if you're worried."

"I did. She's not answering." Kiera took a deep breath. "This is getting way out of hand. We have to come up with some kind of solution." She knew she had said all of this before, but her frustration with Trista—and Nate, for that matter—was reaching a breaking point, and it wasn't just because of her medical problems.

"Come on," Nate said with a dismissive wave of his hand. "Summer vacation's about over. She's probably partying with her friends. I'm sure she's all right."

"She's with Townsend, and you know it, and you and I both know what kind of *partying* they're probably doing."

Nate started to say something but caught himself and remained silent. Kiera stared at him and prayed he would do or say *something* because she was coming up with nothing.

"Look, you and I know Trista's got a good head on her shoulders," Nate finally said. "I'm sure she's being sensible. We raised her that way, right? So we have to trust her judgment."

"Not when she's with people like Townsend." Kiera sniffed with thinly veiled disgust and then sighed and shook her head, thinking, *What's the use?*

"I'm just saying this is getting *way* out of hand, and I can guarantee it won't continue once school starts."

"I agree," Nate said, holding his hand out and shaking it impatiently. "Give me the phone. I'll call her right now."

Before Kiera could do what he asked, the back door opened and then shut quietly.

"See?" Nate said, smiling at her with smug satisfaction. All Kiera could think was that this didn't prove anything, and it certainly didn't solve the problem.

"Trista. Come in here right now," Kiera called out when they heard footsteps moving stealthily down the hallway.

"Oh . . . You're up . . . Both of you," Trista said, blinking with surprise as she entered the family room. Her eyes flicked back and forth between her mother and father. Her hair was disheveled, and her clothes looked rumpled.

"We'd like to talk to you," Kiera said.

"About what?"

"For one, we'd like to know where you've been." Kiera put as much iron into her voice as she could, but she wasn't convinced it was working.

"Out," Trista said with a shrug. Her expression looked pinched.

"We *know* you were out." Kiera didn't have a whole lot of patience for her daughter's usual dodges. "We want to know *where* you were and who you were with."

"Friends," Trista said.

"I want names," Kiera said as her anger spiked. She wanted to ask Trista why, whenever they questioned her, she answered in single words, but she wasn't ready for the *you're the one who's defensive* argument.

She glanced at Nate for support, but he was hanging back, looking like he wanted to get between mother and daughter about as much as he wanted to step into an alligator pit.

"You know . . ." Trista said. "Just friends."

"Names," Kiera insisted, and then, before Trista could answer, "Have you been drinking or taking drugs?"

"Christ, why the third degree?" Trista asked, looking wounded.

"Watch the language," Kiera snapped.

"I was just out with my friends and—no, we weren't drinking or doing drugs. You want to give me a urine test or something?"

"That's not necessary," Kiera said, "but I don't appreciate your sarcasm." She was getting angrier by the second, and again she looked to Nate for support, but he just stood there silently watching.

"Can we talk tomorrow, Mom?" Trista made a little half turn to leave. "I'm really not up for this right now."

"You *are* aware what time it is?" Kiera said, so mad she couldn't stop herself. "How many times do we have to tell you to *call* if you're going to be out past eleven?"

"Sorry . . . I forgot." Trista shrugged and looked like she was ready to bolt as soon as she could.

Kiera had no idea what to say next, and Nate was useless, so she finally waved her off and said, "You're right. We *will* talk about this in the morning. And there *will* be consequences."

"Whatever," Trista said, and without another word, she turned and darted away. Her footsteps stomped a little louder than necessary on the stairs.

"Thanks for all the help," Kiera said, turning back to Nate and glaring at him.

Nate shrugged. "It's not in our control anymore. I think we raised her right, and we just have to trust her."

"We need to set and enforce limits."

"Come on. Remember what it was like when you were her age?"

Kiera froze, her mind instantly flashing on what had happened to Billy Carroll.

"I do," she said shakily. "That's what worries me."

"She's got to figure things out on her own. You know, we're not always gonna be around to help her."

Although Kiera knew he hadn't meant it to, his words cut her like a razor. Everything she had been through today came rushing back, almost overwhelming her. She shivered at the thought that she had gotten a death sentence with the doctor's diagnosis.

"So why can't you sleep?" Nate asked. He took a few steps closer to her but didn't reach out to touch her. His gaze was fixed on the computer screen, not her. Kiera realized he was trying to see what she'd been reading, so she clicked the window shut, closing the site so quickly Nate jumped back.

"What don't you want me to see?" he asked. "You checking out porn sites or something?"

His feeble attempt at a joke didn't go over well. Kiera scowled, her lower lip trembling as she looked at him.

"I was just . . . checking out some . . . ahh . . . medical sites." It took effort to keep her voice from cracking.

Nate softened his attitude and knelt down beside her. Taking her hand in his, he gave it a tight squeeze. Kiera knew he was trying to reassure her, but it didn't help. She felt such a distance between them, she wasn't sure anything he could say or do would help.

"I'm sorry," he said. "I didn't mean . . ."

"It's okay," Kiera said, fighting back tears. "You didn't know." She took a breath to steady her nerves. "I was just looking over what—" Her voice broke again, and she had to swallow before she could continue. "—looking over what might be going on . . . you know? . . . inside my head."

"You think that's a good idea? If you read that stuff, you're gonna start thinking worst-case scenario."

"Like I'm not already?" Tears began to fill her eyes, and when she looked at her husband, she was filled with anguish because of the immense gulf between them.

Nate looked at her, his eyes glowing softly in the blue light from the computer screen.

"What can I say?" he asked, and Kiera saw the desperation in his eyes. "You have to believe the doctor knows what he's doing and that everything will be all right."

"I know. It's just so scary, some of this stuff."

Nate nodded but said nothing.

Kiera swallowed hard, hesitating for a moment. She was desperate to talk to *someone* about what she was going through. Left to her own devices, her imagination got much too carried away.

"I was researching vestigial twins."

"Vestigial twins?" Nate shook his head. "I've never heard of that."

Kiera eased back in her chair and let out her breath. Just minutes ago, she had been absolutely convinced that's what was going on inside her head, but saying it out loud made her think how foolish she was. She wanted to dismiss it all as just late-night worries, but the expression on Nate's face urged her on.

"It happens more than you'd think. They think it might even happen one out of every five or six pregnancies."

"What happens?"

Kiera took a deep breath, hoping to clear her mind and wishing she could detach herself from all of this. "What happens is, when a woman gets pregnant, twins often develop. Before long, though, one of them will absorb the other."

"Absorb?" Nate didn't look convinced.

"There are thousands of cases of people who have tumors removed later in life, and the doctors find fingernails and teeth growing inside the tumor."

The disbelief on Nate's face told her he wasn't buying any of this, and she had to admit that saying it out loud made it sound ridiculous.

"It's been medically proven," she said. "Some researchers think people who develop multiple personalities and serious psychological disorders like schizophrenia might really be expressing the thoughts and feelings of their absorbed twin who is still alive, in a way, and still has its own thoughts."

Nate was silent for a few seconds as he let this sink in, but she could tell by the expression on his face that he still didn't believe her.

"And you're saying—what? This growth in your brain is a twin that was never born?" He shook his head and rubbed his face with the flats of his hands. "Come on, Kiera. That's just . . . bullshit. What you need is a good night's sleep, not sitting up so late, worrying. Let's go to bed."

Kiera started to get up but hesitated. Her gaze shifted to the computer monitor, and she considered doing a bit more research. Instead, she shut the computer down. Her bare feet scuffed the carpet as she and Nate went upstairs, but after the lights were out, and she was tucked into bed, she still couldn't stop the flood of worries and fears that swirled through her mind.

It was a long time before she finally drifted off to sleep, and even then, her sleep was thin and disturbed by vivid dreams and a faint voice that kept asking her—

"Where's Billy . . . ? Where's Billy Carroll . . . ?"

~2~

"It's really weird," Kiera said. "And I'm really scared."

Worried that Nate or Trista would overhear her, she cupped the phone close to her mouth. She was in the living room with early morning sunlight filtering through the front windows. The rest of the family was still in bed, hopefully asleep. From the sound of his voice, Kiera was certain she had awakened Jon, even though he insisted he was already up because he was leaving for the airport soon. In the background, she could hear Liz going on about something. Kiera wasn't sure if she was on her cell phone talking to someone else or complaining to Jon about taking a call so early in the morning. She heard something that sounded like "the crack of dawn."

"You have every right to be concerned." Jon's voice was low and mild in spite of Liz's jabbering, which continued nonstop. "I'm just saying . . . I wish you had said something to me before now."

"I would have," Kiera said, "but I didn't want you to worry. I figured I had to deal with this on my own."

"Oh, really? And what do you think friends are for? And how about Nate? You certainly told *him* about this."

The back of Kiera's neck prickled, and she looked at the living room doorway, expecting to see Nate—*or someone else*—standing there, but the doorway was empty.

Who did you expect to see? she asked herself.

She had described vestigial twins to Jon, and he had listened patiently while she explained how she was now convinced that's what was happening to her.

"You're filling your head with ideas that are really out there because you're scared," Jon said mildly.

Kiera hadn't dared to tell Jon about the phone call she'd gotten yesterday, where the voice—she was convinced it was a woman's—had asked her what had happened to Billy.

"I'm going to be in Boston for the next five days at a real estate conference, but I want you to promise me one—no, two things, all right?"

"What's that?" Kiera asked, cringing at the tightness in her voice.

"First. Stop worrying. I know it's easy for me to say, and if the situation was reversed, I'd probably be freaking out like you are. But you have to trust that your doctor has got everything under control. Even if it's your worst fear—even if the growth is cancerous, he said it was small and because of the location, relatively easy to remove."

"Brain surgery is *always* dangerous," Kiera replied. "*That's* what he said."

"Of course. I'm just saying you can't stay up all night, losing sleep surfing the Web and getting all worked up about this . . . this *bullshit* you're reading."

"It's not—"

"How valid are these reports? For all you know, they could be some whack-job, writing fiction."

Kiera exhaled softly through her teeth as she looked around the living room. It was brightening steadily, but—like last night—she had a creepy feeling that she was being watched.

"Yeah . . . Okay," she said, "I'll try to stop worrying."

"There is no try. There is do and do not," Jon said, using a voice that she assumed was supposed to sound like Yoda.

Kiera didn't laugh as she said, "All right. What's the second thing?"

"Easy. Call me," Jon said. "I don't care what time, day or night, if you're upset or freaking out, *call.*"

"Okay."

"And after the surgery, as soon as you can, call and tell me how it went."

"That's really three things." Kiera said, but what she was thinking was, *after the surgery, I might not be able to call anyone because I might be in a coma . . . or dead.*

"Okay, so even when you're worried, you're still a pain in the ass."

They both chuckled at that, but Kiera didn't really feel like laughing. Again, she considered mentioning the phone call from yesterday, but she decided not to. If Jon was on her case so much for worrying about her upcoming surgery, what would he say about that . . . especially since, besides her, he was the only person who did know what had happened to Billy Carroll?

And the more she thought about it, the more that whole event had taken on the cast of a half-remembered dream that didn't really happen. No matter how hard she tried to recall the tone and timbre of the voice, she no longer had a clear memory of it. There had been so much static, the voice had been distorted. Now, she wasn't even sure if it had been a man or a woman. She began to wonder if, like the visual effects she was getting with the migraine, it had been an auditory hallucination.

If so, she didn't feel reassured. She was all the more frightened, and she had every right to be worried no matter what Jon or her doctor or anyone else said.

"Promise me?" Jon asked.

Kiera had been so distracted by her thoughts it took her a moment to remember what they'd been talking about.

"Umm—yeah . . . yeah. I promise."

The instant the words left her mouth, she told herself it didn't matter anyway, because tomorrow, after the surgery, she wasn't even going to be alive . . . and even if she was, she wouldn't be the same person she was now.

~3~

The palms of Kiera's hands were slick with sweat as she listened to Dr. Martindale describe the procedure he would perform on her tomorrow morning. He explained that they would put her under general anesthesia and then drill a small hole into her head, what was called a "burr hole," so they could extract a small piece of brain tissue for analysis.

After they got the results, cancerous or not, Dr. Martindale would then operate to remove the mass.

The first step, twenty-four hours before the actual operation, he would either cut or clamp the blood supply to the growth to make it wither, so when he removed it, it would come out more easily.

"Hopefully, that's all we find, and we'll suction it out through the same burr hole," Dr. Martindale said. "Of course, because it's so close to your optic nerve, we have to be extremely careful—"

"Or I could end up blind," Kiera said, remembering something she'd read on the Internet last night.

Dr. Martindale shifted in his chair.

"Well . . . yes, in one eye. There's always that danger," he said. "But looking at the CAT scan, I don't expect much difficulty. I really don't. Look, Kiera—" He leaned forward across his desk, his expression almost pleading. "I know how worried you are. You have every right to be."

"That's what my friends keep telling me," she whispered.

Nate shot her a curious look but didn't ask, *What friends?*

"I've reviewed the scans with two specialists, and I honestly don't expect any complication. We have to be cautious, of course. We always do when we're dealing with the human brain, but if I were a betting man, I'd lay solid odds this is not cancerous. We'll know more tomorrow."

Kiera nodded and started to stand up to leave, but then she said, "When you make this . . . *burr* hole, will you have to shave my head?" She twiddled a strand of her long, red hair between her fingers.

"Probably not, but I can't guarantee it." Dr. Martindale softened a little, obviously aware that there was an element of vanity behind her question. "We may have to shave your left temple. It really depends on what we see on the CAT scan that we'll do just before the surgery."

"I have to go through *that* again?"

"We have to check the tumor against the previous scan to see if there's been any significant change. By the looks of things, I'd say this has been the same size for a while. It could have been something you've had since you were young. You may even have been born with it."

"Born with it? Could it be—?" But she stopped herself after glancing at Nate.

"We can't know why the symptoms presented now. It *could*—and I emphasize the word *could*—indicate recent growth. Do either of you have any more questions?"

Kiera shook her head, but it was obvious something was bothering Nate. She wasn't ready for it when he asked, "What are the chances this could be a vestigial twin?"

Dr. Martindale sniffed and shook his head as he eased back in his chair. He was silent for a moment; then he pursed his lips and said, "I've been a doctor long enough to know that weird things can happen, Mr. Davis. I know there are numerous reported cases with . . . unusual circumstances. But in Kiera's case, a vestigial twin is pretty close to one hundred percent impossible."

"Why's that?" Nate asked, shooting Kiera an *I told you so* look.

Kiera felt betrayed that he had even mentioned her concern, but like the mysterious phone call yesterday, she realized getting so worried last night was bordering on paranoia. In the clear light of day, her fears seemed to lose their potency.

"And why is that?" Nate repeated, glancing at Kiera.

Kiera couldn't believe he was doing this to her. Was he trying to embarrass her? Make her look like a fool? It was almost like he was mocking her and making fun of her fears.

"For one thing," Dr. Martindale said, "a vestigial twin occurring in the human brain has never been reported, at least that I know of. In the vast majority of cases, any such growth is detected in the lower abdomen, usually in the genital area. I suppose there could be the odd case of some embryonic material being found in a person's skull or brain or any other part of their body, but . . ." He shook his head again, and it looked to Kiera as if he was trying not to laugh out loud. "It's just highly unlikely."

Crossing his arms over his chest, Nate looked at Kiera with an almost smug look of satisfaction on his face. She felt all the angrier and—worse—hurt.

What do you think you're doing? she wanted to scream at him, but she was too upset even to speak. Blushing with embarrassment, she looked at Dr. Martindale, who regarded her with what she thought was a sympathetic look.

Silence settled in the room, but then the doctor cleared his throat and said, "I don't know what either one of you has been hearing or reading, but trust me. While no brain operation is ever routine, you have absolutely no need to worry. We'll take care of this over the next few days, and you'll be back to your old self in a matter of weeks."

"I hope you're right," Kiera said even as she thought that couldn't possibly be true. She was positive that, after the operation, things were never going to be the same.

~4~

Three days later, it was all over.

Kiera awoke in the recovery room feeling as though time had simply disappeared . . . slipped away into a black hole. She had no memories . . . no dreams . . . nothing but an empty void that she thought must be what death is like . . . except death never ends.

She regained consciousness very slowly. First, she was only aware of voices and activity around her. Sneakers squeaked on the floor; metal banged against metal. The sound of louder voices and laughter came through every now and then, and someone—she was pretty sure it wasn't her—kept groaning as if in terrible pain.

She took her time coming back to reality. She liked where she was and didn't want to force herself to get closer to consciousness any quicker than absolutely necessary. Sounds were muted, and nothing seemed threatening. The voices were pleasant-sounding and happy. Sometimes they were calm and reassuring.

". . . coming around, I see . . ." a woman who seemed to be quite close to her said.

Kiera was positive she replied, but there was no response from the person who had just spoken, so she let herself slip back down into the darkness where it was so comfortable and safe.

There was no time where she was, so she had no idea how long it had been, but she felt like a bubble, rising from the muddy bottom of a pond. One time, along with the voices, she could hear a steady *beep-beep-beep* that sounded like the warning buzzer of a truck that was backing up. Only much later did she realize it was some sort of medical equipment.

"Hey there, sleepyhead," a woman's voice said. "How are you feeling?"

It might have been the same person who had spoken before. Kiera couldn't tell. She tried to peel open her eyes, but the hazy brightness through her eyelids hurt, so she kept them closed. Her chest shuddered and made a watery rattling sound when she inhaled deeply.

"I'm—" she said, but that was all. Her throat was so parched it closed off as small waves of panic ran through her.

Where am I? . . . What happened?

"You did just fine," the woman said mildly. "Don't push. You have all the time you need."

Kiera licked her lips, aware of the rough, sandpaper feeling. "How is . . . ? Is it over?" she managed to say.

"Everything went just fine. Would you like a sip of water?"

Kiera nodded, relieved to find it didn't hurt to move. She had been expecting the slightest motion to send shooting pain through her head when she moved. She still had her eyes closed when a straw slipped between her lips, and she sucked gently. She reveled in the sudden wash of cool wetness that flooded her mouth and throat.

"Easy. Not too much," the woman said as she pulled the straw away.

Kiera was mesmerized as she stared into the hazy glow that penetrated her eyelids. Indistinct colors and smeared shapes swirled before her like melting pinwheels. She raised her left hand and touched her forehead, feeling the padded bandage that was wrapped around her head. The strange thing was, she could barely feel her fingers, pressing against her head.

"Did they . . . shave my head?" she asked. She realized how vain she must sound, but she had to know.

"I wasn't in the OR," the woman said, "but I don't think they shaved much . . . if any. Right now, your head's bandaged."

Kiera accepted that she wouldn't get an answer right away, so she exhaled and settled her head into the pillow. It felt as cool and comfortable as a cloud, so she let herself drift away again.

The next time she came to, she was a little more aware of time passing. She groaned when she tried to open her eyes. It seemed like she was losing the struggle against the harsh glare, but once her eyes were opened a slit, she found the muted amber light of the recovery room soothing. No one was at her bedside, but there was activity close by. She decided the nurse must be assisting someone else who was coming out of the anesthesia.

Rolling her head to one side, she tried to make sense of her surroundings. The solid reality of medical equipment gave her some reassurance, but she felt like she might still be dreaming. She was startled when a young woman wearing a hospital blouse and pants with a bright purple flower pattern came around the partially drawn curtain.

"Hey. You're awake," she said.

Her voice sounded familiar, and Kiera figured she must have been the one who gave her a drink when she first came to.

"Yeah," Kiera said, noticing how weak she sounded.

The nurse walked over to her bed and did a quick blood pressure check, then glanced at the monitors and IV. She nodded with satisfaction and made some notes on the chart.

"You're looking good," the nurse said, "but we'll wait a little while longer before we move you up to your room."

"My . . . room?" Kiera asked, confused.

The woman nodded. "Looks like you're going to be here for a day or two. For observation."

A rush of fear went through Kiera.

"I'm okay, aren't I? I mean, the operation went well, right?"

"Oh, absolutely," the woman said, "but after surgery like yours, most people usually don't waltz out of here after a couple of hours."

Kiera realized she was tensed up, so she let out a loud sigh and settled her head back into the pillow.

"I'll let Dr. Martindale know you're awake," the nurse said. "I'm sure he'll stop by before you go to your room."

Kiera heard and understood everything the woman was saying, but she closed her eyes and let it all slip away as she drifted off to sleep. It took her a while to remember that it had been only three days since Dr. Martindale had met with her to describe the procedure he would do. And now—just like that—it was over.

Or is it? a voice in the back of her mind asked. She couldn't stop thinking that it *wasn't* all over. In fact, the voice in her head kept telling her it had only just begun.

~5~

"Hey."

"Hey yourself."

"You're looking pretty good, considering."

"Yeah . . . thanks . . . considering what, that I just had my skull opened up?"

"Yeah. There's that."

"What do you mean?"

A tingle of apprehension stabbed Kiera when she realized

she had been gently pulled out of sleep while carrying on a conversation with this unseen person. She wasn't ready to open her eyes. Since the other voice belonged to a woman, she assumed it was the nurse who had been by earlier to check on her, but now she realized that this voice sounded different. It must be later. The evening shift was on, and this was someone new. Kiera felt unaccountably uncomfortable. She had felt so secure with the other nurse, but now she felt . . .

Vulnerable . . .

"Am I going up to my room soon?" she asked, still not daring to open her eyes.

"How should I know?" the woman replied with a coldness that made Kiera shiver.

What's going on? . . . This is no way to talk to a patient.

"I'm awfully thirsty," Kiera said. "Could you get me—"

"Get it yourself. What, you think I'm your slave?"

Startled, Kiera opened her eyes and raised her head. Looking around, she saw an indistinct figure at the foot of her bed. It wasn't much more than a dark smear against the bright light coming through the window. She could see that it was a woman, but if she was a nurse, she sure had a lousy bedside manner. If it was someone stopping by to see how she was doing, they had obviously gotten off on the wrong foot.

"Who are you?" Kiera asked, blinking her eyes and trying to make out the woman's features.

There was something vaguely familiar about her silhouette, but Kiera couldn't place it until the woman stepped around the corner of the bed and came closer. When she leaned over her and smiled, Kiera had to choke back a scream when she found herself looking up at her own face.

"This has been as hard on me as it has been for you," the woman said. "Truth is, it's been really confusing."

Kiera couldn't speak or breathe. She was convinced she was looking into a mirror, but the "reflection" didn't match anything she said or did. She had a vague memory of something like this happening before, but she couldn't recall when. Kiera knew her head was bandaged, but this woman's shock of long, red hair framed her face and fell down over her shoulders. Her eyes were a shimmering green; her mouth was set in a firm line that showed little sympathy.

"Who are you? How did you—?" Kiera's voice cut off, too weak to call out for help.

The woman's upper lip curled into a faint sneer as she glanced to one side and scratched her cheek thoughtfully.

"Isn't it obvious who I am?" she said. "But *how* I got here . . ." Her voice cut off as she shrugged and shook her head. "That is one heck of a conundrum." She snapped her fingers and pointed at Kiera. "Tell you what. If I find out, you'll be the first to know. Deal?"

She held her hand out to Kiera as if she actually expected her to shake with her, but Kiera shrank as far away from her as she could. Looking at the cloth curtain that separated her from the other recovering patients, she wished she had the strength to call for help, but her voice was lodged like a stone in her chest.

"I can't stay," the woman said. "This place gives me the willies." Without another word, the redheaded woman turned and moved away from the bed.

A hazy, gray shadow shifted across the curtain and then dispersed like smoke. Kiera blinked and, when she looked around, saw no trace of the woman other than the shifting of the curtain as if a gentle breeze was blowing. A sudden constriction gripped her throat, making it almost impossible for her to breathe. She sucked in a tiny breath of air and then let out a surprisingly loud shriek. In an instant, the nurse who had been tending her before appeared at the bedside.

"What is it?" she asked, her eyes wide with concern.

Kiera stared at her, vaguely aware that her lips were moving as she gulped air like a fish out of water. Tears flooded her eyes, and in her panic, she batted feebly at the nurse as she leaned closer.

"Take it easy," the nurse said, her voice firm but reassuring. "You're all right. Everything's all right."

Swept up by a surge of panic, Kiera looked at the nurse and tried to make sense of what had just happened. Was it a dream or a hallucination? Nothing made sense. Her pulse was racing so fast her neck and wrists ached with every throb. She took a few short, wheezing breaths.

"I was . . . Someone just . . . Oh my God! My heart's beating so fast . . . I was . . . scared."

The nurse took the glass of water from the side table and held the straw to Kiera's mouth so she could have a sip. That helped a little, but as Kiera looked around, she was gripped by a sense of impending danger. Even the faintest shadows seemed fraught with menace. Her eyes kept darting back and forth as she looked for any sign of the woman who had just been there, but she was gone.

She couldn't have been real, Kiera told herself. *Hospital staff would never treat a patient like that.*

But no matter how much she tried to rationalize it, she found it impossible to settle down. The faintest sound, the slightest glimpse of motion in the corner of her eye made her jump and tense up, expecting to see that woman again.

Then in a flash she remembered where she had seen the woman before. It had been when she was taking the CAT scan. And there was another time. A few days before, when she had been fixing her hair and looking into the bathroom mirror, she had noticed that her reflection didn't match what she was doing. It had been like looking at a duplicate of herself.

"I *have* to be imagining this," she whispered, not aware she was speaking out loud.

"What's that?" the nurse asked, glancing at her with a raised eyebrow.

"Huh . . . ?" Kiera shook her head, realizing what was going on. "Oh, nothing . . . I was just—"

She wanted to tell the nurse what she had just seen, but what good would it do? While it was possible someone on the hospital staff who looked like her had just stopped by, she was sure she either imagined or dreamed the woman.

"Do you think I'll be able to go up to my room and get settled in soon?" Kiera asked.

The nurse shrugged and said, "The doctor has to check on you first. Your husband's been in the waiting room all morning. Do you feel ready for a visitor?"

Kiera flushed and nodded. She hadn't even thought about Nate, but suddenly the thought of him coming to see her made the feeling of dread even worse. He was a reminder of the life she had been living, but now, for some strange reason, Kiera knew things had changed. The operation had been like a watershed of some kind, she just didn't know what yet.

But *something* had changed, she knew that much.

The nurse left, and as she lay there in the bed, waiting for Nate and Dr. Martindale to show up, she tried to figure out what had changed. In a curious way, she felt liberated, as though she had changed for the better somehow. Still, the cold, churning uneasiness in the pit of her stomach hadn't gone away and, if anything, was only getting worse.

She didn't have long to prepare herself before the curtain parted, and Nate walked up to her bed. He smiled at her, but Kiera saw something in his expression that bothered her. It was in his eyes. She was suddenly convinced that he was hiding something from her, but she could sense it, no matter how much he tried to mask it.

"Hey," he said as he came close enough to give her a quick kiss on the cheek. Then he backed away, looking like he didn't know what to do next.

"Hey yourself," Kiera replied. "Well, I guess I lived through it." She narrowed her eyes and raised a hand to the bandage on her forehead. "It's crazy to think that, just a few hours ago, they were operating inside my head."

"I've already talked to Dr. Martindale," Nate said as he dragged a chair close to the bed and sat down. "Wanna hear the scoop?"

Kiera nodded groggily. Now that Nate was here, she realized just how out of it she really felt. She kept stealing quick glances at him, telling herself she should appreciate the love and support he was expressing, but it rang hollow, and she couldn't ignore the yawning distance there was between them. She had never seen it so clearly before.

"I know what they did. They took out my brain and put it in a freezer. They're just waiting for someone who needs a new one."

Nate chuckled but, unlike the old days when he would have played along with one of her jokes, he didn't have a comeback. It pained her to see how much things had changed between them. Or maybe they had never been good. Could she admit to herself that their marriage had always been missing . . . something . . . something that neither one of them could provide?

She felt a deep sadness as she looked at him and realized he was part of her previous life, but he wasn't—or could no longer be—a part of her life now.

It's over.

And then it hit her. She had thought it . . . she had suspected it, but it was so obvious she was almost embarrassed she hadn't admitted it to herself before. She knew now, with total certainty, that Nate was seeing someone else, that there was another woman in his life.

"Like the doctor said," Nate said, "it wasn't very serious. The tumor was benign, like we'd hoped. It looked like it had suddenly started to grow again, but other than pressing on the optic nerve, it wasn't tangled up with—uh, anything else."

"So that accounts for the hallucinations, the flashing lights and everything," Kiera said. Even as she said it, though, she knew it wasn't true, because just then she caught a hint of *something* moving across the field of her vision like a smoky figure behind her husband's back. She fought back a rush of panic.

Maybe it just takes time . . . Maybe my nerves are still firing after the surgery . . . Or maybe something's still there inside my head . . .

She had the frightening feeling that whatever it was, it was still there and it would *always* be there, surgery or not.

Shifting her eyes, she tried to track the hazy streak as it floated by behind Nate, but it moved along with her eyes, so she could never look at it directly.

Before Nate said anything, the curtain was raised again, and Liz O'Keefe entered, holding a large vase filled with roses and baby's breath.

"Well look at you," Liz said, smiling as she placed the roses on the windowsill and then approached the bed. When she leaned down and gave Kiera a kiss on the cheek, Kiera caught a whiff of her perfume and sneezed. The sudden motion sent a dull ache through her head, but—thankfully—the pain quickly faded.

"What do you think of my new headgear?" Kiera asked, touching the bandages that swathed her head. "Just the most stylish thing, don't you think?"

Liz pursed her lips and tried to smile, but she obviously felt uncomfortable. She hadn't even bothered to say hello to Nate, and Kiera wondered if she was picking up on the weird vibes between her and her husband. Then again, Nate didn't really like Liz or Jon. They weren't his kind of people, he told her. Moving away from the bed, he glared at Liz, looking annoyed that she had intruded on their privacy.

"Where's Jon?" Kiera asked, glancing at the curtain as though expecting to see him lurking nearby.

"Still at that real estate agent's meeting in Boston," Liz said. "Don't you remember?"

"Oh, right," Kiera said, nodding. She vaguely remembered him telling her something about that. "It must've slipped my mind. God, you'd think I needed brain surgery or something."

"Look," Liz said as she started backing away from the bed. "You're just coming round. I'm sure you need all the quiet time you can get. I was in town doing a little shopping, but I'll drop by later."

Kiera started to protest, but another, stronger throb in her head made her realize Liz was right. The truth was, she wished Nate would leave, too, but she knew he planned on staying at least for a little while longer. Thankfully, there was no sign of Trista yet. Kiera didn't want to face any of *that* tension.

"Sure thing," Kiera said. Her eyes went unfocused as she heaved a sigh. "I am pretty beat."

"What do you expect?"

Kiera was startled by the male voice and looked up as Dr. Martindale walked over to the bed. He was smiling as he placed a hand on Kiera's shoulder.

"So, how are we feeling?" he asked.

"Well *we* are absolutely wiped," Kiera answered honestly.

As she looked at him, she had the odd sensation that he seemed farther away than she knew he was. He almost didn't look real, like she was looking at him through the wrong end of a telescope, and he appeared to be at the far end of the room.

"I'll come back during visiting hours," Liz said as she backed away. "It's good to see you came through all right. I'll let Jon know."

Kiera smiled and nodded. The feeling of dissociation that had started when she looked at the doctor was getting steadily worse. Her eyes flickered and closed for a moment, but the feeling of falling backward in a slow-motion tumble startled her and made her jump. When she opened her eyes again, the room looked like it was swaying from side to side, like the deck of a boat on a storm-tossed sea.

"You want me to wait outside?"

She recognized Nate's voice, but he, too, sounded so far away he might have been shouting to her from far down the corridor.

"I'd appreciate that," Dr. Martindale said.

Kiera wondered why she suddenly couldn't keep her

eyes open, even though she was terrified of what would happen when she closed them. Through narrowed slits, she watched Nate leave the room. All she could see was a featureless gray blur that only vaguely resembled a person.

"So," Dr. Martindale said as he looked down at Kiera. "Are you really feeling all right?"

Kiera was sure that the panic bubbling up inside her would make it impossible for her to speak, but she licked her lips and said, "Not really . . . I'm . . . Just now, I started feeling . . . really disoriented."

"Disoriented?"

Kiera listened to the rolling echo of the doctor's voice and struggled to focus, but no matter how hard she concentrated, her eyesight kept twitching back and forth.

"I . . . I'm not sure," she said, fighting back a chilling rush of panic. She took a breath to try to pull herself back from the dizzying rushes that were sweeping through her, but she could feel herself sinking deeper. "I just feel . . . really kinda . . . messed up."

"The anesthesia will do that to you. Plus the pain meds you're on could make you feel a little fuzzy."

"Yeah . . . fuzzy," Kiera said and then chuckled. "I'm feeling kinda . . . fuzzy."

She was slipping deeper. The warm darkness inside her head—even with the spinning, backward fall—seemed safer than reality. A faint voice in her head asked if she felt safer because Nate had left the room.

"Fuzzy Wuzzy . . . was a bear . . . Fuzzy Wuzzy had no . . . Yeah . . . No hair . . . You didn't shave my head . . . did you?"

She raised her hand and touched her head, but she couldn't tell through the bandage if there was hair there or not.

"Your hair is fine," Dr. Martindale said, his voice echoing now like he was shouting in a canyon. "I think we'd best get you up to your room so you can get some rest. It'll take a while for the anesthesia to wear off."

"Uh . . . Yeah . . . That sounds . . . like fun," Kiera said, "fuzzy wuzzy fun."

Her own voice was so faint and dreamy it sounded like someone else was talking for her. She had been afraid before, but now she no longer cared as she squeezed her eyes tightly shut and let herself drift into the darkness that reached up to embrace her.

And in that darkness, she dreamed . . .

~6~

Kiera jumped when she heard a car door slam shut. The sound echoed like a cannon shot through the huge, all-but-deserted parking garage. It was night, and she was on the top floor that looked out over a fantastic view of Portland's brightly lit skyline.

Moving with a swift, gliding motion that felt like flying, she wove her way between the cement pillars until she came to a single parked car. A woman was bent over as she struggled to fit a key into the lock. Kiera could sense the woman's rising frustration when the key didn't go into the lock the way it was supposed to.

Wanting to help, Kiera came closer. It didn't strike her as at all odd that she was flying, her feet a few inches above the oil-stained cement floor, and it never occurred to her that she must be dreaming.

"Maybe I can get that for you," she said, but her voice was no louder than the hiss of a soft breeze through dry grass. It wafted the woman's hair, making her look around, but she obviously didn't see Kiera, who was surprised to see her friend, Liz O'Keefe. After a moment, Liz went back to fumbling with the key, trying without success to get it into the door lock.

"Gotta be the wrong key," Liz muttered in frustration.

She was obviously talking to herself, so Kiera didn't bother to answer. Then, stepping back, Liz looked at the key ring in her hand and started to chuckle. Hovering behind her, Kiera looked at the key ring, too, and saw that it was a remote. When Liz pressed the lock button, the car's lights flashed, and the horn beeped twice. After smoothing her clothes, Liz turned and started toward the bank of elevators that would take her down to ground level.

Kiera could sense that Liz was in a hurry. She looked anxious as she practically ran toward the elevators. They were at the far end of the building, and Kiera wondered why, if Liz was so concerned about being alone up here, she had parked on the top floor of the deserted building. Her shoes clicked on the cement, echoing with an odd reverberation in the vast darkness.

Liz was panting heavily by the time she reached the elevators. Leaning against the wall, she let out a loud gasp as she pressed the Down button. Kiera realized that, in her hurry, Liz hadn't noticed the handwritten Out of Order sign taped beside the metal door. The message was hastily scrawled with dripping red letters.

"It's not working," Kiera said, but once again, her voice was as soft as a whisper in the night.

"Damn it," Liz muttered when she finally stood back and saw the hand-lettered sign. She turned around to the stairway behind her and was about to start down the stairs when both she and Kiera sensed motion behind them. In the shadows, Kiera couldn't see who was approaching them, but whoever it was, he was moving fast.

Kiera's vision suddenly telescoped, and she felt like she was falling backward. She blinked her eyes and realized she was looking at Liz from the far end of the garage. She watched, unable to move, as the person—nothing more than a black silhouette—came up behind Liz and slammed into her hard enough to knock her against the wall.

"No!" Kiera cried out, but her voice was muffled by the darkness that surrounded her.

Liz also let out a strangled cry as she swung her purse around, trying to hit her attacker in the face. Kiera was frozen helplessly as Liz kicked and punched at her attacker, but the person was stronger than she was and started pushing her toward the metal railing of the stairwell.

Anger and fear filled Kiera as she watched the struggle. Closer . . . closer they came to the wide, gaping hole of the stairwell that went straight down three stories to the cement floor.

"Express elevator . . . going down," a high, twisted voice whispered like the rasp of metal against metal.

The assailant slipped his hands under Liz's armpits and lifted her off her feet. She squealed and continued to struggle, kicking and thrashing wildly, but to no avail. One of her shoes flipped off and shot between the railings. As she was pushed facedown over the opening, she—and Kiera—watched the shoe drop, twisting and turning end over end until it hit the bottom of the stairwell and bounced out of sight. A man's face suddenly appeared at the bottom of the stairwell as he leaned over the railing and looked up with shock and surprise in his eyes.

"Help me!" Liz and Kiera shouted in unison.

But Kiera watched helplessly as Liz was lifted up over the railing. She fought back valiantly. Her arms and legs banged against the metal railing, making it ring like a gong. But her flailing didn't do any good. The person forced her over the railing and then, with one last, powerful shove, he let her go.

For a moment, Liz was airborne. Kiera wondered why Liz couldn't hover in the air like she could. Her arms flapping uselessly, Liz twisted around and made one last, desperate grab for the railing. Her hand smacked against the metal railing, and then she dropped out of sight.

Kiera cringed as she listened to the long, fading shriek, and Liz's cry blended with Kiera's as she cried out and sat up in bed, her eyes wide with horror.

The hospital room was dark, and she was alone. For a long time, she sat there in bed, listening to her pulse racing in her ears. Only much later was she able to relax and drift back off to sleep.

CHAPTER 6

Yellow Dust

~1~

"No, you *can't* have a word with her. Not right now. She had surgery yesterday, and I don't think she's up to seeing anyone."

Nate's voice, coming from the corridor, sounded both angry and nervous as it drew Kiera out of the thin sleep she had drifted into sometime before dawn following a terrible dream that—thankfully—was already fading from her memory.

For a few seconds, she thought she was home in bed. Even after she opened her eyes, it took her a while to realize where she was. Dazed and confused, she looked around the hospital room. It was suffused with a dull gray light that looked like a thin haze of smoke. The shades were drawn, and it looked like it was a cloudy day.

"Can I ask what this is all about?"

Kiera thought Nate sounded nervous. She rolled her head to one side and looked at the partially open door. Someone—it had to be Nate—was blocking the entrance, but the dark silhouette reminded her of something from her dream, which made her shiver. Beyond him were two indistinct silhouettes.

"And you are?" one of the men said. His tone was flat and humorless.

"Nate Davis. Her husband. And I'm telling you, she can't see you right now. She needs to rest."

"We just have a few questions, Mr. Davis," said another, more pleasant-sounding voice. "We won't take more than two minutes of her time."

Nate was silent for a moment. He glanced into the room at Kiera, but she wasn't sure if he realized she was awake. Whatever it was, it sounded important, and she wanted to signal that it was okay, that she could see whoever was out there, but she remained motionless. Looking down at her hand, which was lying outside of the covers, she experienced an odd feeling of dissociation. She remembered the feeling she'd had earlier—*when was that?*—of floating in darkness, and she wondered if she was dead or dreaming this now.

"Hon . . . ?" Nate whispered, moving silently into the room. "You awake?"

Kiera tried to speak, but the only sound she could make was a faint, guttural grunt. She cleared her throat and finally managed to say, "Yeah."

The feeling of dissociation grew steadily stronger, and with it came an inexplicable rush of fear. She had a sudden impulse to bolt upright in the bed and scream at Nate not to let these people in, but it was already too late. Helpless to move, she watched as Nate stepped aside, and two figures entered the hospital room. In the thin morning light, she couldn't see their faces clearly until they were close to the bed.

"Mrs. Davis?" one of them said. "I'm Detective Fielding. This is Detective LeRioux. Can we ask you a few questions?"

"Sure," Kiera said even though the sense of dread was steadily mounting inside her. She glanced at Nate, who looked grim and maybe a little frightened.

"You don't have to if you don't want to," he said.

"No. It's okay," Kiera said. "What's this about?"

"You're friends with Elizabeth O'Keefe?" Fielding asked.

The tension Kiera had been feeling before suddenly jolted her as a fragment of the dream she'd had last night came back. Her eyes widened as she looked from the detective to her husband and then back to the detective. She took a shallow breath that clicked in her throat. The feeling that she was floating rushed over her, making her feel giddy.

"Liz? Yeah. Sure. She's a good friend." Even to her, her voice sounded weak. "Is something the matter? Tell me what happened."

"Ms. O'Keefe had an accident last night," Fielding said simply.

"An accident—?"

Panic surged inside Kiera. Her heart started racing, high and fast. Each pulse made her vision twitch.

"She fell down the stairwell in a parking garage in Portland last night."

"Oh my God! Is she—?" Kiera started to say, but judging by their faces, she knew the answer. In a flash, she had a clear mental image of the parking garage, almost as if she had been there herself. She saw the wide stairwell and, crumpled at the bottom, looking like a rag doll that had been tossed aside, a figure she recognized.

"I'm sorry to tell you this, but she's dead," Fielding said. His voice was still emotionless, but Kiera caught a hint of sadness in his eyes. His partner, LeRioux, had a harder, more suspicious look in his eyes.

"My God! You can't be serious."

"She either fell or was pushed over the railing," Fielding continued. "But I was wondering if you could explain how this—" As he spoke, he reached into his coat pocket and withdrew a clear plastic bag. Inside was a slim plastic card. "—got there?"

Kiera looked at the thing until she recognized it.

"My driver's license. Where did you find that?" Panic coursed through her body.

"It was on the floor of Ms. O'Keefe's car. On the passenger's side," Fielding said simply. "Someone in the parking garage last night reportedly saw Ms. O'Keefe struggling with someone. He didn't get a good look at whoever it was, but he says he saw someone with red hair in the parking garage. Since you match the description . . ."

"What? You think *I* was there?" Kiera asked, astounded.

"She hasn't left here since the surgery yesterday," Nate said.

"My license was in my purse, which I left at home when I came in yesterday for the surgery," Kiera said.

"Then how did it get into Mrs. O'Keefe's car?" Fielding asked, taking a step closer to the bed.

"Whoa, hold on a second there," Nate said, turning on the detectives. "What the hell are you suggesting? There's no way Kiera had anything to do with this."

Fielding turned and regarded Nate with a steady, blank expression. "I'm not *suggesting* anything," he replied in a low, controlled voice that slammed into Kiera's ears like a hammer on metal. "I'm simply following up on a lead that might help us find out what happened to Mrs. O'Keefe last night."

Nate's face flushed with anger as he looked back and forth between the detectives and Kiera.

"She had goddamned brain surgery yesterday, for Christ's sake." His voice was tight with anger. "She's been drifting in and out of consciousness ever since."

Tears filled Kiera's eyes as she leaned her head back into the pillow and tried to process what was happening. Fragments of her dream last night came back, but they were only fragments. She couldn't put them together to make sense. Her pulse was beating so fast her neck ached. Worried that she was going to faint, she clenched her fists and struggled to stay conscious.

How can Liz be dead? . . . But there was something . . . I saw it . . . but that's not possible!

"Ms. O'Keefe is married," Fielding said, ignoring Nate's outburst as if it hadn't happened. "We found her home number on her cell phone, but her husband's not answering. Do you have any idea where he is?"

It took Kiera a few seconds to realize he was talking to her. Blinking her eyes, she stared at him blankly as she struggled to catch a single, rational thought through her confusion and panic.

There's no way Liz can be dead, she kept telling herself, even though she had the weird feeling that—somehow— she had seen it happen. The cold emptiness in the pit of her stomach told her it was true. This wasn't a dream or some flight of imagination. These detectives were real, and what they were telling her had really happened.

"Mrs. Davis?" Fielding had a sympathetic look in his eyes as he looked at her. "Do you know how we can get in touch with Mr. O'Keefe?"

"He's at a . . . a conference . . . for real estate agents," Kiera said distantly. She was still too stunned to focus clearly. "He—ah, sells properties . . . here in town. I thought he . . . he left . . . I'm not sure. A couple of days ago." She raised her hand to her head, applying pressure to the bandage as if that would help her remember. "I—I'm not really sure, but he's supposed to be gone all week. I think he said he was going to Denver . . . or maybe was it Boston?"

"Thank you very much," Fielding said. "You've been a big help. I think that's all we need right now." He glanced at his partner, who simply nodded. "Would it be okay for us to come back if we have any follow-up questions?

Still stunned by the news, Kiera stared blankly at him before nodding and saying, "Yes, yes . . . Of course."

"Thank you for your time, Mrs. Davis," Fielding said. "Sorry to trouble you." Without a word to Nate, the two detectives turned to leave.

"One question?" Kiera asked in a broken voice.

The detectives stopped in the doorway and turned back to her.

"My license . . . When can I have it back?"

"We'll return it after we dust it for fingerprints," Fielding said without emotion.

"If it's mine, I . . . I have no idea how it got into Liz's car."

She closed her eyes and rubbed her bandaged forehead. Mentioning her friend's name drove home the grief again, and tears filled Kiera's eyes, turning everyone and everything in the room into a watery blur. Once the detectives were gone, Kiera settled down in bed and listened to the receding *click-click-click* of their shoes on the linoleum. After a long silence, still struggling to process what had just happened, she looked at Nate.

"I can't believe it."

Her voice choked off, and a thick, salty taste filled her throat. She looked helplessly at Nate, who was standing at the foot of the bed.

"I can't either. What gives them the right to come in here and grill you like that?" Nate's face flushed with anger, and his eyes twitched from side to side as though he didn't know where to focus. "Can they do that? Can they just keep your license?"

Kiera shrugged even though the slightest motion pained her neck and shoulders. "But Liz—" she whispered, her voice twisting off again. "How can she be . . . dead?"

Nate sat down on the edge of the bed and took her hand, giving it a firm squeeze as he stared into her eyes and sadly shook his head.

"I don't know," he said softly, but Kiera thought she detected a distance in his voice. For whatever reasons, Nate had never liked Liz or Jon. Maybe he just didn't like that she had friends she did things with while he only socialized with other teachers, usually on poker night. He always complained about how boring they were because all they ever talked about was work.

"And Jon . . . He doesn't even know yet? He's gonna be devastated when he finds out." Kiera's eyes were brimming with tears.

"I know," Nate said, still squeezing her hand. "I can't imagine . . ." He shivered. "But you can't let this get to you. You have to rest and get better yourself."

Looking at him, Kiera realized just how wide the distance between them was. A volatile mixture of grief and rage flared up inside her, but she had no idea what to say or even where to start expressing to him how she felt.

At that instant, a nurse Kiera didn't recognize poked her

head into the room. She was tall and thin, and she was smiling as she walked over to Kiera.

"And how are we this morning?" the nurse asked, apparently oblivious to what had just happened. She went about her business, checking Kiera's blood pressure and vital signs without saying much, and then she left after informing her that Dr. Martindale would be by soon to check in on her. Kiera forced a smile and watched as the nurse left, but the coldness that had wrapped around her heart made her shiver. She didn't like being alone with Nate. When he started to speak, she cut him off sharply.

"I don't want to talk right now," she said. "I really . . ." She took a deep breath. "Would you mind leaving me alone for a while?"

Nate started to say something, but then he stood up and stretched, rotating his shoulders. He remained silent as he regarded her.

"I really need to . . ." but she couldn't finish the sentence as fresh tears welled up in her eyes and streamed down her face. Nate moved closer, but she waved him away.

"Please," she whispered, turning away from him and burying her face in the pillow. "I need some time alone . . . Please?"

Without another word, Nate left the room and closed the door behind him. For a long time, Kiera just lay there as she cried. How could she accept that one of her closest friends was dead? Here she had been so worried that a brain tumor was going to kill her or that she would die on the operating table, and then . . . just like *that* . . .

Out of the blue . . .

Liz O'Keefe was gone.

And I saw it happen, she thought, even though that made no sense at all.

~2~

"Out of the frying pan and into the fire, huh?"

The voice—it was Jon's—wafted like cool morning mist into Kiera's sleep. She stirred in bed but didn't open her eyes. She was too comfortable where she was, floating in a soft, cushiony haze.

"We're really in trouble now, aren't we?" Jon said after a pause. "But I can count on you, can't I?" His voice reverberated with an odd echo effect that made him sound faraway.

Without opening her eyes, Kiera grunted and nodded. She had a vague idea what he meant but couldn't bring herself to deal with it directly. After getting past the first jolt of shock and grief over Liz's death by falling asleep, she'd had dreams that, distorted as they were, filled her with a gnawing sense of uneasiness. Echoes of the dream she'd had the night before where she had seen what had happened to Liz still haunted her. She wished she had been able to see the face of the person who had attacked Liz, but the figure had been lost in shadow.

"I have no idea what I'm going to do now," Jon said, his voice catching as he sobbed.

And then—even with her eyes closed—Kiera looked up and saw him looming over her. His skin was drawn and pale, almost white; his eye sockets were dark hollows, and his eyes were wide and glistening with an unnaturally bright sheen. His mouth was set in a firm, bloodless line, but when he spoke, his teeth looked huge and white, almost too big for his mouth.

"What *can* we do?" Kiera asked as she struggled to push back the rushes of fear inside her. Jon was, after all, probably her best friend, and she had to help him get through the hard times she knew were ahead. "We should have done something about it a long time ago."

His face hovered in front of her like a huge balloon. It seemed to inflate, expanding as his anger boiled up. She had never seen him like this.

"You see?" he shouted. Spittle flew from his lips, and his voice strained almost to breaking. *"That's* exactly what I'm talking about! You can't talk like that! You can't *think* like that!" He took a breath, but his anger didn't seem to abate. "What's done is done. We have to move on, so get used to it!"

"Okay. Sure. *We* can move on . . . but *Billy* can't."

Kiera was trying hard not to say what she'd been thinking. Maybe the pain meds were making the words tumble out of her before she could censor them. She cringed and waited for another outburst from Jon, but the eyes in his balloon face regarded her with a flat expression that was almost impossible to read. It seemed to be part concern, part rage, and part . . . something else that she couldn't quite grasp.

"After all these years," he said, "I hoped I could count on you." There was a wistful trace of sadness in his voice now, but Kiera could feel the rage just below the surface. "With everything else I have to deal with, I was sure you'd be the one person I could count on."

"I am . . . You can," Kiera whispered. She rolled her head from side to side, but it was impossible to get away from the face that loomed in front of her.

"Whoa . . . Take it easy," a voice said.

It took Kiera a while to realize Jon was still speaking, but now his voice sounded closer and clearer, and much calmer. She opened her eyes—*had they been closed all this time?*—and saw Jon standing beside her bed. His face was flushed, but not with anger. Tears glistened like mercury in his eyes, and his lower lip was trembling with repressed emotion.

"Hi," Kiera said weakly, and seeing him instantly brought back the tragedy of what had happened to Liz.

"I'm sorry," Jon said. "I didn't mean to wake you, but I—"

"Oh, Jon . . . I'm *so* sorry."

Kiera started to cry as she raised her arms to hug him. Jon leaned down and hugged her, smothering his hot face in the crook of her neck. His body shook, and he was making a strangled animal sound deep in his throat. His tears dropped onto her skin and ran down her neck, making her shiver. Desperate with grief, she clung to him, trying to think of something she could do or say, but nothing came.

"I can't believe it . . . I can't believe she's . . . gone," Jon said in a strained and muffled voice. Sobs wracked his body. Kiera was surprised how small he felt in her embrace.

Which is the real Jon? she wondered as she struggled to sort out what was happening. She must have been dreaming at least part of their conversation, but she wasn't sure when she had awakened. She must have imagined or dreamed him saying those terrible things about Billy.

"I just got home and came right over," he said, his voice choking on almost every word. "If I hadn't gone away . . . if I had been here . . . this never . . . would've happened."

"Don't say that," Kiera said as she raised her hands and tried to soothe him by rubbing his back. He was practically vibrating in her arms. "You can't know for sure."

"And do you know what the worse part of it is? The police . . . they're treating me like I . . . like I might have had something to do with it. Christ!"

Before he could continue, Jon broke off the embrace and leaned back so he could look at her. His face was pale and slick with tears.

"I know the spouse . . . the spouse is . . . is always a suspect, but how could they . . . ? How could I . . . ?"

His voice choked off, and he couldn't finish. At a loss for words, Kiera decided the best thing was just to wait. He had to know how much she cared for him and how devastated she was over Liz's death. Still, she couldn't get rid of that mental image of him looking at her with such rage when she talked about what had happened with Billy. It frightened her even though she knew she had to have imagined it.

"They have to follow up everything," she said, trying her best to sound reasonable. "They found my driver's license in Liz's car and actually interrogated me, like they thought I might have been involved. Someone reported seeing a woman with red hair in the parking garage."

"Really?" Jon's face drained of blood, and he looked like he was about to collapse.

"I assume they have to follow up on any leads they get," Kiera said. "I know you didn't do it, but . . . but *someone* did, and they—"

Before she could finish that thought, Jon's expression suddenly crumbled as if his face was made of sand that was blowing away. He blinked his eyes rapidly and looked up at the ceiling as he struggled to stem another flood of tears, but he lost control and, covering his face with both hands, let out a long, heart-rending sob.

"I just don't know what I'm going to do," he wailed, his voice muffled by his hand. "I have no idea what I'm going to do."

Kiera's hands were trembling as she reached up and touched his arm.

"You have friends . . . You have *me*," she said. "Somehow, we'll get through it."

"I wish I could believe you," Jon said, looking at her and shaking his head. His expression was silently begging her *how*, but he didn't say a word. He couldn't, and Kiera found that she couldn't speak, either. After a long silence, Jon took a deep breath, straightened his shoulders, and looked at her as if he was seeing her for the first time.

"Jesus Christ almighty," he said in a shattered voice. "And you have *this* to deal with." His expression suddenly softened, and he forced himself to smile. "How are you feeling? I mean, the surgery and all. It wasn't anything serious, was it?"

Finding it odd to be talking about something that seemed almost mundane in comparison, Kiera simply shrugged.

"It was benign . . . the growth. They went in through a little hole here—" She touched the left side of her head, tapping the thick wad of bandage. "—and sucked it out. There's no sign of any other tumors, and the doctor says there's no evidence of any permanent damage."

"Oh, thank *God*," Jon whispered, his eyelids fluttering rapidly. "I . . . I just don't know what I would have done if I . . . if I had lost you, too."

"You're not going to lose me," Kiera said. "Trust me."

It broke her heart to see him shattered like this, but she also couldn't feel comfortable because the more she thought about it, the more she believed it didn't matter if she had dreamed what had happened earlier or not. She had seen a side of Jon, a frightening, angry side of him that really unnerved her, mostly because she hadn't seen it since that night when Billy died.

~3~

"We have to talk."

It was late afternoon. Although the shades were drawn, narrow bars of slanting golden sunlight cast thin shadows across the floor. A faint yellow haze filled the air like thick dust. Vases of flowers and get well cards from friends, and a stuffed bear from Trista were lined up on the windowsill. An eerie silence filled the room, and Kiera, who had been dozing off and on all day, pinched the back of her hand to make sure she was awake and had actually heard the voice.

"I know we do," a voice said.

She'd been expecting to hear Nate and was startled to realize it was Jon's voice again. She rubbed her eyes and looked at the corner of the room where a dark shape was slouched in the chair. After a second or two, she realized she was the one who had said they had to talk. She moaned as she dragged herself closer to consciousness.

"Have you been here all day?"

"No," Jon said. "Just the last half hour or so. I had to go to the morgue and identify Liz." He heaved a heavy sigh. "Then I met with Mark Steensland at the funeral home to start making arrangements."

The chair creaked as Jon shifted his weight forward and clasped his hands in front of him between his knees. He looked bigger now. Kiera thought it was because of the darkening room . . . or maybe it was her nervousness because of what she knew she had to tell him.

"We have to talk," she said again. "There's something I need to tell you.

"And what would that be?" Jon sounded absolutely drained. It must have been a terrible day for him as well as her. Kiera hoped he'd had a chance to doze while she was sleeping.

"You know," Kiera said. "It's about Billy." She licked her lips to moisten them before continuing. "I don't know why, but I've been thinking a lot about what happened back then, and I need to talk about it if only to get it off my mind."

The room was so silent that Kiera thought for a moment that she might have imagined Jon there. She blinked her eyes, trying to make him out in the gathering gloom. The hazy yellow light gave his skin a sickly cast. Even his clothes looked like they were covered by a fine, yellow dust.

"There's nothing to discuss," Jon finally said, sounding tired. He shifted and started to stand up but then sank back into the chair and sighed. "We did what we did. It's done. We can't go back and redo it."

"I know we can't, but—" Kiera said as shivers coursed up and down her spine. "I . . ." She took a shuddering breath and held it, fighting back the panic that was rising inside her. "Do you believe in ghosts?"

Jon frowned at her, a half smile playing across his lips as though he wasn't sure he'd heard her correctly. When Kiera didn't say anything more, he tipped his head back and, looking at the ceiling, stroked his chin.

"Ghosts . . ." he said, his voice soft and low.

Kiera nodded. She wanted so much for him to understand and sympathize with what she was going through.

"Are you saying—" Jon's voice cut off as he leaned forward, gazing at her with a cold, harsh light in his eyes. "You're not going to tell me you've been seeing Billy Carroll's ghost, are you?"

Hearing him say it so bluntly, Kiera couldn't help but think how foolish she sounded . . . if not downright crazy.

"I'm not losing my mind. Honest. I'm not," she said, but even she wasn't convinced because of the shrill whine in her voice. "But I can feel *something* close by. Like . . . I don't know what it is, but I've been getting this creepy feeling, like someone's watching me."

Jon leaned back and shook his head.

"You don't think this might have anything to do with what you've just been through recently?" He paused, letting that sink in. "You just had brain surgery, for Christ's sake. You don't think this . . . this *feeling* might have something to do with *that*?"

"I don't know. I'm not sure of anything anymore," Kiera said with a quick shake of the head. "I can't help but think that maybe the tumor was making me see things that—"

"Exactly!" Jon practically shouted. "Nate told me it had been pressing on your optic nerve."

"Yeah, but . . . I think maybe I was seeing things that are really there . . . Things that have been here all along, but I wasn't able to see them clearly until now. It's like . . . like now that they've taken this thing out of my head, it opened something up. It set something free. I don't *feel* like myself anymore. I'm not even sure who I am—or was—in the first place. It's *really* scary."

"I can imagine," Jon said.

For a long time, neither of them spoke. Now that she had said it, Kiera wished she could take it back. Jon and everyone else was going to think she was losing her sanity, and she couldn't help but wonder if maybe the doctor had missed some of the growth. Maybe there was still a piece of it in her brain, making her see and imagine things that weren't real. But they certainly *felt* real. In ways, they were more real than what she used to take for reality.

"So what makes you think this has anything to do with Billy?" Jon finally asked.

There was an odd detachment in his voice and manner that Kiera found unsettling. This wasn't the Jon O'Keefe she knew as a friend and confidant. She had been so happy to reconnect with him when he first moved back to Stratford, but now she wasn't so sure. He seemed so cold to her.

"You don't think it's just your imagination or maybe a side effect of the operation or the meds you're on?"

Kiera thought about that for a moment but then shook her head and said, "I don't know." She paused, then added, "No. It's real. And even if it's not Billy, something is haunting me. I've even imagined a couple of times—no! I didn't *imagine* it. It was real." She swallowed hard. "I saw myself." John didn't say a word. "I've even had conversations with myself."

The expression on Jon's face was bothering her. She could see that he was becoming genuinely worried about her mental health.

And why wouldn't he?

What she was saying was seriously delusional if not downright psychotic. Maybe the tumor or the surgery or the medications had damaged her brain more than she or the doctors realized.

"Look," Jon finally said, leaning toward her and taking her hand in his. "You've got to get some rest so you'll get better. You were so worried about what would happen, I'm sure you imagined a lot of things. But whatever it is, you *have* to let it go about *Billy*. That was so long ago."

Jon froze and cast an anxious glance over his shoulder when someone walked by in the corridor. Lowering his voice, he leaned even closer to Kiera in the bed.

"I never meant to kill him," he whispered. "You know

that. And I think Billy knew it. It was a fucking *accident*! If I could go back to that night, don't you think I'd change it?"

"Of course you would," Kiera said in a strained whisper.

"We did what we had to do, and like we agreed at the time, we both have to live with it." He lowered his gaze and shook his head, obviously moved. "Maybe our decision wasn't the best one. We were young and scared. But believe me, I think about it more than you could know, but we can never go back and redo it. *Never!*" He wiped the sweat from his face. "There's no statute of limitations on murder, Kiera, so if we report what happened, even thirty years later, the police will charge me—charge *us* with murder. It will ruin both our lives."

"It already has," Kiera said, unable to keep the desperate edge out of her voice. "Living with the guilt has screwed me up so bad it's hurting my marriage and my relationship to my daughter and friends. It's ruined my life."

Jon squeezed her hand so tightly she winced. His face had gone pale, and his bloodshot eyes were wide with fear.

"If you're having any trouble now," he said, "even if you're seeing things—ghosts or whatever—it has *nothing* to do with what happened back then. Trust me."

"You're hurting my hand," Kiera said, but Jon didn't let go or ease his grip. If anything, he tightened it all the more as he brought his face so close to hers she could smell his aftershave and feel the warmth of his breath on her skin.

"Forget all about what happened that night. Please," he said in a deep, grating whisper. "It's over and done with. We can't bring Billy back—even as a ghost, but if you talk about this to *anyone* now, it will definitely destroy us— both of us."

Kiera stared into his eyes and, for a terrifying instant,

thought he was going to move close enough to kiss her; but after a tense moment, he let go of her hand and collapsed back in the chair. His face was shining with sweat, and his eyes had an empty glaze that genuinely unnerved her. He didn't look at all like the friend she knew. He looked like a man teetering on the brink of insanity. She told herself it was because of the grief he felt over his wife's death, but it seemed somehow more.

"Something's happening here." Kiera's voice shattered the silence like it was crystal. "I don't know what. I don't know if I'll ever understand it, but I have to try. If I don't, I know it will drive me crazy."

Covering his face with both hands, Jon leaned forward with his elbows on his knees and let out a loud, racking sob. His shoulders heaved violently. After a long time sobbing, he looked up at her, his cheeks glistening with tears.

"I'm so sorry," he said in a shattered voice. "I . . . I didn't mean . . . any of that. I—I just don't know what I'm going to do now that . . . now that Liz is—" His voice choked off, and all he could do was start crying again. Kiera didn't have the strength to sit up, but she reached out and touched his hand.

"It will all be all right," she whispered.

"What in the world am I going to do?" he asked, staring at her with wide, shining eyes. Without warning, he lunged forward and embraced her, holding her so tightly she almost couldn't breathe. His body was trembling as he cried into her shoulder. Kiera could do nothing but hold on to him and soothe him as best she could while he let out all of the grief that was pent up inside him.

"It will all be all right," she kept repeating, but even as she said it, she felt it wasn't true. As much as she was going to miss Liz and as badly as she felt for Jon's terrible loss, she could tell that something else . . . some much worse tragedy was lurking close by.

So far, it was unknown and unseen, but from the gnawing coldness in her stomach, Kiera knew that whatever it was, it wasn't going to remain unseen and unknown very much longer.

CHAPTER 7

Shadow and Light

~1~

Three days later, on an unusually warm September morning, Kiera was released from the hospital. After teaching for two days, Nate took the day off to bring her home and help her get settled.

The leaves on the trees were just starting to change color, and the snappy, fresh smell in the air filled her with exhilaration and hope when she walked out of the hospital.

"It feels so . . . weird," she said, looking around as Nate took hold of her hand to help her out of the wheelchair he'd used to roll her out the front door. "I can't believe it's been only—What? A week?" She shook her head. "It feels like a lifetime."

Nate didn't say a word before he rolled the wheelchair back inside the hospital door where an aide took it.

"I can imagine," he said when he came back. "You okay?"

Kiera blinked as she looked at the arc of blue sky, so bright it hurt her eyes. The last few days had been overcast, and she took this gorgeous day as a good omen. On the horizon, puffy white clouds moved slowly by, heading east, out over the ocean. From the trees nearby, a blue jay called out its raucous song, and squirrels scurried among the branches whose leaves were veined with bright red and yellow.

"I feel a little weak, actually," Kiera said, stretching out her arms for balance. The world was spinning, and she swayed from side to side. She couldn't suppress a surge of resentment when she had to lean on Nate for support.

She had done a lot of thinking over the last several days, and she thought she had some perspective on a lot of things now . . . not just what she had talked to Jon about when he had visited. The truth was, she questioned if he had really been there. She recalled a curious distance between them during the encounter, and she was more than half convinced she had imagined the whole thing.

One thing she could finally admit to herself—after all these years—was that her marriage was in serious trouble. It might be at the point where, if she wanted to save it, she was going to have to do something drastic, and soon.

The problem was, after so many days with a lot of time to think about everything that was wrong—and right— about her relationship with Nate, she didn't know what she should do about it. Even as simple a thing as how much time Nate had spent with her while she was in the hospital rankled her. If they were truly together, she should have been happy to have him there. But his presence irritated her, and when he wasn't around, all she could think was he was with someone else.

And what about Trista?

For the three days she had been in the hospital, Kiera had barely thought about her daughter. It pained her to feel so alienated from her own flesh and blood, and she would tear up any time she thought about how close they used to be. In many ways, it felt as if Trista was someone else's daughter, not hers. The disconnect between them was frightening . . . and terribly sad, but—like the distance between her and Nate—this, too, seemed so inevitable there wasn't a thing she could about it.

Is that it, then? she wondered as they started down the hospital steps and across the street to the car. *We just quit? . . . I give up?*

The thought made her stomach ache. She wished she didn't feel so feeble, but that was normal, after lying in bed so long. Once she got home, she told herself, once she settled in and started feeling better, things would get back to normal.

But that's what frightened her.

Normal was Nate and her barely relating to each other anymore. *Normal* was arguing with Trista until one of them—usually Trista—got so angry she stormed off, slamming doors behind her. *Normal* was everything that was making her feel so useless she might even be seeing and talking to people who weren't there. Her stay at the hospital already had a dreamy cast to it, making her wonder who of the people she had seen and talked were real, and who were not.

What if I'm seeing ghosts?

In spite of the warm day, her blood turned cold at the thought. When people died, and they weren't ready for it, they supposedly lingered where they had died, haunting the place. If that was true, the hospital should be filled to overflowing with restless spirits who hadn't moved on yet.

Kiera was shaken from her reverie when Nate moved quickly to unlock the passenger's door and help her into the front seat. Once she was settled, he walked around the car to the driver's side and got in. Kiera watched everything he did with a dreamy detachment.

"You feel like you could eat?" Nate asked. He barely turned to look at her as he started up the car. "I was thinking we could stop for breakfast along the way." Before she answered, he shifted into reverse and backed out of the parking space.

Kiera was silent as she parsed every word he'd spoken, trying to assemble them into some meaningful pattern, but her mind felt like an untethered helium balloon that was swaying slowly back and forth as it rose into the sky. The sensation of floating and falling at the same time made her close her eyes.

"Not such a great idea, huh?" Nate said.

His voice sounded thin and distant, like he wasn't in the car. Kiera shook her head no while fighting against the vertigo that gripped her. When Nate took the right-hand turn out of the parking lot, she clutched the door handle like it was a lifeline.

They didn't speak for much of the drive home. Kiera knew Nate was being respectful of how she was feeling, but she couldn't help but feel isolated and a little angry that he didn't at least *try* to connect.

"So what's been happening in the real world while I was away?" she asked.

She was leaning her head against the side window and still had her eyes closed. The sense of motion wasn't quite so bad now, but she imagined she was still a balloon, floating above the road.

Nate started to reply, then stopped himself. His hesitation caught Kiera's attention. She opened her eyes and looked at him. His figure was gauzy and out of focus, with the landscape slipping past his window behind him.

"What is it—?" she asked, knowing he was holding back on her.

It wasn't until Nate slowed down and stopped for a stop-light that he looked at her, a terribly pained expression in his eyes.

"I don't know if I should tell you or not."

Cold gripped her gut.

"Is it Trista? . . . Something's happened to Trista?"

The surge of panic became an icy ball in her stomach. It was all too easy to imagine scores of terrible things that might have happened to her daughter—a car accident . . . an overdose . . . pregnancy . . . suicide. Her heart seemed to stop as she waited for Nate to reply.

"No. No. Trista's fine." He flashed a tight smile. "As grumpy and alienated as ever, but—" The light turned green, and he accelerated through the intersection without looking at her. "I didn't want to tell you this, but Liz's funeral is this afternoon."

"Oh my God," Kiera whispered. She felt suddenly de-flated as she stared at the road ahead. Tears filled her eyes. For a while, she had forgotten that her friend had died. "I . . . I never even thought . . ." Her voice drifted away as she wiped her eyes with the back of her hand.

"You had your own stuff to deal with." Nate reached out and clasped her hand, giving it a reassuring squeeze. Kiera thought her hand felt like a dead fish in his grip . . . cold . . . lifeless . . .

"We have to go," she said, once she gained a measure of control.

Nate took a deep breath and held it for a second, then let it out slowly, and said, "You don't have to, you know."

"Yes, I do."

"You think it's a good idea?"

Kiera looked at him in amazement. *How can he think for even a millisecond that I wouldn't go to the funeral of one of my best friends?*

"You've still got a long recovery ahead of you," he said. "I'm sure Jon would understand if you called and told him you couldn't make it."

But Kiera wouldn't consider not going, even for a second. She *had* to be there if only to give whatever comfort and support she could to Jon. They went back too far. She couldn't let him down when he needed her most.

"I won't discuss it." Kiera's voice was flat and icy. "We're going. What time is it?"

Nate hesitated, then sighed and said, "One o'clock at St. Paul's."

Kiera raised her hand to her forehead and ran her fingertips over the bandage. She would feel self-conscious, showing up in public with her head bandaged and still feeling so out of it from the medication, but she knew she *had* to be there.

"We've got plenty of time to get ready," she said.

"I was planning to go back to school once you were set at home."

Nate still looked like he was keeping something from her. The anger Kiera was feeling fanned higher.

"You expect me to drive to the funeral myself?"

Nate shook his head. "No. No. Truth is, I didn't think you'd go."

"Because you weren't going to mention it." Her face was flushed with anger. "What were you thinking, you'd get me tucked in all safe and sound at home and conveniently forget to mention the funeral until it was too late, like it was something that just slipped your mind?"

"No. Nothing like that." Nate was sounding really defensive now. His knuckles turned white as he squeezed the steering wheel, and the muscles in his jaw tensed and untensed.

"If you really *have* to go back to school, I can drive, you know."

"The doctor said you aren't supposed to for a couple of weeks."

"Then I can get Joanie or someone to pick me up. Or Trista can drop me off."

"Don't be stupid. I'll take you."

"What do you mean, *'Don't be stupid'*? One of my best friends is *dead*. You don't think I want to go to her funeral?"

"That's not what I meant."

Kiera could tell he was getting angry, but he was holding it back. She had a sudden insight that this wasn't just about her recuperating and him wanting to check in on his classes. Something else was bothering him. Again, she wondered if he was seeing someone else, but she was too angry to confront him about it right now.

"I just was thinking . . . after everything you've been through . . . you don't need the stress of a funeral."

Kiera sniffed but said nothing.

"I would think—I'm sure Jon would understand if you didn't make it."

Kiera eyed him steadily, and once again—like she had so many times these last few days—she wondered if she even knew who this man was. He certainly wasn't the man she had fallen in love with and married twenty years ago. Over the years, they had both changed, but the gulf yawning between them had grown so imperceptibly she couldn't say exactly when or where things had changed.

But they definitely had changed. Maybe it had taken the operation for her to see it and finally admit it.

"I'm going," she said as exhaustion swept through her. "One way or another, I'm going."

Nate didn't say a word, but he glanced at her and nodded. The rest of the drive home was in total silence.

~2~

The funeral service at St. Paul's Lutheran Church struck Kiera as a bit hypocritical. She hadn't known Liz nearly as long as she had known Jon, but they had bonded quite a bit after she and Jon moved back to Stratford. If there was one thing Kiera knew about Liz, it was that she was definitely not a "religious" person. Not that she was an avowed atheist, and she certainly wasn't hostile to people who did believe, but she is—*or was*—an earthy person who showed little if any interest in spiritual things.

This must all be Jon's doing, she thought as she sat through a seemingly interminable service with hymns and prayers, a sermon from Pastor Wolfe, and several very heartfelt eulogies from friends and neighbors. Thankfully, Jon hadn't asked Kiera to say anything. She never could have gotten up in front of a crowd and said anything. Liz's brother had died several years ago, and she had no surviving family back in Colorado where she had been raised, so the people in attendance were there because they knew her through Jon.

Throughout the service, Kiera felt terribly self-conscious about her appearance. Everyone, of course, knew she'd had brain surgery. Like any small town, word spread quickly. Before the service began, even people Kiera didn't know very well came up to her and asked how she was feeling. She smiled and told them she was fine, considering, but it was a lie. The loss of her friend was just the beginning of how bad she felt, but there was no one—not even her close friends she'd known since she was a kid—she could talk to about everything she was going through.

It was a foolish detail, she knew, but she was worried most about her hair. Although she acknowledged it was pure vanity, she had always been proud of her bright red hair. It was practically her trademark, an essential part of her identity. She was glad the doctors hadn't shaved off more than they had. She couldn't imagine being bald and having to wait a year or more for it all to grow back.

Still, the large bandage was bad enough. While getting dressed for the funeral, she had considered removing the bandage—or at least taking off the gauze pad and replacing it with something smaller, something she might be able to hide beneath her hair. But she finally decided to go the way she was. No matter how she looked, she knew people would talk about her. The bottom line was, she was there to mourn her friend and celebrate her all-too-short life.

After the service, she and Nate drove with the procession out to the Pine Grove Cemetery, where Liz was interred beside Jon's father and mother.

As everyone gathered beneath the canvas canopy by the graveside, Kiera couldn't stop looking at Jon. He was wearing a dark, three-piece suit, and in spite of his obvious grief, he looked healthy, especially for a man his age. As she stared at him, she found herself thinking that he wouldn't have much difficulty finding another woman, if that's what he wanted. Especially in the last year or so, she had picked up some tension between him and Liz. Although they weren't so close Liz had ever confided in Kiera about any marital stress and strain, Kiera knew that

Liz had been pushing for them to move back to Colorado after Jon's mother died and their primary reason for being in Maine was gone.

And now, here she was, being buried in Maine two thousand miles from her home.

A sense of melancholy filled Kiera as she contemplated how sad life could be. It seemed so limited, so definitive. When you were young, life had so many possibilities, so much potential. Eventually, though, and usually sooner than you wanted, you had to start making choices, and these choices determined how you lived until it seemed—at times anyway—as though your life was no longer under your control. Other forces—forces you couldn't see—started to direct your life. It was like being swept away by the dark waters of a river you couldn't see, and you floated along, doing the best you could until—finally—you went under.

Still, there's all that potential, Kiera thought, shivering in spite of the afternoon sun on her back. *What happens to all that potential, all those possibilities for lives you* could *have lived but never did?*

"Does it all just disappear?" Kiera said out loud.

Nate leaned close and whispered, "What?"

Blinking back tears, Kiera looked at him. His face hovered in front of her, his expression frozen like a mannequin's. Cold sweat broke out across her face and neck.

She shook her head. "Nothing," she whispered, but when she turned away, her gaze went from the freshly dug grave down the grassy slope to the line of mourners' cars. The sun was angled such that it and the blue sky reflected from the windows like mirrors. With the clouds shifting by, the effect it created was dizzying. Kiera stiffened her legs so she wouldn't fall.

She stared at Jon's car, which was parked behind the

hearse, and then at the hearse. The sun reflecting off the black roof was as bright as a welder's torch. The glare hurt her eyes and left trailing afterimages whenever she blinked. The funeral director was standing beside the limo, his arms folded as he leaned against its shiny, black fender for the duration of the service.

And then, as she shifted her gaze, Kiera saw something that made her breath catch in her throat.

A woman's face appeared in the back window of the hearse. One second it wasn't there. Then it was. But Kiera had the impression it had *always* been there. It was only when she shifted her focus that she saw it.

She let out a gasp and staggered, taking a quick step backward, fighting for balance. Nate turned and grabbed her arm, but his touch, distant and cold, didn't help. The muscles in her legs had become unstrung and were about to fold up. Her eyes widened with fear, and she sucked in a quick breath as she stared at the face in the hearse window, unable to look away.

The face hovered in the darkness behind the curved glass that was framed with a black curtain. She almost lost it in the glare of the sun, and it seemed clearest when she didn't look straight at it. The face looked like a photographic negative that was slowly developing, and the longer she looked at it, the clearer it became; but it was maddening because it was clearest only when she looked to one side or the other. When she looked directly at it, it was lost behind the burning glare bouncing off the glass.

There's nothing there! . . . It's just the reflection . . . a passing cloud or something, she told herself, but she didn't believe it. That face with its vacant stare looked directly at *her.* The wide eyes and hollow, dead expression seared her mind.

It's Liz, Kiera thought as chills weaved up and down her back.

But even as she thought that, she knew it wasn't Liz. While the face looked familiar, she was convinced it wasn't Liz or a passing cloud.

Nate leaned close and whispered something, but she couldn't make out what it was. She wanted to look at him if only to prove to herself nothing was wrong, but she couldn't tear her gaze away from the face behind the hearse's window.

"You want to sit down?" Nate's grip on her arm tightened until it was almost painful. Kiera pulled her arm away from him and shook her head.

"I'm fine," she said in a raw, tight voice.

At the grave site, Pastor Wolfe was still intoning the funeral service. When he asked everyone to bow their heads in prayer, Kiera folded her hands, closed her eyes, and lowered her head, but she couldn't keep her eyes closed for long. When she looked down at the hearse again, she wasn't sure what she expected to see. She hoped the face wouldn't be there, that she would see it *had* been just a cloud or an illusion. She wasn't prepared for what she did see.

The woman's face was still there, glaring at her from inside the hearse, but the same image was reflected in the windows of all the other cars that lined the narrow cemetery road.

A small, whimpering sound escaped her. Squeezing her hands together, she looked at Jon, who was standing at the graveside with his head bowed. The sunlight wasn't shining directly on Liz's casket, but the polished wood glowed with an unnaturally bright light. In the swirling wood grain of the casket, Kiera thought she saw a repetition of the face that was watching her from the car windows. In the dark wood grain of the coffin, long strands of dark red hair wafted like they had been caught in the wind.

A sudden clutching at Kiera's throat cut off her air supply. She watched as the face inside the wood grain shifted ever so slightly. Its eyes moved back and forth until they fixed on Kiera with penetrating intensity. She gasped, knowing that those eyes would remain fixed on her, no matter where she went or what she did.

Even worse, though, she recognized the face.

It was a mirror image of herself, frozen as if trapped inside the polished wood grain.

~3~

"... Honey ... ?"

Nate's voice sounded faraway. As Kiera drifted closer to consciousness, she realized she was lying on something hard and uneven. She thought she might still be in a hospital bed, but they weren't as hard as this. She struggled to figure out where she was and how she had come to be here. When she finally managed to wedge her eyes open, she found herself looking up at the sky.

But there was something wrong with the sky. Instead of being blue, it was a wide, undulating swatch of dark tan. As her eyesight gradually adjusted, she saw blurry splotches of darker brown against the arching tan background.

Her throat clicked when she took a breath. The cool flood of air that filled her lungs surprised her. She had been expecting stale air laced with the smell of death and decay, or maybe the antiseptic sting of a hospital room. Figures leaned over her, peering down at her, but the bright beige backdrop behind them made it so she couldn't distinguish anyone's features. She had no idea who these people were.

She was sure that one of them was Nate. He—or some-one else—was much closer to her than the others. As her vision cleared, she saw a worried look in his eyes.

"Are you all right, sweetie?"

His voice still sounded faraway, and when he spoke, his lips were out of synch with his voice; but she winced and nodded and said, "Yeah, I—What happened?"

"You fainted."

The crowd around her murmured, but Kiera couldn't make out anything anyone said. She groaned as she shifted to sit up, but something was pressing her down on the ground. She finally remembered that she was at Liz's funeral.

"I . . . I'm so embarrassed," she said, fixing her eyes on Nate, who was gently caressing the side of her face. His touch was as cool and refreshing as spring water.

"I told you coming here wasn't a good idea. Didn't I?"

The edge of accusation in his voice stabbed her. She had no idea how to respond, but a surge of anger filled her . . . anger at Nate for saying "I told you so" and at her-self for making a scene.

"Come on. Step back and give her some air," someone said. It sounded like Jon, but she couldn't be sure.

Someone moved closer, and from both sides, hands took hold of her, sliding under her armpits, and started to lift her, but the crushing weight pinning her down only got worse. It was almost impossible to take a deep enough breath as pinpoints of white light trailed like fireflies across her vision. A gentle breeze blew across her face, sending chills through her, but that was nowhere near as bad as the embarrassment she felt. Before the day was over, people would be talking about how she had fainted because of the brain surgery, and there would be speculation that she was suffering from irreparable brain damage.

She finally got to her feet but still didn't feel stable. Holding on to Nate helped. She realized the beige sky was the canvas awning that had been erected over the grave site in case of rain. She was humiliated that she had disrupted the burial by fainting. She felt like everyone was staring at her, and she wondered if it was up to her to let the minister know he could finish the service.

A small measure of relief passed through her when the people turned their attention back to Pastor Wolfe, who began to intone the remainder of the ceremony. Leaning close to Nate, she whispered, "I'm going down to the car."

"You want to go home now?"

Kiera shook her head. She wouldn't consider the suggestion even for a second. She had to go to Jon's house after the interment if only to talk to Jon. She didn't know how she knew, but she was convinced that whatever was happening to her was connected to Jon somehow.

"I just need to catch my breath." She stared at the open grave for a moment. "I'll be fine if I can just sit down."

When she started to walk away, Nate tagged along with her, keeping his arm around her waist to support her.

"I just need a little time," she said.

"You've got all the time you want," he said, but his words made her shiver, because she knew it wasn't true. She was painfully aware that she was running out of time. Remembering the cold, lifeless stare of the woman who had been watching her from inside the hearse chilled her. And as impossible as it seemed, she was suddenly convinced it was *her*, trapped in the back of the hearse.

~4~

"How you holding up?"

Kiera forced a smile when she looked at Jon and saw the genuine concern in his expression. It broke her heart to think that an hour or two after burying his wife, he seemed to be more worried about her than he was about himself.

"I'm really sorry . . . about what happened at the cemetery," she said.

Jon's house was filled with relatives, friends, and colleagues from work who had stopped by after the funeral. Several people had provided food and drink, and the conversation was dominated by talk of Liz. She had only lived in Stratford for a little less than two years, so not many people could say they really knew her. But many of them had known Jon from childhood, and they were there to console and commiserate with him. When Jon was out of earshot, people also talked about how she had been murdered, and that the police had no leads and no suspects in custody.

It struck Kiera as odd that Jon didn't seem to need all that much consolation. He never came right out and said it, but she knew him better than most of the people here, and she sensed something different in his demeanor that convinced her, at least, that he wasn't as broken up about his wife's death as he might have been.

Maybe he had changed more than she realized in the time he'd been away. How could she say she really knew him? She remembered the high school boy, not the man. Maybe he was keeping his grief to himself, bottling it up, but it certainly seemed like he was detached from everything going on around him.

"Can we go outside for a sec?" Kiera asked. She pulled at the collar of her black dress and added, "It's getting kind of stuffy in here."

Without a word, they walked out the back door and onto the deck that looked out over a wide field leading down to a narrow stream that marked the edge of Jon's property. As they stepped outside, Kiera caught a glimpse of Nate, who was talking to Pete Johnson, a teacher at the high school and one of his poker buddies. Nate seemed not to notice that she was leaving with Jon, and she felt a mild twist of guilt. As if she was trying to sneak something.

The day was still unusually warm. The fair-weather clouds scudding across the sky cast the field with rapidly shifting swatches of shadow and light. The effect was a little like the rapid flashing of a strobe light, which gave Kiera a feeling of vertigo. She gripped the porch railing for support.

"So . . . still no leads?" Kiera asked. "The cops have no idea who did it?"

Jon's expression froze as he fought to contain his emotion. Then he shrugged and shook his head.

"Nothing." There was a note of bitterness in his voice, and who could blame him? "They say it must have been a random act of violence. Whoever did it was probably trying to rob her, and it just got out of hand."

Kiera sighed and closed her eyes, letting the sunlight wash across her face, but a mental image flashed across her mind of the woman she had seen in the hearse. She made a soft whimpering sound and quickly opened her eyes again.

"I'm not cracking up, you know," she said without preamble as she looked at Jon, who was looking at her with a bemused expression.

"I never said you were," Jon said, "but you know—sometimes I think *I* might be."

"Why do you say that?"

Jon didn't reply as he gazed at the shadows shifting across the field.

Kiera gave him a sympathetic smile and said, "I don't wonder. What happened to Liz was horrible."

Jon inhaled sharply and nodded, looking like he was fighting back tears. "That's not all," he said softly.

"What do you mean?"

Jon still focused on the horizon. The clouds shifting by so rapidly cast his face into shadow and light, but Kiera thought he looked more frightened than anything else. His shoulders were so hunched he seemed to be cowering.

"You—" he said, but then he stopped himself and looked at her with an intensity that Kiera found unsettling.

"What?" she said. "Talk to me. We're old friends. You can tell me anything."

"You didn't get out of the hospital until today—this morning, right?"

Not sure where he was going with this, Kiera nodded. Jon didn't speak for a long time, but she could tell something was weighing on his mind.

"Tell me. What *is* it?"

He took a deep, shuddering breath and, pursing his lips, shook his head like he was desperate to say what was on his mind but also unwilling or unable to.

"Last night . . . I got back from the funeral home really late, and I . . ."

He snickered softly and shook his head, but Kiera didn't see a bit of humor in the way he was acting. The truth was, she was a little afraid of him. Maybe she had been wrong about how strong he was. Maybe Liz's death had hit him a lot harder than she realized. When he looked at her again, a gleam lit up his eyes, a crazy light that actually unnerved her. Her first thought was that his mind might have snapped because of his wife's murder.

"No . . . It's nothing," he finally said with a quick, firm shake of his head. "I just . . . I saw a car outside my house last night, and I . . . I could have sworn it was you."

"What?" Kiera was stunned and didn't know what to say. She shook her head slowly from side to side, and all she could think of was the face—*her face!*—in the hearse window and in the swirling wood grain of the coffin.

"No . . . It couldn't have been me," she said, struggling to maintain control of her voice. "I was in the hospital."

"I know . . . It's just been so . . . so—" He sighed and covered his face with his hands. "I mean—*shit!* You've had your own mountain of shit to deal with." He lowered his hands and, for a moment, seemed to regain control. Putting one hand on her shoulder, he gave her a reassuring squeeze. "I can't believe how incredibly strong you are."

"What are you talking about?" Kiera said. She knew he wasn't leveling with her now. Something was bothering him. She gritted her teeth, even though it sent a bolt of pain through her head sharp enough to make her eyes sting, and told herself not to cry. It was just the rapid changes of sunlight and shadow that were affecting her vision.

"I . . . I just don't see how anyone can deal with something like this," Jon said.

She searched his face for some sign that—at least with her—he felt secure enough to let his guard down. But he looked at her with a cold, impassive stare, as if he somehow was above it all. After an uncomfortably long silence, he took another breath, held it, and let it out.

"You want to know the truth?" he finally said, taking his hand from her shoulder and grabbing the porch railing. He squeezed it so tightly his knuckles went white. "Just between you and me . . . ? As old friends . . . ?"

Kiera bit down on her lower lip to keep from saying anything she might regret. Was this really what she wanted? Because back in a corner of her mind, a tiny voice was screaming at her that Jon was about to tell her something she definitely did not want to hear. A cold gnawing twisted in her stomach, but she nodded slowly and said, "Jon, you know you can tell me anything."

He shot her a tight smile, then sniffed with laughter and shook his head while staring deeply into her eyes. His face shifted in and out of sunlight and shadow as the clouds passed by overhead, and Kiera had the unnerving sensation that she was seeing two versions of Jon. There was the one face everyone saw in the sunshine—happy and confident, strong and secure. And then there was the other face—the dark side he kept to himself and fought to hide from everyone—even her.

"Liz and I weren't going to make it," he finally said, his voice low and strained.

Kiera pulled away from him. She didn't like hearing him put it so bluntly, but he continued talking before she could say anything.

"You've known it all along. You've sensed it. And as mean as this sounds—I know you guys were friends—but this—" He tossed his head back and clenched his hands into fists as though he couldn't find the words to express himself. "What happened, happened for a reason, and I—"

He cut himself off abruptly and shivered. It didn't matter if his face was in sunlight or shadow, it looked pale and drawn, the skin almost translucent as it appeared to collapse in on itself.

Kiera's body was tingling with tension because she suddenly knew exactly what he was going to say next, and there was no way she wanted to hear it. Not now. Not here. The thought was already so clear in her mind he might already have said it out loud, and she was just remembering it. No matter how much she didn't want him to say it, at least not now, right after his wife's funeral, it was as unavoidable as a train wreck.

Jon's hand went to her shoulder again, but this time his touch was a gentle caress. She wanted to pull away from him, but the rapid alterations of sunlight and shadow on the field made her feel dizzy. She didn't dare close her eyes, not when there was the danger of seeing that face—*her face!*—staring back at her from inside the hearse.

"We can't . . ." she muttered. "I don't want you . . . or either of us to say something we might regret."

Jon shifted closer to her, his blue eyes glistening like wet marbles. His lower lip was trembling, and the corners of his mouth twitched.

"I mean it," she said, but his arms slid down her back and hugged her. Before she could stop him, he pulled her close until her face pressed against his chest. She inhaled, smelling his aftershave and body sweat. She listened to his heart, thumping in his chest—or maybe it was her own, skipping fast with fear.

Is it fear? she asked herself as she slowly put her arms around his waist and pulled him to her. Her legs buckled, and she sagged in his arms, letting him support her. After a dizzying moment, when she eased away from him, they looked deeply into each other's eyes. Neither one of them said a word because they both knew that words were unnecessary. Then, in unison, they let go of each other. Kiera felt her strength return and was grateful she didn't fall down.

"I want to see you . . . after all this is all over—" With a flick of his head, he indicated the house filled with people.

Confused by the conflicting emotions raging inside her, Kiera didn't know whether she should laugh or cry or run screaming from the house and vow never to see Jon again. She was trembling as she took a breath—the first, it seemed, in the last five minutes or more.

"Not now," she said, surprised by the strength of her voice.

Feeling as if everyone in the house knew what was going on and was staring at them, Kiera backed away from Jon and nervously smoothed her clothes. Still feeling painfully self-conscious, she ran her fingers lightly over the bandage on her head.

"Are you okay with this?" Jon asked, his eyebrows rising with what looked like genuine concern.

"With what?" Kiera asked, so confused and frightened by what had just happened she had no idea how to respond. After a moment, she looked at Jon and nodded.

"I'm just really exhausted," she said. "I'd better go home."

"Can I call you later?"

Kiera caught the desperation in his voice and smiled to think how much he sounded like a teenager tortured by infatuation. And she wanted to believe that's all it was. Neither of them was thinking this through. This was how they had behaved in high school, when they were sweethearts. She couldn't let any foolish infatuation or whatever this was proceed. But even as she told herself this, she nodded and said, "Yes . . . We'll talk."

With that, she walked back into the house, feeling unsteady and disoriented. She found Nate still chatting with his poker buddies, but when they made eye contact, she couldn't help but feel a rush of guilt.

Did he see us? . . . Does he know what just happened out there?

She felt as though her guilt must be written all over her face. And even if Nate hadn't seen them, even if he didn't suspect a thing, someone must have noticed what was going on. It had to be obvious. And it wouldn't be long before more gossip was flying. She told herself if Nate or anyone else ever mentioned it, she would play it off like she was just consoling Jon, who was, after all, one of her oldest and closest friends.

But she didn't like the way she was feeling. Deep inside, a voice was telling her that life was all about choices—the ones you make and the ones you don't make—and every now and then, something big happens—like the death of a spouse or divorce—and you can make a choice, take a new direction. Maybe when you make that choice, you change on so basic a level you become someone else. And maybe—eventually—you turn into the person you were supposed to be all along if it hadn't been for something that happened long ago that took you off your path.

"You sure you're feeling okay?" Nate asked as they started for the door.

Kiera was so drained her body was shaking, but she hid it as best she could and said, "Sure. It's just been a tough day. I want to get home. I haven't even seen Trista since I got out of the hospital."

Nate didn't say anything, and he was so silent throughout the drive home that Kiera was sure he had seen what had happened out on the deck between her and Jon. He must at least suspect something was wrong.

As confused as she was, she was convinced what had happened *wasn't* wrong.

It might be the most "right" thing that ever happened to her.

CHAPTER 8

River's Edge

~1~

"You're sure that's all it was?" Nate asked.

He had both hands on the steering wheel and didn't take his eyes off the road to look at her. The muscles in his jaw worked back and forth as he ground his teeth the way he did whenever he was really agitated.

Kiera's chest ·ached with sadness because she knew there was no way she could tell him about what had happened with Jon. It was hard enough sorting out her own feelings, but the truth was, what Jon had said, the feelings and thoughts he had stirred up had hit her hard. And the truth was, it wasn't really unexpected. She was frightened and confused because at least some part of her felt the same way about him.

But how much?

Why would she even consider jeopardizing her marriage by following through with this?

"Jesus, Nate. Think about it for just one second, will you?" Her confusion fueled her anger, and she couldn't hold back. "He just lost his wife. And she didn't just *die*.

She was killed. *Murdered!* And so far, the police don't have a damned clue who did it. He's freaking out, and I think you should cut him some slack!"

Nate shook his head and said softly, "Hell, he probably did it."

The casualness with which he said it only fired Kiera's anger all the more.

"Don't you *say* that! Don't you even *think* it!" she shouted so loud Nate glanced at her with genuine worry in his eyes.

"I didn't mean it." He reached out and placed his hand on top of hers. "It's just . . . You know, on cop shows, whenever someone's wife dies, the husband's always the prime suspect."

"Jon would never kill anyone!" Kiera said, but as soon as the words were out of her mouth, a prickling rush of panic went through her. She turned and looked out the side window at the passing scenery because she knew—all too well—that Jon not only *could* kill someone. He *had* killed someone.

The blood drained from her face, and a chill radiated a dull ache all through her body as the memory came rushing back.

It was an accident, she told herself even though, after all these years, she only half believed it. *He didn't mean to kill Billy . . . not on purpose.*

Even as she thought it, another voice in the back of her mind—a voice that had been there ever since that night said, *You know he meant to kill him . . . You were there.*

Uttering a soft moan, she leaned her bandaged forehead against the passenger's window and stared into the distance as the memory came rushing back.

~2~

Ever since junior high, Kiera had been attracted to Jon, but they didn't start dating until the beginning of their senior year. The first few times Jon asked her out, she hadn't taken him seriously. It was too much to hope for. Besides, she and Billy Carroll had been going steady for over a year, and she didn't want to hurt Billy's feelings.

Still, she was flattered someone as cute and smart and popular as Jon would even notice her. After a few weeks of Jon calling her and them sneaking off together "to talk," as hard as it had been, she had broken up with Billy. One Saturday night in late October, they had driven out River Road to a deserted picnic area beside the Hancock River where they could be alone.

Somehow, Billy found out where they were going, and he followed them. That night, Kiera and Jon were the only couple out there. They had parked and, for over an hour, had been talking and making out when Billy suddenly appeared. He must have walked more than four miles from town, and he was furious when he saw what was going on. He started banging on the car's windows, accusing Jon of stealing his girlfriend. Billy dared Jon to get out of the car and fight "like a man."

As surprised and angry as he was, Jon maintained his cool. Kiera thought it was because he was confident she wanted to be with him, not Billy. No matter how much Billy ranted and pounded on the car and challenged Jon to get out of the car and face him, Jon locked the doors and sat there, stubbornly refusing to move. As frightened as she was, Kiera was glad Jon didn't act like a macho shit head and get out of the car to fight. She couldn't stand idiotic behavior like that. Besides, Billy was much stronger than Jon.

She wished he would just accept that their relationship was over. No amount of shouting and posturing would make her love him again.

She told Billy to go away, to give up and leave them alone. She told him she didn't love him anymore, but that only fueled Billy's anger all the more. Finally, after yanking on the car door to no effect, he went down the slope to the river and returned in a few seconds with a huge rock. Kiera knew he was crazy enough to throw the rock through their windshield, but before she could say or do anything, Jon started up the car and floored it.

"Leave us the fuck alone!" he shouted as the car's engine roared, spewing exhaust. In the harsh glare of the headlight, Kiera watched as Billy walked toward the car, the rock raised high above his head. Crouching low, he prepared to throw it at the car.

Just then, Jon slammed the car into gear and took his foot off the brake. The tires spun in the dirt, kicking up a cloud of dust as dense as fog in the red taillights. Instead of moving backward as Kiera had expected, the car suddenly jolted forward. A loud impact rocked the car, and Kiera saw Billy go flying backward. The rock he'd been holding above his head dropped.

After that, everything seemed to happen in excruciatingly slow motion.

Billy fell backward as the rock slipped from his grip and peeled a swatch of skin off his face. For an instant that seemed somehow to last forever, pink flesh and exposed bone glistened wetly in the harsh glow of the headlights. Blood started to flow, and Billy's eyes bulged from their sockets with a look of numbed amazement. His arms reached behind him and flapped uselessly as he struggled to keep his balance, and then he dropped out of sight below the front of the car. He disappeared so quickly it was almost like he had never been there.

Stunned for a moment, Kiera wanted to believe none of this had just happened. It had all been an illusion, a trick of the eye or something, but a part of her numbed brain was screaming at her that this was all too real.

Jon jammed the gearshift into neutral and jerked the emergency brake up so fast the car heaved to the side and stopped with a lurching jolt that threw Kiera forward. Her head slammed against the dashboard so hard a spray of stars exploded across her vision. She never knew if she lost consciousness or not, but ever since that night, whenever she thought about what happened, it felt as though she had lost an indeterminate span of time.

Something else happened that unnerved her even more.

The instant her head hit the dashboard, she felt as though—somehow—her consciousness was separated from her body. The memory was hazy and confusing, and over the years whenever she thought about it, she was convinced she must have imagined it or else modified it until it became something it couldn't have been; but she had the odd feeling of being in two places at once. As she slumped over in the car seat, her head spinning and throbbing with pain, she felt as though she also was outside the car, standing beneath the trees and watching everything that was happening.

She viewed this memory with a cold, almost clinical detachment because it was like watching a movie of something that had happened to someone else a long time ago. The sense of unreality was dizzying, even when she tried to convince herself that none of it could ever have happened.

Certainly not to me, she thought, but the details of what

happened next, of what she and Jon had done were too real
to pretend it had never happened.

Jon's face was as pale as a mask of white porcelain. His
eyes were wide and staring as he looked at her. He seemed
not to notice the blood that was gushing down her face.

"What did I do?" he asked in a thin, frightened voice.

Kiera looked at him and nodded. Jon killed the engine
and snapped off the headlights, plunging their surroundings into impenetrable darkness. Kiera remembered hearing someone sobbing, unaware it was her. The only other
sound was the rapid clicking of the car's engine as it
cooled. The metallic taste of blood seeped into the corners
of her mouth. Her skin was sticky and cool when she wiped
her face, and her hand came away slick with blood.

"We have to see if he's—" she said, but then stopped
herself.

There was no point in checking to see how badly Billy
had been hurt. That frozen glimpse she'd had of him when
the front bumper hit him had been enough. She had no
doubt he was dead. No one could have survived an impact
like that. Even if he was still alive, he wouldn't live long.

"We have to get help. We need an ambulance," she said,
but Jon just sat there, immobile, until after what seemed
like several minutes, he finally spoke.

"We can't do that," he said.

"Why not?"

In the darkness, she could barely make out Jon's expression, but the impression she got was that this wasn't even
him. It was someone else, some heartless creature posing
as her boyfriend. His lower lip was trembling, and he
whimpered as he took a short, gasping breath.

Kiera started to open the passenger's door to get out, but
Jon grabbed her by the upper arm and pinned her against

the car seat. Their faces were close as they eyed each other, barely able to see each other in the darkness.

"We have to take care of this ourselves," Jon said.

Kiera struggled as he held her back until she realized it was useless to resist.

"What do you mean . . . 'take care'?"

After another long silence, Jon said, "Do you realize what will happen to *me*—to *both* of us—if anyone ever finds out?"

"I didn't do anything," Kiera said, her voice tight with fear. "It was an accident. Even if he's . . . dead . . . It wasn't your fault. It was an *accident*!"

"You think anyone will believe that?"

Jon's grip on her arm got painfully tight. He shifted in the seat until he was between her and the windshield. Raising his other hand, he pressed her shoulder against the car seat and leaned so close his breath was warm on her face.

"This will *ruin* me," he said. "I want to go to college. If I—Jesus, no college in the world will accept me if I've been arrested for *murder*."

Kiera was so scared she was afraid she would wet herself, but she told herself to calm down. She could make him see that they had to do the right thing.

"You didn't *murder* anyone," she said. "It was an accident. I'll swear to it."

But even as the words left her mouth, she had her doubts; and all these years since, she still had her doubts. It had all happened so fast she could never be sure, but she couldn't forget how, as soon as Billy stepped in front of the car with the rock over his head, Jon had floored it and driven ahead on purpose.

"We have to check him," she said.

After a long, intense moment, Jon relaxed his grip.

Kiera didn't think she had the strength to stand up, but somehow she opened the door and stepped out onto the uneven ground. The injury to her head made the world spin uncontrollably.

"Turn the headlights on," she said.

Jon, still in the car, didn't do as she said. She saw him lean down and fumble around in the car until suddenly a flashlight came on. He shined the light into her eyes, blinding her for a moment. She covered her eyes quickly, but after he shifted the light beam away, a streaked afterimage made it impossible for her to see clearly.

"Thanks," she said as she reached into the car and grabbed the flashlight from him. "You coming?"

For a long time, Jon stayed where he was until, finally, he opened the door and got out. By then, Kiera's eyesight was better. She swept the beam of light back and forth across the ground. The river was close by. It looked like a wide sheet of black plastic as it flowed with a deep gurgling rush of water over stones. A short, rock-covered bank led down to the river's edge. Waist-high weeds and small saplings grew between the rocks.

When she didn't see Billy's body in front of the car, she felt a spark of hope that maybe this really hadn't happened. If only it could all be a dream that would be over soon . . .

Maybe Billy had seen the car coming at him and ducked out of the way.

Maybe he was hiding in the brush or already running back to town.

But then she froze. The narrow beam of light came to rest on a human hand that lay across a rock. The fingers were curled up, looking like a hawk's talons. Even in her initial shock, Kiera knew there was no strength left in that hand. It wasn't clinging to the rock. It just rested there motionless . . . lifeless.

She heard footsteps behind her and turned around, shining the light on Jon, who was walking toward her. When he stopped beside her, she shined the light back on the hand, moving the beam slowly, following it up to Billy's elbow . . . then his shoulder. A sour, sickly taste filled her mouth, and she almost vomited when the light showed Billy's head. He was facedown on the rocks, so she couldn't see his face, but the glistening splash of dark blood on the ground told her everything she needed to know.

No! . . . He can't be dead!

A sense of total unreality swept over her. Jon was standing behind her, but she had the distinct feeling that someone else—someone hiding in the deepest shadows of the night—was watching them, waiting to see what they would do next.

Billy's head was oddly distorted. One side was dented in, and something that might have been a piece of bone was sticking out from underneath his hair. Kiera wanted to believe it was just a trick of the light, but she knew the rock had smashed his skull when he fell. There was blood everywhere, and the sight of it made Kiera's stomach heave.

"Satisfied?" Jon asked simply.

His voice made her cringe.

"You *killed* him," she whispered, her voice so weak she wasn't sure he heard her or even if she had spoken out loud. Moving the flashlight beam away from Billy, she tried not to think how, only seconds ago, he had been a living, breathing person.

And now—just like *that*!—he was gone.

It was incomprehensible. Even at the time, Kiera knew

she would never be able to comprehend this, much less accept it. She lost any sense of the time as she stared into the swelling darkness across the river. The faint gurgle of water became a soft backdrop that lulled her, making her feel as though she was floating downstream.

"What are we going to do?" she finally asked.

Jon was standing right behind her. She couldn't see him, but she could feel his presence the same way she felt the other presence that was somewhere close by, watching her with eyes that she was sure could see in the dark.

"There's nothing we can do," Jon replied solemnly.

Kiera was relieved to hear a sympathetic tone in his voice. She wanted to believe this had all been a terrible accident. She had to, if only for her own sanity.

"We can't just leave him here." She heard the hollowness in her voice and cringed. "Someone will find him. It will come out eventually."

Jon didn't say anything for a while, but then he cleared his throat. Even with him behind her, she could feel him looking at her like a hawk about to swoop down.

"It doesn't have to," he said.

Too numbed to know what she was feeling, Kiera turned and looked at him. His silhouette was etched against the starfilled sky. Behind him, the trees lining the riverbank looked like black lace against the dark sky. She caught a hint of motion as something moved in the densest shadows under the trees, sensing that someone other than Jon was watching her. A powerful feeling of dissociation came over her.

"You have to stop and think," Jon said. "Both of us will end up in jail. Even if they believe it was an accident, we'll go to jail."

"It will be worse if we don't report it. Hit and run is a lot worse if we get caught."

"So," Jon said with a shrug, "we won't get caught." He came down the rocky slope until he was at her side. "You broke up with him to go out with me, right?"

Kiera nodded even though she thought the motion was wasted in the darkness.

"And he's been really depressed about it ever since, right?" Jon said, pressing.

Again, she nodded.

"And everyone at school knows it. He never stops talking about how much you broke his heart."

I did break his heart, Kiera wanted to say, but she was too frightened and too numbed to speak. She no longer felt like she was standing on the riverbank. She had become a disembodied soul that was hovering in the darkness by the river. It occurred to her that maybe the *someone else* she thought was watching her from out of the darkness was Billy or his ghost.

"If we roll him into the river, and he floats downstream, and someone finds him, they'll think he committed suicide, right? They'll think he jumped into the river to kill himself."

"Jon . . . Please, don't."

"Even if his head's messed up, they'll figure he banged against some rocks or something in the river. And that's only if they find him. They might never find him."

I can't believe you're even saying this, Kiera wanted to scream at him. Instead, she nodded agreement. She was numb with grief and guilt and fear, and she couldn't stop wondering how she'd ever be able to go on with her normal life, pretending this had never happened. She was sure of one thing—she would *never* be able to face the consequences of what they had done and were thinking of doing.

It was *an accident,* she kept repeating to herself. *And there's nothing I can do about it now.*

"Think you can hack it?" Jon asked.

She flinched from the steely tone in his voice as he came close and put an arm around her shoulder. She shivered as he pulled her close and wanted to push him away and scream at him that it didn't matter what he wanted to do; she was going to the police to report the accident. She had to do it. It was the right thing . . . the *only* thing to do. She owed it to Billy.

"Can I . . . Can I hack what?" she asked, dreading the answer but knowing what Jon was going to say before he said it.

"Knowing we killed someone and didn't tell anyone."

The feeling that someone was watching her was still there, but Kiera closed her eyes and nodded, wishing desperately she could be someone else . . . someone who wasn't here . . . someone who didn't know what she knew and would have to live with for the rest of her life.

The feeling of dissociation was still strong, and she felt like someone else, not herself, when she finally said, "I guess I'll have to."

She had the distinct impression the words weren't coming from her, that someone else was speaking for her. The feeling of being detached from reality was only getting worse as she considered what she was about to do.

Could she really do it?

"Okay, then," she said softly.

"Keep the flashlight down . . . in case anyone comes by," Jon said. "If someone sees the car, they'll think we're parking and probably leave us alone."

"Unless it's the cops."

Jon cast a worried glance up the slope, but from where they stood, they couldn't see their parked car.

"We'll have to hurry then."

He made his way down the slope to Billy's body and knelt down beside it. He pressed his fingers against Billy's throat and obviously didn't detect a pulse. Kiera sat down on the rock-strewn riverbank. Shielding the lens of the flashlight with her hand to dull the glare, she watched in mute horror as Jon lifted Billy's body and dragged it down to the water's edge.

"He's heavier than you'd think," he said, sounding entirely too blasé about what he was doing.

"Just hurry up."

"I could use some help down here."

The edge in his voice frightened her, and for the first time, Kiera wondered if Jon would have acted the same way if *she* was the one he was dumping into the river. She cringed at the hissing sound Billy's body made as Jon dragged it over the rocks. Finally, when he was close to the water, he made sure his footing was good and then lifted the body.

Kiera lowered the flashlight so she wouldn't have to see what happened next, but her imagination was bad enough. The cold inside her made her chest and stomach hurt, and she cringed as she imagined Billy's ghost, lurking in the darkness, watching everything they did. She wished she had the courage to yell to Jon, to tell him they couldn't do this! They *had* to report the accident. Maybe things wouldn't be as bad as he thought if they both swore it was an accident.

And it was *an accident, wasn't it? . . . Jon never would have killed Billy on purpose.*

Before she could say anything, she heard a loud splash from the darkness below. She let out a low groan when she saw a dark ring of disturbed water spread out from the shore and then flatten out with the fast-flowing current. Something dark that she tried to convince herself wasn't really a human body drifted slowly away from the shore, spinning as it was floated away downstream.

"Fuck!" Jon shouted as he staggered away from the riverbank. "I almost fell in with him."

Kiera didn't say a word as she watched the dark shape move downstream and dissolve into the darkness. Gasping for breath, Jon clambered back up the slope to her.

"You okay?" he asked, placing a hand on her shoulder.

Kiera was speechless. She couldn't believe what they had just done, and she wondered how she'd ever be able to keep this to herself. In the end, though, that's exactly what she had done. For almost thirty years, she shared this horrible secret with Jon and no one else—not even her husband when she got married. Even after Jon moved to Colorado following college, this secret bound them in ways she had never fully understood.

But now, for some reason, that bond was beginning to break, and the thought of what might happen terrified her.

~3~

"You okay?"

Nate's voice was soft and full of sympathy, and it pulled Kiera away from the memory of that night more than twenty-five years ago. Still lost in her thoughts, she stared at him with a blank expression on her face. They were driving west, and the sun was setting, so a rich golden glow illuminated his face in stunning detail. Kiera tried not to think how much it reminded her of Billy's face in the glare of Jon's headlights.

"I didn't . . . You know I didn't mean to upset you," he said.

Kiera licked her lips, wishing she could think of something to say, but chaos and confusion filled her mind.

"I shouldn't have said what I said." Nate glanced at her quickly before looking back at the road ahead. The tenderness she saw in him made her heart ache. "I'm sorry."

"It's okay," she said, even though she wasn't sure exactly what she meant by that. She was having a hard enough time tearing her thoughts away from that night so long ago.

What's okay? she asked herself, and a voice inside her head answered, *Absolutely nothing, that's what!*

It bothered her that she couldn't tell her husband what was bothering her, but it had been like that ever since they got married. What she had to admit to him now was too huge.

He'd never understand why I kept this from him . . . It's too late . . . for both of us. Sadness pressed down on her, making it difficult to breathe. After a long, uncomfortable silence, Nate leaned forward and glared into the rearview mirror.

"What the *fuck* is his problem," he whispered.

It took Kiera a moment or two to realize he was talking about the vehicle behind them. She turned and saw a dark car tailgating them. The sun glinted off the windshield with a laserlike glare, so she couldn't see the driver.

"Slow down and let the idiot pass," she said tiredly, but she'd lived with Nate long enough to know it didn't take much for his road rage to kick in.

"Fucking *asshole*," he muttered as he sped up a bit even though they were on a stretch of road where the person could have passed them.

It didn't matter, though, because the driver seemed intent on tailgating them, not getting past them. He sped up just enough to stay close on their tail.

"Will you slow down? Please?"

"Com'on. I'm just driving here," Nate said, shooting her a harsh glance. "What's his problem?"

"What's *your* problem, is more like it? Just slow down and let him pass. It's not a race."

She looked at him and saw the grim set of his jaw and knew he wasn't going to give an inch.

What is it about men that makes them take offensive driving as some kind of personal insult? Why can't they just let it go?

"Our turn's coming up," Nate said, sounding almost disappointed that the duel or whatever it was would be over.

Kiera was relieved when he eased up on the gas, slowing for the turn. The problem was, the car behind them was also slowing down. She knew Nate must be tempted to step on the brake pedal just to give the jerk a scare. Instead, he clicked on the turn signal and slowed for the turn.

"Why the *fuck* do people have to drive like that?" he said. His face was flushed, and not just from the glow of the setting sun. She could tell he was furious, and she wondered what he might have done if she hadn't been in the car with him. They probably would end up pulling over and getting into a shouting match or a fistfight.

"As long as *you* don't drive like that, let the fool go his own way." She wanted to inject some humor into the situation, but Nate's lips were compressed into a thin grimace when he looked at her. Kiera shrugged, all helpless innocence, and said, "Hey. I'm just saying."

"When he passes us, get his plate number," Nate said. "You got something to write with?"

"What are you going to do, call the cops?" Kiera sniffed with laughter.

"It wouldn't hurt to report the jerk in case he causes an accident up the road."

She didn't know why, but having a car follow them so close bothered her a lot more she was letting show. She felt suddenly light-headed, as if she'd had too much to drink. When she turned and looked back at the car, she had the freaky sensation her head kept turning until it rotated in a complete circle. A wave of nausea swept over her, making her stomach feel like it was floating. She let out a faint whimper and fought the feeling that she'd lost her balance and was going to fall. She grabbed the back of the car seat for support.

Nate was driving with such intensity he didn't even notice her reaction. His gaze flicked back and forth between the road ahead and the rearview mirror where the car was practically on their bumper. Kiera thought he was still going too fast for the turn, and she braced herself as they went screaming around the corner. The tires squealed loudly on the asphalt.

Caught up in her panic, Kiera didn't know what to do. She was so off balance she felt like she was in free fall and had no idea which direction was up. When she turned her head, the motion, combined with the motion of the turning car, made it feel as though they were spinning out of control.

Somehow, she followed the car as it whizzed past them. The slanting rays of the setting sun reflected off the windshield, but through the side window, she caught a glimpse of the driver that made her heart stop in her chest.

"You get the number?" Nate asked, his voice laced with agitation.

Kiera couldn't respond. Like earlier today at the cemetery, the person in the car looked exactly like her. She forgot to exhale and held her breath until her chest burned like it was on fire. Gasping loudly, she finally expelled the last traces of air from her lungs, but the dizziness that gripped her only got worse. As Nate straightened out the car following the turn, it felt as though they had hit a patch of black ice and were spinning around and around in wide, lazy circles.

Through her confusion, Kiera somehow kept focused on the car that had been following them as it sped down the road. There was no way she could make out the license plate number, and in a flash, the car disappeared around the bend, swallowed by the intervening trees that lined the roadside.

"Did you get it?"

Still swept up by vertigo, Kiera couldn't respond. She braced herself with both hands on the car seat, and after taking another deep breath, somehow managed to speak.

"Stop the car! Now!"

Nate applied the brakes, and the car coasted to a gentle stop, the tires hissing in the dirt on the side of the road. Before the car even stopped moving, Kiera swung the door open and, leaning out while clinging to the door handle, vomited onto the roadside. Wave after wave of nausea rushed over her, bathing her body with cold sweat.

"Christ, Kiera," Nate said.

The sick, sour taste of vomit filled her mouth and throat, gagging her. She exhaled and tried to take another breath, but fluid got into her lungs and made her cough before more vomit gushed from her mouth, splattering the roadside and the inside of the car door. Nate placed his hand on her back and patted her gently, but his touch didn't seem to matter.

When she tried to speak, her stomach convulsed again. She closed her eyes, convinced she was going to die where she was, and she almost wished she would. The pain in her stomach was intolerable. It felt like she was being ripped apart by huge, invisible claws inside her. Staring into the flickering darkness that spiraled behind her closed eyes, she imagined a voice was calling to her. It was faint and faraway, and there was no way she could make out what it was saying above the rumble of the car's engine and her own violent retching sounds, but one thought cut through everything else.

She could hear a voice—her own voice, calling to her. She couldn't tell what it was saying, but it seemed to be getting closer, and when it did, she was terrified that she would hear what it had to say all too well.

⋅⋅4⋅⋅

"She *what*?"

Kiera was sure she couldn't handle another shock today, and she wanted to believe she hadn't heard Nate correctly, but the expression on his face told her otherwise.

"She's moving out . . . She's already left."

Stunned and filled with sudden rage, Kiera stood there in the kitchen, her mouth hanging open as she looked around the house. The second they got home, Kiera had rushed to the kitchen sink for a glass of water to rinse the aftertaste of vomit from her mouth. She had splashed cool water on her face and was reaching for a hand towel when she had asked where Trista was. It was then that Nate told her Trista had moved in with Robbie.

"You knew about this?" she shouted. "And you didn't tell me all day? You let me . . ."

After everything else that had happened today, she was too wrung out even to stand. She couldn't believe she could feel this angry. Her pulse pounded in her head, and her vision blurred as she listened to the total silence of the house.

"Why didn't you tell me? Why didn't you stop her?"

Nate shrugged as he stared at her. He looked so helpless, so utterly useless it was almost ridiculous.

"When did she leave?"

Nate bowed his head and focused on the floor.

"She told me this morning, before I left to pick you up." His voice broke the terrible silence of the house.

"I want you to call her right now! *I'll* call her. I want her home *now!*" She paused and swallowed hard, still tasting the residue of vomit. "No. Call the police. We'll report that she's a minor and she's with an older man. If that scumbag even so much as *touches* her, I'll charge him with rape, the lousy son of a bitch. This is my daughter we're talking about!" She paused and looked wide-eyed at Nate, overwhelmed by a sudden feeling of betrayal. "But how *could* you . . . ? How could you let her do this to me?"

"What choice did I have?" Nate said with a shrug. He could barely make eye contact with her, and Kiera wondered if he realized just how ineffectual he sounded. "While you were in the hospital, we talked about—"

He stopped himself, and Kiera could see he didn't want to say what he was going to say. After everything else she had been through today, she was so exhausted she didn't think she could handle this. She closed her eyes and wished with all her strength that this last bit of news would finish her off, kill her so she wouldn't have to deal with it anymore. If she was *dead*, she wouldn't have to face the train wreck her life had become.

"About *what*?" she asked in a low, shattered voice. Nate looked at her, his eyes shining with a distant gleam that only emphasized how far apart they had grown.

"She said she really appreciated not having you around, that when you weren't here, she finally realized how much tension and hostility you added to the family."

"Me?" Kiera sagged back and had to support herself with both hands on the counter. The strength drained out of her as a heady, floating feeling took hold of her. When she looked down, she was surprised to see that she was not lying flat on the floor.

"That I add to the family . . . ?" she said, more distantly.

She recognized her own voice but had no sensation of speaking the words out loud. They echoed inside her head like a far-off rumble of thunder. When she looked around the kitchen, she had the sensation that her head kept rotating. She was carried away by that same unnerving, disconnected feeling she had experienced on the drive home.

"I'm sorry," Nate said, "I should have told you sooner, but I wanted to prepare you for it."

"This is how you prepare me for it?"

Kiera locked eyes with him, and he stared back at her, his gaze cutting through her with such intensity it made her feel uncomfortable, and she had to look away. No matter where she looked, she could imagine someone she couldn't see was lurking nearby, watching her. The dissociated feeling got so strong she was suddenly convinced it was herself—her real self—who was watching this with a cool, clinical, almost amused detachment.

"Nate," she heard herself say. "I can't . . . after everything else that's happened, I just can't take this."

"I know," Nate said, but Kiera's only clear thought was, *Do you really?*

She wanted to run upstairs and dive into bed. If she could just go to sleep, maybe all of this would go away . . . maybe she'd wake up and find out this had all been a dream, but there was no way she could sleep. She wondered if she should take a little extra pain medication to get to sleep . . . or maybe knock back a belt or two of whiskey, but she doubted even that would help.

I have to do something—anything—to get away from this!

She knew she was as close as she had ever been to having a complete nervous breakdown . . . That was, if her mind hadn't snapped already and she just didn't realize it yet.

Maybe that's it . . . Maybe I'm already so far gone I don't even realize how crazy I am . . . I never had an operation . . . There was never a growth in my brain . . . I had a mental breakdown, and I've been in a psych ward all this time . . . I'm so out of it I don't even know how bad off I am!

A small, rational part of her mind told her this wasn't true—it couldn't be—but she had been under so much stress lately that any explanation seemed not only reasonable but probable.

"I . . . I have to lie down," she said in a voice not much more than a gasp.

"Let me help you," Nate said, moving forward and offering his arm for support.

Kiera leaned against him, but she was surprised how distant and cold he felt. Even when he helped her, Nate didn't seem to really *be* there for her. A terrible sadness gripped her as she contemplated just how much she and Nate had lost.

"We have to do something . . . about Trista," she said feebly as they moved down the hallway toward the stairs.

"I will. I'll call and tell her she has to come home."

As they started up the stairs, every step made Kiera feel weaker and weaker. Her insides were vibrating like jelly, and her vision was blurred. When a thick, sour taste filled her throat, she was afraid she was going to vomit again, but there was nothing left in her stomach to throw up.

"Make sure you do," she said. "Promise me you'll get her home, 'cause if you don't, I'll drive over there myself and drag her home."

"There's no need to talk like that," Nate said. His calm, reasonable tone only made Kiera's anger at him flare all the higher.

Once upstairs, they made their way down the hall to their bedroom. When Nate pushed the door open, Kiera thought the bed looked too far away and too high for her to get onto, but she collapsed face-first onto the mattress.

"You want me to help you undress?" Nate asked.

Kiera snorted and shook her head, rubbing her face against the pillow. Wave after wave of darkness was dragging her down, but still, she couldn't quite let go. She desperately clung to consciousness until she heard Nate on the phone. She assumed he was talking to Trista and wanted to stay awake until her daughter was safely home, but she couldn't resist the dreamy, downward fall that was pulling her down . . . down . . . down . . .

~5~

Kiera wasn't sure when the voices had started, and for a long time, she thought she might have been the one talking. No, not talking—yelling. One voice in particular rose higher than the other, which at first she assumed was Nate.

But it wasn't Nate. As alienated as she felt from her husband, his voice never made her feel the way this voice did, so gruff and demanding.

"You said you wanted more beer . . . So get it."

Kiera strained to see where she was, but darkness surrounded her, closing in around her like a wet woolen blanket. She found it difficult to breathe the humid air. Even so, the man's voice sent chills through her.

"Why d'you want something to drink?" the man's voice said. "We're relaxin' now, ain't we?"

Kiera's stomach muscles clenched when she finally recognized who was speaking. It was Robbie Townsend. So that other voice—the woman—must be Trista. Chills ran up Kiera's back when she realized—somehow—she was hearing an argument between Trista and her boyfriend.

Did she bring him home?

Are they in her bedroom?

Would she have the nerve to do something like that?

She realized Robbie's voice was slurred. It was obvious he'd been drinking.

"Whassa matter? You ain't relaxed? You can't relax without somethin' to drink? S'that it?"

"No."

That was definitely Trista. The tightness she heard in her daughter's voice filled Kiera with concern for her. Something bad was happening here.

Why can't I wake up?

Why isn't Nate doing something about this?

As she listened, the light began to brighten around her, and she saw two figures—Trista and Robbie. They were sprawled on a couch in a room that looked like a bomb had gone off. Litter was strewn everywhere—empty beer bottles, fast-food wrappers, pizza boxes, dirty clothes, newspapers . . . It was a total mess, and Kiera wanted to tell Trista to get out of there, but for some reason, she couldn't make her mouth form any words.

"Come on," Robbie said as he stood up and wiped away the drool that was leaking from the corner of his mouth. "Whadda' yah say we go to bed?"

"I don't want to," Trista said in a low and controlled voice. "Not right now, anyway."

"That's fucking bullshit."

Kiera watched, helpless to move, as he jabbed his forefinger at her, hitting her on the breastbone hard enough to make her wince.

Get out of there! Kiera wanted to shout, but her voice was trapped inside her.

"I don't have to *prove* anything," Trista said as she backed away from him.

Kiera watched as she turned to the door. Robbie, still sprawled on the floor, shifted forward so he was balanced on his knees and started to run his zipper down. Before he got far, he lost his balance and fell backward, hitting his head on the edge of the couch.

Trista squealed, her hand shaking as she threw open the deadbolt lock and darted out onto the porch.

"Where the fuck you going? Get back here!" Robbie bellowed, but Trista slammed the door shut behind her and ran down the stairs to the parking lot.

The scene shifted, and Kiera found herself moving along beside her daughter as she ran across the parking lot to the alley beside the darkened apartment building. Just before she ducked out of sight, the apartment door swung open so fast Kiera heard the glass rattle when it hit the wall. A dark silhouette reeled out on the porch.

"You'd better get yer ass back here right the fuck now, or you'll be goddamned sorry!"

Kiera cringed as Robbie's voice filled the night, echoing from the surrounding buildings. He stumbled and almost fell as he came down the stairs and ran over to his car. After looking up and down the street, he got into it and started it up.

With the fluid transition of a dream, Kiera now found herself moving down a long, winding dark road. Ahead of her, she could see two red taillights and knew she had to catch up with them.

She knew Robbie was driving the car, but she wasn't sure if Trista was in the car or not. She had a sense that her daughter was hiding in the darkness somewhere, afraid to move, but Kiera was moving and, although it wasn't the result of anything she did, she found that she was rapidly closing the gap between her and the car in front of her.

I'll get you, you son of a bitch, she thought as the darkness slid past her. She could see her hands on a car's steering wheel in front of her, but she had an unusual sense of flying. There was no engine sound . . . no wind through an open window . . . just a dizzying sensation of flying along the dark curves of the road until she found herself beside a fast-moving car.

Fear gripped her as she looked to the right and saw Robbie at the wheel of the other car. His face had a ghastly blue glow from the dashboard lights, and his eyes were focused on the road ahead of him.

You'll leave my daughter alone! Kiera thought, but it was as if she had spoken the words out loud, because Robbie's head slowly swiveled around until he was looking straight at her. His eyes held a dull, red glow that sent a spike of fear through her.

"Fuckin' bitch!" Robbie shouted as he glared at her and banged his clenched fist repeatedly against the steering wheel. "Who the *fuck* do you *think* you *are*?"

He kept driving without looking at the curving road

ahead. The bright wash of his headlights splintered into fragments of light that hurt Kiera's eyes.

Kiera didn't recognize where she was. The houses, fields, and trees that flashed past her all looked unfamiliar. She noticed that every house she passed was plunged into darkness, as if there had been a massive power outage.

You can't do what you're doing to my little girl! Kiera thought, although the thought was so clear in her mind she was positive she had shouted it. She was convinced she had when Robbie turned and looked at her again, his face contorted into a wild, angry sneer.

Suddenly, Kiera was no longer beside him. She was still moving silently through the night, but the only light came from two yellow circles in front of her. As she watched breathlessly, the circles resolved, and Kiera realized they were headlights, and they were coming straight at her.

"Are you fuckin' *nuts*?" she heard someone—it must have been Robbie—shout. She saw him clearly through the windshield of the approaching car now. He gripped the steering wheel and pulled it hard to the right. Tires squealed like banshees on the asphalt as Robbie lost control of his car. It lurched heavily to the right when its wheels ran off the edge of the pavement. The chassis hit the ground with a loud *clunk* that sent sparks flying out from under his car.

It was all over before Kiera knew what was happening. Suddenly she was no longer moving, although she had no sense of stopping or slowing down. She watched in mute horror as Robbie's car careened down into a gully and then flipped over. It had been going so fast it rolled over five or six times before finally coming to rest. When it did, it was a twisted wreck, lying upside down more than fifty feet off the road. Steam hissed loudly, and smoke curled lazily up into the night sky to be whisked away by a gentle breeze.

Robbie was dead in an instant. His head had smashed through the windshield, and a huge splash of blood washed the crumpled hood of his car and dripped from the dashboard onto the floor. His sightless eyes were wide open and staring up at the night sky as though he couldn't believe what had just happened.

Chapter 9

Phantom Limb

~1~

Kiera woke up earlier than usual, but she wasn't at all surprised she hadn't slept any longer because of the dream she'd had. In the early morning light, the memory of it was already fading, but it left behind a feeling of discomfort that she couldn't shake as she got out of bed and washed up.

On her way downstairs, she poked her head into Trista's bedroom and was surprised to see her daughter asleep in her bed. She had no idea when Trista had come home last night, but it must have been late. Her dream had had something to do with an argument between Trista and Robbie, and she wondered if Trista actually had the gall to have her boyfriend up to her bedroom. She wished she could recall more details of the dream, but they were melting away.

While she was scrambling eggs, making enough for Trista if she bothered to show up for breakfast, she heard the shower start upstairs. Nate had already showered, so she knew Trista was awake and apparently planning to ride to school with her father as usual.

When she came downstairs, Trista acted as if everything

was perfectly normal. Kiera waited for her to say something about her being home from the hospital, but Trista was typically uncommunicative. It was just as well, Kiera decided. She intended to wait until after school and Nate was home before she confronted Trista and told her in no uncertain terms that she would never allow her to move out of the house while she was still in high school.

After perfunctory good-byes and a peck on the cheek from Nate, he and Trista left for school. Kiera was still trying to dredge up a clear memory of the dream that was still haunting her, so she was glad to see them go.

A little before nine o'clock, just as she was settling down on the couch in the living room with a cup of coffee, the phone rang. The caller ID showed that it was Jon. Kiera's first impulse was to ignore it, but she knew he'd leave a message and then try her cell. She answered it because she couldn't think of a good enough excuse not to.

"Hey there," she said, a bit surprised by her cool, aloof tone of voice.

"Hey yourself. How you feeling?"

"Okay, I guess. How are you doing?"

Kiera sensed a chill between them, and she wondered if it was mutual or if it was all coming from her.

But what could she do?

After what Jon had said to her yesterday, how was she supposed to feel about him? He had all but asked her to leave Nate and run off with him. It wasn't like she could just pretend he hadn't said the things he'd said.

After a short silence, Jon cleared his throat and said, "We, uhh, need to talk."

"I'm listening," Kiera said. She hated that she was treating Jon with such detachment. She didn't have to remind herself that he had buried his wife yesterday. No matter what happened between them, he was her closest, dearest friend. What she'd been through seemed almost insignificant compared to his recent loss. She should be kind and forgiving, not cold and angry.

"About yesterday . . ." Jon said, sounding weak and hesitant. Kiera could easily imagine how uncomfortable he was feeling. Maybe he was embarrassed about what he'd said and had called to apologize. If he had said what he said because he wasn't thinking straight because of grief, she should let him know that she still cherished his friendship.

But she also had to make it clear that's *all* they were. Just friends. It was *never* going to go any further than that.

Or could it? whispered a faint voice in the back of her mind. *Maybe he said what you've been thinking all along . . . what you've been wanting but afraid to admit . . . even to yourself?*

"Look, Kiera. I can't do this over the phone. Can we meet for lunch or something?"

Kiera sucked in a breath and held it, struggling to sort through the confusion in her head. She was exhausted after such a lousy night, and she didn't think she had the energy for this . . . not now, anyway.

"Maybe in a day or two," she finally said. "I've been . . . I'm still pretty wiped out from the surgery, and Liz's death really affected me."

"Me, too," Jon said simply, but even through her confusion, Kiera detected an insincere note in his voice. Her lower lip started to tremble, and tears misted her vision as she looked around the living room, wondering if Jon had been in love with her all along, and not Liz.

Could he have been carrying a torch for me all this time . . . ever since high school . . . and I never even knew it?

Or did I . . . is this what I've wanted all along?

"I want you to know how concerned I am about Trista, too," Jon said.

His words sliced her like a razor. A chill took hold of her as a surge of panic rose in her stomach.

"What are you talking about?"

"Oh, Jesus." Jon sighed in frustration. "You hadn't heard? It's on the news this morning."

"What's on the news?" Kiera choked back a scream she could feel building up inside her. Fragments of her dream flashed through her mind, a vague memory of moving down a long, dark road, watching the red taillights of a car ahead of her until she saw it careen off the road.

"Her boyfriend—Robbie what's-his-name—died in a car accident. They found him out on Cold Spring Road. Rolled over a couple of times and went right through the windshield."

"Oh my God," Kiera said, stunned. Her vision narrowed until she was staring at a small square of the floor at her feet. Her senses seemed to be shutting down. She wasn't aware of anything other than Jon's voice inside her head.

"The first reports indicate he was drunk," Jon continued. "You're damned lucky Trista wasn't with him."

Kiera tried to speak but couldn't as she listened to Jon and the loud rush of her blood in her ears.

Robbie Townsend's dead?

How was this possible?

If Trista hadn't been with him last night, where had she been? Did they have an argument? Had she walked all the way home from his place? If she had been with him, she no doubt would have been killed, too. It frightened Kiera to realize that right now, if things had been just a little bit different, she would be trying to cope with the loss of her only child. That she had seen Trista this morning, even though they had barely spoken, seemed almost a dream now.

"Are you still there?" Jon asked.

Kiera swallowed, but the dryness in her throat didn't yield.

"Yeah . . . I . . . I'm here."

"Damned cell phones. You can never tell when you have a connection or not." Jon inhaled heavily. "So . . . she must be pretty broken up about it, huh?"

"I . . . I don't think she even knows about it. She was her usual self this morning . . . not upset or anything. I—" Kiera rubbed her bandaged forehead and shivered. "I don't know what to think."

She found it difficult if not impossible to focus. She wasn't surprised that the news didn't really upset her. She had almost been expecting it, but she didn't know why, unless it was because of that dream she'd had last night. As cold and heartless as it made her feel, her only concern was how Trista would react to the news when she found out. She was going to be devastated, but Kiera could only feel immense relief.

"From what you told me, you should be pretty happy, huh?" Jon said. "It's not like that creep was doing Trista any good. Am I right? I was just . . . you know . . . worried how Trista was dealing with it."

"I don't know," Kiera said. Dozens of conflicting thoughts crowded her mind. Because of the dream she'd had last night she had the unnerving feeling that—somehow—she had been involved with the accident last night, that she was responsible for it.

"I can't believe he's dead," she said.

"It's on the news. Put your TV on. Hey, this is what you wanted, right?"

Jon's words, so heartless and echoing her own thoughts, stung her. She had to be honest with herself and admit this was *exactly* what she had wanted. If Trista was going to be so stubborn about seeing Robbie, then—yes, she had wanted him dead. But getting what she wanted at the expense of someone else's life was almost too much to handle.

"Even Trista will get over this," Jon continued. "With any loss, it's just a matter of time until the pain goes away and you forget about it."

"No," Kiera said as an image of Billy Carroll rose unbidden in her mind. "Some of them, you *never* forget."

"You might be right," Jon said, still sounding much too casual about this. Kiera couldn't stand how he sounded so empty of emotion. She wanted to scream at him, but she was too drained and numbed to react.

"But eventually, the immediate pain goes away," Jon said. "All I'm saying is, she'll be fine. Don't worry about her. She'll get over it. It's just gonna be rough for a while."

Kiera couldn't take any more of this. It didn't matter what Jon said; he was really irritating her, mostly because she was so twisted up with guilt. Just because she had *wanted* Robbie Townsend to die didn't mean she should feel guilty because he had. It was an accident . . . just like what she had spent most of her life trying to convince herself had happened to Billy. It wasn't like she was responsible for it.

Or was it?

She wasn't so sure, because the more she thought about the dream she'd had last night, the more she was convinced—somehow—she had known what was happening and maybe even had something to do with it.

"Look . . . Jon . . . I'm really not feeling so good," she said. "I have to lie down."

"Oh, yeah. Sorry."

Once again, Kiera was struck how much this didn't sound like the friend she knew . . . the friend who had just buried his wife yesterday.

"I'll call later this afternoon. Maybe we can get together for a late lunch."

"Tomorrow might be better," Kiera said, and she hung up before Jon could say anything more.

She focused on the view outside the living room window as a powerful wave of dizziness swept over her. Nausea filled her stomach, and she sagged back, feeling like she was about to pass out. She grabbed the arm of the couch with both hands, her heart beating high and fast in her throat. Every pulse made her vision twitch. When she took a breath, her chest ratcheted as tiny white spots of light swam across her vision.

"This can't be happening," she whispered as she squeezed the couch arm, holding on desperately. The room seemed to be heaving up and down like a storm-tossed ocean.

Somehow, she managed to get up off the couch and make it into the kitchen, where she went over to the sink and turned on the tap. Cupping her hands, she filled them with water and splashed her face several times, blubbering and sputtering. The cold wetness washed over her without seeming to penetrate her, and she had a dissociated feeling as if this was happening to someone else, not her. She grabbed a dish towel and rubbed her face, but she still felt frighteningly disconnected from her senses.

"I have to lie down," she muttered, but she wasn't sure she could make it back to the living room. Her vision narrowed as darkness closed in from all sides. Just before she collapsed onto the kitchen floor, although she had been thinking about Robbie Townsend, a face appeared before her.

It was Billy Carroll, and he was smiling.

~2~

Kiera came to an hour or so later when she heard the telephone ringing for what seemed like a hundred times. Finally, the answering machine clicked on, and Nate's recorded message played. After the beep, Nate spoke.

"Hello, Kiera. You there?" And after a pause. "I have some really upsetting news."

Even through her confusion as she struggled to sit up on the kitchen floor, she registered the agitation in his voice.

"Last night . . . Robbie Townsend was killed in a car accident."

Kiera dragged herself closer to consciousness, wishing she had the strength to get up and reach the phone before he hung up.

"All I could think was—thank *God* Trista wasn't with him! We're at school, and she just found out. Needless to say, she's devastated. I . . . I don't know what to say. I— I'm taking the day off to bring her home, so we'll there soon. Hope you're feeling better. See you in a bit. Bye."

The answering machine beeped again and then clicked off. Kiera sat there on the floor, her legs splayed in front of her as she rubbed her face and struggled to process what she had just heard. She still wasn't fully conscious, but something—not Nate's news—something else was bothering her . . . a lingering memory that left her with a clear mental image of the accident. She hadn't actually seen the accident; it was more like someone had told her about it . . . had whispered the details to her while she was passed out.

As she struggled to clear her mind, the memory faded until all she was left with was an empty, hollow feeling. She couldn't stop thinking she was forgetting something vitally important.

"Damn it," she whispered as she struggled to stand up. Nate and Trista would be here in a few minutes. She had to pull herself together enough, at least, so they wouldn't see her falling apart like this. She couldn't shake the feeling that, no matter what she did, no matter how freaked out her husband and daughter were, they—especially Trista—would know something was wrong with her. And she couldn't shake the feeling that she didn't just know about Robbie's accident. Somehow *she* had been involved with it and—even worse—she was somehow responsible.

"That's not possible," she whispered as she moved stiffly to the kitchen sink.

She groaned and covered her eyes with both hands as she leaned against the wall and tried to force herself closer to consciousness. But the closer she got, the faster that vague memory faded, no matter how hard she tried to hold on to it. Once it was gone entirely, she was left feeling like it was a phantom limb—an amputated arm or leg that still experienced sensation. No matter how much she tried to scratch it, the limb was no longer there, so she was never going to be able to relieve the irritation.

She was still leaning against the wall when a car pulled into the driveway. Shaking her head to clear it, she got ready to put on a false face and pretend she felt terrible about Robbie dying. The truth she could never admit to anyone was she was *happy* he was out of their lives—especially Trista's. She was ecstatic, even.

Feeling tense, she waited to hear the garage door open as Nate and Trista pulled in. After what seemed like a terribly long time, she began to feel nervous. Now that she thought about it, there hadn't been enough time for them to drive all the way home from school.

Someone else is out there!

A cold, clammy feeling slithered under her skin as she walked down the hall to the family room. The windows looked out onto the driveway and the street in front of the house, but there was no car in sight. Her nervousness spiked when she heard an engine rev so loudly it practically shook the walls. The family room windows rattled as the sound rumbled like thunder. A haze of pale blue smoke swirled in the air from around the corner of the garage.

"*What* the *hell* is going *on*?" Kiera muttered.

Why couldn't she see the car she knew was out there? She was tempted to go outside and take a look around, but she held back because a sense of impending danger made the hairs on her neck stir.

One thing she was sure of, this wasn't Nate. If Trista was as upset as she thought she'd be, they would have come directly into the house. She didn't think they'd stay out in the car, having a heart-to-heart talk . . . unless Trista felt so alienated from her mother she didn't want to face her. Did she think Kiera was going to gloat and say, "I told you so?"

But why can't I see the car I know is out there?

It sounded like it was parked in front of the garage, but the angle was bad, and no matter how close she got to the window looking left and right, she just couldn't see it. The street in front of the house was also empty.

As she leaned against the window, wondering what to do next, Kiera's focus shifted, and she found herself looking at her reflection in the glass. She was instantly captured by the frantic, almost insane look she saw reflected in her eyes.

And then something happened.

Something impossible.

As she took a step back from the window, still listening to the throaty roar of the car's engine, her reflection moved, too, but it didn't move in synch with her. Fear rippled through her as she tipped her head to one side and turned it. The face in the window didn't move. Instead, it stared straight at her without blinking.

A frightened whimper that she barely recognized as her own escaped her. As she took another step back, she tripped over her own feet and almost fell, but somehow she kept her balance. She started trembling violently, afraid that she was having a complete mental breakdown. She covered her mouth with both hands to stifle the scream that was about to burst out of her. In the reflection, her hands remained at her sides as she stared back at herself with a cold, unflinching gaze.

"What is *happening* to me?" she said in a raw whisper.

Another strangled sob escaped her as she stared at herself and had to acknowledge that this was no trick of the eye, no illusion. In the reflection, her mouth didn't move when she spoke. The image's lips remained a thin, compressed line, and her mouth twitched only after she stopped speaking. It took her a terrifying instant to realize her reflection was speaking to her. At first, she couldn't hear what it was saying. Then, as faint as the flutter of a moth's wings in the dark, a voice hissed at her in a soft, grating whisper.

"I could ask you the same thing of you," her reflection said. Each word hovered just at the edge of hearing. "*Who* are *you*?"

Kiera was too stunned to respond. She couldn't believe this was happening. She wanted to believe she was asleep on the couch and dreaming this because, if it *wasn't* a dream . . . if she really was awake and this was happening, then she was losing her mind if she hadn't already lost it.

"We have a lot to talk about," the reflection whispered. The voice, a strange distortion of Kiera's voice, was so faint it could have been the wind blowing through the trees. But the windows weren't open, and a dense stillness was hanging in the air and pressing down on her with a hot, steady pressure.

"No . . . no," Kiera said, shaking her head in adamant denial as she watched her unmoving reflection. "I'm asleep. This *has* to be a dream."

She raised her right hand and stared at it, remembering that she had heard how you weren't supposed to be able to see your hands in a dream. Flexing her fingers, she watched as they curled into a fist, the veins and tendons shifting beneath her skin and standing out in sharp relief. She pressed her fist against her mouth to stifle the sounds she was making.

"And you're *not* going crazy," the reflection said softly. "No crazier than I am, anyway. You're the sanest you've ever been ever since you got rid of me."

"Got rid of you? What are you talking about? Who *are* you?" Kiera found it almost impossible to breathe. "I never got *rid* of you.

"Yes you did. You set me free," the reflection said, its voice ending in a long-drawn-out, sorrowful note. "I'm not part of you anymore, but somehow I'm still here. Look, I'm just as confused as you are, but I guess no matter what happens, I'll always be a part of you."

Without realizing it, Kiera opened her hand and raised it to her forehead, touching the bandage that covered the scar from her surgery. In the window, her reflection did the same thing, and the light pressure of her fingers against the incision sent a mild electrical shock through her even as she had the unnerving sensation of not really being able to feel her own touch. It was like watching someone else—a twin—touch her own head.

"Who are you?" Kiera asked, but even before she finished asking the question, she knew the answer. She was seeing a ghost of herself. *She* hadn't died, but a part of her *had*. And that part of her that was dead, the growth Dr. Martindale had cut out of her head, had been alive and now, somehow, it was haunting her.

"What do you want?" Kiera asked, her voice trembling as she leaned forward and stared intently at her reflection. She fought back the fear that rose inside her as the reflection's eyes widened with confusion. She had no idea—even by paying attention to how she was reacting to this—what this pale reflection was feeling. It looked like fear in her reflection's eyes, but it could just as well been caring and sympathy.

Is she afraid for me or for herself? Kiera wondered, but the thought struck her as foolish.

This is *me!* She hit herself on the chest with her clenched fist. The resounding thud startled her.

"Something's coming," the reflection said in a low, grating whisper.

"What's coming?"

"I'm not sure. I'm just as confused as you are. I can't see it clearly, but I can *feel* it. Can't you? I know you can. But all I know for sure is, you have to be careful who you trust."

"Be careful?" Kiera echoed, dumbfounded as she stared at herself and nodded slowly. She was no longer amazed to see that her refection didn't match her movements. As crazy as it was, she accepted that, even if she was dreaming, what was happening was as real as if she was talking to her twin.

But I never had a twin, she thought, and a shiver rushed

through her when she heard—or thought she heard—a voice say, "Not anymore, you don't. But I still want to help."

"Help me *what*?" Kiera asked as a surge of desperation filled her. She felt herself getting lost as she stared into the dark, glazed hollow of her reflection's eyes.

Before she could answer, the reflection began to waver and fade. Kiera refocused her eyes and realized she was staring past the glass to the driveway and the street beyond. The sound of the unseen car was still there, still rumbling steadily. Although she noticed it as if for the first time, she knew it had never really gone away. It had always been there, but as it got louder now, she saw in the distance another car coming up the street. Her blood went cold when she saw a dark Volvo—just like her car—crest the rise a few hundred feet away from her house.

Kiera watched in stunned amazement as the car drew closer. She anticipated that it would slow down and turn into the driveway, and when it did, she knew she would see herself behind the steering wheel.

A blur of motion off to one side caught her attention. She saw her reflection shake its head back and forth, but she couldn't tell if this was meant as a warning or an expression of sadness.

"What are you trying to tell me?" she asked desperately as she adjusted her focus to look at her reflection again. Coldness gripped her heart, and a soft concussion like a muffled explosion popped inside her head. Her reflection remained in the glass, but Kiera no longer experienced that odd feeling of duality, of looking at herself in the window while at the same time looking back at herself from the glass.

At the edge of hearing, she heard a voice whisper something, but it was lost beneath the roar of the car as it approached the house. Kiera watched with steadily rising terror as it got closer to the driveway, but then— surprisingly—it went past the house.

Kiera turned her head to track the car as it sped down the street until it rounded the corner and was out of sight. As crazy and impossible as it seemed, she was positive she had just watched herself drive past the house in her car. She jumped when she looked at the driveway again and saw a car parked in front of the garage.

It was a police cruiser. She watched in stunned silence as two men, one wearing a policeman's uniform, the other a dark business suit, got out and started up the walkway to the front door. Kiera recognized Detective Fielding from that day in the hospital when she had learned Liz had died. Running her hands over her face, she tried to pull herself together but knew she must look a wreck as she went to the door and opened it before the detective rang the bell.

"Mrs. Davis," Fielding said as he reached into his suit coat pocket, pulled out his wallet, and flashed his ID badge. "I'm Detective Fielding."

"I know."

"This is Officer Doyle. Do you mind if we have a word with you?"

"Of course not," Kiera said, taking a breath as she backed away from the door so they could enter. "Please, come in." She led the two men into the living room.

Trembling inside, she sat down on the couch, tucking her feet beneath her while indicating for Detective Fielding to sit down in what was usually Nate's chair. Officer Doyle remained standing in the doorway.

"What can I do for you?" she asked. She wished she sounded chipper and bright, but she was painfully aware of the tremor in her voice. "Have you found out who killed my friend?"

"Not yet," Fielding said. "We're checking out a few things regarding an accident last night involving Robert Townsend."

A cold shock hit Kiera's stomach as her face drained of blood. She folded her hands tightly in her lap to stop them from trembling.

"I just heard about that," Kiera said. "My husband's on his way home now with my daughter."

Detective Fielding nodded, his mouth a thin, grim line. Kiera remembered him being friendlier that day in the hospital, and she wondered if it had all been an act to get her to confess if she had anything to confess to. She was sure she didn't, but she flinched anyway, remembering the clear images she'd had in a dream about what had happened to Liz O'Keefe. She wondered if Detective Fielding noticed, too, and if he took this as a sign that she might be more involved than she was letting on.

Stop feeling so guilty, she told herself . . . Or was it someone else speaking . . . someone she couldn't see who was whispering in her ear? *You didn't do anything wrong.*

"I understand your daughter was dating Mr. Townsend," Fielding said.

"Yes," Kiera replied, praying the detective couldn't see through her façade as easily as she imagined he could.

"And I'm under the impression that you didn't exactly approve of the relationship." Fielding frowned, his eyebrows making a dark V on his forehead.

"No. I don't—I *didn't* approve," Kiera said, struggling to keep her voice from breaking. Sweat broke out across her face, and the trembling inside her stomach got worse. "He was too old for her."

"And what did you do about it?" Fielding asked. He placed his hands on his knees and leaned farther forward, his eyes darkening, his expression even grimmer.

"What do you mean, what did I *do*? I did what any concerned parent would do. I made it perfectly clear to her that I didn't like him and that, to be honest, I suspected he was taking advantage of her."

"What do you mean, 'taking advantage'?"

Kiera stiffened, thinking she had blundered into a trap he had set for her that she hadn't even seen.

"I think you know what I mean," Kiera said, struggling to keep her voice steady. "He was a known drug user, and I thought he was only interested in her for sexual reasons. I did whatever was necessary to make that clear to her."

"Really?" Detective Fielding loosened his posture and leaned back in the chair. "*Whatever* was necessary?"

Kiera frowned and, biting her lower lip, regarded him steadily. She still had the feeling she was playing right into his hands, but she wasn't sure what he was trying to get her to admit.

"This is beginning to sound like an interrogation," she said. "If there's . . . Should I have my lawyer present?"

"That's entirely within your rights," Fielding said, "but I just wanted to ask you a few questions to clear up a couple of things."

Kiera nodded but still wasn't convinced. There was something he wasn't telling her, and she needed to know what it was before she said anything she might regret.

"Maybe we should wait until my husband gets home." She glanced at her wristwatch. "He should be along any minute."

Fielding shook his head. "I don't think that's necessary. What I really came to ask you about is that last night, someone saw Robbie Townsend as he was driving away from his apartment, and they reported seeing a dark blue or black Volvo pull out behind him and follow him."

"Really," Kiera said.

"Since your car fits that description, I was wondering if you'd let me take a quick look at it."

"My car?" Kiera said hollowly. She couldn't comprehend what he was getting at, and was tossed between outrage and steadily mounting fear. Vague memories and fragmented images of two cars racing along a dark, winding road late at night arose in her mind and headlights coming straight at her, but there was no way Kiera could distinguish if these were real memories or fragments of a dream or something she had imagined after Jon told her about Robbie's accident. The images blurred with other vague memories . . . memories from long ago . . . when she and Jon had driven out to the picnic area on the Hancock River and parked . . .

No! she told herself, praying that she didn't say or do anything to arouse the detective's suspicions further. *Don't even* think *about that!*

"Would you mind?" Fielding asked, making a motion to stand up. He made it sound like such a reasonable request as he glanced at Officer Doyle, who stood silently in the doorway.

"Is your car in the garage? It will only take a second."

"What do you expect to find?" Kiera asked. The blood in her veins had turned to ice water, and she hugged herself as she shivered.

"Apparently Mr. Townsend's car was forced off the road by another car. His left door panel and fender were scraped, and we found some flakes of dark blue paint on the bare metal."

"You think *I* had something to do with this?" Kiera asked, too frightened to speak above a whisper. The memories or dreams or whatever they were got more intense, like something she had forgotten and was only now remembering.

"I would just like to have a look at your car," Fielding said simply.

Kiera knew if they went out there and found a dent or some paint missing from her car, she was in serious trouble, and as crazy as it seemed, she would be more surprised if they *didn't* find damage on her car.

Maybe those images weren't dreams. Maybe they were real memories.

She couldn't tell what was real and what was imaginary anymore, but she got up from the couch and led the detective and patrolman out into the garage. Her hand was slick with sweat and trembling as she turned the doorknob leading into the garage. Just as she opened the door, the garage door started rattling as it began to open. Daylight filled the gradually widening gap, and she saw a car—Nate's car—pull into the driveway.

Kiera realized she'd been holding her breath and let it out in a long, whistling sigh.

"My husband's home," she said simply, hoping this would somehow protect her from what might happen next.

Detective Fielding grunted before walking down the short flight of steps into the garage. He folded his arms over his chest and waited for Nate to pull to a stop in front of the now fully opened garage door.

"Trista," Kiera said, pushing past Fielding and walking quickly to the passenger's door. Through the windshield, she could see her daughter staring wide-eyed at her and the police. It was obvious she thought they were here to interview her. Lowering her head, she made no move to get out of the car.

"What's this all about?" Nate asked as he stepped out of the car and started toward them.

Kiera glanced at Fielding, then at her husband. The sense of unreality sweeping over her was so intense her mind was a blank, and she had nothing to say.

"Mr. Davis," Detective Fielding said cheerfully as he walked over to Nate with his hand extended so they could shake. "We just stopped by to ask your wife a few questions."

"My wife?" Nate looked genuinely surprised. "What business do you have with my—"

Everyone turned when the passenger's door opened, and Trista, looking pale and shaky, stepped blinking into the bright sunlight. Her face was red and puffy from crying, and her eyes were bloodshot. She hunched her shoulders and walked briskly toward the house. Kiera rushed over to her and hugged her.

"I'm so sorry," Kiera said.

When she pulled her daughter close to her, she was surprised by how thin and frail she felt in her arms. It reminded her of when Trista was a baby, and her heart ached for her child and what she must be going through.

"I'll just bet you are," Trista said. Her lower lip was trembling when she pulled back and looked at her mother. The only other sound she made was a low groan that started somewhere deep inside her chest before she broke away from her mother's embrace and dashed into the house, shouldering her way past the patrolman who stood close to the door. Once she was inside the house, a long, barking sound filled the air, but it was cut off when she slammed the door shut.

For a few awkward seconds, everyone just stood there looking at each other in stunned silence. Kiera wanted to go after Trista and see what she could do to help, but she knew there was nothing. The chasm between them yawned all the wider.

Finally, Nate cleared his throat and, squaring his shoulders, looked at Fielding.

"So what's this all about?" he said, shooting a quick glance at Kiera.

Fielding's expression never wavered as he indicated the open garage door with a curt nod of his head.

"We got a report that a car fitting the description of your wife's car was seen in the vicinity of the accident last night."

"What are you—? You mean the accident involving Townsend?"

Fielding nodded quickly, and Nate looked at Kiera again, who was standing off to one side with her clenched fist covering her mouth. At that moment, with all three men staring at her, Kiera felt more vulnerable than she had ever felt in her life.

"We'd like to check the car for damage," Fielding said.

Nate took a step toward the open garage as though to block their entry.

"Don't you need a search warrant for that?"

"We can go that route if that's how you want to play it," Fielding said simply. "I was hoping—if neither one of you has anything to hide—you'd allow us to take a look."

Nate shot Kiera a harsh glance. Still stunned and feeling out of it, Kiera shrugged as though there was nothing she could do to stop whatever was going to happen next. Her first impulse was to go into the house, but she didn't want to do anything that would make her appear guilty.

Guilty of what? she asked herself. *I didn't do anything wrong . . . and I certainly didn't have anything to do with Robbie's death last night.*

She wanted to shriek this out loud, but even that might be construed as an admission of guilt. Her only option was to go along with Fielding's request and see what happened.

Nate, who obviously had been considering the pros and cons of cooperating with the police, finally relaxed his stance and, turning on his heel, walked into the garage with the detective close behind him. Kiera was bursting with anticipation and wanted to look with them, but a cold, sinking sensation in the pit of her stomach convinced her that she should prepare herself for the worst.

What if I did do something last night?

What if I don't even remember getting into my car driving over to Robbie's apartment and then following him and forcing him off the road?

What if I wanted him to leave Trista alone so badly I was willing to kill him?

Time seemed to stand still as she waited there in the blazing sun and watched the dark silhouettes of the two men as they inspected the car in the garage. From where she stood, she could see part of her car, but Nate's car blocked her view. Fielding knelt down and inspected the front bumper. Then he stood up and, pointing at the fender, said something to Nate, who nodded and then glanced outside at Kiera.

"Oh my God," she whispered when the two men came back out of the garage and walked over to her.

"Thank you for your time, Mrs. Davis," Detective Fielding said as he held his hand out for her to shake. "I'm sorry for the inconvenience."

Kiera thought her grip was too damp and weak, and broke off the contact quickly.

"Was there—?" she said, but that was all she managed before her throat closed off.

Detective Fielding shook his head sharply. "I didn't see anything wrong." He shot a quick glance at the house and added, "Tell your daughter I'm sorry about what happened."

"I will," Kiera said softly, but even as she said it, she knew she wouldn't. She bristled at the thought that anyone would offer sympathy or condolences to Trista. She and Robbie had only been dating. At least they hadn't been married. Now that it was over, when she searched her feelings, Kiera wanted to smile because, as horrible as it was, at least now she didn't have to worry about her daughter being with a creep like Robbie Townsend.

Nate came up beside her and slid his arm around her waist. Together, they watched as the detective and patrolman got back into the cruiser, started it up, and drove away. The sound of their tires scuffing on the driveway was loud in the sudden stillness of the day.

"Jesus, that was something," Nate said after the cruiser was out of sight. He looked at her and smiled.

"He thought I did it," Kiera said, feeling too stunned to be relieved.

Nate's eyes widened as he sawed his top teeth over his bottom lip.

"He actually thought I forced Robbie off the road to kill him."

"It was an accident," Nate said, but Kiera wasn't convinced by his mild manner. She could sense that he was holding something back. She felt a jolt when the terrible thought occurred to her that maybe *Nate* had done what Fielding had suspected *her* of doing. Narrowing her eyes, she studied him.

Would Nate ever do anything like that? she wondered.

Was he capable of murder?

Time seemed to freeze as she looked at her husband's face bathed in bright sunlight and wondered what secrets he might be hiding from her. If his past was any indication, there might be things she would never want to know, but she twisted with guilt, knowing the terrible secret she had kept from him all these years. More than ever, Kiera was once again aware of the gulf between them. Even with him standing so close to her, she had to admit that they were no longer *together*. Maybe they had never been. Even if Nate didn't have anything to do with Robbie's accident, she knew as clearly as if it was written on his face that he was keeping a secret about *something*.

Nate gave her a quick hug and then moved away from her.

"This is gonna be really hard on Trista," he said.

"Go ahead." Kiera spoke so suddenly her voice sounded like a bark. "Say it."

"Huh? . . . Say what?"

"Tell me the truth."

"The . . . truth? What are you talking about?"

"Admit that you're glad this happened, too. Say it out loud, because I'm not afraid to. I'm *happy* Robbie's dead. You hear me? He was bad for Trista. He was taking advantage of her. And I don't care how or why it happened. I'm *thrilled* that son of a bitch is dead so he won't be pestering our daughter anymore."

Stunned by her outburst, Nate stared at her for a long time. It seemed to Kiera as though her words echoed and reechoed from the house and the woods out back. She wasn't proud about saying what she'd said out loud, but she had to admit that she *did* feel better.

"We have to be honest with ourselves . . . and to each other," she said. Her voice was lower now, almost broken because something deep inside her was telling her that it was already too late. Whatever she and Nate might have shared once upon a time was gone now. Ultimately, it didn't matter what Nate did or didn't admit, because their relationship was irreparably broken.

"Jesus, Kiera," he said, shaking his head and frowning at her. "I can't believe you'd say something like that."

Kiera shot him a hostile look and started to say something, but then she inhaled sharply and exhaled as she lowered her head. The feeling of defeat and loss was total. There was nothing left to say. Without speaking a word, she walked back into the house, leaving him standing there alone.

~3~

"There's nothing you can say!"

Kiera stood in the doorway of Trista's bedroom, leaning against the doorjamb and wishing her daughter would at least invite her into the room so they could talk.

"I know there isn't, baby." Kiera took a step forward but then pulled back. "It's just that I . . . I want you to know how sorry I am for you."

"Yeah, sure." The sarcasm in her voice was raw and heartless. She was lying on her bed with her back to her mother, but she turned just enough to glare at her with eyes that glistened like quicksilver with tears.

Kiera took a sharp breath, wishing she could say just the right thing, but words failed her, and she knew she couldn't fake remorse.

"You were always saying how much you hated him, that

you didn't want me to see him. I would think you'd be *happy* he's dead."

"I'm not," Kiera said, cringing at the lie. Her voice twisted off, and she couldn't continue. Trista's shoulders quaked as another wave of grief washed over her. Kiera wished she could comfort her, but the distance she felt between them kept her rooted where she stood.

"Just leave me alone. Please . . . ?"

Kiera swallowed hard. Every word was like a razor cut.

She's lost to me, she thought. *And nothing I can do or say can ever repair the damage that's been done.*

But who had done the damage?

She had always done what she thought was best for her daughter. If that wasn't enough, it wasn't her fault. Of course she had made mistakes. What parent didn't? She was human, after all. It's what you did *after* you'd screwed up that mattered.

But as hard as she tried, Kiera couldn't say any of this to Trista. Her daughter was so consumed by grief she would twist anything she said the wrong way. All she could do was let her know she loved her and would be there for her when and if she was ever ready to talk. Her heart felt like a cold, dark weight in the core of her chest as she closed the door, turned, and walked away.

Tears blurred her eyes as she walked down the hallway to her bedroom, and all she could think was, *When? . . . When did we lose everything we had?*

~4~

The night was warm with just a hint of a breeze to rustle the leaves in the backyard. Soon, Kiera knew, the leaves would be changing color and falling. The knowledge that autumn was just around the corner filled her with deep sadness. She knew she was being foolish, as young as she was, but for the first time in her life the approach of cold weather made her reflect on her own life, and how sad—no, not sad—pathetic it was that so much of it had passed her by, and she felt as though in so many ways she had never really experienced it, much less appreciated it.

Is it all because of what happened to Billy?

Is that what's ruined my life?

Or were there other, more immediate problems, like the fact that there was nothing left of her marriage—if there had ever been anything to begin with—and what (if anything) she was going to do about it.

Why was she still married to Nate?

Why hadn't she left him years ago when she first found out he'd been having an affair? It was the first—and only—affair she found out about and the first one he admitted to, but she had always suspected it hadn't been the first or last.

Ever since she met him, Nate had always seemed somewhat emotionally aloof. Maybe that was just the way he was, and she should have gotten used to it after all these years married to him . . . or maybe he'd been hiding something from her all these years, that he couldn't help himself . . . that he had to have relationships with other women . . . that she wasn't enough for him!

Like tonight . . .

Where was he tonight?

If they really had a loving, caring relationship, shouldn't he be home with her right now?

Instead, he was out somewhere. She didn't even know where. He hadn't said anything about meeting up with some of his poker buddies or having a meeting at school. For all she knew, he might be with another woman right now, and she'd be none the wiser.

Kiera considered calling him on his cell and asking where he was, but when she was honest with herself, she actually preferred it when he wasn't around.

"Has it gotten *that* bad?" she asked herself, sighing and shaking her head.

Did they have so little left between them that, even when she was feeling as terrible as she did now, when she was scared to death about her mental and physical health, she would rather deal with it on her own than share it with him?

What good is a marriage if I can't share with my husband everything, even my darkest thoughts? she wondered.

And a relationship is a two-way street. Why did he never seem to want to share with her what he was thinking and feeling? She could no longer excuse it as that he was just the reticent type. When she was being honest with herself, she had to confess that she was holding back with him as much as he was holding back on her.

"So where are you now?" she asked the deep silence within the house as she wandered from the living room into the den, where Nate did his schoolwork, correcting papers and preparing lesson plans.

She considered going for a drive, maybe checking the school parking lot and a couple of the bars downtown to see if she could find his car, but she was too tired to go out. She sighed as she sat down at the desk and noticed that Nate's computer was still on. He'd minimized a window and then must have forgotten to turn the machine off. Kiera had no idea what—if anything—she expected to find when she moved the cursor to the small box at the bottom of the screen and brought up the window.

It was a list of names, and it didn't take her long to realize it was his class and homeroom lists for the new school year. But something caught her attention right away, and a rush of anger and trepidation went through her as she scanned the screen. The name Katherine Burroughs in Nate's homeroom list immediately jumped out because, although it was in the same font size as the other entries, the home phone number was highlighted in red.

"Interesting," Kiera muttered as she leaned back in the chair and stared at the number.

She recognized the name, of course. Katie was a senior, like Trista, but Trista and she weren't friends . . . not anymore, at least. Back in elementary school, they had been best friends, but once they entered junior high school, they had drifted apart as they sought out other peer groups. From what Kiera knew, Katie had gravitated to the "smart" kids, the college-bound students who were on the honor roll and active in sports and extracurricular activities. Trista had gravitated to the less academic crowd . . . the "losers" and "stoners," as they were called.

A sense of lost opportunity and regret filled Kiera as she faced the fact that somewhere along the line, she had lost touch with her daughter. Or maybe, more honestly, her daughter had lost her way. Even now with Robbie Townsend dead, Kiera knew there would be more Robbies in the future. She didn't see how she could get Trista off the path she was now following, not without something major happening.

Until junior high, Trista had been a bright and accomplished student, but the older she got, the more detached and hostile she became. She had threatened to move out of the house and move in with Robbie but, for whatever reason, she had come home last night . . . the night Robbie died. Kiera knew without being told that they'd had an argument, but she had no idea what it had been about. Trista certainly wasn't talking to her.

As she leaned back in the chair, her eyes kept being drawn to the highlighted phone number on the screen, and she kept asking herself, *Why is it highlighted?* She was half tempted to call it and ask if Nate was here.

And then another thought hit her . . . a thought that, at first, she wanted to dismiss as being totally ridiculous; but the more she thought about it, the more it made a twisted kind of sense.

Was it Katie's mother Nate was seeing, or was he having an affair with one of his students?

What if he's been dating Katie Burroughs?

"No . . . that's just . . . wrong," Kiera whispered as she shook her head in adamant denial. She knew that Katie's parents, Roger and Teresa, were getting a divorce. If Nate was fooling around, it made a lot more sense that he was trying to get something going with Mrs. Burroughs. He wouldn't . . . he *couldn't* be having an affair with someone the same age as their daughter . . .

Could he?

Kiera wished she could convince herself that she was just being paranoid, but Nate hadn't always been loyal to her. She should recognize the warning signs by now—the uncommunicativeness, the emotional distance, the perfunctory way he dealt with her even after her surgery. If it wasn't Katie Burroughs, it certainly was her mother Nate was pursuing . . . and—maybe—had already caught.

More than ever, Kiera was tempted to call him on his cell or else go out looking for him; but the truth was, she didn't have the energy to confront him about anything right now. She would wait and watch for more indications that he was fooling around.

Besides, what if her suspicions were unfounded?

Worse, what if she was projecting onto him what *she* was really feeling?

What if she was at the point where she finally had to admit that she wanted to leave him?

Putting it so bluntly staggered her, but she had to admit that's what was on her mind. The question was, how—and when—did she begin to approach it?

Heaving another sigh, she minimized the window on the computer, got up from the desk, and left the room. The darkness both inside and outside the house seemed to press in on her. As she walked upstairs, she had to fight the impulse to run to her bedroom, slam the door shut and lock it, and hide there.

"Hide . . . from what?" she asked herself in a tight, trembling voice. "From being honest with myself?"

She knew that Trista wasn't home, either, and as she passed her daughter's closed bedroom door, she considered going into there to have a look around. Maybe she would find something that would clue her in on what was bugging Trista. She hesitated outside the bedroom door, her hand poised to turn the doorknob as she debated what she was considering doing.

It wasn't really fair to Trista, she knew, to snoop around in her room. What did she expect to find, anyway, a stash of drugs . . . or something worse?

What could possibly be worse? Kiera wondered, and

she watched as if someone else was doing it as she turned the doorknob and opened the door. Reaching inside, she snapped on the light and then moved slowly into the room. She didn't want—or dare—to touch anything, because she knew Trista would be able to tell she'd been here, but she wandered around the room, checking things out without touching or moving anything.

All in all, it was a typical high school girl's room, with posters of rock bands—at least Kiera thought they were rock bands—on the wall, dirty laundry piled up on the bed and floor, and CDs and DVDs scattered around on the windowsill and the table with the stereo system and TV. A wave of nostalgia came over her when she remembered the cute, loving little girl her daughter had been. She seemed like another person now.

When she glanced at the things on Trista's desk, Kiera saw something that made her heart skip a beat. Right out there in plain sight was a home pregnancy test kit.

"Oh my God," Kiera muttered as she covered her mouth with one hand and shuddered.

So *this* was the "something worse!" Trista thought she might be pregnant. It was no real surprise to learn that her daughter was sexually active. They had talked about it, and Kiera had told her numerous times to use protection for a variety of reasons, but the possibility that she was actually pregnant—and it would have to be by Robbie Townsend—was devastating.

Is this why Trista was so upset last night?

Is this why she and Robbie had been arguing?

Was this why she had come home right after she made such a big deal about moving out of the house?

If she was pregnant, Kiera wondered what she planned to do about it.

Had she been pressuring Robbie to marry her so they could have the baby together, and he had refused?

The side flap of the box was torn open, but Kiera couldn't tell if the test was still inside the box or not. She was tempted to pick up the test kit and inspect it to see if it had been used yet, but she was afraid Trista would know if she moved it.

In a way, though, Kiera thought it didn't matter. Just the concern that Trista *might* be pregnant was reason enough to worry.

No, a voice inside her head told her. *It's not really any of your business . . . Trista has her own choices to make . . . her own life to lead . . . and you really can't influence it . . . not anymore.*

At the same time, another voice in her head was telling her that it absolutely *was* her business.

Trista's your daughter . . . if she's in trouble, it's definitely your duty . . . as a parent . . . to talk to her and help her figure out what to do next.

Her daughter might be about to make one of the most momentous decisions of her life, and Kiera knew she should help her make her decision whether or not she wanted or appreciated her mother's help.

At least Trista wasn't home right now, Kiera thought, so she had plenty of time to think about how she would handle this. After another quick glance around the room, she turned and left, closing the door quietly behind her. As she was turning to go down the hall to her own bedroom, she found herself staring at the closed door to Trista's bathroom. Without a moment's hesitation, she opened the door and went in. When she turned on the light, her gaze went immediately to the full-to-overflowing wastebasket. Right there on the top was the pregnancy test.

"Please don't let it be . . . Please don't let it be," she muttered as she bent down and picked it up. Her breath caught in her throat when she saw two narrow pink lines on the test strip.

She knew what they meant.

Trista was pregnant with Robbie's Townsend's baby!

CHAPTER 10

Breaking Point

~1~

If anything, the next morning things were worse than ever. Kiera was so filled with anxiety, doubts, and fears that she couldn't even think straight, much less decide which of these feelings were legitimate and which were products of her imagination. Worst of all, though, was the nagging feeling that she had lost some vital part of herself. At times, she was certain some portion of her brain functions were shutting down or gone entirely. She wondered if there might be another growth in her brain, only this time, of course, it would be cancerous.

Her clearest, most reasonable thought was that this was just part of her recovery from surgery. The operation had to have changed her in some fundamental ways, but maybe these changes were more serious than her doctors or she suspected.

As scary as that thought was, it made sense.

Even if the tumor they'd removed *wasn't* cancerous, it must have been putting pressure on other parts of her brain. Depending on how long it had been there, over the years the undetected growth must have forced her brain to function in certain ways. Now that the pressure was relieved, it was inevitable that she would perceive things differently.

That made perfect sense, but it wasn't just worrying about her physical health. There were other things weighing her down that she needed to sort out. For one, she still hadn't fully dealt with her reaction to Liz's death.

Her murder, she reminded herself.

She'd been so preoccupied with her surgery and recovery she hadn't had time to grieve. To the best of her knowledge, the police still hadn't made much—if any—progress finding the killer. She couldn't talk to Jon about it because, frankly, she was afraid of him. Her impression was that the police were treating this as a simple robbery that had gone wrong. They were doing their best to solve the crime, working with the state investigative unit, but until they actually had her killer behind bars, no one—not she or Jon or anyone else—had any sense of closure.

Kiera still couldn't think about Jon without shuddering at the memory of what he had said to her the day of Liz's funeral. How could he come on to her like that as if he hadn't just buried his wife? It was beyond insensitive—it was downright creepy. If he thought for one second they could somehow rekindle their relationship, he was seriously deluded. Every hour, awake or asleep, she dreaded hearing the phone ring because it might be him, wanting to talk to her.

As for Robbie Townsend's death . . . as guilty as she felt about it, she had to be honest with herself and admit that she was relieved, almost happy when she'd heard the news. Of course, she had to express sympathy and concern for Trista's loss, but the tension and distance between her and her daughter were getting to be too much to bear. Things were only worse now that she was convinced her daughter was pregnant. When she was honest with herself, Kiera had to admit to herself that she had neither the energy nor the desire even to try to repair the damage to her relationship both with Trista and Nate.

Following the surgery, she felt in so many ways as if she literally had become a different person. It didn't help that she was hallucinating and having dreams that were much too vivid to be just dreams. She wanted to believe she had imagined what had happened yesterday, before the cops came, when her image reflected in the window hadn't moved when she moved and then actually spoke to her. There was no other way to look at it. She had engaged in a two-way conversation . . . with herself. The added pressure of suspecting Nate was fooling around behind her back— *maybe even with one of his students!*—and the strong indication that Trista was pregnant made her feel like she was about to lose her mind . . . if she hadn't already.

Was she schizophrenic or suffering from some kind of psychosis or other mental disease?

When she got out of bed in the morning, she couldn't shake the feeling that someone was lurking nearby, watching her. She was terrified that, any time she turned around and looked anywhere in the house or out a window, she would see something that the rational part of her brain would tell her couldn't possibly be real.

No matter what else she thought, she was absolutely convinced that what had happened yesterday had been real. She had no doubt that if she looked in any window or mirror in the house, she would see that part of her she had lost. Someone or something was definitely close by, just out of sight, and it drove her crazy that she couldn't figure out what it was. All she had to do, she told herself, was adjust her senses a little . . . just shift the way she looked at things, and she would see and hear her other self.

But if there really was a piece of her that had somehow separated from her, what was she trying to tell herself? And why, after all these years, was she still so obsessed about what had happened to Billy all those years ago?

She wished she could ignore these thoughts, but she couldn't push them aside as she went downstairs and busied herself with making breakfast for Nate. He was already in the shower, getting ready to go to school. He had come home at some ungodly hour last night, well past midnight. Kiera had been lying awake in bed for hours, trying to fall asleep when she heard him clumping around downstairs. At one point, she'd heard a glass clink and knew he was pouring a drink. When he had finally come to bed, she had pretended to be asleep, but she had noticed that after he washed up and got into bed with her, he never said a word to her . . . not even a kiss and a whispered, "Good night." Lying on his side with his back to her, he had fallen asleep long before Kiera had finally drifted off.

"I'm losing it . . . I'm really *losing* it," she whispered. Her vision blurred with tears as she filled the coffee carafe with water and then dropped two slices of bread into the toaster. In spite of the gnawing coldness in her stomach, she didn't really feel like eating. She couldn't even muster up enough enthusiasm to make breakfast for Nate before he went off to work. He could make do with a bowl of cold cereal. As for Trista, Kiera wasn't sure if she had come home or spent the night with a friend. If she was home, Kiera figured she'd spend the day in her bedroom.

And where does that leave me? she wondered as she mechanically moved around the kitchen, barely paying attention to what she was doing. The toast popped . . . the coffee started to sputter in the carafe . . . the sound of running water from upstairs cut off, and all the while, the apprehension winding up inside her got steadily worse.

Something was going to happen, and soon.

Who can I talk to? she wondered.

There had to be *someone* she trusted enough to confess to about what she was going through . . . but who? One by one, she went through her family members, friends, doctors, even the minister of the church she had stopped attending many years ago. There wasn't a single person she felt comfortable about approaching.

That left her with just one thought.

Looking up, she stared at her reflection in the kitchen window over the sink. The bright daylight washed out most of the details, making her appear transparent, and that's exactly how she felt—like a ghost that was fading away. She studied the thin line of her mouth and the narrowed, worried squint of her eyes. She held her breath and stared at herself, waiting for her reflection to move independently of her, but both she and her reflection remained motionless, staring into each other's eyes until she lost all sense of who or what she was, herself or her reflection.

"Ummm . . . that smells good."

Nate's voice, speaking suddenly behind her, surprised Kiera, so she let out a tiny squeak of surprise as she spun around to see her husband.

They locked eyes for a moment, but then Kiera turned away. It unnerved her to realize that she couldn't stand to look at him right now. What she really wanted to do was ask him where he had been so late last night, but she was afraid if she spoke now, she would scream at him and tell him to get out of the house and leave her alone.

A surge of irrational anger swept over her like a fast-moving thunderstorm. Her body was trembling as she stepped to one side so Nate could pour himself a cup of coffee.

"You eat already?" he asked, his voice sounding *oh* so casual as he spooned sugar into the cup, added milk, and stirred.

"Not really," Kiera said hollowly.

She was staring at the window again, looking past her reflection to the yard beyond.

Is that what I've become in my own home . . . ? A fading ghost . . . ? She struggled to control the emotions welling up inside her. *No kiss? . . . Not even a touch or a quick peck on the cheek? . . . I might as well not even* be *here.*

Nate was perfectly capable of taking care of himself. What would it matter if she just disappeared? He and Trista and everyone else in her life would get along just fine without her . . . maybe even better.

"This for me?" Nate asked, indicating the toast when it popped.

Kiera bit down on her lower lip to keep from saying something she might regret and nodded.

"Thanks." He grabbed the two slices and put them on a paper plate. "You having anything?"

"Not just yet," Kiera said, amazed that she could speak at all.

She was still staring out the window, past her ghostly reflection, when a crazy thought entered her mind. She was suddenly convinced that she wasn't looking at *her* reflection in the window; she was seeing a version of herself that was standing on the back lawn and gazing back at her in the kitchen. And Kiera thought that this person who *looked* like her and *moved* like her really *was* her. It didn't make rational sense, but she was sure that the "her" she thought she was, the person standing by the sink in the kitchen, was no longer the real "her."

~2~

Kiera squealed and jumped when the telephone rang. She hadn't been able to eat breakfast and was lying on the couch, trying to quiet the thoughts that still raged in her head. She grabbed the phone and looked at the caller ID, surprised to see that no number was displayed.

Probably a telemarketer, she thought as she considered whether or not she would answer it. The phone rang a second time and, not wanting to disturb Trista, who might be in her room asleep, Kiera pressed the Talk button.

"Hello?" she said. Her throat was so constricted she thought her voice sounded like someone else's.

There was a moment of silence when the caller didn't say anything. Kiera was about to hang up when she heard . . . something . . . a faint noise like a long, low sigh.

"Hello," she said again as a chill rippled up the back of her neck.

The person on the line sighed again, louder this time. The sound made Kiera's stomach lurch as icy cold rushed up into her chest.

"Who *is* this?" she said, but no answer came.

She wanted to hang up, but she pressed the phone to her ear, straining to hear. After another few seconds that seemed to stretch into minutes, a voice spoke; but it sounded far-away, and she couldn't make out what it said.

"We must have a bad connection," Kiera said, but even as she said it she knew that wasn't the case.

The voice spoke again—or was still speaking—but no

matter how hard she strained to catch even a word or two, Kiera couldn't make out anything. The dense, muffled silence seemed to mock her. Kiera wanted to believe this was a prank call, but she knew better.

"I'm hanging up now," she said. "Don't call again," but before she took the phone away from her ear, a single word came through to her.

"Don't."

It was so faint she thought she must have imagined it, but the tension in her stomach intensified.

"Who is this? What do you want?" she whispered. She was trying to keep her voice down so she wouldn't disturb Trista, who was still in bed.

Again, the voice spoke, but Kiera still couldn't make out anything. She was convinced that, whoever this was, they were trying to tell her something important. She thought she caught the words "meet me" but wasn't sure.

"Are you on a cell? Call me back. Maybe you'll get a better connection."

She thought the person said, "not much time," but again wasn't sure. She braced herself and said, "Call me back. I want to talk to you," but she wasn't sure she really wanted to. The voice conveyed a sense of urgency, of desperation and confusion that matched her own. Her hand was trembling as she pressed the button to disconnect. Her shoulders dropped as she exhaled and slumped back against the couch, staring blankly ahead.

Will they call back? she wondered as she squeezed the phone in her hand. She was almost convinced she had imagined what had just happened, that she had fallen asleep on the couch and dreamed it. She was waiting for a call that was never going to come.

The living room glowed with warm, golden sunlight.

Kiera could tell it was going to be a beautiful day. Nothing in the room looked out of place, but somehow, everything was . . . wrong, somehow. The living room looked foreign, as if she didn't belong in it. She was afraid the problem was in *her*, but she couldn't shake the feeling that someone was close by, wanting to communicate with her. But as nervous and worried as she was, she also was positive at least some of what was wrong wasn't just in her head.

It was out there . . . somewhere, and it was trying to find her.

"What do you *want*?" she whispered, trembling as she looked at the phone in her hand.

Just calm down, she told herself, but the feeling of not belonging was getting steadily stronger. The telephone was sweaty in her grip, and as she stared at it, she was filled with a rush of disappointment that the caller hadn't called back.

Maybe it had been just a telemarketer who had gone on to the next number on the list. If the call was really important, the person would have called back right away. It could have been anyone—Nate or Jon or maybe Marsha or Joanie, calling to see how she was doing and then deciding not to bother her.

As much as she wanted to believe that, something deep inside was telling her that something was seriously wrong. The twisting feeling of panic and desperation was so strong inside her she wanted to scream. At the same time, she wished she could curl up somewhere and hide. She jumped when the phone suddenly rang again—once, sharply. The sound drilled her ears.

"Hello!" she said, practically shouting as she thumbed the Talk button and put the phone to her ear.

The only sound was the high-pitched buzz of a disconnected call that droned in her ear like an angry wasp. When

Kiera swallowed, the sound was distorted over the phone with a curious echo effect, sounding much louder than normal.

Tears flooded Kiera's eyes, turning the shadows in the room into gauzy, gray smears that shifted wherever she looked.

I'm losing my mind, she thought as warm, slick tears streamed down her face. Her hand dropped to her side, and she loosened her grip on the phone. It fell to the floor, hitting the carpet with a hollow thud that sounded faraway.

Something's really wrong with my brain.

As that thought sank in, another thought, even more frightening, rose in her mind, and she was suddenly convinced that the operation hadn't fixed anything . . . It had only made things worse . . . and now she was going to die.

~3~

Kiera awoke and found that she was lying on the couch in the living room. She blinked her eyes and groaned as she came to. Nate was standing in the doorway. She had no idea what time it was, but the angle of sunlight made her think it was late in the afternoon.

"What happened?" she asked when she saw his face, pale and blank as he took a step closer to the couch.

"At school," Nate said, staring straight ahead as he sat down on the nearest chair. His eyes were bugging from his head, and his lips were thin and compressed against his teeth as he lowered his gaze and shook his head. "We had . . . One of our students . . . a senior . . . died last night."

"Oh my God!" Kiera said as she sat up on the couch, forgetting for a moment her own problems. "Who was it? What happened?"

"Katie Burroughs," Nate said, barely able to say the name.

Kiera couldn't help but notice the way his voice twisted off when he said the name, and the first thought she had was about the highlighted phone number on his computer screen. He covered his face with his hands and shook his head.

"She—They're not sure what happened." His shoulders shivered when he sighed. "Of course, there are rumors she ODed or committed suicide, but the authorities think it might have been a . . . a heart problem. Supposedly, she had a heart murmur when she was a kid, but I . . ." He leaned back in the chair and stared up at the ceiling.

"That's so sad," Kiera said. "I . . . I can't imagine losing a child like that."

Even as she said it, she thought about Trista, who must still be upstairs, wallowing in her own misery. It struck Kiera as sad that she and her daughter hadn't communicated with any depth since Robbie's death. In a very real way, she felt as though she, too, had lost her daughter. Maybe the loss wasn't as final as death, but it was just as real.

"Her parents . . . They're divorced, right?"

Nate visibly tensed as he glanced at her and then nodded. Kiera was positive she saw the guilt written all over him, but she wasn't about to say anything now.

Nate took a breath and said, "There's a memorial service at the high school tonight. We want to help the students—especially the seniors—process this—"

His voice caught again, and Kiera could see how deeply this was affecting him and couldn't help but wonder if it was Katie, not Teresa Burroughs, he'd been seeing. She was convinced it was one or the other.

"Do you want me to come with you?" she asked.

Nate raised his gaze and looked at her, confusion on his face.

"What do you mean?"

"To the memorial. Tonight. If you want me to, I'll come with you."

Nate let out another long sigh as he leaned forward, his hands folded and his elbows on his thighs as he shook his head slowly from side to side, his chest hitching with repressed sobs. If anything, he reminded Kiera of a cornered, frightened animal.

"I . . . No. You don't have to. I—we didn't really know her parents that well. She was living with her mother. But I . . . No. It's not necessary."

"Are you sure?"

Nate looked up and gave her a long, steady stare. Kiera could see that he wanted to say something, but he remained silent. Once again, she was aware of the impossible distance between them. For so long, she hadn't even been aware of it; now that she *was*, she knew it was already too late to do anything about it.

"I'm sure," he said. The knuckles of his hand were white because of the grip he had on the armrests of the chair. "How's Trista doing? You talk to her?"

Feeling suddenly guilty about falling asleep on the couch, Kiera shook her head and said, "No. She hasn't been down all day."

Nate started to say something but obviously thought better of it and just shook his head as he got up from the chair. Without another word, he went upstairs. A moment later, Kiera heard him knock on Trista's door.

"Mind if I come in?" he said.

His voice almost didn't carry downstairs, and Kiera couldn't make out what Trista said in reply. But she heard the bedroom door open and shut. For the next fifteen or twenty minutes, she just sat there on the couch, listening to the buzzing of their voices upstairs. She couldn't hear what they were saying, but every now and then the conversation was punctuated by loud sobs as Trista cried.

Why can't I go up there, too? she wondered, feeling frantic and helpless.

She wanted to believe she was wrong, but she didn't feel welcome. She didn't belong up there with them, sharing their daughter's grief, and she was convinced there was nothing she could do or say to get any closer to her husband or her daughter. Whatever was missing from their lives, whether she was imagining it or not, it had taken a terrible toll on both her and her family.

Even worse, a voice hissed inside her head. *It's only going to get worse.*

~4~

"It's late. Where've you been?" Kiera asked sleepily. She rolled over in bed and blinked when a sudden burst of light filled the bedroom.

"Just out," Nate said.

Kiera heard his voice slur and knew he'd been drinking. She was still disoriented after being awakened so suddenly and watched as Nate staggered into the bathroom that adjoined their bedroom. She listened as he urinated, a long, noisy stream, and then flushed. Without bothering to brush his teeth, he came over to the bed, peeling off his clothes as he came. He almost lost his balance and had to hop a few times when he was taking off his pants, but he made it to the bed and sat down heavily before kicking his pants free.

"You're loaded," Kiera said, feeling more sadness than

anger. This was one more thing that highlighted the distance between them, and she wondered if she'd ever get used to feeling so alone.

"Umm . . . So?" Nate said, exhaling noisily as he peeled his shirt off and threw it onto the floor. Wearing nothing but boxer shorts, he collapsed back onto the bed and let out a belch. Kiera caught the sour stench of beer on his breath and wrinkled her nose in disgust.

"So how was the memorial?" she asked. She wished she could feel as though they could still communicate the way they used to, but she was convinced they both had become different people from the people they were.

"How do you think? . . . It sucked." He belched again. "What were you doing there?"

"Me? What are you talking about?"

"Were you following me?"

Kiera looked at him and shook her head.

"No. I never left the house."

"You sure?" He slurred the words. "I could've sworn I saw your car in the parking lot."

"I swear to God, it wasn't me," Kiera said, but as soon as the words were out of her mouth, she froze.

But what if it was me? . . . What if I drove down to the high school to check up on him because I don't trust him? . . . What if I did it and don't even remember doing it?

Nate hadn't turned off the bedroom light, so Kiera reached out and flipped the switch, plunging the room back into darkness. She felt safer in the darkness, but she knew he was too drunk to know what she was thinking or feeling.

"It must have been difficult. Tell me about it," she said as she settled down with her back to him. "It's not like you to get so drunk."

Nate grunted but said nothing. For a long time, he lay

there, breathing heavily in the darkness. Kiera thought he must have fallen asleep or else passed out, and she felt a surge of resentment. She had been sound asleep, but now she was wide-awake, so she lay there, staring into the darkness and wondering what was going on.

It *wasn't* like him to get drunk like this, but he might be just as aware as she was that their relationship was heading toward a brick wall.

"Nate?" she whispered, poking him with her elbow.

Nate groaned and snorted, then let out a loud fart, but he didn't move. Kiera thought he might be awake and faking being asleep because he didn't want to talk. Maybe he was afraid he'd end up confessing that he'd been having an affair with Teresa Burroughs . . . or Katie.

The bitterness of that thought made her throat burn. She couldn't take a deep enough breath, and her chest ached.

"Nate," she said, a little louder. "We have to talk."

"Talk . . . 'bout what?" His voice was thick and slurred.

Kiera shifted around so she was facing him and leaned on her elbow. Her eyes had adjusted to the dark, and she could see the rounded contours of his body beneath the covers. She wanted so much to reach out and touch him, caress him like she used to, but she couldn't bring herself to do it. Her skin crawled at the mere thought of touching him, and that only made her sadder.

"Maybe we could start with why you decided to get so drunk tonight."

Nate let out a blubbering sigh that filled her nose with the sour smell of beer.

"It just . . . happened," he said, sounding a little impatient. "I was . . . The memorial was tough, so I went out for a few."

"More than a few."

"Aw right. More than a few. What's the big deal?"

"Besides driving drunk, you mean?" Kiera sighed, not liking the direction this was taking. "Why did you do it? What's really bothering you?"

For a long time, Nate didn't say anything.

In that time, Kiera thought of dozens of things she could say. She knew she should tell him that she was afraid their marriage was in jeopardy, that they had nothing holding them together except their daughter. She wanted to tell him that she could see her whole life crumbling down around her and that she was afraid she was losing her mind, that she felt alone and deserted and wasn't sure she even wanted to live with him and Trista anymore.

Or maybe she should tell him what was at the bottom of it all, that her guilt about what had happened nearly thirty years ago to Billy Carroll—what she *had* and *hadn't* done that night—was eating away her sanity.

"Nate . . ." she said, her voice choking as tears filled her eyes.

The atmosphere in the room seemed to change abruptly. Kiera sensed rather than saw vague figures, shifting in and out of sight in the darkness. If she hadn't been crying, if she could see clearly, she was sure she would be able to see Billy Carroll standing at the foot of their bed, glaring at her with cold, dead eyes.

"You saw him kill me . . . and you didn't tell anyone!"

Kiera covered her mouth with her clenched fist to stifle the scream building up inside her. The feeling that *someone* was in the room was so strong it became a burning pressure inside her chest . . . a pressure that was going to burst out of her no matter how hard she tried to contain it.

"Can we talk about this in the morning? I hav'ta sleep."

Nate's voice sounded cold and cruel. "Would you *please* lemme sleep?"

The rush of panic inside Kiera didn't diminish. She listened to the rapid hammering of her pulse in her ears. The skin on the back of her neck was tingling, and her breath came in short, burning gasps.

"No," she said, almost a whimper, but then, as clearly as if the person was in the room with them, a voice said, *"You know it wasn't an accident! . . . You know he did it on purpose!"*

Kiera thought she recognized Billy Carroll's voice, and no matter how much she wanted to believe it was all in her head, she suddenly realized that it didn't matter whether she imagined it or not . . . It didn't matter whether the voice was real or not . . . what it was saying was painfully true, and *that's* what she had to face.

That night by the river, Jon hadn't stepped on the accelerator by mistake. He had done it on purpose. He had gripped the steering wheel with both hands and aimed the car right at Billy because he wanted him dead. He wanted to *kill* him. All these years, she had denied the truth, and that's why Billy's ghost—real or not—was haunting her.

"I can't take it anymore," she whispered in a strangled voice.

She was lost in misery as she lay there in the dark, listening to the heavy pounding inside her head. Darkness swirled around her, closing in, squeezing tighter and tighter until she could hardly breathe. Vague, vaporous shapes drifted around the bed, looming in close and then receding, fading away whenever she looked directly at them.

"Can't take what?"

Nate spoke so suddenly Kiera wondered if he had spoken

at all, or if it was in her head. She shivered as she sucked in a shallow breath, but she couldn't speak.

"You don't believe me? 'S that what you're saying?"

Nate spoke louder now, and Kiera caught the hostile edge in it.

"You *really* wanna know why I got drunk?"

The bed creaked as he rolled over to face her. His eyes seemed to glow with an unnatural light in the surrounding darkness.

"I got drunk tonight because I realized something about myself . . . and about us."

Oh, Jesus, Kiera thought, bracing herself. *Here it comes! . . . I'm not ready for this . . . Not now.*

Nate sat up suddenly, tossing the bedcovers aside. He got out of bed and started pacing back and forth. Kiera cringed, afraid he was going to lash out at her and hit her, but he paced back and forth at the foot of the bed. She sat up in bed, pulling her arms and legs protectively to her chest.

"No," she said. "Don't do this." She wasn't even sure if he heard her. "Don't say anything we'll regret. You've been drinking, and you—"

"Well, one of us has to say it, goddamn it!" Nate's voice was still slurred, but it was loud enough to fill the room. "One of us has to admit that this is it . . . our marriage is down the shitter."

"Please, Nate."

"Jesus, Kiera! Don't be such a fool! *You* know it and *I* know it! It's just not there anymore. And do you wanna know what I was gonna do? Do you?"

"Please, Nate. Come back to bed. We can talk about it in the morning when we're both feeling better."

"No, goddamn it! We're gonna talk about it now! You

wanna know why I got drunk." He took a rasping breath. "I got drunk because for the past several months all I've been thinking about is how I could get the fuck out of here . . . out of this marriage."

Kiera was crying as she shook her head from side to side. She shrank back as his words slammed into her like sledgehammers. His body was a huge, dark silhouette that loomed threateningly in the darkness. All she could think was that he was going to lose control and hurt her. The rage coming out of him so suddenly was terrifying.

"Stop it. Please. You'll wake up Trista. She's got enough to deal with."

Somehow, her words got through to Nate. He stopped pacing and let out a long, groaning sigh as he sat down on the foot of the bed and hunched over.

"We have to be honest with each other," he said, his voice low and controlled. "Even now . . . 'specially now we have to be honest."

"I know," Kiera said, fighting the impulse to reach out to assure him. This wasn't how she had imagined it would happen, but—finally—it was out there.

"There's something else I have to tell you."

Oh, God, Kiera thought. It felt like a cold spike had just pierced her heart. *Here it comes.*

"That girl who died . . . ?" Nate said, his voice hushed now. All the anger had drained away. "Katie Burroughs. I was—"

"No," Kiera suddenly shouted, cutting him off. "Don't say it." In a quick, fluid motion, she got out of the bed and headed for the door. "I'll sleep downstairs. We can talk about this in the morning when we're both more rational."

"Kiera. Wait. It's not what you—"

But whatever he was going to say was cut off when she

stepped out into the hall and slammed the bedroom door shut behind her.

"Don't you *dare* come downstairs! I don't even want to *see* you right now!"

She clenched her fist and pounded it against the door so hard it hurt. Clutching her hand to her chest, she turned and ran downstairs to the living room, sobbing like a wounded animal. She threw herself onto the couch, feeling so full of rage and hurt she couldn't think straight. All she knew for sure was, if Nate had been about to confess that he had a crush on a high school girl, that he'd been *screwing* someone their daughter's age, she couldn't stand to be in the same house with him.

"I should leave . . . right now," she whispered heatedly. "I should go back upstairs. Get dressed. Grab a few things, and leave!"

The house was unnaturally quiet. The only light in the living room was the streetlight that filtered in from outside. Kiera trembled as she cowered on the couch, convinced Trista had heard them but was too afraid to let them know. It wasn't like this was the first time. Kiera had no idea what to do. Should she try to talk to Trista . . . or run screaming from the house . . . or bury her head under a pile of pillows and blankets and wish she could just die? Maybe she should go back upstairs, confront Nate, and tell him he was absolutely right. Their marriage had been a sham from the start, and she had never trusted him. All they had to do now was face up to it and get a divorce.

Because the truth was, she *did* want out of the marriage, and tonight she had finally reached the point where she could admit it to herself. It had nothing to do with Liz's murder, her operation, Robbie's death, or even Billy Carroll's death. It had *everything* to do with the fact that if there had ever been any genuine love and affection between them, it was gone now.

Kiera was paralyzed. As much as she wanted to do something right now to resolve things, she knew she had to calm down so she could think things through. She let out a shrill shriek and jumped off the couch when the telephone suddenly rang. For a blinding second, she couldn't believe it had actually rung, but before it rang again, she picked up the receiver and pressed it to her ear.

"Hello?" she whispered, hearing the heavy sound of her breathing through the receiver. She waited for a reply, but when it came, it was so faint she couldn't make it out. It almost sounded like an echo of her own voice when it said, *"Hello?"*

"Who is this?" Kiera said, struggling to keep her voice down so Nate and Trista wouldn't hear.

Again, the only sound was an echo of her voice, saying, *"Who is this?"*

Convinced the line was dead and she was just talking to herself, she was about to hang up when a woman's voice said, *"I have to talk to you."*

Kiera froze, her heart suddenly heaving in her chest. Even though the voice was distorted, it sounded exactly like her own. She had a quick but sharp impression that she was someplace else, talking to someone—a stranger who was sitting on the couch in her living room. She suddenly snapped back and, swallowing hard, said, "Tell me where and when."

For several heartbeats, there was no reply. Then the voice came, even fainter. *"Oh, you know where."* After a short pause, the voice said, *"Go there right now. It's the only way I can get through."*

There was a soft click, and then the high-pitched buzzing of the dial tone.

Kiera's heart was racing in her throat. She found it all but impossible to take a breath as a sheen of sweat broke out across her face. Her hands felt clammy as she slowly, mechanically replaced the phone on its base and then raised them to touch the bandage on her forehead.

Even if the voice wasn't real, she knew what she had to do.

A chill wound slowly through her body. She wasn't sure she had the strength to get up off the couch, much less get dressed and drive out to where she knew she had to go, but she had to find it.

"She said to go there *now*," she whispered harshly, trying to bolster her courage, even though she was left with the impression she had been talking to herself on the phone.

Kiera slowly got up off the couch and, moving like she was in a dream, went back upstairs to the bedroom. Nate was already asleep—or else passed out—and snoring loudly.

Thank God, she thought as she turned on a light and for several seconds just stood there, staring at him. Bitterness and hurt filled her, but when she tiptoed over to the closet, she knew she was doing the right thing by leaving him tonight—maybe forever.

She grabbed a clean pair of jeans and a T-shirt, then took a pair of socks from her bureau drawer and got dressed. Without a backward glance, she walked out of the bedroom, closing the door quietly behind her, and went downstairs. She put on her sneakers, then grabbed her jacket, purse, and car keys, and walked out to the garage before the faint voice in her head could tell her to turn around and go back.

As frightened as she was, she had to follow through with this, even if she had imagined it all. If nothing else, she needed to get out of the house and get away from Nate so she could clear her head. There was no way she was going back upstairs and getting back into bed as if none of this had happened.

And maybe, she thought, *a drive out to the river is just what I need.*

CHAPTER 11

Mirror Image

~1~

I can't believe I'm really doing this.

A disturbing sense of unreality gripped Kiera as she drove through downtown Stratford, heading out to River Road. It was well past two o'clock in the morning, and most of the houses and businesses were dark except for a couple of homes where the blue-green flicker of some insomniac's television lit up the night. She couldn't help but wonder how many of the lives being lived in those houses were as sad and confused as hers.

Stop it with the self-pity, she chided herself time and again, but she couldn't let it go. *When is a good time for self-pity if not now?*

Her grip on the steering wheel tightened, and she slouched down in the car seat when, up ahead, she saw a parked police cruiser. It was idling in the town park next to the war memorial. A cloud of exhaust rose behind it like a small tornado. Wondering why she felt so guilty, she silently prayed that the cop wouldn't pull out behind her. The last thing she needed was anyone asking her what she was doing out so late at night. She didn't exhale until she was well past the cop and, glancing at her rearview mirror, saw that he hadn't moved.

The truth was, she wasn't sure about what she was doing. She knew well enough where she was going, but she had no idea how or if that would solve anything. For more than twenty-five years, she had tried to convince herself that Billy's death had been accidental, and she and Jon had done the right thing by not reporting it.

Why ruin both their lives by admitting to murder?

It certainly wouldn't bring Billy back.

But she had to admit the truth, at least to herself. It *hadn't* been an accident. Jon had purposely gunned the engine and run Billy over. She wanted to believe he hadn't intended actually to *kill* Billy. Maybe he'd just wanted to scare him so he'd leave them alone. But the end result had been the same.

Billy was dead. Cut off in his youth. He never got to live his life, and for almost thirty years, her life and her sanity had been all but destroyed by the guilt of knowing—and denying—what had happened.

What did Jon think about all of this, if he thought about it at all?

Ever since he returned to Stratford, Kiera had sensed something wasn't quite right with him. They'd rekindled their friendship right away, picking it up as if the intervening years hadn't mattered. Thankfully, neither of them had said or done anything to try to take it any further . . . until the day of Liz's funeral.

That didn't mean Kiera hadn't *thought* about it. Even after more than twenty years with minimal contact, usually Christmas and birthday cards, she would have been lying if she said she wasn't still attracted to Jon at least a little bit.

But that day at his house, he had said things that made it clear that he thought about her romantically, too, and she wasn't sure what she thought about that.

Regardless, that didn't explain the shipwreck her life had become . . . especially, it seemed, since her surgery.

It might be as simple as that.

Maybe she was feeling so threatened because the surgery had forced her to face her own mortality head-on. The surgery might have done nothing more than highlight the pathetic truth that she wasn't living the life she had imagined she would all those years ago.

Who really does? she wondered. *Does anyone get to live the life they imagined? . . . Or is life simply a matter of how well or how poorly you handle the random disasters that happen to anyone?*

Thoughts like this occupied her, so she was barely conscious of driving. Only after she had passed through town and was heading out on River Road did she snap to and realize the import of what she was doing.

Her nervousness was like a heavy iron ball in the pit of her stomach. She wondered if she actually had talked to someone on the phone, or if she imagined it all.

Would there even be someone out at the river to meet her, or had she lost her mind and was blowing things way out of proportion? Even if someone was there, how would that solve the more immediate problems in her life?

"Just relax," she whispered, but she maintained such a tight grip on the steering wheel that her arms and shoulders ached. She wanted to believe she was just taking a late-night drive to clear her head after arguing with Nate.

"That's all it is . . . Nothing's going to happen," she said, not really believing it. Even when she got to the place where Billy had died, no one would be there. Nothing was going to happen. She could park the car and sit there a while and think things over. Maybe she'd stay until the sunrise, and then she'd drive home to face Nate. Once he was awake and sober, they could talk rationally about what they had said last night. Maybe by then she'd have a better grip on how she felt and whether or not she really wanted to leave him.

"Just clear your head," she whispered, but when she glanced into the rearview mirror and saw her eyes illuminated by the dim dashboard lights, she felt as though she was looking into the eyes of a stranger, someone who had died a long time ago.

"Nearly thirty years ago," she said as the chill that gripped her got stronger.

The crescent moon had already set in the west. Darkness filled the woods that surrounded her. Her headlights pushed the darkness back, but they seemed nowhere near strong enough to hold it at bay for long. The weight of the night crushed her with a steadily mounting heaviness that made it difficult to breathe. Her heart started racing when, up ahead, she saw the turnoff and the dirt road that led to the river.

Just drive past it, whispered a voice in her head. *No one's out here . . . Nothing's going to happen.*

She felt like a helpless observer, unable to stop herself from pressing her foot down on the brake and slowing for the turn.

~2~

The night was alive with the sounds of crickets and night birds as Kiera parked the car and killed the engine. When she turned off the headlights, the parking area was plunged into darkness. For a long time, she sat there, letting her eyes adjust to the darkness as she stared out across the river and listened to the clicking sounds the engine made as it cooled down. The river glowed with a faint iridescence that, without the headlights, made the distant shore look all the darker. Faint wisps of mist blown by the cool night breeze rose from the water, twisting as they drifted through the trees.

"Okay . . . All right. I'm here," Kiera whispered, trying to calm down as she looked around. "What now?"

She rolled her window down and leaned her head out, taking several deep breaths. The damp smell of the river was strong. Tilting her head back, she looked up at the sky. The trees were etched against the dusty field of stars like black lace. Fitful gusts of wind shook the leaves. To the east, she couldn't see even a hint of approaching dawn.

Kiera was mildly surprised that no other cars were out here. When she was in high school, couples came out to the river all the time. But it was late, and times had changed since she was young. High school kids didn't "go parking" anymore. The idea struck her as quaint, almost sweet, even though, back when she was doing it, her parents didn't think it was very cute or amusing.

As she scanned the surrounding woods, Kiera couldn't get over the feeling that she wasn't alone. Somewhere out there, unseen in the darkness, someone was watching her. When she thought it might be the ghost of Billy Carroll, a quick chill shot through her, but she ignored it. She didn't *really* believe in ghosts, even though, in a place like this, it didn't take much imagination to think that within that tangled, vaporous mist she might catch a fleeting glimpse of a lost soul.

Her heart was racing so fast it felt like weak hands were trying to choke her, but she opened the car door and stepped out. The sudden glare of the dome light hurt her eyes, and she ignored the *ding-ding* warning that the keys were still in the ignition. She slammed the car door shut, cutting off the dome light, and straightened up to look around. She couldn't stop feeling vulnerable, and she was suddenly convinced that if someone was hiding in the shadows, they were a danger to her.

How long have they been waiting?

"Hello?" she called out. Her voice was feeble and twisted off to nothing as she took a few steps away from the car.

She wanted nothing more than to get back into the car and drive out of here, but she had to be sure no one was here. It was crazy, coming here so late . . . and all alone. There could be real dangers out here . . . rabid foxes . . . or bears . . . or whatever.

"So leave," she told herself, but she knew she wasn't going to do that. She was confused about a lot of things, but she knew one thing for sure—she couldn't face Nate just yet, not after what they had said to each other.

Kiera glanced to her left, knowing as soon as she did that she was looking at the spot where Jon had run Billy over. She hadn't been out here in almost thirty years—not since that night—but she knew exactly where it had happened.

At the edge of the parking lot of hard-packed dirt was a large oak tree. As much as she didn't want to, she remembered how Jon's headlights had illuminated everything with bright, glaring light. Even now in the darkness, she could imagine seeing it replayed here, night after night. If she closed her eyes, she might even be able to hear the faint sound of a revving engine . . . the scuff of tires in the dirt . . . the sudden thump that had thrown her forward so hard her head slammed against the dashboard.

She let out a low moan as she raised her hand to her forehead and touched the bandage. She started to massage her head, and a subtle tingling spread across her scalp. At first, she thought it was just the chilly night air, but as the cold touch spread down her face and neck, she started to become frightened.

Her vision telescoped as the surrounding night caved in on her. The night air felt like water washing over her skin, and she gasped when she saw a barely discernible figure standing in front of the tree.

No, my eyes are just playing tricks on me, she told herself, but even before she completed the thought, panic slammed into her like a fist.

It's not possible . . . There can't be anyone there!

Her heart skipped a few beats, and her knees started to buckle, but she caught herself and stared at the figure, willing it . . . daring it either to resolve more clearly or else fade away like the illusion she hoped it was.

Without conscious effort, she took a few steps forward. She knew she was hyperventilating. Tiny spots of light weaved across her vision like a swirl of fireflies. The pressure clutching her throat got so bad, her eyes felt like they were popping from her head.

"Who's there?" she called out, surprised that she could speak at all as she took another few steps forward.

She raised her hands as though in supplication, and

once again thought this had to be Billy Carroll's ghost. It now seemed like a perfectly rational thought.

"Are you . . . ?" Her voice choked off when the figure moved. She wanted to believe it was still just a trick of the eye. It had to be the night shadows playing on her overactive imagination, making her believe this illusion. But when she took another step closer, the vague silhouette of a person emerged from the night.

"Who are you?" she asked in a trembling voice. She wasn't sure she dared to get any closer to whoever this was and confront them. She knew she should run back to her car, lock the doors, start it up, and get the hell out of there, but she was frozen where she stood. She stared at the figure as it shifted in and out of focus, blending with the darkness.

"Who are *you*?" a woman's voice replied. The sound sliced through the night like a thin blade cutting cloth.

Kiera knew it hadn't been an echo of her voice, but she was left with that impression as the voice faded into the night. Once it was gone, she felt as though she hadn't really heard anything, that she was still imagining things, but then the figure shifted forward, moving closer to her.

"Who are you? What are you doing out here? What do you want?" Kiera asked, her voice cracking as fear spiked inside her.

"I came to see you, of course," the voice said.

Once again, even more strongly, Kiera thought the voice sounded frighteningly like her own. Not exactly the same, but close enough to unnerve her.

The figure halted, still lurking under the deepest shadows of the tree, but there was something familiar about the way this person stood. Her shoulders were squared, her hips cocked to one side. A wave of light-headedness swept over Kiera, and she staggered back a few steps, struggling to maintain her balance.

"Who *are* you?" Kiera asked in a desperate, shattered voice.

"I'm Ariel . . . Ariel McKinnon."

"Ariel," Kiera echoed. Just hearing that name filled her with alarm. A rush of memories came roaring back, convincing her all the more that she had to be dreaming or hallucinating.

"You can't be . . . How can you be . . . Ariel?"

Her voice choked off, and in the silence that followed, Kiera tried to convince herself that none of this was happening. How could anyone be standing there?

"I've come a long way to see you," the woman said. When she spoke, the voice sounded so familiar that Kiera was convinced she was listening to herself. That odd feeling of duality, of being in two places at the same time, returned, making her nauseous.

When the figure moved even closer, Kiera fought back the impulse to run back to the car. She couldn't move. She knew she must have lost her sanity.

When they were less than twenty feet apart, the woman stopped. If it had been daylight, they could have looked into each other's eyes, but that was the one thing Kiera feared most. She was afraid of who—or what—she would see.

"How did you get here?"

"I'm not entirely sure," the woman said, sounding genuinely mystified.

"But Ariel . . . Ariel was the name of—"

"I know . . . of your imaginary friend," the voice said. "But see? I'm not imaginary at all. I'm right here."

Kiera clenched her teeth to stop them from chattering as

she shook her head from side to side as if by denying what she was hearing and seeing, she could make it go away. The night was closing in with a steady, rising pressure. The stars cast faint shadows of the trees across the ground. The branches looked like claws, reaching out to grab her.

I must be losing my mind . . . she kept thinking, but she also knew that she had to trust her senses.

"I've been Ariel ever since I can remember," the woman said mildly. "You've been just as real to me as I've been to you."

"But I . . . I haven't believed in you . . . I haven't even thought of you in . . . *years*."

The woman stood her ground, her hands on her hips as she stared at Kiera. Again, even stronger, the feeling of being in two places at once came over Kiera. It seemed as if, simultaneously, she was staring wide-eyed at this person who was telling her she was her childhood imaginary friend and—somehow—she was also inside Ariel's head, watching herself cower where she stood.

"No. This is . . . impossible," Kiera whispered. "This can't be happening."

She was struggling to make sense of the situation, but no matter how hard she tried, she couldn't see how any of this was possible.

The woman lowered her head, and Kiera heard a soft sniff of laughter.

"At first, that's what I thought, too," Ariel said. "I haven't thought of you in years."

"What do you mean?"

"I mean, I had my own life, and then—I have no idea how or why, but I started thinking about you all the time, and then . . . I ended up here . . . back in Maine. It feels like a dream."

Taking a step back, Kiera was finally starting to accept that whatever was happening, it had to be real. She didn't know how, but this person who claimed to be Ariel had somehow insinuated herself into her life and was messing with her.

But why? . . . And how?

"Where did—Where do you live?"

"Montana. For more than twenty years. Right after college, I left Maine and moved out there. I couldn't stand to be around Stratford after what happened . . ."

"You mean with Billy?"

Ariel nodded. "Yeah," she said, "but then it all . . ." Her voice faded away, and Kiera panicked, thinking she was going to disappear.

"It all *what*?" she asked, moving forward, hoping to keep Ariel here so she could figure out what was going on.

Ariel raised her head and looked at Kiera, her eyes shining with a dull, lambent light.

"My life . . . before I came here . . ." Ariel's voice was now as light as the wind, hissing through the leaves overhead. "It all seems so . . . distant now . . . like a dream that never really happened."

"I know what you mean," Kiera said, nodding in agreement. "In a lot of ways, I feel like my life has been like that." She paused and glanced up at the night sky, sighing as she shook her head. "It all seems so . . . unreal—especially since the surgery."

"What do you mean, that I'm just something you made up? That I only became real after the surgery, once they cut me out of you?"

"I have no idea," Kiera said simply, shaking her head.

"Maybe," Ariel said, "it's been this way ever since that night."

What night? Kiera was going to ask, but they said the same words simultaneously.

"The night Billy died."

Realization hit Kiera so hard she staggered. She stared at Ariel, torn between wanting to believe she was really there and convinced this was all a delusion.

"What happened?" Kiera asked, hearing the tension in her voice. "What really happened that night?"

"The night Jon killed Billy?" Ariel sounded strained, as if it took an immense effort just to speak. Kiera saw that the woman's body was trembling and glanced over her shoulder, ready to run if there was any trouble.

"I know he did it on purpose," Kiera said. "I didn't want to believe it. All those years, I tried to convince myself it had been an accident, but he did it on purpose. He meant to kill Billy, didn't he?"

For a long time, Ariel was silent, and Kiera could almost believe the figure was fading away, melting back into the shadows.

Maybe she wasn't really there, Kiera thought, but as Ariel withdrew, Kiera felt abandoned and afraid. She moaned as an aching sadness filled her, but then Ariel spoke and, once again, her words were the exact words Kiera had been thinking.

"Yes, he did," Ariel said hollowly, "and he paid for it."

"Paid for it?" Kiera said. "How?"

"I reported what happened to the cops," Ariel said. "They arrested him later that night, and Jon spent the next twenty-five years in Warren for murder. He just got out earlier this year."

Kiera was stunned by what she heard. It was obvious that Ariel believed what she had said, but that wasn't what had happened. On some level, though, maybe Ariel was right. It *could* have happened that way. Unconsciously, she raised her hand to her forehead and rubbed the bandage above her eyebrow.

"I don't remember everything that happened that night," she said. "I banged my head on the dashboard, and I—"

Before she finished, another thought hit her. It was crazy. Impossible. But on some level it made perfect sense.

"Do you think . . . that night . . . *two* things could have happened?"

"What do you mean?" Ariel asked.

Kiera took a few steps closer to Ariel until she was less than ten feet away and held her hands out to her, beckoning her to come closer.

"I don't know what happened," Ariel said in a soft, wounded voice. "I have no idea what's real and what isn't anymore. I have memories of my life, but they . . . they're all so distant now. So vague. Like my whole life was just something I imagined."

"I feel that way, too," Kiera said. She shivered. "I don't know what happened that night . . . not everything."

She was still rubbing the spot on her head just above her eyebrow. As she applied more pressure, her mind seemed to clear. She became more aware, more perceptive. The night filled with a hazy blue glow that illuminated the area under the trees. She wasn't surprised to find herself staring at herself. It was like looking into a mirror.

"So who's right?" she asked. Her voice was thin, but it didn't break. "Did *I* create *you*, or did *you* create *me*?"

Ariel stared at her with a blank expression until she finally said, "I have no idea."

"Or could it be that *both* of our lives are real? Maybe I just *thought* I made you up. Maybe you were real, and when I was younger, I thought of you as my imaginary friend. But if you're real, maybe what happened that night set you free. And everything both of us experienced in our lives really happened."

While Kiera was talking, Ariel looked at her with a perplexed expression. Her skin was translucent in the darkness, and Kiera thought she might be talking to a ghost . . . a ghost who had memories of a life that never was . . . at least in the world Kiera knew.

"Because in *my* life," Kiera said, "that night, I never told the police or anyone else that Jon killed Billy."

Ariel's eyes widened with shock. Her mouth opened, but she didn't speak.

"Jon dragged Billy down to the river and rolled him into the water. His body was never found, and Jon . . . Jon never went to prison. He graduated from high school and went to college, and he got married and lived in Colorado for the last twenty years."

Ariel was shaking her head slowly from side to side as though she couldn't or didn't want to believe what she was hearing. Her expression gradually shifted until she looked absolutely terrified. Kiera knew how frightened she was, because she was just as scared. In ways neither of them could understand, they had a deep connection.

"You think that explains . . ." Ariel said, but then she paused and, raising her hand to her left eyebrow, massaged her forehead. "Is that why I'm here and why I feel so threatened?"

"What do you mean?"

Ariel looked at Kiera with the most pathetic expression she had ever seen.

"I have no idea how I got here," Ariel said. "I think I remember my life before now, but since I found myself back here, my life seems more and more distant, and I have this feeling of danger, of impending doom that just keeps getting worse and worse. Once I realized who you were, I did everything I could to contact you because . . ." She paused and took a shuddering breath. The air whistled through her teeth. "I thought *I* was the one in danger, but I realize now it's *you*."

"*Me?*" Kiera was unable to stop the chill that gripped her. "What do you mean? What danger?"

She knew it wasn't just the disconnect she felt with Nate and Trista; it wasn't just the worry of having brain surgery; and it wasn't just the grief she felt over Liz's death. It was the feeling that someone was actively trying to scare her. Someone was using her fear and insecurity to manipulate her.

In a flash, it hit her. She knew *exactly* who it was.

"That son of a bitch," she whispered.

~3~

It took a few seconds, but eventually Kiera realized the glow in the surrounding night was getting steadily brighter. At first she thought the light was coming from Ariel's face, which shined with a bluish luminosity.

She's a ghost or something I made up . . . She's not real.

When she heard the sound of an approaching car, she realized the increasing light was a car's headlights, shining through the foliage.

Ariel tensed, her eyes wide as she scanned the road. Kiera was praying the driver would drive past and not even notice her car parked a short distance down the narrow dirt road. A spike of fear went through her when she saw the car slow down and then turn down the road.

"Quick! Hide!" Ariel said.

Needing no further prompting, Kiera ran down the slope toward the river and ducked behind a thick clump of brush. Ariel was right beside her, and both women crouched on the mulchy forest floor as they watched the approaching headlights.

"You think it's the police?" Kiera asked, glancing nervously at Ariel, still not believing she was real. It amazed her how much she looked like her twin. Even the way Ariel craned her head forward and bit down on her lower lip reminded Kiera of herself.

"It's not the cops," Ariel said breathlessly.

"Who is it?" Kiera asked, her voice almost breaking with tension.

Moving slowly so she didn't disturb the brush, Ariel pointed toward the car as it pulled up beside Kiera's. Once again, Kiera had the impression she was seeing double, because the car was a dark-colored Volvo just like hers.

The driver, barely visible behind the windshield, sat there for a long time with the engine idling. The headlights were aimed toward the river, the beams just missing Kiera and Ariel where they hid. Strands of mist rose from the water into the cool night air. This close to the river, Kiera could hear the wind in the trees above and smell the warm, resinous scent of pine. The faint gurgle of the water as it rolled over rocks and reeds filled her ears.

After what seemed like several minutes, the driver stopped the engine. After another tense moment or two, he finally opened the car door and got out. After slamming the car door shut, he walked to the front of the car and stood there, blocking the headlights.

Kiera couldn't see who it was, but she was suddenly positive it was Jon O'Keefe.

It had to be him.

She couldn't help but flash back to the last time she and Jon had been out here more than twenty-five years ago. Time telescoped crazily, and she held her breath, almost expecting to see Billy Carroll.

"I see your car's here, so you must be," Jon called out. His voice boomed in the night and echoed from the opposite shore, making him sound closer than he was.

"Come on, Kiera. This is no time to play games."

Kiera cast a furtive glance at Ariel, who was watching Jon with intensity. Her lips were moving as if she was silently rehearsing something. Kiera tapped her on the shoulder to get her attention, surprised that she felt contact with a real body. She asked with a shrug of her shoulders what they should do.

For a moment or two, Ariel didn't respond. Then she leaned close to Kiera and whispered, her breath warm on Kiera's ear.

"Stay right here. Don't move or make a sound, no matter *what* happens."

Kiera started to protest, but she cowered back when Ariel suddenly stood up and walked quickly up the river bank from their hiding place.

"Hi, Jon," she said. Her voice was low and controlled, but Kiera caught the fear in it. "What are you doing out here this late?"

Jon laughed, a deep, rolling laugh that filled the night.

"I could ask you the same question," he said.

He didn't move from where he stood, but Kiera watched as Ariel came closer to him. Her shoulders were hunched defensively, and she moved at an angle, shuffling to the right as though looking for a chance to run.

"I asked you first," Ariel said, sounding like a little kid.

Again, Jon laughed, and then he said, "Your husband

called and asked if you were at my place. I knew you'd come here." He took a breath and exhaled. "It's pretty late to be out driving around, don't you think? Especially someplace as lonely and isolated as this. There might be some dangerous people hanging around."

"I'm not breaking any laws, am I?" Ariel asked, still sounding like a wise-ass kid.

Kiera tensed as she watched Ariel getting closer and closer to Jon. Was she going to try to fight him, or was she going to make a break for it in hopes of drawing him away from Kiera's hiding place?

"Nate said you were really angry when you left the house. So you're finally leaving him?"

When Ariel hesitated, Kiera knew she didn't know who Nate was. How was she going to fake Jon out by pretending to be her if she had no clue what her life had been up to this point?

"I just went out for a drive," Ariel said simply. "I needed some time to think."

"Time to think . . ." Jon sniffed with laughter. "About what?"

Kiera caught the edge in his voice. He still hadn't moved away from the front of the car. He was keeping the head-lights behind him so she was illuminated, but she couldn't see him in the glare.

"I think you know what I was thinking about," Ariel said. The firmness in her voice surprised Kiera. "About what you did out here, and how you still haven't paid for it. Not in *this* life, anyway."

Kiera caught the double meaning but wasn't sure Jon did. He chuckled again and then, clenching his fists at his sides, took a single step forward. His feet crunched in the gravel.

"For killing Billy, you mean? Is that still bugging you?"

Instead of laughing again, he snorted and spat onto the ground at his feet. In the harsh glare of the headlights, Kiera saw the glob of spit raise a little cloud of dust when it hit.

"You know why I did it."

Ariel stopped moving, turned, and faced him directly.

"Do I?" she said.

"You know goddamned well why I did it!" Jon leaned his head back and looked up at the night sky for a moment. The tendons in his neck stood out in sharp relief as though he were in agony. "Don't you get it? I *wanted* you! And I had to get *him* out of the way. He was . . ." The sudden rush of passion seemed to ebb, and he finished more calmly, "He was bothersome. But I wanted you then, and I want you now."

Kiera froze at his words, tensing as a slight whimper escaped her. Jon apparently heard her because he suddenly turned and looked in her direction. Fortunately, the headlights weren't shining directly on where she was hiding. Leaning forward, he peered into the darkness.

"You don't get it, do you?" he said, not looking at Ariel. "You don't get that I would do *anything* for you."

"Even murder?" Ariel asked, her voice a high-pitched blend of fear and barely disguised outrage.

"You think Liz's death was an accident? You think it was a botched robbery like the cops think? How naïve are you?"

As Kiera listened to him, a chill gripped her, squeezing her. A wave of dizziness swept over her, and she almost fainted.

"You want the truth?" Jon asked, sounding mocking now. "The truth is, *I* did it. Of course I did. I wanted Liz dead so I could have *you*."

"Well, you can't," Ariel said simply as she started inching her way again toward the road. Kiera wondered if Jon was too distracted to notice she was getting ready to bolt.

How far can she get before he catches her? Kiera wondered. *Can she outrun him? . . . She can't outrun his car.*

"You never could have me," Ariel said. "Not after the things you did."

"But I did them for *you.* Don't you understand that?" He raised his hands, pleading with her now. "I was through with Liz. You're the only person I've ever wanted. My whole life. I got rid of my wife. I got rid of that creep who was hanging around your daughter. I even did in that little high school slut whose mother—"

"What—?" Ariel shouted.

Kiera knew Ariel had no idea what Jon was talking about. Cold fear took hold of her heart and started to squeeze.

He's crazy! . . . He'll say and do anything!

"You don't know? You didn't even guess?" He leaned back and roared with laughter so loud it echoed across the river. "He was screwing around on you behind your back with that girl's mother."

"So you killed her?" Ariel said.

Kiera knew just from her tone of voice that she had no idea what Jon was talking about, but she did. Jon had killed Robbie Townsend and Katie Burroughs as well as Liz, all in an attempt to win her affection.

"Don't you get it? I did it all for you!" Jon's voice rose higher with a frightening waver that convinced Kiera he was teetering on the edge of sanity. "Once I realized good ol' Nate was screwing around on you, I followed him out to the Burroughses' house. I was afraid he saw me, but that wouldn't have mattered. The mother wasn't home, but I killed the girl, figuring they'd pin it on Nate and maybe . . . just maybe that would finally drive you to me." He paused and took a deep breath, panting heavily. "Let me show you something."

He walked back to the driver's door and opened it. Leaning inside, he fished around until he found what he was looking for and straightened up. In his hand was a tangled red . . . something. He wasn't standing in front of the headlights, so at first Kiera couldn't make out what it was. When he lifted the object and, using both hands, pulled it down onto the top of his head, she understood.

It was a *red* wig.

Are you out of your mind? she wanted to scream, but fear kept her silent as she watched with mounting horror.

"Jesus Christ on a crutch! You still don't get it!" Jon sounded deranged as he raised his arms above his head and waved his hands wildly. "The dark car like yours? The red wig? It was all so if someone saw me in the parking garage or driving around town or whatever, they'd give the cops a description that matched *you*."

Ariel stopped moving and stood there, staring at him in amazement. The headlights lit her from the side, and once again, Kiera had an overpowering feeling of seeing herself as if in a dream. It was like being in two places at once.

"Why . . . why would you do something like that?" Ariel asked, her voice trembling to the point of breaking.

"Jesus Christ, Kiera. I wanted to keep you off balance. Keep you scared. I never really trusted you to keep your mouth shut about what happened to Billy. I'm surprised you lasted as long as you did." In the glare of the headlights, Jon's eyes glistened with a frightening, insane glow.

Ariel regarded him with a steady stare and, in a low, calm voice, said, "How do you know I haven't reported you?"

Jon froze, but then he snorted derisively.

"I'm not in jail, am I?" he said, his voice rising. "Okay, so I killed Billy, and I killed my wife and that loser Robbie Townsend and that Burroughs girl. Who fucking cares? No one can prove a goddamned thing. Now that I know I can't fucking trust you . . ."

As he turned his head slowly and stared at Ariel, he slipped his hand into his jacket pocket and pulled out a small revolver. He gave her a thin smile as he aimed it at Ariel.

"You don't know how sorry I am, Kiera," he said, sounding genuinely disappointed. "I was hoping I could scare you enough so you'd see me as your only hope. I realize, now, that I'm going to have to give you up, too . . . forever."

Kiera stopped breathing, and time seemed to stand still as she waited to see what would happen next. She wanted to help Ariel, but she was too frightened to move. With the headlights shining directly on her, Ariel cringed like a frightened animal. She glanced over her shoulder toward the road as though estimating how far she could get before he shot her, but then she squared her shoulders and faced Jon.

"If you shoot me, they'll know it was you." She was obviously struggling to keep her voice low and steady. "The cops will connect you to it, and even if they don't, even if you throw the gun into the river, they'll eventually put it all together."

"Like they did with Billy?"

Again, Jon laughed, but there wasn't a trace of humor in it.

"They won't investigate if it's ruled a suicide," he said.

Before he finished what he was saying, Ariel wheeled around and started to run. She was heading for the brush out of the range of the headlights, but she tripped on something on the ground and went down.

Jon ran over to her, covering the space in a few long strides. Still wearing the red wig, he stood over her and aimed the gun at her head. In the brush, Kiera shifted her position so she could see what was happening. She watched in horror as Jon cocked back his arm and smacked Ariel on the side of the head with the gun.

Kiera covered her mouth to stifle a scream as she watched Ariel slump to the ground without a sound. A gash on the side of her head started bleeding.

"You *stu*pid *fuck*ing *bitch*! I warned you, didn't I? Didn't I? But, no. You wouldn't listen." Jon straightened up and, wiping his face, scanned the deserted parking lot. He looked foolish with the red wig, but the crazed fire that lit his eyes terrified Kiera. She cringed and hunkered down in the brush, clasping the earth.

Please don't let him see me . . . Please don't let him see me . . . she kept repeating in her mind. She lay on the ground as flat as she could get, positive Jon knew *exactly* where she was. It was just a matter of time before he came and got her.

Convinced that Ariel was already dead, Kiera couldn't decide if she should try to make a run for it now or if she should stay where she was and hope Jon didn't know she was there. She *had* to get out of this so she could report him to the cops.

Bending over, Jon picked up the unconscious—or dead—woman and settled her on his shoulder with her head hanging behind him. Moving slowly and struggling with the weight, he carried her toward the car. At first, Kiera thought he had finally come to his senses and was going to take her to the hospital, but he walked past the car and started down the path toward the river.

"No," Kiera whispered, trembling and unable to move as Jon and his burden disappeared from sight down the slope. She knew now was the time to get up and run, while Jon was out of sight, but she was positive he would hear her and come after her. She didn't want to end up in the river like Billy and Ariel.

Cold emptiness filled Kiera when she realized that Ariel really was dead. The woman's existence—even when she had been standing right beside her—had always seemed so tenuous, so ephemeral it was like she hadn't really existed. Kiera could easily convince herself that she had fabricated her, but when she heard a faint splash from down by the river, she knew Jon had pitched the woman's body into the water. A frightening sense of déjà vu overcame her as memories of that night almost thirty years ago when he had thrown Billy into the river blended with what was happening now.

Her fear spiked when, moments later, Jon came back up the slope and walked over to their parked cars. His headlights still illuminated the parking lot, making his eyes shine with an insane light. He was still wearing the red-haired wig, but when he got to his car, he yanked it off, opened the door, and tossed it onto the front seat.

Kiera was praying he would get into the car and drive away, but he folded his arms across his chest and, turning, surveyed the area. She trembled with fear as she hunkered down on the forest floor and watched him carefully. She was waiting for some indication that he knew she was there. She was paranoid that Jon was toying with her, pretending he didn't know where she was hiding before coming after her.

Moving slowly, he walked over to Kiera's car and stood there for a while, staring at it as though considering what to do next. It was obvious he was unfazed that he had thrown what he thought was her body into the river, but if he really wanted to make it look like suicide, he should have put her behind the steering wheel and rolled the car down the bank and into the water.

After a moment, Jon walked over to a clump of brush close to where Kiera was hiding and broke a leafy branch off a sapling. For the next five minutes or so he walked back and forth, sweeping the branch across the ground, obliterating most of the footprints he had left. Then he got into his car, started it up, and backed it out onto the paved road. With the headlights shining on the parking area, he came back and wiped away his tire tracks.

Kiera was crying as she watched all of this. He was obviously setting this up so, when someone eventually found her car, the cops would conclude she had come out here and drowned herself.

Once this was done, Jon walked went back to his car, got in, and drove away. Kiera's body throbbed with tension as tears burned her eyes. She couldn't help but feel a huge hole in her heart and soul . . . a hole that ached for the loss of someone she still wasn't even convinced had really existed.

Exhaustion and grief finally won out, though, and as uncomfortable as the ground was, she fell asleep. When the first faint streaks of dawn lit the sky, and the woods filled with the songs of birds, she awoke, sat up, and looked around. In the pale predawn light, the horrors she had witnessed seemed like a terrible dream. As the day brightened, the parking area looked remarkably mundane. It was impossible to believe what she had seen and gone through had been real.

She moaned softly as she stood up, shivering as she stretched. She brushed the dirt and mulch from her face and clothes, feeling bone-deep aches in every part of her body. Every joint and muscle felt like they were on fire.

Kiera felt shattered, emotionally and physically, and had no idea what she should do now. She jumped when she looked at the spot where—as impossible as it seemed now—Ariel had crouched next to her last night. There was something on the ground. Her hand was shaking out of control as she reached down and touched it. After a few heavy heartbeats, she realized she was looking at a purse.

It wasn't hers. Hers was still in her car. This must belong to Ariel.

"Maybe you *were* real," Kiera whispered, her eyes wide as she looked around, still afraid that Jon would suddenly appear and attack her.

For a long time, she was afraid to bend down and pick up the purse. She considered leaving it there for the police to find when they investigated. Still feeling as though she was trapped in a nightmare, she stared at the purse, wondering what to do. When she exhaled, the chilly morning air turned her breath into a white mist. Her teeth were chattering loudly, but after taking a few deep breaths, she found the courage to pick it up.

Tears spilled from her eyes, but she wiped them away as she looked down the slope toward the river. It was impossible to imagine that Jon really had carried Ariel's body down there and thrown her into the river. Shreds of mist rose into the steadily brightening sky, and it was all too easy to imagine they were the ghosts of people who had drowned in the river.

Clutching Ariel's purse to her chest, she walked over to her car and opened the door. For a long while she stood there, unable to bring herself to get in.

Where would I go? . . . What would I do?

Her jacket was on the front seat. She was chilled, so she grabbed it and put it on. She was hungry, too. When she looked toward the river, all she could think was that Ariel's body must be far downstream by now.

"Oh, Lord . . . Oh, sweet Lord," she whispered, covering her mouth with her hand as more tears filled her eyes. She whispered a silent prayer, but she cried out when a terrifying image flashed in her mind.

She saw Billy Carroll . . . or what was left of him after nearly thirty years. He was lying in the black ooze on the bottom of the river, staring up at the sky that shimmered above him like quicksilver. Kiera knew what he was looking at, and she watched with him as a dark figure silhouetted against the glowing surface floated by above him. As the figure resolved, she saw Ariel—*or was it herself?*—drifting slowly down . . . down . . . until she joined Billy in the dark, murky depths. A smile spread across Billy's skeletal face as he reached up to embrace her with arms that were black with rot and river muck.

"Dear Lord in heaven, she's gone . . . gone forever," Kiera whispered. The sound of her voice startled her, and she had the distinct impression that someone else—maybe Ariel—was standing close beside her, whispering to her. When she looked around, she saw that she was alone, and that only made the feeling worse.

She's really gone . . .

The sadness that filled her was coupled with the horror

of what she had witnessed here last night and nearly thirty years ago. She finally accepted fully that what had happened here so long ago had left a permanent stain on her soul.

She took a deep breath and looked around as daylight pushed back the darkness, and the woods filled with the songs of birds. She took a deep breath and smelled the warm scent of damp earth and pine. A gentle wind that stirred the leaves was warm and soothing on her face, and she felt a surge of new life inside her.

"She's gone forever," Kiera whispered to the breeze, "and so am I."

CHAPTER 12

Unbroken

~1~

My God, there's an awful lot of money here, Kiera thought as she leaned back in the cushioned booth and looked up at the ceiling. It was difficult to control the sudden rush of emotions as she dropped Ariel's wallet into her lap and squeezed it shut. She had stopped counting when she got over five hundred dollars, most of it in fifties and twenties. Her hands were shaking as she placed them on the table and looked around, fearful that someone had noticed her reaction and was watching her.

It was late in the afternoon, and she was seated in a small restaurant called Becky's Diner on Commercial Street in Portland. She hadn't taken a shower since yesterday morning, and after hiding in the woods by the river until she was absolutely positive she was safe, she needed to freshen up.

She certainly had enough money to rent a hotel room in Portland for the night, and she needed time to think about what to do next. The money in Ariel's wallet certainly would buy her that, too.

"Refill?" the middle-aged waitress said as she came up

to Kiera's table. The name tag above her blouse pocket read Sally. Her cheeks were pitted with old pockmark scars, but she had a warm, friendly smile and bright eyes. Kiera looked at her, fighting the impulse to tell her about what had happened last night. She needed to confide in *someone*, but she also knew she needed to be careful . . . especially if she really was going to do what she was thinking about doing.

"Yeah . . . That'd be great," she said, leaning back and sliding the purse out of sight beneath the table as Sally filled her cup and dropped two cartons of dairy creamer next to the saucer.

"Looks like you had a rough day," Sally said, smiling sympathetically. When Kiera smiled and nodded, the waitress hesitated, then turned and walked away, obviously knowing when someone was going to talk or not.

Kiera stared blankly ahead, her mind filled with concerns about what she might do next. Moving mechanically, she ripped open two packets of sugar and dumped them into the coffee. Then she opened and stirred in the creamers. The spoon clanked on the sides of the cup, setting her teeth on edge. She cringed at the sound, hoping it didn't draw anyone's attention to her.

Take it easy, she told herself. *You didn't do anything wrong.*

But even as she thought that, it seemed like the voice in her head was Ariel's, not her own.

She blew over the top of the cup before taking a sip and, rotating her shoulders, eased back in the booth. She had taken the seat at the back of the diner so she could keep an eye on the door, although she had no idea who or what she was so afraid of. Her biggest fear was that Jon O'Keefe would suddenly walk in, but that didn't seem very likely.

Kiera forced herself to relax by sitting back and watching the steady routine of restaurant workers and customers, but the purse in her lap was a heavy weight that seemed to be crushing her legs. Finally, she mustered up the courage to open it again and look through the contents.

First, she shuffled through Ariel's wallet. She checked out her driver's license. It was from Montana and gave her home address as 128 Creek Circle in Bozeman.

"Montana . . ." Kiera whispered as her gaze shifted out the diner's front window. She smiled as she looked at the busy street lined with old warehouses and storefronts. When she was young, she used to fantasize about moving out west . . . to Montana or Wyoming.

It was unnerving to see how much Ariel's ID photo looked like her. There was no *way* this wasn't her. She stared at the picture for a long time as a thought that was forming in the back of her mind became clearer.

Sighing and shaking her head, she looked through the rest of Ariel's purse. There were the usual things—makeup, loose change, receipts from stores in and around Bozeman. Kiera's heart skipped a beat when she found a bankbook in a thin, plastic protective case. She swallowed hard and looked around guiltily again, convinced someone had noticed what she was doing and was calling the cops.

What am I doing with a dead woman's purse?

Her heart was pounding fast in her neck as she slid the savings book out of its protective case and opened it. There were several pages denoting deposits and withdrawals, but on the fifth or sixth page, she saw the bottom line.

"Oh my *God*," she said with a gasp.

She sagged back in the booth and clamped the savings book shut, marking the place with her forefinger. Sally shot her a questioning look as if to ask, *Is something wrong? . . . Find something floating in your coffee?*

Kiera signaled that she was all right, but she could tell her face was sheet-white as she slowly lowered her gaze to her lap and opened the savings book again. The final figure with a date of less than a month ago after another deposit was a little over three hundred thousand dollars.

The diner walls seemed to close in, and the air got much too stuffy. Kiera had an urge to get up and leave just to be doing something, but she didn't want to draw any more attention to herself than was necessary.

This has to be a mistake, she thought. *Maybe the money's not in the bank now . . . Maybe Ariel closed the account before she came to Maine . . .*

Still, the question remained: how *did* Ariel get to Maine? Even she had expressed surprise and confusion about how she had gotten here.

And now she's dead, Kiera thought with a shudder. She almost screamed when she turned and looked at her pale reflection in the diner's window. She knew who was really supposed to be dead.

She was . . . not Ariel.

Jon had left last night, obviously convinced Kiera was dead. The weird thing was, as she stared at her reflection in the window, she had the distinct impression she was looking at Ariel, who was sitting in Becky's Diner. Kiera Davis was dead. She had been murdered, and her body had been thrown into the Hancock River.

The disoriented feeling swept over her, and she was sure she was about to collapse or else dissolve away to nothing if she didn't keep staring at her reflection in the window. That was the only thing that anchored her to reality.

Who are you? she wondered, but she didn't have the answer. Looking at the bankbook again, she realized that she could just as easily *be* Ariel as Kiera.

And why not?

She had lost everything she had ever valued or thought she valued. Her marriage was over . . . her daughter had no love or respect for her . . . and she'd lost her friends and any sense of belonging in Stratford, Maine. How could she trust anyone ever again? Her husband had been cheating on her with a student's mother. The person she thought was her best friend had killed his wife and two other people, not counting Billy. Everything she had lived for, everything she had believed in and trusted was a sham, and now it was all gone.

So why not be *Ariel McKinnon?*

The thought filled her with a racing thrill.

The life she had known was over. It had been over for a long time. It no doubt had ended almost thirty years ago, when Billy died. So she should take this opportunity to live another life . . . a better life. In the end, maybe that's all that was happening here. Maybe through Ariel she had finally discovered the life that should have been hers all along. And even if it wasn't—even if she didn't really know what she wanted, at least she now knew what she *didn't* want.

Kiera shivered, wondering if she really could follow through with this. She had a home in Montana to go to. She had plenty of cash in hand and more than enough money in the bank to start a new life. If Nate reported her as missing, and the police found Ariel's body, they wouldn't need to examine her body too carefully to identify her. So why not head out to Montana and establish herself as Ariel McKinnon?

This is your only chance to live the life you should have

had all along, said a voice that sounded more like Ariel than herself. *So don't be a fool . . . Take it!*

She caught Sally's attention and signaled that she was ready to pay her tab. When the waitress came over to the table and handed her the receipt, she hesitated and looked at Kiera with a perplexed expression.

"You sure you feeling okay?" Sally's brow furrowed with concern.

Kiera was afraid what her voice might sound like if she spoke, but she forced a smile, nodded, and said, "Sure. I'm fine."

She took a twenty from Ariel's wallet and gave it to Sally, smiling widely when she said, "Keep the change."

"But you only had a cup of coffee," Sally said, but Kiera was already out of the booth and heading toward the door. At the door, she slipped her jacket on and said, "I'm better than fine."

Slinging Ariel's—no, *her* purse over her shoulder, she stepped out onto the sidewalk. The September sun was warm on her face as she walked down Commercial Street. She debated whether she would fly out to Montana or take a bus . . . or maybe rent a car and drive there, but there was one more thing she had to take care of.

She waited until she was in the Greyhound station in Worcester, Massachusetts. Just before the bus left, heading for upstate New York, she found a pay phone and made a call to the Stratford Police. For added insurance, she dialed *70 so the number wouldn't show up on caller ID. When she got the dispatcher, she told her that if they wanted to know who had killed Robbie Townsend, they should check the front fender of a blue Volvo, which was probably parked in Jon O'Keefe's garage. If and when they found the car, they might also find a red wig, which Jon wore to shift suspicion onto Kiera Davis.

"As for Kiera Davis . . ." Her voice caught when she thought about herself in the third person. "Jon O'Keefe lured her out to the parking lot on River Road. He killed her and threw her body into the river. Check his alibi for the night his wife died, too. He was supposed to be in Boston, but he came back to Maine and killed her in the parking garage. He also may have killed a girl—Katie Burroughs."

"May I ask who's calling?" the dispatcher said, but even before he finished his question, Kiera replaced the phone on the hook and practically ran from the booth. Not more than five seconds after she ended the call, a voice over the PA announced that the bus for upstate New York was now boarding. She was relieved that it hadn't happened while she was on the phone. It would have made it easier for the cops to trace the call.

She rushed through the lobby to where the bus was idling and got on, taking a seat almost—but not all the way—at the back. She knew she had to blend in as much as possible.

What are you so afraid of? Ariel's voice kept asking her. *You didn't do anything wrong.*

It wasn't like she had faked her own death to pull off an insurance scam or anything. The truth was, she was trying to take hold of her life in ways she hadn't since . . . well, since that night nearly thirty years ago. Because of that night, she had lived a life she never should have led. But she was about to change all that.

"I got it back," she whispered as the bus lurched and started moving out of the station.

She told herself to relax, that the farther she got away from Maine and New England, the less likely it was that she would hear about a woman who was missing and presumed dead in a small town in central Maine. Unless Ariel's body was found, it probably wouldn't even make national news.

It was hard to relax because of the guilt she felt about leaving her husband and daughter, but she assured herself that they'd eventually get over her death. What bothered her the most was wondering who Ariel really was.

Was it possible that *she* really *was* Kiera . . . or a version of her that existed in some alternate reality? Was she from a parallel timeline where Kiera *had* reported Billy's death, and her and Jon's lives had changed dramatically?

Or what if the brain surgery had somehow freed Ariel, who really was just a figment of her imagination? Maybe that had made it possible for Ariel to become real and enter Kiera's reality.

It was much too confusing and frightening to contemplate. Maybe she had simply imagined Ariel. The truth was, even though she had spoken to her and had Ariel's purse and IDs as proof of her existence, Kiera's memory of her already was slipping away like a half-remembered dream.

Or was it the other way around?

Maybe *she* really *was* Ariel, and Ariel had dreamed Kiera's life right up to this moment. Her life with Nate certainly felt like it had happened a long time ago to someone else. Maybe she was just returning to the life she had always lived in Montana.

In the end, Kiera accepted that she might never figure out what had happened. None of it made sense, but as the bus lumbered out of Worcester onto Route 290, other questions filled her mind . . .

What's my home in Bozeman like? . . . Am I married? . . . Do I have kids? . . . What do I do for work . . . if I have a job? . . .

Three hundred thousand dollars is a lot of money for

*anyone to have in the bank . . . How did I get it? . . . Did I
get it legally? . . .*

   *Am I a good person? . . . Am I the kind of person I al-
ways thought I was or, at least, wanted to be? . . .*

   *Did I report Jon to the cops when he killed Billy or
didn't I? . . . Did he spend twenty years in prison? . . .*

   . . . and perhaps the biggest question of all . . .

   *Who's more real—me or Ariel? . . . Or on some plane of
existence, are we both real? And why did she die instead
of me?*

It was all too confusing and frightening to contemplate,
and as tired as she was, she found she couldn't sleep as the
bus headed out on the Massachusetts Turnpike.

When they pulled into a rest stop, Kiera was tempted to
use the pay phone to call home—just once—to say goodbye to Nate and Trista. She knew what she was doing
wasn't fair to either of them, but if she was going to start
living an authentic life, leaving them was absolutely necessary. It was a good thing she had left her cell phone in her
car. Her purse and cell phone would help identify her if
and when they found her body downriver. Maybe the police wouldn't check too carefully to ID her. Or maybe
they'd never find Ariel's body, like what happened to Billy.
Maybe she'd even meet a version of Billy Carroll out in
Montana.

And who knew? Maybe someday she would contact her
family and tell them what had happened. Imagine the
shock and surprise. But that wouldn't happen until she understood better what she had been through.

One thing gave her comfort, and that was the knowledge that Nate and Trista and the friends she'd left behind
would know she had been murdered, that she hadn't committed suicide.

Kiera was trying to be optimistic about the new life that lay before her, but she also had no delusions. It would be a life like any other life, filled with mysteries and surprises and—yes, hardships and heartbreaks, losses and maybe even love . . . just like her previous life.

But her previous life had been broken because of a decision she had made when she was young. She had known it was wrong, even at the time; but from now on, she was determined to live as honestly as she could and be true to what she knew was right because—finally—*this* life was *her* life.

This life wasn't broken, and she had every intention of living it to the fullest.

Afterwards, I learned that the best way to manage some kinds of painful thoughts is to dare them to do their worst; to let them lie and gnaw at your heart 'till they are tired; and you still have a residue of life they cannot kill.

George McDonald, *Phantastes*

THE HOTELMAN

by

Jerry Seelbach

Best wishes

Jerry Seelbach

BOOKWORLD COMMUNICATIONS CORPORATION
3418 Frankfort Avenue
Louisville, Kentucky 40207

© Copyright 1976 by Jerry Seelbach
All Rights Reserved

International Standard Book Number: 0-914242-07-5

Library of Congress Catalogue Card Number: 75-5296

Published by:

Bookworld Communications Corp.

3418 Frankfort Avenue

Louisville, Kentucky 40207

Printed in the United States of America

To my wife Doris,

and

To Jim, and LaVerne Yocom

Part I

"There are shades in all good pictures, but there are lights too, if we choose to contemplate them."

DICKENS - *Nicholas Nickelby*

John Broker sat on a park bench viewing the tranquil scene before him. The river, still muddy from the spring floods, moved its silt and driftwood downstream in a turbulent pattern. Big cottonwoods lining the banks were in full bloom and spawning down seeds that floated in the air like soft snowflakes, aimlessly looking for a place to land. A soft breeze blowing in from the river afforded a relaxing comfort to the warm rays of the mid-morning sun shining down through a cloudless sky.

John Broker thought how strange it was that he could content himself sitting there most every day, passing away the last years of his life. With little strength for anything else, there was ample time to reminisce about the disappointments and rewards that engulfed the full life behind him.

As he sat there, dressed in a comfortable business suit, with his hickory cane hanging from the back of the bench, he raised his head and looked up through a patchwork of green leaves that contrasted with the blue sky. Then, lowering his head he thought of his boyhood days at Fern Lea, the stately family home situated in the prestigious South Hill section of Lexington, Kentucky. Located in the center of beautifully landscaped acreage, complete with a fine stable, it stood elegantly with its high roof, flanked by enormous chimneys and pointed gables. John's father had acquired considerable wealth in the 1800's as the owner and manager of the Zenith

Hotel in Lexington. It was one of the largest in Central Kentucky and a gathering place for many affluent sportsmen associated with the fertile Bluegrass farms that surrounded Lexington.

Mr. Broker spent long hours at the hotel overseeing every little detail about the business. Demanding perfection in the work of all the employees, he made the hotel a Kentucky showplace. Brass door plates and railings were highly polished, crystal chandeliers sparkled with immaculate cleanliness, thick carpets were spotless, and wide expanses of oak and terrazo flooring through the building were scrubbed and polished with regal splendor.

The Zenith was one of the first buildings in Lexington to be equipped with electricity, and each room had a three-lamp ceiling fixture. Wrought iron floor lamps placed near leather-covered chairs added a new, unique reading comfort for guests.

John had to learn about activities at the hotel from his mother because his father seldom mentioned the business. By the time he was fourteen he had been inside the building on only two occasions. Mr. Broker purposely kept his family away because of the environment.

Like most hotels of its size, the Zenith had its share of gamblers, prostitutes and shady characters. Mr. Broker wanted to shield his youngsters from these people. Then too, he looked forward to his sons pursuing careers in the field of medicine or law.

John's mother kept busy looking after the household, and placed special emphasis on seeing that the children were educated in the best schools.

Brenlyn, the oldest, had long golden curls that hung down over her shoulders, and greatly resembled her mother with her clear sparkling blue eyes and delicate features. Margaret was next in age. She wasn't as pretty as Brenlyn. However, her personality made up for anything she lacked in looks.

John was two years younger than Margaret and far different in his interests. For one thing, he despised school and, consequently, was a poor student. He also disliked the social life in which the family was so heavily involved. Instead, he liked to be around the hired help at the Broker home. The employees were fond of him too. The cooks liked to have him visit the kitchen and always had treats for him to enjoy, and the grounds-keepers and grooms enjoyed having him around to join in the fun as they laughed and joked with each other.

Frank was the youngest in the family. Unlike John, he was an excellent student. He was forever making clever remarks and Brenlyn and Margaret enjoyed showing him off to their friends.

John's boyhood days seemed to speed by quickly, but his interests didn't change. He managed to get passing grades, but in his senior year in high school he felt he had little to look forward to in life, as his father had made plans to enroll him as a medical student at an eastern university.

He dreaded the thought of leaving the carefree life he lived at home. He had his own saddle horse and, after school, would ride out to visit with friends who worked at neighboring horse farms. He often helped them with their work; feeding and watering the horses, bandaging ailing shanks, changing straw bedding in the stalls and polishing harnesses.

He even helped deliver a number of foals and assisted in doctoring horses with liniments and medicines. He loved working at the farms and envied the freedom of his friends. If he had been free to choose his own career at that time, no doubt he would have obtained employment at one of the farms hoping to eventually become a trainer of thoroughbreds. He dreamed of saddling a fast three-year old in the Kentucky Derby and proudly walking at his side to the coveted winner's circle.

He planned a number of ways all of this might be done. The one that suited him best was to wait until he was sent away to college. He would simply leave school and go to a city where there was a major racetrack and get a job as a stablehand.

He was well aware that one day he'd inherit a substantial amount of money from his father's estate. He didn't relish the thought of his father's passing away, but it would happen sometime. After that there would be ample funds to invest in a stable of his own.

******

As the children grew older, the parties and balls at Fern Lea became more prevalent. Fine carriages drawn by well-groomed horses were driven along the tree-lined roadway leading to the courtyard in front of the home. Uniformed doormen would hold their horses at bay as young ladies and their beaus stepped down to the stone pavement. The night air would ring with sounds of lively music being played inside the spacious home.

John would be at most of these events on orders from his parents. While he despised the forethought of attending, he'd sometimes become infatuated by the attention he received from pretty young ladies. Some thought him the most handsome man they had ever seen. Just a little over six feet in height, he had broad shoulders and long, slim legs. His dark brown eyes were close set and seemed to dance in a happy sparkle whenever he was amused. He parted his wavy coal-black hair on one side, and habitually ran his fingers back through the coarse strands to keep them from falling across his forehead.

John danced with girls to his liking, teased them, sometimes walked them to the porch railing, kissed them and found great enjoyment in their company. This would continue until one of them wanted him to accompany her to another social event. Then he would quickly sever his relations and retreat to the family stable and pull off his coat and tie and mingle with the employees. He seldom gave the girl another thought and never cared enough to realize how they were hurt by his sudden loss of interest.

While John lolled in the sanctuary of his stable retreat, the parties would continue to the full enjoyment of the others. Brenlyn's beauty radiated as she moved from one place to another, laughing and talking with guests, and honoring handsome young men by complying with their requests for a lively dance.

Brenlyn had studied voice since she was five years old, and as she reached her early twenties was an accomplished vocalist. During the summers she played minor roles in a number of operettas in several major cities along the Ohio Valley.

Among the handsome young men who tried to win her affection was Neil Hathaway, a Harvard graduate and son of a wealthy grain dealer. Brenlyn liked him much better than any of the others, but was careful not to show it.

******

The spring of 1898 was lovely in the Bluegrass countryside and one of the most delightful seasons that long-time residents could ever remember. Balmy air swept over the grass and clover and whistled along the soft limestone ridges and creekstone fences. Horses grazed contentedly in rich pastures surrounded by newly whitewashed fences. Rye, wheat, corn, barley, hemp, oats and other plants were rising out of the rich, cultivated fields. Covers were removed from hotbeds and tobacco plants were being transferred to the fields.

Just as the lovely weather brought prosperity to Kentucky farmers, so did the economic growth that swept throughout the continent bring good times to the cities.

Lexington was no exception. Served by the Kentucky Central, Chesapeake and Ohio, Cincinnati Southern and

Louisville and Nashville railroads, it became an important and busy railroad center.

New shops and stores were being constructed along city streets while many newly built homes were taking shape in residential areas.

The Zenith, under Mr. Broker's efficient management, prospered to such an extent that it was necessary to enlarge the building to provide more accomodations. A large cellar was remodeled and equipped with bowling alleys, billiard tables, a barber shop and toilet rooms.

Mr. Broker kept long hours at the hotel. From early morning until late at night he closely followed all that was going on. He inspected newly made rooms, checked the quality of food delivered to the kitchen storeroom and helped prepare daily menus. He checked bookkeeping, greeted guests as they arrived and sampled prepared food before allowing it to be served in the dining room.

He closely supervised banquet set ups and watched over the waiters as guests were wined and dined until late hours of the night. Then before going home he would see that the day's receipts were secured in the office safe.

Though it would be close to midnight when he arrived home, Mrs. Broker would always wait up to greet him and to fill him in on the day's activities at home.

Brenlyn and John were a source of worry. Brenlyn seemed to be losing interest in all social life. She would attend Mass each morning at St. Paul's Catholic Church then spend a lot of time in her room studying. She attempted to discourage Neil Hathaway from calling on her but he insisted on seeing her anyway. In answer to his questions about John Mrs. Broker explained he was seldom at home and still lacked interest in studying. He preferred visiting friends at the stock farms to joining in with family friends. This greatly perplexed Mr. Broker.

"Has he ever shown any resentment about going

away to college?'' he asked.

"Never," Mrs. Broker replied. "In fact I believe he's actually looking forward to it."

"Has he said anything about what he wants to do during summer vacation?"

"Well, I know you're going to be surprised but he told me he wants to work at one of the horse farms."

"Horse farms?" Mr. Broker shook his head in amazement. "What kind of work would he do there?"

"I really don't know but you know how much he loves horses. Maybe he wants to help out with the buying and selling."

Mr. Broker raised his eyebrows in disgust. "Or maybe he wants to clean stalls!"

"Surely not!" Mrs. Broker said in astonishment. "Surely he would never do anything like that."

"Well, I don't know what's going on in his mind but I'm going to find out. I'll have a talk with him and maybe there'll be a change in his plans."

Mrs. Broker's face took on a pondering look. "I wouldn't be too hard on him. This will be his last summer vacation before leaving for college. And I do want him to enjoy it."

"Right now I'm not too sure he'll be going away to college."

"Not go to college?" Mrs. Broker was puzzled. "What will he do?"

"I'm not sure just yet. I want to think more about it. I may decide to put him to work at the hotel."

"At the hotel? But you've always said you'd never want either of your sons in the hotel business."

"Yes, that's what I said, and I prefer it that way; never-the-less, I may have good reason for changing my mind."

Mrs. Broker started to speak, but was interrupted. "I prefer not to discuss it any further tonight. Let's call it a day and talk about it later."

Walking toward the staircase, he stopped for a moment and called back.

"Not a word to John about this until I've fully made up my mind."

"I understand," she answered, wishing she did.

******

John Broker felt elated as he sat through his English class at Fayette High School. Only three more days of school and he'd be graduating. There would be no problem in getting passing grades. They wouldn't be high grades, but they wouldn't be failing either. He knew he could do better if he really tried. He just didn't like to take time to study. He didn't worry about it and that's the way it was. The boredom of classrooms would soon be over.

He gazed out an open window and filled his nostrils with the delightful aroma of newly plowed fields. He listened to a pair of raucous Bluejays heckling and screaming as though a hawk were trespassing on their feeding grounds. He caught a glimpse of them darting in and out of a tree as they fussed at the intruder. The countryside seemed magical, and John was happy that his vacation days were so close at hand. Then he'd be free to spend full days in the open country he loved so much.

The school day ended and John joined a group of classmates as they walked along a tree-lined path leading homeward. As they laughed and joked along the way, Harriet Metcalfe managed to walk at his side.

"Well, John, your sister Margaret tells me you'll be leaving us next fall and going away to college."

"Yes, indeedy," John answered casually. "I'll be leaving good ole' Lexington and heading for one of the New England states."

"You don't know where?"

"Oh, it'll probably be Dartmouth; that's in New Hampshire, you know."

"Looking forward to it?" Harriet liked John but she seldom saw him except during school hours. She hoped to get him to pay more attention to her now.

"Yes, sort of." John hid his real thoughts. He looked forward to being on his own. Dartmouth was only going to be a short stopover before he'd make his break and pursue a career in training racehorses.

"I hope you'll be coming to some of the parties this summer."

"If my parents have their way, I'll be making quite a few of them." John smiled to indicate he'd be attending at their choice.

Harriett raised her eyebrows in delight. "Then I hope they'll have their way."

"Why is that? Do you enjoy seeing me so miserable?" John was teasing. He sensed her interest in him.

"If I have anything to do with it you won't be miserable."

John laughed. "Well, we'll just have to wait and see about that." He was pleased at her inference and gave her a warm smile as he turned to take the road leading to Fern Lea.

Harriett waved a farewell. "I'll be looking forward to seeing you."

John shook his head to let her know he understood and walked briskly toward home.

Walking up the front steps, he heard his mother calling.

Turning, he saw her sitting in a wicker porch chair and went to her side. She raised her head and he leaned over and gave her a quick kiss. She started to speak, but John interrupted.

"Do you know that you're very fortunate?"

"Well, I think I am in many ways," she said, smiling. "But is there some special reason for you to mention it now?"

"Sure is." John cocked an eyebrow in an entertaining

gesture. "Do you know there's hardly a pretty girl in Kentucky that wouldn't give all she owns for a kiss like that from me?"

Mrs. Broker laughed. "And I wouldn't blame them either. Did you have a good day in school?"

"The last five minutes were real enjoyable."

They both laughed. Then Mrs. Broker's expression changed. "John," she said, "I don't want you to be alarmed, but your father came home early today. He's waiting in the library to see you."

John was surprised. His father seldom left the hotel early, and to be home now and waiting to see him meant something was wrong.

"Wants to see me?" he asked solicitously.

"Yes, but just as I told you, there's nothing to be alarmed about."

John nodded but was still puzzled. Once before his father had come home early to talk to him and that time it pertained to his lack of interest in school. He dreaded facing him again.

"Did you say he's in the library?"

"Yes, and you better go now. He's been there for some time. She wished she hadn't mentioned his wanting to work around the horse farms when she talked with Mr. Broker earlier. She was not aware of her husband's reasons for wanting John to learn the hotel business. Mr. Broker hadn't told her about having severe pains in his chest and this being diagnosed by a physician as an acute heart condition.

The doctor had ordered complete rest but he would not comply. This was his main reason for having John come to work at the hotel as soon as school ended. He wanted him to be in a position to oversee the hotel's operation in case anything happened. He insisted that the doctor keep his health problem confidential.

As John approached the doorway leading to the library he saw his father seated at a table in the center of the room. Seeing John, he looked up. "Hello, son. I didn't expect you so soon. I guess the time passed faster than I thought. I was browsing through several volumes of our new set of encyclopedias."

John managed a warm smile. "Hello, sir," he said, feeling tense.

"This is a mighty fine set of books. Have you had a chance to look through them?"

"No sir. But I plan on doing that real soon."

"I wish you would. There's so much to learn from them."

"I'm sure there is, sir."

Mr. Broker gestured for John to be seated.

"I'm sure you're anxious to know why I want to talk to you."

"Yes sir, I am," John answered politely. Mr. Broker rubbed his chin as he collected his thoughts. He seldom hurried into anything and as he began his voice was low keyed.

"There are several things I want to discuss with you. They're concerned with your future. Have you given this any thought?"

John felt blood rushing to his temples. He worried what his father would say when he told him about wanting to do farm work. He knew he'd have to get it over with.

"Yes sir, I have." For a moment he had to stop and clear his throat. "You see, sir, I feel this may be my last summer of complete freedom and I'd like to do some kind of physical work. I'd like to build up my body. A physical instructor at school was telling how important this is for eighteen year olds." He amazed himself as he came up with this fabricated explanation.

Mr. Broker listened intently. Yes, go on," he said, confident what was coming next.

John knew there was no turning back now. He had a pessimistic feeling about the outcome.

"Well, sir, if it wouldn't be objectionable to you I'd like to work at one of the big horse farms. You see, I've met some of the people who work at them and I think I'd be able to get hired without any trouble."

Mr. Broker pursed his lips. John waited, anxiously, for him to speak. "And just what kind of work would you be doing?"

"Well, sir I think I can get on at the Rolling Ridge Farm. You see, I know the head trainer there. In fact, his two sons are near my age and we've become close friends."

"What are their names?"

"Carl and Fred Rint."

"Sons of Bradley Rint?"

"Then you know him?" John's hopes began to build up.

"Yes, Bradley is a fine man."

"Then you have no objections?"

"Oh, I didn't say that," his father replied, his voice still in low key. "What kind of work would you be doing?"

"Well, I guess I'd be doing all kinds of work. I'd probably exercise horses, help take care of them, feed and water them and other things like that."

Mr. Broker looked across the room and studied the bookshelves. "Well, son, I can understand your interest in wanting to do something physical, but there are more important things to think about at this time."

The words were a bitter disappointment to John. He saw the stern look on his father's face and wondered what was so important to keep him from fulfilling his own wishes.

His father continued, "In fact, I've given much thought about your future and have decided that it's best that you go to work at the hotel."

"At the hotel?" John couldn't believe what he heard. "You mean I won't be able to work at Rolling Ridge?"

"No, son, I feel that would be a complete waste of time. You need to spend more time preparing for the future and there's absolutely nothing to gain by working on a farm."

"But sir, I'd like to be the owner of a horse farm some day and this would be a great opportunity to learn all I can about their operation."

"If you should ever have enough money to own one you can hire all the skilled help you need. However I'm not interested in your getting into farming. It's more important that you become a hotelman."

"A hotelman?" John was dumbfounded. "But I'll be going to college in the fall. You've always wanted me to study medicine."

"I've changed my mind about that. You know son, the hotel business has provided us with a high standard of living and someone must be ready to take over if anything should happen to me."

John wanted to object strongly but feared his father too much for that. Restraining himself he pleaded, "I would hate to give up my studies." This was a lie but he hoped it might forestall working at the hotel.

"Yes, I realize that," Mr. Broker replied, then pursed his lips again as if to collect his thoughts. "Well as much as I hate to talk about it, I'm getting up in years now and my health is certainly not as good as it used to be. Of course I'd like for you to continue your schooling but I'm greatly concerned about the business and what would happen to it if something did happen to me."

Mr. Broker stood and walked to a bookshelf and ran the tip of his forefinger up and down the edge of a book. Then looking toward John he continued. "I know it won't be easy for you son, but after you get started you might find that you will like the work."

John pretended to understand but understood nothing. In the first place his father didn't seem old and he could never remember his staying away from the hotel because of illness. All he could think of was being tied down at the hotel for long work days every day of the week and every week of the year. That was the way his father had worked for as long as he could remember. The thought brought on a feeling of hopelessness and he thought of refusing but was afraid.

Then he thought about his mother. He could usually persuade her into thinking his way. But against his father's wishes it might be different. At least it was a ray of hope. All he could do was wait and see. He got up from his chair and saw that his father was waiting for him to reply.

"I'll do my best, Father."

Mr. Broker placed his hand on John's shoulder affectionately. "I know you will, son." Then they walked out of the library.

That evening John went to his mother's room to discuss his predicament with her. He was surprised his father had already talked with her about it. She was sympathetic but despite his pleading she too seemed intent on his going to work at the hotel.

"It's a wonderful opportunity for you, John, and it will make us all very proud of you."

John knew he must abide by his parents' wishes although he had a strong feeling he would not be able to live up to their expectations.

******

On the same Monday morning that John went to work at the hotel there was much cause for excitement at the Broker home. Mrs. Broker had just received the morning mail and as she sorted the letters she noticed two of them were for Brenlyn. Looking up at the parlor clock she knew her daughters would be coming in the door before long. They would be returning after attending a weekday Mass. After reading her mail she again looked at the letters for Brenlyn. One was postmarked Philadelphia and the other St. Martin, Ohio.

When the girls returned they carefully removed their wide-brimmed hats and took turns at a hall mirror combing their hair. The maid told them their mother was in the parlor and they went to see her.

Mrs. Broker handed Brenlyn her mail. Sitting on a couch, she opened the Philadelphia letter first. Her eyes followed each line of print closely. After she finished she handed the letter to her mother and asked her to read it aloud so Margaret could hear.

It was a letter from Orin Rupert, the noted director of a Philadelphia Opera House. It contained an offer for her to take a major role in summer opera. "Your beautiful voice is an equal match to your own loveliness," it read in part. Then it went on to say that everyone at the Music Hall was anxiously looking forward to her acceptance and informed her of the date rehearsals were to start. After Mrs. Broker finished reading she and Margaret looked at Brenlyn to show their delight. Brenlyn hardly noticed. She was engrossed in the contents of the second letter.

Mrs. Broker was overwhelmed with excitement. "Oh, Brenlyn, I can hardly realize it. A major role at the Philadelphia Opera House. I'm so happy for you!"

Brenlyn looked up, exposing soft teardrops running down her cheeks.

Margaret took her hand. "Go ahead and have a good cry," she said, "because I'm going to cry too and I'll feel better if someone cries with me." Brenlyn managed a smile and quickly regained her composure but had little more to say as they expressed their delight in anticipation of going to Philadelphia with her.

Brenlyn managed to change the subject. "I wonder how John is getting along at the hotel?"

"Oh, I feel sure he is doing fine," Mrs. Broker replied. "Of course it's bound to be a big change for him at first but after he gets acquainted I'm sure he will adjust quickly."

"I can't help feeling sorry for him," Brenlyn said. "He's always had so much freedom."

"Well I think it's time he settled down," Margaret interjected. "He needs to have something to think about other than loafing around smelly stables."

Mrs. Broker agreed. "Yes, I think it's best."

"Let's just hope that he does like it. That'll make it so much easier for him," Brenlyn said, then excused herself and went to her room. Purposely she refrained from mentioning the contents of the second letter.

******

John was dissatisfied at the hotel. He hated wearing business suits and the stiff-collared shirts that rubbed against his neck each time he moved. His highly polished, button-top shoes caused him to feel awkward when he walked.

Mr. Broker instructed Byron Hargrove, the chief clerk, to escort John on a tour of the hotel and to explain the fundamentals of working behind a lobby desk.

They walked through the lobby and saw the tufted chairs that were placed around large round columns supporting the upper floors. Between the columns matching divans gave relief to the wide expanse of flooring. Red, plush drapes hung from each window and were neatly tied back at the sides to permit a view of the street. Portraits of generals, noted politicians and other dignitaries were mounted in heavy gilt frames along the walls.

A modest-sized crystal chandelier, glowing with an array of incandescent lights hung from the ceiling.

As they walked down a long hallway, Mr. Hargrove explained the numbering system for the many paneled doors on each side. Some of the doors were open and maids were busy sweeping floors and making beds. They entered a newly prepared room and Mr. Hargrove explained it was typical of most of the rooms in the hotel.

It had an iron rung double bed, dark walnut chest of

drawers, matching table and chairs and a flowered Belgian carpet. A white water pitcher centered the top of a smaller table beside the bed and a white porcelain sink with running water was fastened to a side wall. A bell rope was placed near the bed so that guests needing service could pull it and a system of cables and pulleys caused a bell at the desk to ring designating the room number. A polished brass spittoon was placed beside one of the chairs.

Mr. Hargrove took John along the hallways in the upper third and fourth floors then they rode an elevator down to the basement. They looked at the four-laned bowling alley, the public bath and storage rooms.

They walked up to the main floor into the dining room and then to the kitchen where employees were preparing dinner. John smiled and nodded a greeting to each employee as he passed.

Mr. Hargrove looked at him disapprovingly.

Afterwards they went to the desk and Mr. Hargrove introduced him to the clerk on duty. "This is John Broker, Mr. Broker's oldest son. And this is Ben Gadby."

Each eyed the other as they exchanged handshakes. Gadby was a round-faced man of medium build. He was bald except for a small crop of hair along each side of his head and had a neatly-trimmed black moustache. He was well dressed complete with a small diamond stickpin in his tie and a white carnation in his lapel.

"John will be working at the desk with us," Mr. Hargrove said. "Of course it will be some time before he can be expected to be on his own.

This was the first inkling John had of what he was to do at the hotel.

"Yes, he is rather young for a desk clerk." Gadby's face was expressionless.

They both expressed pleasure in meeting. John, personally, felt he had no reason for saying so, and thought that Gadby probably felt the same.

Mr. Hargrove had John sit on a straight-back chair next to a roll-top desk, and Gadby sat in a swivel chair facing the desk. John looked around the clerk's working area. He saw numerous pigeon holes in a cabinet on a back wall. Some contained only a room key while others had sealed envelopes addressed to room holders.

Mr. Hargrove asked Gadby to bring him the register and then proceeded to explain the proper way to register guests. John held the book in his lap and turned the pages, reading names and cities. He was amazed at the variety: New York, Kankakee, Kansas City, Jacksonville, Richmond, New Orleans, Memphis, Cincinnati, Cleveland, Atlanta, Washington. Mr. Hargrove reached for the book. John started to close it but Hargrove held it open. "Never close a register book," he said. "It's bad luck."

"Bad luck?" John wondered if Hargrove was joking.

"There's not a clerk in the country that will close a register book. Business would be bad the rest of the day."

John wished he knew of a way to escape the place. He longed to be riding across the fields where there were no formalities and office procedures.

Mr. Hargrove explained the method of assigning rooms and caring for guests. He warned about free loaders and souvenir hounds. "A man will jump his bill, leaving behind a cheap suitcase filled with catalogs or bricks. Study everyone's face without their knowing it. Sometimes these cheats make a second trip."

John listened intently.

"We have our share of hotel hermits here too," Hargrove explained. "Most are nice fellows but will talk your head off if you let them. These fellows are usually bachelors or widowers and are permanent guests at the hotel. You'll have to learn how to get rid of them if they hang around the desk too long."

John nodded to let him know he understood.

Mr. Hargrove explained the method of accounting for daily receipts and other procedures then instructed John to spend the rest of the day behind the desk. "You can watch Ben and learn from him." Mr. Hargrove walked out into the lobby and disappeared through a side door.

John spent the rest of the day in misery. Gadby seemed to resent his presence and vaguely answered his questions. John thought it was a complete waste of time and wondered what Carl and Fred Rint were doing at Rolling Ridge. He felt like walking out of the hotel and riding out to see them. It was one of the few pleasant thoughts he had that day.

John had lunch with Mr. Hargrove in the hotel dining room. His father was seated at another table with a group of men. All were well dressed and were quite jovial as they dined. John wondered what they were talking about and occasionally looked at his father to see if he were aware that he was in the dining room. His father never looked his way.

John asked Mr. Hargrove who the men were. "The fat one with his hair parted down the middle is a state senator from Glasgow; the one on his right is a Fayette County attorney. The one on his left is the state banking commissioner and the other one is a state representative from Louisville. They think an awful lot of your father." Then he added, "He's a prominent man in this state. If he didn't have to spend so much time looking after the hotel he'd be one of Kentucky's leading politicians. Might even be governor. Yes sir, might even be governor."

John felt proud but this feeling lasted momentarily. He had a premonition that he could never live up to his father's expectations. He remembered his saying he wanted him to take over the hotel some day but wasn't even sure that he could qualify as a desk clerk.

He felt melancholy as he surmised it was not likely he

could ever become a trainer. If his father had only followed through and sent him away to college, then he could have made his break and would have done what he wanted. He felt chained to the hotel. There was no means of escape in sight.

John did not see his father again that day until it was time to go home. They had been at the hotel eleven hours and John had hated every minute of it.

One of their drivers met them at the hotel door and they sat side by side in the back of the carriage. Both were tired. His father asked how he liked hotel work.

"Not too well sir," he answered. "I don't feel that I'm qualified for this kind of work."

Mr. Broker patted John's knee. "That's because you're so young. You'll learn to like it. In fact once the hotel business gets into your blood you won't want to think of anything else. Just wait and see. Each day will be better."

"I hope so, sir," John replied but he felt that there was little to look forward to.

After they arrived home John went to his room. He thought of getting into more comfortable clothes and riding out to see the Rint brothers but decided it was too late for that. Instead he stretched out on his bed and fell sound asleep and his problems were suspended for the night.

******

John was in his third week at the hotel when Brenlyn made a startling announcement. She hadn't planned on making it at that time but Neil Hathaway's insistence that they get married made it necessary.

Neil met Brenlyn at church on the Tuesday morning of that week and was glad to see that Margaret was not with her. Neil was not as devout as Brenlyn but occasionally joined her on week days at St. Paul's as an excuse to be with her.

As they were walking home Neil knew he must try to

find out why she tried to avoid seeing him.

"You know what?" he said light heartedly. "While we were in church I wondered what it was you were praying for and I think I know the answer. You're praying that I'll ask you to marry me. And you know what? I'm going to answer those prayers by setting the date right now."

Brenlyn hated to hurt him. "Neil, you're such a wonderful person but you must forget about our ever being married. I've told you this so many times and I know you deserve to know the reason but I just can't talk about it now."

"You just can't put me off like this anymore, Brenlyn. You know how much I love you and I could never be happy without you."

"You mustn't feel this way, Neil," Brenlyn pleaded. "I wish I could explain but I just can't talk about it now."

Neil shook his head dejectedly. "When will I know?" There was a hint of anger in his voice. "Or can't I know that either?"

"Have dinner with us tonight and I'll tell you afterwards." Brenlyn hardly realized what she had said.

Arriving home she went to her room and looked out over the lawn. Sighing deeply she walked to her dressing table and looked in the mirror. "You can't go on like this," she said to herself. She picked up a pearl handled hair brush and raised it to stroke her hair hesitating as she collected her thoughts. Then quickly she brushed it smooth and went downstairs to talk to her mother.

She found her in the dining room arranging cut flowers. Brenlyn admired and loved her mother greatly. Greeting her with a kiss she asked if she could talk with her.

"Why of course you can, Brenlyn," she said smiling. "You know you don't have to ask." Mrs. Broker laid the flowers on a tray.

She and Brenlyn went to the parlor and sat on a divan.

Brenlyn folded her hands in her lap trying to hide her anxiety. Her mother sensed something was wrong. "What is it, my dear?" she asked solicitously.

Brenlyn took her mother's hand. She had to force herself to speak. "Mother, what would you say if I told you I want to become a nun?"

For a moment Mrs. Broker was lost for words. She knew how devout Brenlyn was but had never thought of her being a nun. "Surely you're not thinking of doing that!"

"Yes, Mother, I have decided that's how I want to spend my life."

Mrs. Broker's mind was quickly crowded with questions. "What about your singing career? What will your father say? What about Neil?" Mrs. Broker could no longer control her emotions and burst into tears. She managed to restrain herself quickly and gently blotted her eyes with a handkerchief.

"I've been thinking about this for a long time," Brenlyn said. "But I just wasn't sure. Now I know I've made the right decision. I know it's going to be difficult for father to understand and I have continually tried to discourage Neil. He is such a dear, sweet person. It hurts me so much to know how he feels." Then with strained countenance she added, "Oh, Mother, there are just so many problems right now. I hope I won't cause a lot of unhappiness."

Mrs. Broker took Brenlyn in her arms and caressed her. "I have often thought I would like for one of my children to become a member of a religious order but I never dreamed you'd be the one. You have so much to give up."

They talked for a long time. Brenlyn explained she had been corresponding with the Brown County Ursulines at St. Martin, Ohio, and they had agreed to accept her as a postulate.

St. Martin was located in the center of a great and picturesque Ohio farm belt and the town had only a general store, a graveyard, a church, eleven houses and a three-story inn that was owned by the nuns and operated privately by the parents of one of the nuns. It afforded a place for other parents to stay when they wanted to visit their daughters at the convent.

The convent and grounds were big and the nuns operated a prestigious boarding school with more than two hundred students. They also managed a convent farm that boasted a dairy farm and produced crops for the convent dining room.

Brenlyn learned about the convent from a friend who received her high school education there and had visited the school several times with the girl's family. Brenlyn had never forgotten the place and longed to be a member of the community of Ursulines ever since.

Later in the morning Brenlyn told Margaret about her plans. Margaret was not greatly surprised because she and Brenlyn had discussed the possibility of going to a convent together but Margaret realized she was not suited for that kind of life.

Frank, who was vacationing in Michigan with neighbors, would be told when he returned home.

Mr. Broker and John would learn about Brenlyn's plans when they returned home from the hotel.

Mrs. Broker explained to Margaret that Neil Hathaway was to have dinner at Fern Lea that evening and Brenlyn would tell him afterwards about her plans. Nothing was to be said at the dinner table.

Neil was in unusually good spirits during the dinner. He entertained Mrs. Broker and the girls with amusing stories.

After dinner he and Brenlyn went to the flower garden and walked through the neat winding paths that encircled the plot. Neil thought how the beauty of the flowers matched the girl beside him.

"Brenlyn dear, I'm afraid you're going to have a much changed boy friend before long," he said.

"Why is that, Neil?" she asked curiously.

"Well, my father called me into his office and told me about his plans of turning a portion of the business over to me and making me a vice-president of the firm."

For a moment Brenlyn forgot about the unpleasant task before her and thought only of how important Neil would be with his new position. "Oh, Neil, I'm so happy for you," she said joyfully.

He smiled. "Let's put a happy ending to this by setting our wedding date." He looked longingly at her and waited for her answer.

Brenlyn knew she must not wait to tell him why they could never marry. The thought filled her with fear. A sense of dizziness overcame her and she felt her body becoming limp.

Neil saw the paleness in her face and felt her trembling hands. He helped her to a nearby bench and sat down beside her. Her body slumped in faintness and he held her in his arms to prevent her falling. He gently rubbed her wrists.

"What's the matter, darling?" he asked, and touched his lips to her cheek. "Are you all right?"

She felt weak and helpless. His voice brought back the agonizing thought of the reason she had fainted.

She tried to speak but Neil tenderly placed his hand over her lips. "Don't try to say anything now," he whispered. "I only wish I could hold you like this forever."

Brenlyn motioned for him to let her speak. "Oh, Neil," she sighed, "I have something I must tell you and I just don't know how to say it because I know it's going to upset you terribly."

"Not now, darling. It'll keep until you feel better."

"No, I must tell you now," she insisted.

"Whatever it is, it can wait. We better get something

to bring back the color to those pretty cheeks."

"Neil, you must listen to what I have to say."

He had never seen Brenlyn so distressed and sensed a feeling of terror in her voice. "What is it, darling?" he asked, somehow feeling as though he never wanted to hear the answer.

"I'll be going away soon," she said, dropping her head because she couldn't stand to see the troubled expression on his face. Oh Neil, please don't let this hurt you." She struggled to continue. "I'm going to enter a convent to become a nun."

His face took on a puzzled look. "What are you saying to me?"

"I have made arrangements to enter a convent in Ohio." She had to force the words to make them come out.

Neil couldn't believe what he heard. He leaned forward and picked up a pebble from the walkway. Then he stood and as he did he slowly rolled the pebble between his thumb and forefinger. Then in a sudden burst of anger he threw the pebble to the ground and turned toward Brenlyn. "What made you ever think of such a thing ?"

"Please don't make me explain right now, Neil. Please try to understand."

"Understand? What is there to understand?" His face became flushed. "Are you asking me to understand your telling me you plan to be cooped up in a convent? Why nuns can't do anything. They can't do anything at all! Surely you can't be serious about this."

"Please Neil. Please don't talk that way."

He looked down into her eyes and held her arms. "I'll never let you go! Never! Never!" He felt his fingers pressing deeply and released his grip in dismay.

Brenlyn knew it was hopeless to continue talking until time could ease the tension. She asked him to take her back to the house and as they walked silently side by side

Neil thought how different the flowers looked now. They resembled poison spears darting out at him and he felt as though he wanted to destroy them all. He refrained from speaking until the stairway to the house came in view, then he took her hand. "How long have you been thinking about this?" he asked.

"For a long time."

"Do you actually think you could ever be happy in such a place?"

"Very happy."

Neil felt his anger returning. "What about us? What about me?"

Brenlyn tried to be cheerful. "You'll soon forget and find someone else much nicer than me."

"Sounds easy. Real easy. But it just so happens that I'm in love with you and there'll never be anyone else."

"Neil, please don't make it so hard for me. You know that I never once promised to marry you. I pleaded with you time after time to go out with other girls. If I could have just made up my mind before this maybe I could have spared us all this unpleasantness. Please try to understand. I would never want to do anything to hurt you and if there was the least doubt in my mind that I would want to remain in the outside world, I wouldn't be going away."

Neil refrained from talking further until they reached the porch steps. Then he took her hand letting her know he wanted to pause before going into the house. Somehow he felt he shouldn't ask the question but knew he could never rest until he did.

"Brenlyn, have you ever really loved me?"

She shook her head sadly as she looked up into his handsome face. "Neil, if I would have ever married it could have never been anyone but you."

He wanted to take her in his arms but she turned and ran up the steps to her room.

Instead of going home Neil purchased a bottle of

whiskey and checked in at the Midland Hotel. He drank until his senses were numbed. Then he lay across the bed and for the first time in his adult life cried himself to sleep.

******

When Mr. Broker came home that night he was very tired. Mrs. Broker dreaded telling him about Brenlyn but knew she must. He could usually control his emotions but she knew he would have strong feelings about this and waited until they retired to their bedroom to tell him.

After she explained about Brenlyn he walked back and forth in deep thought. He was always too busy at the hotel to give much thought to the spiritual side of life. He managed to attend Mass on Sundays but never took the time to seriously meditate about matters of faith. As he paced the floor he could only think of his lovely daughter in a convent hidden from the world. He had always been very proud of her. Secretly she had been his favorite since the day she was born. He had always managed to attend her recitals and concerts and felt proud when she walked out on the stage. Her beauty and charming voice thrilled him to no end. And now this he thought to himself. The thought angered him.

"This order of nuns. What are they like?"

Mrs. Broker explained all she knew about them.

"How often can she come home?"

Mrs. Broker wished she could say it would be often but explained that their rules prohibited them from ever visiting in any home including their own.

Mr. Broker's face brightened. Then she won't stay. Perhaps it's just a whim and she will quickly change her mind when she is away from her pretty clothes and the happy life she is accustomed to. "Yes, that's the way it'll be. That's the way it'll have to be."

After the lights were turned off and they retired for the night Mrs. Broker asked, "I hope her going away will not upset you too much." Mr. Broker did not answer. He was too tired to think about it any longer and was lost in sleep.

Mr. Broker and John were having lunch together in the hotel dining room the next day when Mr. Broker told him about Brenlyn. He was surprised that John seemed so unconcerned. He meant to discuss this with him but a waiter interrupted by handing him a note from the assistant manager. He left John alone to think about Brenlyn.

His viewpoint of her leaving was not from a religious standpoint. He looked at it as an escape from society. There were times he had thought of entering a monastery to escape having to do things he objected to in social circles. So he looked at Brenlyn's reason for entering a convent as an escape. He was wrong about that but he had no way of knowing what it was like to have a calling for the religious life.

******

As the 1898 spring moved into summer John was infatuated with Lexington's changing scene. The streets acquired a new look. Steel rails were laid and electric trolley cars transported passengers throughout various streets. Electric horseless carriages came into being and caused great excitement. Many residents complained that they made the streets unsafe because they frightened the horses and various ordinances were passed limiting their use.

John was fascinated with the horseless carriages. Occasionally one of the cars would stop at the Zenith and he would step outside to look at it and find a way to converse with the owner.

One driver complained about the laws that hampered the use of the cars. He handed John a copy of a periodical called *Toots*, published by a newly-formed automobile club in Louisville.

"Just look at this," the driver said, pointing to an open page. "It shows what we're up against!" Then he added, "At least these people are trying to do something about it."

John carefully read the item, word for word.

"It is always best to give heavily loaded teams the best part of the road. Of course, many wagon drivers are known as 'road hogs', but it does no good to stir up an argument with these people just because they are hogs. When traveling in the country, speak to everyone you meet. A polite good morning, or good evening, produces better effect than hours of arguing.

"Many times, if the machine is brought to a standstill facing a horse showing some nervousness, it is almost certain to invite disaster; where if the machine is taken quietly by, it is all over before the horse make up its mind to do anything. Great care has to be exercised in passing an over-taken vehicle; where some of the occupants, especially women, are liable to jump out right in front of the machine."

John was awed as he studied the machine and vowed that he would one day own one.

Business houses and residences had telephones installed as a luxurious convenience. Mr. Broker had telephones installed in the better class rooms at the Zenith.

John was fascinated with the many new devices that gradually became commonplace in Lexington. Although he still dreaded the confinement of working at the hotel there were many things that detracted from the day to day restriction of having to be there.

He enjoyed talking to the guests and often became engrossed with attractive young belles as they accompanied their parents through the lobby.

One Saturday afternoon three college students checked in at the hotel and later were showing signs of heavy drinking as they frolicked in the lobby. One student appeared more sober than the others and John called him to the desk. He greeted the young man with his personable smile and tactfully explained that he and his friends were putting him in an awkward position.

The student reached out and shook John's hand. "Don Kent's the name. Tell you what," he said good-naturedly, "I'll get my two buddies and go up to our room if you'll join us for a drink." He pulled his coat open and patted a bottle placed in an inner pocket. "Straight corn whiskey. The best!"

John had never drunk hard liquor before but didn't want to admit it. "Sure," he said, enthusiastically. "You all go on up and I'll get someone to take my place. I'll join you before long."

Don waved his hand to acknowledge his approval. "See ya up there."

John got another clerk to cover for him and went to the room. After a quick introduction to his friends, Red Burton and Al Roberts, Don poured a drink for each one then held up his glass and uttered a toast. "Drink to your heart's content." He squinted his eyes and tried to think of a rhyme to complete it. Before he could do so Al held up his glass and helped him out. "And soon you'll be as drunk as Don Kent." This brought hilarious laughter from them all.

They touched glasses and John watched as they raised them to their lips. He followed suit and gulped heavily. He started to say it was good but felt he was going to choke. A burning pain caused him to bend over. Dropping the glass on the floor he began coughing as if his insides were coming out. He rushed to the wash basin and found relief.

Don was sympathetic but his friends were laughing. "You guys get out of here," he ordered, "and not a word about this to anyone."

After they had gone, Don apologized. "Why didn't you tell me you don't drink?"

John shrugged his shoulders. "I thought I could handle it." He tried to offer another apology.

Don stopped him. "You drank too fast."
"Want me to show you how to drink without having all that pain?"

"I'm going to have to learn sometime."

"Sure you are." Don handed him the bottle. "Now take a drink and hold it in your mouth for awhile. Then swallow it easy like and you won't have any trouble."

John hesitated concerned whether he could handle it. Then he raised the bottle slowly and let a small amount of whiskey seep through his partially closed lips. He waited in anticipation. It stung but didn't burn.

After a few moments Don told him to swallow slowly. John felt a little discomfort as it went down. He waited until it settled then smiled proudly. "I made it all right."

They continued drinking and talking and John was glad to vent his problems to someone. He explained how he wanted to train racehorses and about his father's insisting he become a hotelman.

"Hell, my old man is just as bad," Don said, dejectedly. "He's got me enrolled in the agricultural college. Wants me to be a farmer. Imagine, me a farmer. Messing around with pigs and plowing cornfields." He grimaced. "I don't wanna' be no farmer," he said in disgust.

John bobbed his head as he asked, "What would ya like to be, Don?"

"Ya know what I wanna' be? Well, since ya asked, I'll tell ya." He held the bottle up triumphantly. "I wanna' be a bum. A plain ole' hoboin' bum."

John laughed at him. Don set the bottle down and his arms dropped limply at his sides. He puckered his lips as if he had just issued a great proclamation.

Don's two friends returned and they continued drinking. John was enjoying it as much as the others.

There was a knock at the door. A bellhop asked to see

John.

"Send him in and give him a drink," John blurted out and they all laughed.

The bellhop was surprised. The room reeked with the smell of whiskey. "Your father said for me to tell you to come to his office right away."

"Tell him to send up a wheel chair and he'll be right down." Red Burton added with a thick tongue.

"Or a stretcher," Al Roberts chimed in and they laughed more.

John stood up and started to walk toward the door. His shoulders swayed and his legs buckled and he fell flat on the floor.

The bellhop was dumbfounded. "This is bad! Real bad!" he said, shaking his head. "Mr. Broker ain't gonna' like this at all. He ain't gonna' like it one bit."

"Well, he don't need to know about it," Don shot back. "Tell him he left the hotel and won't be back for a couple of hours."

"Oh, I can't do that," the bellhop replied. "Mr. Broker is sure to find out. I've got a wife and five children. Mr. Broker would fire me in a minute when he found out I was lying. I got to tell him. I just got to!"

He started to leave and Al reached out to grab him. Don interferred. "Let him go. He's right. His old man is sure to find out." The bellhop hurried out the door.

When Mr. Broker and the house detective entered the room, Don was bathing John's head with a wet towel.

Mr. Broker went to him and bent over to look at his face. "How much has he had to drink?" he asked.

"Quite a bit," Don answered. All three of the students had sobered up to the degree that they were worried at the outcome.

Mr. Broker looked around the room. Two empty bottles were in a trash can and a half-empty bottle sat on the dresser. He turned to the detective. "Pour that stuff down the drain." Then he addressed the three students. "We don't want to hear another word out of you for the rest of the night. If we do, you'll be put out of the hotel."

The detective got John to his feet and assisted him to an unoccupied room. Mr. Broker watched as the capable detective pulled the covers back and laid John on the bed. As they pulled off his shoes and loosened his collar, John opened hs eyes and tried to speak but found it too difficult. Mr. Broker shook his head. "We'll talk about this tomorrow," he said before leaving the room.

John was awakened by sounds coming in an open window. The din of horses' hoofs clopping and steel-rimmed wheels pressing and galling against cobblestones was different from the sounds at Fern Lea.

He felt different too. His head ached as if he had been struck by a hickory club. His stomach racked with pain. He opened his eyes and realized he was not in his own bedroom.

He wondered how he happened to be in a hotel room. His memory was clouded but he remembered the drinking party. Then he remembered his father's being there. He rose from the pillow and thought about having to face him. It was an ugly thought.

He pushed the covers back and sat on the side of the bed. His head felt like it was charged with gushing blood. His throat was dry. He went to the sink and filled a glass with tap water. His hands trembled and his body felt unbalanced.

The water was soothing to his parched throat but his head continued to ache and there was no real comfort. He walked back to the bed and laid crosswise, backside down, with his legs dangling and his feet on the floor. He heard the town clock strike eight and realized he should have relieved the night clerk an hour earlier. He forced himself to rise on his elbows. A feeling of weakness forced him back down. His eyes felt heavy and his body felt as though it weighed a ton. His thoughts drifted and he dozed back into a deep sleep.

Mr. Broker instructed a bellhop to take a pot of coffee up to the room and awaken John, and to inform him that he would be up to see him shortly.

After the coffee, John's head cleared up considerably. He stood at the window watching pedestrians on the sidewalks going about their business. Their life and his seemed two worlds apart. His viewpoint of them was that they were free to do what they pleased. Whether he was right about that, or not, didn't matter. They looked that way to him.

He felt angered when he thought about himself assigned to the hotel and under the continual scrutiny of his father. In less than three months he would be twenty years of age and he wanted to be free to do as he pleased.

When John pictured his father's reprimanding him about drinking his anger increased. "After all," he thought to himself, "he was the one who brought me to the hotel. What was I supposed to do all day? Stay behind the desk and cater to the whims of a bunch of stuffed shirts?"

His mind was made up. As soon as his father started berating him about drinking he would let him know how he felt about the hotel life. If he didn't like it he would simply walk out on him.

The door opened and Mr. Broker entered the room. "Did you have a good night's sleep?" he asked in his usual soft voice.

"I slept real well." John's voice was terse. He was ready for battle. He purposely left off the "sir."

"I instructed them not to awaken you." Mr. Broker was smiling. "I thought you could use the sleep."

John shook his head in agreement. He wondered about the smile wishing his father would begin the reprimanding so he could let him know his own feelings.

"Rodney Carter is working the desk in your place," Mr. Broker said.

John decided that he would get the argument started by telling him he was not going down to relieve Carter. Before he could speak his father continued, "You may as well take the rest of the day off."

"The rest of the day off?" John's eyes brightened at the thought. He felt less hostile. "I guess I made quite a fool of myself last night?"

Mr. Broker's eyes were downcast. "Well, I don't intend to make a big issue of this. There's nothing wrong with a man's taking a drink but it's just important to know how much to drink. A man who can handle his drinks is a real man. A man who lets his drinks handle him is a fool. I never wanted another man to think of me as a fool and I don't want any man to ever think of you as one."

After saying this he walked toward the door but paused before opening it. "You mean a lot to me son. I know it's going to be difficult for you to adjust to hotel work but you must be patient. Learn all you can about the business and you'll become a fine hotelman." He opened the door and waited for John to leave. As they walked downstairs to the lobby he continued, "I almost forgot to tell you Margaret is having a small group of friends over at the house this afternoon for a little farewell party for Brenlyn. It's mostly girls from South Hill. Anyway your mother wants you to drop in to see them. I'm sure Brenlyn would appreciate it. You go ahead and enjoy yourself."

John had planned on riding over to see Carl and Bob Rint, but he stopped in to see Brenlyn and the other girls gathered in the living room.

Brenlyn saw him and went to his side. "I'm so glad you came. Some of the girls asked if you were here."

Brenlyn was dressed in a plain black dress which John found distasteful.

"Must you dress this way so soon?" he asked.

"Oh it's not as bad as all of that. Besides, I'm very

comfortable.''

She took John's arm and led him to the gathering of girls. Harriett Metcalfe was the first to greet him. John thought she looked much prettier than he remembered her during their school days.

Most of the girls' faces brightened as they talked with John. He used his best manners. When she got the chance Harriett moved in close. She asked where he had been keeping himself. ''I hoped to see you a lot this summer but you haven't been around at all.'' Her Kentucky accent drawled out each word in melodiously pleasant tones.

John laughed. ''That's because I've had to spend so much time at the hotel.''

''I suppose you're happy working there?''

''Not really,'' he said. ''It's like being in prison -- too confining.''

''Well, you must have some time to yourself. You're not working now.''

''This is my first day off since starting to work.''

John was interrupted. Brenlyn wanted him to meet a new girl who had recently moved to South Hill. After the introduction John excused himself saying he had to leave. He exchanged pleasantries with the guests and started to leave the room when Harriett caught up with him. ''It's been a dull summer for me too,'' she said. ''I thought maybe we could go someplace together. I'm awfully good at cheering up people you know.'' She raised her eyebrows in anticipation of his answer.

''But you're not free now.'' John was intrigued with her invitation.

''I can be, though.'' She smiled coyly. ''I can tell them I have to leave early.''

''Then what?'' John asked curiously.

''You could be taking me home. It's a fine day for a drive in the country.''

''But it's only a short walk to your home.''

"You said you planned on visiting with friends. You could be dropping me off along the way." She cocked her head mischievously as she waited for an answer.

"I'll go back to the stable and get a runabout hitched up and meet you at the porch steps."

Harriett shook her head in delight. "I'll be waiting for you."

John watched as the pair of matched chestnut mares were brought from their stalls. They looked beautiful as they pranced to the shed area and were fitted to the harness and carriage.

John was just as proud of the carriage as he was the mares. His father had bought it from a NewEngland firm, and there was no finer around Lexington. The open body was built of bird's eye maple. The shafts and wagon wheels were golden oak. Its wide single seat was neatly trimmed in brown leather stretched over steel springs. The four wheels were fitted with forged steel rims and the body was mounted on leaf springs. The stable hands kept it in top condition.

He was anxious about Harriett and was glad when the men hitched the traces to singletree laprings and tied the reins to the brass whipsocket. He jumped in the carriage, loosened the reins and held them firmly in his hands. When the brake was released the mares lunged forward and John held them in check as they stepped spiritedly along the driveway toward the house.

Harriett was standing at the top of the steps and seeing the runabout she gracefully walked down the steps and waited. She smiled anxiously.

John pulled the team to a halt and locked the brake. As he helped her into the carriage he felt the warmth and softness of her hand.

The team half-trotted along Spring Hill Road and Harriett removed her wide-brimmed hat making her hair flutter back from the sides of her face exposing the rosiness of her cheeks.

When they reached open country John let the mares have their bits and they shook their heads and moved into a fast trot.

John looked at Harriett and smiled. She returned the smile approvingly. They passed along miles of whitewashed paddock fencing, hay barns, stables and exercise tracks. Then they came to farming country where rows of tobacco and corn were growing out of the rich soil. Occasionally they would see a farmhouse but these became more scarce as they traveled along a dirt road. Soon they came to a wooded area where tall sycamores lined each side of the road and a rippling creek came into view. A deer jumped out on the road ahead of them and disappeared quickly in a thicket. They laughed at his fast getaway.

Coming to a grove of trees John checked the team and guided them through a winding road barely wide enough to let them pass. Harriett admired the way John handled the reins and held the mares to a slow walk as the wheels jolted around jagged rocks and depressions.

His hair disarrayed and his eyes glittering with excitement John had an air of confidence that made Harriett feel secure and happy. As they picked up speed the air felt fresh and invigorating. It fanned their cheeks ruffled their clothes and mussed their hair.

"Have you ever heard of a 'Thank-you-m'am-rock'?" John shouted to be heard above the hoof beats and bouncing carriage wheels.

"I'm afraid I haven't," Harriett shouted back.

"I'll show you one," John called out at the same time glancing back and forth at her but never completely losing sight of the road.

Suddenly a front wheel struck a jagged rock and the carriage jolted sending Harriett scooting along the seat to John's side. Instinctively she grabbed him around the waist.

"Thank-you-m'am," he said.

"Thanks for what?"

John laughed. "That was a 'thank-you-m'am-rock' we just hit."

"You mean you purposely hit it?"

"I sure did and if you take your arm away I'll hit another one."

"Then I won't turn loose for anything."

John looked down at her smiling ecstatically.

Harriett looked up admiringly as he slapped the reins against the mares' backs.

They came to a clearing and saw a stream of swift water gushing over and around rocky obstructions. John checked the team and guided them a little farther to a spot where a two-foot waterfall was before them. He pulled them to a halt then jumped down and tied them to the trunk of a dogwood tree.

The roar of the water filled the air with the muffled sound of surging turbulence. John helped Harriett down from the carriage then continued to hold her hand as they stood looking at the falls.

"What do you think about this?" he asked almost sure of what the answer would be.

"Oh, it's beautiful! Just beautiful! I never dreamed there was a place so pretty."

"I like it too," John replied.

Walking to a rocky ledge closer to the falls they sat down. The rocks along the banks were covered with deep green velvety moss. Graceful willows with their draped branches hung listlessly over the creek. Higher, carpets of meadow grass covered the ground.

The water was calm and tranquil above the falls but after it crashed over the natural dam it gushed and spurted through numerous tributaries wild with motion.

Harriett was thrilled. "How did you ever find this place?"

"I've ridden all over this countryside. I could show you lots of places like this but this is my favorite."

"Then you come here often?"

"Whenever I want to. I've even been here when the ground was covered with snow and there was ice on the falls."

"I'll bet it's pretty then," Harriett said then looked at the ground as she asked, "Do you always have someone with you?"

John shook his head. "Most of the time I'm alone."

Harriett wiggled the toe of her slipper digging the tip into the sandy soil. "Have you brought other girls here?"

John stood. "Hey young lady, you ask an awful lot of questions. Next thing you'll be asking if I've ever made love here."

"Have you?" she asked, looking up into his deep set eyes.

"No, not really."

She wondered.

He took her hand and she stood facing him. Her lips looked inviting and her cheeks were pink with excitement. He drew her close. Their lips met and they wanted each other.

The grass smelled fresh and sweet and the earth was warm and inviting. A wood thrush scolded them for intruding on his domain but they didn't hear. They were lost in a world of happiness.

******

The day that Brenlyn was scheduled to leave for St. Martin a cold gusty rain fell on the Bluegrass country. A reminder that summer was drawing to a close and winter was not far away.

Sparrows sheltered themselves under roof eaves. Robins searched lawns for worms, fattening themselves before joining others for the long migratory flight to the deep South.

Brenlyn's train was scheduled to depart from Lexington's depot at five in the afternoon. A number of friends came to Fern Lea in the late morning hours to exchange farewells and any signs of sadness were overshadowed by Margaret's ability to keep everyone happy.

After lunch Brenlyn retired to her room. She lay across her bed and kicked off her black pumps then buried her face in a soft pillow. She offered prayers, asking for strength during the last hours before leaving her home, family and friends.

She turned and saw the big windows that overlooked the picturesque front lawn of their home. She stared at the delicate pink lace curtains hanging gracefully across the spotless panes of glass. Looking around she saw the fine pieces of furniture that adorned her room and gazed at the louvered doors that served as an entrance to the racks where her pretty clothes were kept. She thought of all the parties and balls that she loved and never being able to attend them again.

Closing her eyes she was overcome with grief. "Do I want to give all of this up?" she asked herself, pensively. "Can I be happy in a convent?" She was filled with despair and tears gathered in her eyes.

Desperately she fought the sorrow that engulfed her and buried her head in her pillow to blot the tears. Never before had she realized how much she loved her worldly life.

The thought of giving it up was almost too much to bear. She rose and sat on the side of the bed. A missal on the bedside table gained her attention. She picked it up and opened it to a marked page. She read a verse she knew from memory but wanted to read again. Many times, lying in bed at night, she had said the words over and over. It was taken from *The Imitation of Christ*."

"Thou canst not possess perfect liberty, unless thou wholly deny thyself. All self seekers are bound in fetters; full of desire, full of cares, ever unsettled and seeking ways always their own ease, not the things of Jesus Christ; but often times devising and framing that which shall not stand. For all shall perish that cometh not of God. Hold fast this short and perfect word; forsake all, and thou shalt find rest. Consider this well, and when thou hast put it to practice thou shalt understand all things.''

Suddenly there was a knock at the door and she heard her mother asking to come in. She laid the missal down and quickly wiped away the tears. Opening the door she saw her mother's pretty face and her grief was temporarily relieved.

Mrs. Broker kissed Brenlyn's cheek. ''I thought we might have a little talk before you leave.''

She could readily see that Brenlyn had been crying. ''A little nervous about it all?'' she asked compassionately.

''Just a little,'' Brenlyn answered with a faint smile. Then under her breath she kept saying over and over, ''I can't cry now. I just can't.''

Mrs. Broker put her arm around her and spoke in almost a whisper. ''Maybe it would help if you'd let yourself have a good cry.'' It was just what Brenlyn needed to relieve the tension. She burst into tears as she held tightly to her mother.

******

As the cooks and helpers prepared a luxurious dinner, they felt sad about Brenlyn's leaving. Clara, the head cook, had been with the family a long time and couldn't understand Brenlyn's decision at all. Most of the time she managed to keep her opinions to herself about the Broker's personal life but this time she could not hold back her feelings.

She smacked her lips in disgust. ''I jest think it's a cryin' shame that Miss Brenlyn's gonna' give up all dose pretty clothes and gonna' have to start wearin' dose ole' black robes with her purty little face stickin' out like a turtle er sumpin'.'' Then, throwing her shoulders back and shaking her head, she repeated, "I jest think it's a cryin' shame!"

******

A light, cold rain continued to fall as the Brokers arrived at the railroad station and the warmth inside felt comforting. A pretense of happiness prevailed as the Broker family sat and talked until it was time for Brenlyn to leave.

John told them about talking with an Ohio railroad engineer who had spent the night at the hotel. The man told him about plans to construct railroad tracks from Cincinnati to Chillicothe, Ohio, that would pass through Blanchester, which was only a short distance from St. Martin. John further explained to Brenlyn this would make it convenient and simple for any of them to visit her. This was especially good news for Mrs. Broker who dreaded the thought of riding fifty miles in a bouncy stagecoach.

When the station master announced that it was time for passengers to board their train all signs of happiness diminished. Brenlyn kissed each one. As she went to her mother she saw tears in her eyes. Neither one could restrain her feelings and they embraced in compassionate sorrow.

Mr. Broker gently held Brenlyn's arm and shook his head dejectedly. It grieved him terribly to think of never seeing her at home again.

As the train pulled away from the station Brenlyn looked out her window and waved affectionate farewells to her family.

Continuing to look out the window she saw a figure at the end of the platform. It was Neil Hathaway. Instinctively she waved frantically to attract his attention. For a fleeting moment she thought he wouldn't look up but he finally raised his head. He smiled and covered his lips with the tips of his fingers then slowly extended them toward her as the window moved from sight.

Brenlyn closed her eyes. A feeling of loneliness and fear overcame her. She reached down in her handbag and pulled out her prayerbook and opened it to a specific page and began reading:

"We must leave the beloved for the sake of the beloved; for Jesus will be loved alone and above all things. He that clingeth to the creature shall fall with its falling. He that embraceth Jesus shall be firmly rooted forever. Love Him for thy friend, who, when all will go away will not forsake thee, nor suffer thee to perish in the end.

"Sooner or later thou must be separated from all, whither thou wilt or no. In life and in death keep thyself near to Jesus, and entrust thyself to His fidelity, who alone can help thee when all others fail."

******

The winter months seemed to pass quickly as John continued working at the hotel. There were a number of reasons for this. He had cultivated a taste for bourbon and working as a room clerk, he could readily step back in a cloak room and drink from bottles stored in a nearby supply cabinet. Then too he persuaded his father to let him make several trips to various large cities and spend several days at the better hotels. He told his father he would keep notes about any constructive features he might see that could be incorporated at the Zenith.

He visited hotels in Philadelphia, Chicago and Detroit. Making the rounds of saloons he met a lot of people including frivolous girls who were infatuated with his good looks and personality. He learned about the latest men's fashions and purchased a tremendous wardrobe and listened to stories told by seasoned hotelkeepers and people of all walks of life. In return he fascinated many of them with stories and legends about

Kentucky.

Most everyone listened intently as he talked about the thoroughbred horse farms and the life of the owners and trainers. When he returned to Lexington, he had not only attained a better knowledge of hotels, he had also learned that he got along with all the people he met. This gave him a feeling of confidence he had never known before. Guests often gathered around him as he repeated amusing stories he had heard on the trip.

One of the stories he liked to tell was about a grumpy guest who insisted on being seated at a choice spot in a hotel dining room each day. A couple of salesmen paid a waiter handsomely to shave a quarter of an inch off the brim of his hat daily without his knowing it. The salesmen watched as the grump put his hat on each day, unaware that the brim was smaller. Finally, after most of the brim was removed he put his hat on and detected it did not feel right. He walked over to a mirror and immediately threw the hat in a trash can. They heard him mutter as he went out, "Why in hell did I ever buy such a stupid looking hat in the first place?"

John also told his father about the constructive things he learned. One thing Mr. Broker accepted was his suggestion that they modify the front of the building to make stores and shops along the ground floor. A men's fashion store was built into the front corner of the Zenith and was rented for a nice return on investment.

On John's advice Mr. Broker instituted several other money-saving devices. Some had to do with unnecessary employee services which resulted in a reduced payroll.

These suggestions greatly pleased Mr. Broker despite the fact there were other things John did that provoked him to no end. His drinking habit was a source of trouble and he often made mistakes totaling bills for guests as they checked out. John was rather careless about these things, which usually was due to his becoming too preoccupied while talking to guests or watching some pretty belle.

Mr. Hines, the office manager, would report all of John's accounting mistakes to Mr. Broker which would result in his getting a severe reprimand.

Mr. Hines disliked John from the first day he started working at the hotel. He resented his working there because he hoped to become assistant manager someday and knew that John would most likely be selected over him. He reported anything unfavorable about him to Mr. Broker in hopes he might become so displeased he would send him away to college rather than trying to make a hotelman out of him.

******

No one in or around Lexington welcomed the spring of 1899 more than John Broker. Yet there were times when he was greatly depressed. This was mostly in the mornings as he dressed for work. He hated to think of spending the day indoors at the hotel and again longed to ride his horse over the countryside through the woods along the creeks and over the rich bluegrass pasturelands where the stock farms were.

But spring did make work at the hotel more pleasant than the dull cold days of winter. The doors and windows were opened and the air in the lobby and desk area was refreshing and stimulating.

John took advantage of the weather and walked along Lexington's streets as often as he could. He'd walk down Main Street past the seemingly endless rows of shops and stores, stop by harness shops and look at new livery equipment, inspect clothes displayed in tailor shops, watch tickers in the telegraph office and stop by a saloon and have a refreshing glass of cold beer.

He usually carried a bag of sugar cubes in his pocket to feed scraggly looking horses as they stood at the curbs hitched to their wagons. He realized it did little to ease their hunger but it would be worth something.

There were aways a lot of racehorse people staying at

the hotel during the weeks of spring. Some came to buy horses. Others came to sell leather goods, wagon, farm equipment and other commodities. Travelers often stopped overnight before continuing to Louisville to attend the running of the Derby at Churchill Downs. John was always interested in the Derby and listened as he heard the event discussed.

He learned that Churchill Downs was having financial problems and might have to close its gates after the 1899 spring meet. Some said the track had never shown a profit since the day it opened.

There seemed to be little national interest in the Derby and never enough starters to create much enthusiasm. The distance had been shortened from one and a half miles in 1896 to one and a quarter miles in hopes more horses would be entered but many trainers still felt this shorter distance took too much strength out of a three year old so early in the spring. Consequently only four horses had started in the 1898 Derby.

John's pulse quickened as he heard the Derby discussed. He had never been to Louisville and decided to ask his father's permission to attend. He would stay at the famous Galt House he had heard so much about. He would tell his father he would learn all he could about the hotel's operation. The Derby was to run on May the fourth. That was only five days away so he would have to see his father at once.

Mr. Broker was not receptive to John's request saying he needed all the help he could get during the busy spring season. "I know how much you would like to go but we need all the trained help to get us through these next few weeks." John was disappointed. Knowing his father's decisions were final he did not pursue the trip any further. As he started to leave his father's office to return to the clerk's desk his father continued to speak. "I've been giving some thought to giving you a week off a little later on though."

John was pleasantly surprised. "A week off?"

"Yes it'll probably do you good to get away from the hotel for awhile."

"I'd sure appreciate that, sir," John said gratefully.

"I hope it'll make you take more interest in your work when you return. You've been extremely careless lately. I'm in hopes a vacation will result in your being more careful in the future."

"I feel sure it will," John answered. "When can I go?"

Mr. Broker looked at a calendar on his desk. He thought for a moment. "The first week in June."

John thanked him and returned to the desk feeling happier than he had for a long time.

That evening he rode out to visit Carl and Fred Rint to tell them the good news. He asked if they could get away for the same week and was assured their father would let them off. They talked about the different things they might do.

"How about a fishing trip?" Fred suggested enthusiastically. Then looking at Carl, he continued. "Remember that isolated spot on the South Fork of the Cumberland?"

"Yeah, we camped in an abandoned lumber mill. Wonder if it's still there?"

"Probably is."

"Best fishin' we ever done."

"Yeah. We musta' caught a ton of Black Bass."

"You mean a short ton of course."

"All right, Carl, if you want it that way. Make it a short ton."

"Well, it would be better to call it a string of bass."

"I will next time," Fred replied. Showing his annoyance over arguing about such a trivial subject.

"Hey you guys sound like a couple of brothers arguing," John interjected. "How did you guys ever find out about this place?"

"An uncle of ours took us there several years ago."
Fred answered. "He had a friend in Tyrone that told him
about it."

"Sounds like an ideal spot. How do we get there?"

"We'll take a train to Burnside, then hire a driver to
take us there by horse and wagon. You got two choices
after leaving Burnside, go across a bunch of hills or take
a dirt road that's got ruts as deep as the Red River
Gorge."

"How deep?" Carl asked.

"There you go again."

"Well, it is hilly." Carl said in appeasement.

"In fact, there ain't a piece of land bigger than a skillet
bottom where you could drop a walnut and it wouldn't
roll down hill."

"It's mighty pretty country though. You gotta' admit
that, Carl."

"Yeah, it is," Carl agreed, nodding his head. "Uncle
Jess used to say, 'If God made the Cumberland Valley
any prettier He woulda' fenced it in with roses and
honeysuckle and put heaven there.' "

"Yeah, that's what he used to say all right."

John was enthused about the trip. "What will we need
in the way of equipment?"

"We got all the stuff," Fred advised. "Cooking
utensils, lanterns, blankets, candles, fishing gear, and
we can buy the food in Burnside. That way we won't have
to lug it on the train."

"What about something to drink? We'll need a gallon
or so of good corn whiskey, won't we?" John asked,
cocking an eye.

"To be sure," Fred agreed, then repeated it
wholeheartedly, "To be sure!"

******

John thought the time might drag slowly while waiting
to leave on the trip. Instead, it sped by. This was because
he was extremely busy. Late evenings he would ride out to

Rolling Ridge to help Carl and Fred with plans and packing. The days were well occupied at the hotel too. It was Derby time and the house was heavily booked with racehorse people. It was the twenty-fifth running and there was heavy speculation on the outcome.

Only five horses were entered. Fontainbleu was heavily touted to win but many felt that Corsine or Manuel would beat him in the stretch. The other horses, Moza and His Lordship, had few followers. John liked Moza though and arranged for one of the permanent guests going to the Derby to place a five dollar win bet on him. Later he placed another bet on Fontainbleu at a Main Street saloon just in case he should happen to win.

On Derby Day he anxiously waited for the late edition paper to come out so he would know the results. He was not so eager to win the money as he yearned the prestige of being able to say he picked the winner.

In late afternoon a newsboy burst into the lobby yelling, "Hey, extra, extra, read all about the Derby!"

John called him to the desk, handed him a coin, then spread the paper on the desk top. There it was in bold headlines.

"Manuel with Fred Taral in the saddle wins Derby."

John was greatly disappointed. He looked to see how the other horses finished. Corsine was second; Moza, third; His Lordship, fourth; Fontainbleu, last.

Other guests bought papers and stood near the desk.

"Look at the time," one of them said. "Two minutes and twelve seconds -- and the track was fast. Hell, I could have beat that time riding a fire horse."

"And you would have had time to put out a fire along the way," John added. It was evident none in the group picked Manuel.

"Who did you have, John?" A friendly hotel hermit asked.

"I had all my money on Corsine." He lied, feeling no

need to mention his bets on the third and fourth place horses. He hated himself for doing so but just couldn't bear to say his pick was worse than second place.

The heavy activity at the hotel held John's interest and caused him to do a lot of thinking. He realized for the first time that the work fascinated him. He didn't like working for his father mostly because of the father and son combination. However he felt that if he were on his own at a big hotel in another city he might want to make a career of being a hotel manager.

He liked the contact with people and though the hours were long there was plenty of time for enjoyment. Women were always available; drinks could be had throughout the day; and there was always time for a game of billiards or a quick turkish bath and rubdown. If a need was felt for gambling there was always a game of some kind going on in one of the rooms. Then too there was excellent food in the dining rooms and good Havana cigars could be bought at lobby cigar counters.

The more John thought about these things the more enthused he was about following hotel work. He wondered if his father would back him to open a hotel in St. Louis or Atlanta? He thought of other cities. A hotel of his own! That's what he wanted more than anything. Maybe his father would be receptive if he asked. He was confident his father would do it. He had no way of knowing about his father's heart condition and his dire need for him to remain at the Zenith.

******

John thought there couldn't have been a more beautiful June morning; clear skies, sunshine, warm balmy air. Overhead fans hummed new sounds in the lobby as they were turned on for the first time. Well dressed sportsmen crisscrossed the lobby eagerly looking forward to an exciting day at the Lexington trotting track.

John was extremely happy. It was the last day of work

and he would soon be joining his friends for the trip to
Burnside. The Rint brothers would be arriving at the
Lexington station at noon and would have all the
equipment. John had purchased the train tickets the day
before and his satchel was packed and safely stored
behind the desk. He made arrangements with Byron
Hargrove to be relieved of duty at one o'clock. Then he
would make the short walk to the station on Limestone
Street and he and his two friends would board the
one-twenty-five train and be on their way.

He collected receipts from his cash drawer and picked
up his daily ledger and delivered them to Mr. Hines in
the accounting office. He went back to the lobby
restroom to wash, told a bellhop to take his satchel to the
outside entrance, then went to his father's office to thank
him again for the week off.

Mr. Broker was talking with several guests, so John
waited at the office doorway. The visitors left. Mr. Hines
came in a side door and spoke in a low voice as he laid
several envelopes and a ledger on Mr. Broker's desk.

Mr. Broker read a note attached to one of the
envelopes then opened the ledger. John impatiently
waited for him to finish. He coughed to remind him he
was waiting. His father looked at him momentarily, then
moved a pencil point up and down a column of figures.
He put the pencil down and began counting a package of
currency.

John tapped his foot nervously as he looked at a wall
clock. It was twenty-five minutes before train time. Carl
and Fred would be wondering about him. John was
annoyed. If his father didn't finish soon he would have to
leave without saying goodbye. Three more minutes
passed.

Mr. Broker pushed his chair back and looked up at
John, motioning for him to come to his desk. He shook
his head despairingly.

"I sometimes wonder where your mind is," he said

disgustedly. "Just look what you've done. Here's the ledger and receipts you just turned in to Mr. Hines."

It was obvious to John that he had made a mistake. He picked up the opened ledger and studied his last entry.

"You've made a thirty dollar mistake." His father continued, "You charged Doctor Harris and his family sixteen dollars and his bill was actually forty-six dollars!"

Mr. Broker banged his fist on the desk top. His voice was straining with anger. "I won't have that kind of carelessness in my business. I just won't have it!"

John had never seen his father this angry before. He felt uneasy. He began an apology. "I'm sorry, Father, I guess —"

His father cut him off. "Sorry, hell!" he shot back and at the same time rose from his chair and began walking back and forth across the floor.

Mr. Hines looked at John contemptuously and then left the office, feeling vindictive.

John looked at the clock again. The train would be gone in fourteen minutes. He knew he must leave at once.

"What in the world were you thinking about when you added up that bill?" his father asked. There was less anger in his voice but it was evident he wanted an immediate answer.

John could offer no reasonable explanation. He had to force himself to speak. "Father, it's almost time for my train to leave. When I get back I'll work without pay until the loss is made up. I must leave right away."

Mr. Broker had momentarily forgotten the fishing trip. "What train?" he asked. "Where do you think you're going?"

"On the fishing trip, sir. Don't you remember?"

"You can just forget about the trip. You stay here and work until you learn to keep your mind on what you're doing."

It wasn't the loss of money that upset him. He had always been impatient with anything but perfection in his business. He just couldn't tolerate these kinds of mistakes.

The words stunned John. He realized unless he left immediately the train would leave without him. He knew Carl and Fred would be anxiously waiting. For a moment he was overcome with a feeling of hopelessness. He thought about his father's promise of a vacation. A surge of anger engulfed him. He felt his heartbeat quicken. "I'm going on that fishing trip," he shouted.

His father's face took on a stern questioning expression.

"You'll do what?" His voice was trembling with rage.

John's anger was subdued with fear. He felt a cold sweat over his body. He was ready to back down but the thought of missing out on the trip offset this. There were five minutes left and it would take that long to get to the station. He turned to leave then looked back momentarily. "I'm going whether you like it or not!"

Mr. Broker looked at him in disbelief. Never before had any of his children talked back to him. "If you leave this office I don't ever want to see you again," he said in a voice filled with determination. "Do you understand? Never!"

John didn't look back. He ran out of the office and through the lobby. Grabbing his satchel he picked up speed running down Limestone Street to the station. He joined his bewildered but relieved friends and quickly boarded the train as it began moving out on the tracks.

No sooner had John run out of the office than his father felt an imminent attack coming on. First there was severe pain in his chest and arms. It frightened him and he tried to call out but it took all of his effort to breathe. He slumped back in his chair and immediately went into shock and fell, helplessly sprawled on the floor.

Fortunately Mr. Hines was entering the lobby and saw

John running toward the door. After a moment of reasoning he turned and went to Mr. Broker's office. When he saw him lying there his first thought was that he had been attacked by John. Rushing back to the lobby he told the clerk to get in touch with a doctor at once and send him to Mr. Broker's office.

Mr. Hines' face was ashen. He was extremely unnerved.

"What's wrong?" the clerk asked excitedly.

Mr. Hines stared at a back wall, almost in a state of shock. "John struck him! John struck Mr. Broker! Get a doctor at once!"

There was a doctor in the hotel and the clerk summoned him to Mr. Broker's office. He recognized the symptoms right away and had him carefully moved to a room on the first floor. Mr. Broker's well-kept secret of why he had not been feeling well and his reason for needing John at the hotel could no longer be kept from his family.

******

Shortly after the train departed John uncorked a bottle and passed it to Fred who drank heartily. Smacking his lips, he handed it to Carl who also gulped down a generous drink. When Carl handed it to John for his turn he rested the bottom of the bottle on his leg and stared out the window in deep thought.

He saw rolling fields, some newly plowed and planted; a long line of fence rails; a herd of Black Angus grazing contentedly on a sloping green meadow; a sturdy looking log cabin rested along a tree-lined creek. Each came in view momentarily then disappeared as the train sped along the rails.

They were little more than insignificant sights to John because he was thinking of his father and the ugly way he had run out of his office. He wondered why things like that ever had to happen. If Mr. Hines had only waited a little while before reporting the mistake how different things might have been. He and his father would have exchanged farewells on pleasant terms.

John felt remorseful and wished that he could live the moment over. Why hadn't he let the train leave without him and talked with his father longer. He might have consented to let him catch the next train. He wondered if he should get off at the next station and catch the first train back. He was thinking about this when Fred punched his arm.

"Hey dude," he said smiling. "You look like you lost your last friend. Drink up!"

"Sure, sure," John answered, not realizing he had been in deep thought.

"You're not homesick already?" Carl asked jokingly.

John managed a smile. "No it's nothing like that. I was thinking about something I should have done before I left."

"Anything serious?"

"No not really. I can straighten it out when I get back."

He raised the bottle to his lips and felt a pleasant burning of his throat as he swallowed. There's no use in spoiling this trip for all of us he said to himself. It happened. Its over and there is nothing I can do about it now. I've worked long and hard for a vacation. It's mine to enjoy and that's the way it's going to be. He raised the bottle again and took a second drink.

After crossing the heavy steel bridge over the South Fork of the Cumberland the train stopped at the Burnside station. John reached up to pull a bed roll from the storage shelf and losing his grip, fell awkwardly back into an empty seat across the aisle. Carl and Fred laughed and John grinned sheepishly back at them.

"The longer I get," he said, still lying on his back, "the drunker I drink."

Carl and Fred thought their sides would split as they laughed hysterically at his twisted remark.

Carl waited at the depot while Fred and John went into a general store and bought groceries. Afterwards they walked down the street and hired a driver to take them to the abandoned mill.

Because they would be traveling seven miles over rough terrain the driver selected an open plank bed wagon with sturdy spoked wheels for the trip. He hitched a big black work horse between the shafts. Loading the groceries in the wagon they instructed the driver to take them to the station to get Carl and pick up their gear.

The driver was a big man with a long hatchet face and an oversized nose that hung over his face like a thick banana. He sat up on the buckboard with his upper body in a slightly humped position and his lower lip dropped as if it were weighted down at the center and supported at the ends only. John and Carl overheard someone at the livery stable call him by the name of "Moose" and there was little doubt in their minds how he got the nickname.

John and Fred were still wearing their dress clothes. Their attire greatly contrasted with the clothes Moose was wearing; faded bib overalls and a shabby wide-brimmed straw hat, badly discolored from long exposure to sweat and weather. As they approached the depot many of the townspeople stared in wonderment at the unusual sight.

Moose pulled up to the station platform and Carl climbed in the wagon with the equipment bundled loosely in his arms. His shoe hit a warped floor board and he was sent sprawling across the wagon bed. John looked down at him and laughed. "That had to be the most graceful approach I ever saw."

"Yeah," Fred answered. "It's a good thing he hasn't been drinking or he might have sailed all the way up where ole' Moose is sitting."

Moose turned around. "Looks to me like he's half

drunk. You sure he ain't been drinkin'?'' His hung-down expression didn't change.

The trio laughed and Moose shook his head, wondering what was so funny. John pulled out a bottle and held it high in the air proposing a toast. "Here's to our friend Moose who can't tell when a guy is juiced."

They laughed again and each had another drink, leaving the bottle half filled.

Fred handed the bottle to Moose. "Here, have a drink of the best corn whiskey ever made," he said.

Moose wrapped his long bony fingers around the bottle and stuck the spout in this mouth and curled his lips around it. He drank the entire contents down with big gulps that made his adam's apple bobble up and down like a bouncing ball.

After reaching open country Moose pulled the wagon off the dirt road and drove the horse in a walk over open country. The terrain was bumpy but they didn't mind as they drank and laughed and joked and felt elated at their joyous escapade.

"You suppose ole Moose knows where he's going?" Fred asked.

"I doubt if he even knows his name right now but I'll ask him," John answered, then called out to him. "Hey, Moose, do you know you're not on the road anymore?"

Moose turned around. The ends of his lips curled up in a comical smile. "Yeah," he said, "this here way'll get ya' there a helluva' lot faster."

As they traveled farther the surface became more hilly and Moose's head began bouncing uncontrollably from side to side. He held on to the wagon seat with one hand while he drove with the other.

Traveling along up a long sloping hill, the horse struggled to keep the heavily loaded wagon moving. Moose jumped down and grabbed a wagon shaft to keep from falling. He told the others to get out and push.

Moose walked staggeringly at the side of the wagon

and urged the horse on as John and the two brothers pushed. As Moose walked up the hill holding on to the reins he occasionally lost his balance and would quickly grab anything handy to keep from falling to the ground. Sometimes he grabbed a wheel, sometimes the brake handle, sometimes the horse's tail, and sometimes he would miss everything and tumble past the others as they pushed against the wagon.

Traveling downhill, the effect was the opposite and Moose would stagger forward, traveling ahead of the horse while clinging to the reins. The sight was so comical John and the Rints roared with laughter.

They reached the top of a hill and John pointed out the long sloping downhill terrain before them and mentioned how few obstructions there were. He suggested that Moose drive the horse down on a run so they might gain enough momentum to be able to go up the next hill without having to get out and push.

Moose tried to voice his objection, but the words wouldn't come out. He motioned with his hands that he had something to say. His lips merely curled up in an awkward grin. Then his expression took on an inept look and he fell helplessly to the ground.

John and his friends decided to go ahead with their plan. They laid Moose in the wagon and John and Carl crawled in beside him. Fred jumped up in the driver's seat and gripped the reins. He looked down the long, sloping hill, then turned and looked down at Moose. "Everybody all set?" he asked, grinning.

"Yeah, ole'Moose is ready for anything," John answered. "Hasn't moved a muscle."

Carl looked at Moose's prostrate form. "That's what you call nerve." He raised a bottle and proposed a toast to Moose's nerve.

After John and Fred had another drink Fred braced his feet against the buckboard. "If this piece of horseflesh can run like I think he can we'll be down at the bottom of this hill mighty soon," he said, as he released the brake and snapped the reins across the horse's back causing him to lunge forward in a startled movement.

Everything seemed under control as Fred skillfully handled the reins and applied just enough brake pressure to prevent the singletree from bumping against the horse's back legs. Then, the wagon began to sway from side to side. John and Carl held to the sides to keep from falling.

Suddenly, the horse broke to one side and a front wheel struck a stone jutting out from the ground. The wheels turned sharply and the wagon jackknifed over on its side. The confused horse struggled free of the broken shafts and ran up a hill and disappeared from view.

Fred jumped clear of the spinning wheels and landed in a clump of weeds. John and Carl, along with Moose, rolled out of the wagon and except for a few cuts and bruises were unhurt. Fred had a slight cut over one eye and a torn shirt but suffered nothing else.

Recovering from the shakeup they got Moose to his feet and explained what had taken place. They located his horse and gave him some money to cover part of the damage and promised to send the rest after they returned home.

Moose mounted the horse. His long legs dangled down limply at the animal's sides. His face had a solemn look and his lips seemed to hang down lower than ever.

"Ole' Moose didn't have much fun did he?" Fred remarked.

"Oh I don't know, " John answered. "He's had a lot of free drinks and a long nap. Now he's got money in his pocket and some unforgetable memories of three nuts who hired him to take a simple trip down to the river.

"Yeah," Fred chimed in. "I'll bet that's more excitement than he's had for a long time."

Laughing they gathered their equipment and hiked the short distance to their campsite.

******

Dusk was setting in when they arrived at the mill. Fred pointed out a huge saw table to John. A rusted shaft and pulley were the only remnants of machinery once used to cut lumber. Carl led the way to a long low-roofed building and opened a badly deteriorated screen door. As they entered the building he explained to John that this had been a screened-in porch where the workers loafed in their off time. He pushed the door open. "This is the old bunk house," he explained.

It was dark inside but John could see there were rows of wooden bunks at each side of the building. They laid their equipment on the two bunks closest to them and lighted their lanterns.

John counted eight bunks along each wall. The bunks nearest them were plainly visible in the pale yellowish light. The others looked like square crates in the gray darkness. They were made crudely. Oak planks nailed to two-by-four beams and these supported by four-by-four posts. Ten inch planks were nailed to the sides. The interiors were filled with discolored straw.

"Just like home," Carl said.

They laughed.

"Here, I'll show you the kitchen," Carl added. He picked up a lantern and walked down the aisle between the bunks to another doorway at the far end. They entered a rather small room and Carl held the lantern over an old fireplace. The sides were built up with stone and a steel plate was mounted on top.

A long table was placed near one side of the room with wooden benches along each side. John noticed that they had been permanently nailed to the floor. A half empty jar of preserves, an empty flour sack and a dirty, enameled dishpan were on the table.

Carl picked up the jar and ran his finger across the top to check for dust. "Looks like someone else camped here recently," he said. He looked at the others. "Shall we build a fire and fix something to eat?''

John grimaced. "I couldn't eat a bite." He felt half sick from the drinks.

"Me either," Fred said.

"I'm not hungry," Carl added, "but I'm dead tired."

They walked back to the bunks and each selected one. They began rolling their blankets over the straw and a field mouse scurried out of Fred's bunk. "Wonder how many more there are?" he said. He picked up a stick and poked around in the straw. "Guess he was a loner." He rolled a blanket out, crawled in and pulled it over his body and fell asleep.

John picked up the stick and poked the straw in his bunk. Nothing appeared but he was skeptical about sleeping on the straw. He turned to ask Carl if he thought they might be better off to remove it and sleep on the planks. Carl was in his bunk snoring.

John spread his blanket and cautiously crawled in on top of it. He pulled another blanket over his body. He wondered if a mouse might have built a nest in the straw. "What if he did?" he asked himself. His eyes felt heavy and his arms and legs were tired. Soon he too was sleeping soundly.

******

An hour before sunrise a nesting robin broke the morning stillness and quiet by calling out to its mate with continuous melodious songs. Soon the cardinals and thrushes filled the air with their enchanting calls and it wasn't long until the entire bird kingdom around the mill was in full song.

Fred was the first to hear them. He pulled the blanket over his head in hopes it would soften the noise so he might sleep longer but it didn't help.

Finally the sun peered over a distant hill and it looked as though someone had sprayed the surroundings with a mist of gold. A slight breeze fanned the leaves of the poplars, sycamores, birch and other trees. The air was rich with the smell of honeysuckle, goldenrod, dogwood blossoms and mountain flowers.

It was chilly but Fred knew he must get up if they were to get an early start for fishing. He climbed out and searched his pack for a wool slip-on sweater. Finding it, he poked his arms through the sleeves and pulled the larger opening over his head and tugged at the waist until it was down under his belt line.

He pulled on a pair of boots and went to the kitchen. Luckily someone had left a pile of chopped logs. He crumpled up a bundle of paper and placed it in the stone pit. After covering this with several logs he lighted the paper and welcomed the glowing heat. He called out to John and Carl to wake them up.

John opened his eyes but wished he hadn't. His forehead and temples throbbed with pain and his stomach burned with a sickening feeling of nausea.

Feeling a demand to go outside for relief he sat on the side of the bed and draped a blanket around his shoulders to ward off the damp and chilly air and made a mad dash out the door.

Carl and Fred unpacked their equipment and set their fishing gear on an empty bunk.

Carl agreed to walk along the shoreline to a point upriver where a lone fisherman lived on a shanty boat. There he would rent a skiff for the week and pay him extra to pick up the boat at their makeshift dock after they had broken camp.

When Carl returned his breakfast was ready. John had gone back to bed. He told Fred he was too sick to eat and wanted to sleep off his hangover but would join them later for fishing. The two brothers went on and said they would be back at mid-afternoon to pick him up.

When John awoke the second time the sun was high and the morning haze had cleared away. He looked for Carl and Fred then remembered they had gone out on the river. He climbed out of the bunk and felt a surge of dizziness. His head ached as though a bucket of coal had dropped on it. Feeling the need for a hot cup of coffee he went back to the bunkhouse kitchen and felt the fireplace. It was merely warm. Looking around he saw the food was unpacked and stored on shelves. He found a can filled with coffee and held it in his hand looking back toward the fireplace.

He wanted to kindle the fire but didn't feel up to it. He went back outside and stretched out on the saw table. The sun had grown stronger and it felt good as it warmed his body. He dozed off to let time and nature ease his discomfort.

Before long the sun's rays became so hot that it made sleeping uncomfortable. He saw a stream of clear water springing out from a rocky ledge and drank his fill of cold water then splashed a generous amount on his face. He felt the stubble of two days' growth of beard and ran his fingers through his uncombed hair. It felt coarse and grimy. Remembering he had not bathed since leaving Lexington he felt that a swim in the river might be refreshing.

Descending a short flight of stairs he hesitated and looked at the river valley. He was awed at its magnificent beauty. The banks were lined with rocky cliffs surrounded by green foliage and wild flowers. He followed a path to the river and stood at the water's edge marveling at the sparkling clear water. He stooped to dip his finger in the stream and was glad it felt warm.

Stripping his clothes off he waded out on the sandy beach until the water was at his hips. Plunging headlong there was a momentary chill but this quickly disappeared as he swam a short distance and then swam back to the shore and gently cleansed his body with warm sand. Afterwards he waded back in the water and took another plunge to wash the sand from his body.

Back on shore he dried himself with his shirt and put on his trousers. After gathering the rest of his clothing he climbed back up the hill to the campsite.

Reaching the top he stopped to catch his breath and looked out towards the river to see if Carl or Fred was in sight. He was a handsome figure as he stood there. His skin had acquired a dark copper color. His coal black hair and heavy beard blended well with his tanned face, and his deep-set eyes sparkled in the refreshing air.

Turning to walk back to go to the bunkhouse, he heard a noise. A feeling of fear gripped him because he felt certain it came from inside. There was another sound. He cautiously moved to a place between two windows and pressed his body against the building and waited. There were footsteps!

Slowly he moved toward one of the windows until his head touched the frame. He could feel his heart pounding and his breathing was deep and heavy. He carefully moved his head forward and peered inside. Someone was moving toward the door!

The intruder's back was toward him. He saw long wisps of brown hair and a slight, shapely body. It was a girl! She was carrying a basket filled with food.

John made a quick dash toward the door and waited for her to come out. Seeing him she was overcome by fear and dropped the basket. John offered a friendly smile. He eyed her up and down. Though shabbily dressed, she was quite attractive. He judged her to be about twenty years old. Her face was filled with fear. She pulled at her cotton dress in an effort to ease her embarrassment.

John attempted to relieve her anxiety. "There's no need to be afraid," he said in an assuring voice. "I won't hurt you." He looked down at the spilled food and recognized items which they had bought at Burnside.

"You must be awfully hungry to be carrying all that food?" Getting no answer, he stooped and began picking up the food and placing it back in the basket. Then he set the basket down beside her.

"You can have it all if you want it," he said, smiling. Seeing she was starting to walk away, John introduced himself. "My name's John Broker. What's yours?"

She hesitated a moment then answered shyly, "Ellen."

"That's a very pretty name." John saw this pleased her. "Where do you live?"

She motioned in a direction back toward the hills. "Over that way a piece."

"Live with your folks?"

She motioned her head to indicate she didn't.

"Married?"

She dropped her head then moved it up and down, indicating that she was.

"Is he waiting for you to bring the food to him?"

She moved her head negatively.

"Where is he now?"

"At a lumber camp."

"Be home soon?"

She shook her head again.

"When?"

"Friday night."

John was infatuated with her. Since she was in the act of taking their food he thought she might be hungry and decided to play a hunch. "Can you come in and cook something for me to eat?"

"Anyone else with you?" she asked.

"Oh, there's a couple of fishing buddies but they won't be back for a long while."

She was hesitant.

"Please," he begged. "I'm so hungry I could eat a barrel of food and I don't know anything about cooking. In fact I once cooked a pan of flour gravy that turned out so bad we used it for paste."

She smiled for the first time and it pleased John.

After eating, they went outside and sat on a bench facing the river. John managed to get her to talk about her life in the hills.

Her husband was a teamster in a lumber camp. He was home only on weekends. He drank most of the time and continually abused her. She was always glad when Monday mornings came and he went back to the camp. He never left her with enough provisions or money, so her only means of getting more food was to beg or steal.

John asked how she had met her husband and came to marry him. She told him she was one of five children reared in a three-room cabin near the Kentucky-Tennessee border. Her father was an alcoholic who drifted from one place to another, cutting hair at lumber camps and coal mines. Most of the time he was too drunk to work.

As a result the family had to use any possible means of getting money for food and upkeep. Sometimes they cut and sold firewood. Often they had to beg or steal when they became destitute.

Ellen could never remember her father's showing any kindness to any of them. Their life was filled with sadness and fear. He cursed and beat them as if he hated the ground they walked on.

When Ellen was twelve her mother arranged for her to live with an aunt in Somerset. Her aunt was very kind to her and she was glad to have escaped the unhappy life at home. She had pretty clothes to wear, attended school and made friends with many of her classmates. She never let herself think about her earlier life. She was happier than she had ever been before.

But her happiness was short lived. When she was fifteen her aunt died suddenly and she was forced to go back to her parents' home and she had great difficulty adjusting to her former crude life in the hills.

Her only desire was to escape but she knew that her mother needed her. Then too she realized if she did run away her father would find her and there would be no end to the punishment he would inflict on her.

A year after she returned home her father introduced

her to a lumberman named Jed Boone. Jed worked at one of the lumber camps where her father cut hair and the two men had struck up a friendship. One evening her father brought Jed to their cabin. They sat at the kitchen table and drank until the early hours of the morning.

It was difficult for any of the family to stay out of the room because the kitchen doorway was the only exit in the house. Each time Ellen had to walk through, Jed stared at her desirously. Seeing his interest her father stopped her on one of her trips. "Ellen, honey, come back over here. I want you to know this here friend of mine."

Ellen stopped and hesitatingly turned and faced the table.

"Jed," her father said with a thick tongue, "this here's my daughter Ellen. She's my purtiest daughter."

Jed eyed her up and down. "Yeah, she is purty." He said, grinning. "Real purty."

Ellen could never forget how repulsive he was as the memory of that night came back to her.

He had large lips that protruded outwardly against uneven rows of tobacco stained teeth. His face was round and puffy. His reddish hair curled up close to his scalp in small ringlets. His nose was pocked and fleshy and his eyes looked as if they would pop out of his head at any moment.

He was heavy set and his arms and shoulder and chest looked oversized for the rest of his body. His hands were knobbed and scarred from years of working with timber.

Thinking of him as she sat there in the open with John she shuddered in fear that he might learn she had been talking to another man. But she needed to talk to someone. She never dared to talk to any of her neighbors. She couldn't risk the chance they would tell him. She was sure he would beat her unmercifully and make her life more miserable than ever. It was a great relief to talk to someone about Jed and she was confident

John would never see anybody she knew.

She looked at him. "I ought not to be talkin' to you like this. He'd skin me alive if he ever found out I was talkin' about him to another man."

"He won't know about it," John assured her.

"I really better head on back home." She started to get up but John beckoned her to sit back down.

"No, I want you to tell me more. It might do you good to talk about it."

She looked up at him in appreciation and told him the rest.

The morning after meeting Jed she was returning from a spring with a bucket of water and saw her father sitting on a bench at the side of their cabin. He called and said he wanted to talk to her. Ellen set the pail down and nervously walked to his side. Seeing him close she wondered how he could be anyone's father. He was unkempt, lazy, irresponsible and usually so full of whiskey that he never knew what he was saying. He had a repulsive habit of sucking saliva through a cavity in one of his front teeth, making an ugly hissing sound which added to his unsavory appearance.

"Ellen, honey," he said, curling his lips and making the sucking noise. "Me and Jed Boone talked quite a spell last night and he wants to marry up with you."

Ellen couldn't believe what she had heard and began walking backward as if to escape. Her father stood and walked toward her. She was gripped with fear and turned and began running toward the house. Realizing there would be no refuge there she fell to the ground in hopeless resignation.

Grabbing her by the arm her father pulled her to her feet. "You're going to marry Jed Boone if I have to hitch ya to a post," he said in a booming voice.

Ellen shook her head frantically. "No! I won't! I won't! Please don't make me," she pleaded, crying. "Please!"

Her father raised his arm and struck her across the face and sent her sprawling to the ground. "That'll learn ya never to talk back to me," he said, then turned to walk back to the house.

Ellen didn't know how long she lay there but when she got up she realized how completely useless it was to try to escape her father's wishes. She thought of going to her mother but she too feared him. She thought of running away but knew that Jed or her father would eventually find her. She thought of killing herself but knew she could never do that.

With no way to escape Ellen became Jed Boone's wife and had not known a happy day since.

John felt great pity for her. "You must let me find a way to get you away from here."

She shook her head hopelessly. "There's no way to get away. I've thought about it and thought about it. There just ain't no way fer me to ever leave. Why, if he even knew we were sittin' here talkin', he'd kill both of us, for sure."

"What if I bought you a train ticket and provided you with money to live on?" John didn't have that much but thought he could borrow it somewhere.

"Where would I go? I wouldn't know which way to turn."

John had to agree. If she were just a little older it might be easier but he realized how difficult it would be for her to get along in a strange place.

Wanting to make their situation more pleasant, he looked at her and smiled. "Ever do any fishing?"

"Sometimes," she answered.

"I'll get a couple of cane poles and we'll go down and try our luck."

"I better not," she said, shaking her head.

"Come on, maybe we will catch a big catfish and you can take it home for supper."

They both laughed. John went into the bunkhouse and

selected two poles. Returning, he saw Ellen waiting at the top of the path leading to the river. She was much more attractive than he had first thought her to be. She followed him as he led the way down to the river. John came to a sharp drop-off and tossed the pole down ahead of him; then jumped down grabbing hold of a willow branch to maintain balance. After getting a foothold in the sandy soil he reached up for her hands. As she jumped she too landed off balance and he grabbed her around the waist to prevent her from falling.

She laughed at her inability to stand and turned to see if John was amused too. She saw a different look on his face and in a split second he pulled her close to him. Instinctively, she tried to pull back but couldn't. In another second his lips pressed against hers and she didn't have strength to pull away.

She was stunned. "You had no right to do that!"

John pulled her forward to kiss her again. This time she managed to pull back.

"I thought you might be different," she said, resentfully, then turned and ran up the bank.

John ran after her but when he reached the top she was gone. He called out to her. There was no answer. She had disappeared into the woods.

******

When Fred and Carl returned to the camp they showed John their catch. They had a string heavy with blue gill, catfish, black bass and crappie. Carl held the string up for John to see. The fish lashed and pulled in a futile attempt for survival.

John complimented them on their success but couldn't help feeling sorry for the fish. He wanted all wild life to be free and thought that was the way it should be. He wondered what right man had to remove any living creature from its natural environment. He wished he weren't so softhearted but could not help himself. He seldom spoke to anyone about this because so few would understand.

After cleaning the fish, Fred dipped the filets in corn meal and dropped them in a skillet of hot grease. John shucked a half dozen ears of corn and placed them in a pan of boiling water. Under Fred's direction he cooked a pot of green beans with bacon for seasoning, brewed a pot of coffee and sliced half a loaf of bread.

He did these things without saying a word. He wanted to tell Carl and Fred about the day's events but felt they wouldn't understand. Ellen needed help so badly and he might have been the only person who would ever be able to help her. He was disgusted with himself and ate sparingly of the food.

Carl and Fred saw that he was troubled. This they thought was because he was probably still feeling the affects of the heavy drinking. They shrugged it off feeling confident he would feel better in the morning and would join them for a day of fishng.

After retiring for the night John lay awake for a long time thinking about Ellen. He wondered why he was so concerned about her. Why should he worry about apologizing to her? Why should he care how she felt toward him? He knew he must find her and convince her he was different from the other men who had made her life so miserable.

He tried to think about other things. Without realizing it his thoughts drifted back to Lexington. He wondered about his father saying he never wanted to see him again. Would he still feel this way? Should he go back home? Then he thought of Louisville. If he went there he would be unknown and free to do as he pleased. It was a wonderful feeling. He wanted to see Churchill Downs, the Falls of the Ohio, the Galt House and the business section on Main Street. He had heard so much about these places and felt thrilled about seeing them.

His eyelids became heavy, his thoughts waned and his senses dulled as he drifted into a deep sleep.

At breakfast the next morning John told Fred and Carl about Ellen and explained she needed help. He told them he wouldn't be fishing with them again that day because of wanting to find her and to see if there was anything he could do. Carl and Fred were greatly disappointed. They warned him of the trouble he might get into. John could think of only two things; helping Ellen and going to Louisville.

He entered a wooded area in the general direction where Ellen had indicated she lived. Before long he found a narrow path and followed it until he came to a mountain spring where water flowed down a wooden trough making it accessible for drinking. He cupped his hands and drank freely of the cool water.

He checked the surroundings. A well worn path led down along a valley. Realizing the spring was probably a public watering place, he wondered if Ellen might be one of the users.

Walking a little farther down a hillside he stopped abruptly as a small village came into view. There were about twenty shabby looking cabins spotted along a hillside along the bottom of a desolate looking valley. Most of the cabins were supported by upright timbers on the front while the backs were butted up against the hillside. They were low-roofed, one-story cabins with rough, unpainted wood sidings. Each had a small side porch with a flight of wood stairs leading to a doorway.

He took a position in a cluster of dogwoods and rhododendron. It afforded a view of the cabins yet obscured him from anyone who might be walking along the path. Sitting on the ground he rested his back on one of the trees and waited. It wasn't long until he heard someone talking. Standing, he saw a slightly bent and frail looking woman walking toward the spring. Two small boys with yellowish hair walked in single file behind her. She was wearing a long gingham dress that was faded and threadbare. Her gray hair was combed tightly back across her head and tied at her neckline. She carried a wooden pail in each hand. When she reached the spring she set the buckets down making a dull thudding sound that echoed back and forth across the valley.

John could hear the sounds of water as she filled the first bucket. At first it was high pitched, gradually changing to a deep, fluidic tone as the water neared the top. He heard the sound repeated a second time; then heard the woman ask the youngsters if they wanted a drink. There was a new sound of splashing water as they took turns quenching their thirst.

He heard the children talking as they walked back down the path and saw the woman carrying the heavy buckets of water. Her fingers gripped the handles tightly and her downstretched arms strained under the load. He continued watching until they entered one of the cabins.

John watched hopefully for Ellen. Others made trips to the spring during the morning hours but there were no signs of her living in the valley. Hordes of sweat bees continuously swarmed around his face and he brushed them away with his hand when they became too annoying.

Finally his patience was rewarded. Ellen walked out of one of the cabins and he was pleased to see she was carrying a pail. There was no doubt she was coming to the spring. Remaining in his hiding place John waited anxiously for her. Then he saw someone else nearing the spring. It was an elderly couple. This alarmed him. They would be there when Ellen arrived. If they didn't leave right away he might not be able to talk to her because he had to see her alone. It would be too risky to chance someone seeing him and telling Jed. A horsefly lighted on his cheek and he slapped it away cursing it and his luck at trying to see Ellen.

He watched closely. The old couple reached the spring first. After filling their buckets the old man complained of his legs hurting and said he wanted to rest. Then Ellen walked up to the spring. It made him feel good to see her at close range again.

The old lady began gossiping about current events. Someone had stolen John Bledsoe's chickens; Effie's son came down with the measles; Charlie Hawkins shot a fox in his back yard; Roy Hopson got a job working in Pickerill's coal mine. John wondered if she would ever stop talking.

Ellen began filling her pail. The old lady started talking about her rheumatism. She explained every pain, and talked about the many patent liniments and home made medicines she had tried. Ellen sympathised with her, then picked up her pail to leave.

John was desperate. He had to gain her attention. The old couples' backs were turned toward him and he had to take a chance. He stepped forward quietly poking his head above a cluster of foliage and moved his arms.

Ellen looked up. John quickly placed a forefinger upright over his lips signaling her to remain quiet. Her face took on a startled, puzzled look. Every nerve in her body trembled in fear. She lowered her eyes, wondering what to do.

The old man got up. "Wa'll," he said, "We're a goin' on back if'n you wanta' walk along with us."

Ellen hesitated for a moment. "No," she said, trying to hide her nervousness. "I been wantin' to see if the blackberries will soon be ready for pickin'."

"Oh, they hain't gonna' be ready fer a long time," the lady replied.

"I reckon you're right about that, but I think I'll look around, anyway."

"Wa'll, you better watch out fer rattlers. This here place is full of 'em."

When John heard this he cautiously looked at the ground surveying it for any signs of movement. He felt uneasy.

Finally, the old couple decided to leave. After they were out of sight John stepped out in the clearing.

"It's good to see you again, Ellen," he said, smiling.

"You oughtn't be here," she said in a frightened voice."

She started to pick up her pail to leave. "I got to go before someone sees us."

"No, Ellen. Please, I must talk to you."

She started walking away.

John followed her. "You must listen to what I have to say," he insisted.

She stopped to object. "You got to get away from here. Someone will be seein' you and there'll be a heap of trouble fer sure."

Seeing she was too frightened to stay, John decided he would bargain with her.

"I want you to come back to the mill so we can talk. I promise nothing unpleasant will happen like it did yesterday."

"No. Someone is bound to see us."

"Then I'll just follow you down the path and sit on your cabin steps until you decide to listen to what I have to say." It was a bluff. He waited for her answer.

She was in deep thought. She knew she must do something to get him to leave. "You go on back to the mill and I'll be there in a short while."

******

It was late morning when she came to the mill. John was seated on the saw table facing the woods. Seeing her come out from the trees he stood up and walked to meet her.

"I ought not be here," she said in a worried voice.

"Let's go inside and talk." John motioned toward the bunkhouse door.

She was hesitant. John took hold of her arm. "Come on. Didn't I promise there wouldn't be anything like yesterday?"

Inside they sat at the table and John told her of his plans to help her.

"I'll get you a train ticket to St. Louis and provide you with enough money to take care of yourself until you write to me. Then, I'll see that you will have enough money to live on." He had no idea where he would get the money. Since he was never without ample funds this did not pose a problem. He would find a way.

Ellen refused the offer. "There ain't no place I could ever go where Jed wouldn't find me. My life here would be like heaven compared to the awful things he would do to me after he caught up with me."

She thanked him for wanting to help then asked him to let her go back home and for him not to worry about her any more. "I ought not to have said anything to you about my life here. I wouldn't have told you about it if I knew you wuz goin' to be feelin' pity for me. Life up here in these parts ain't very easy on nobody. We know we can't do no better, so we don't notice it as much as you do." She continued with a grateful smile. "It really did help to tell you about it, though. It makes me feel good to know that somebody knows what I been through."

John looked away in despair. He had never felt so helpless. He wanted to take her in his arms and caress her. He felt his eyes watering. "I'll never forget you, Ellen. I don't know where I'm going when I leave here, but as soon as I get located I'll find a way to let you know."

"No," she insisted. "We can't take that chance." She reached out her hand. "I thank you fer being so nice."

John held her hand tenderly. He wanted to kiss her but knew he shouldn't.

"Won't you let me give you some money?"

She shook her head. "Jed would ask me where I got it."

"You could tell him you stole it."

"No, there'd be too many questions." She pulled her

hand from his. He could see the sadness in her eyes as she turned to leave.

"We'll be leaving most of our things here," he said, "too heavy to carry back to town." He hated the crudeness but it was the only thing he could do for her. He walked to the door with her and watched her walk away. She looked back. "You must never try to see me again." She tried to smile. Her lips trembled as she lowered her head and walked away. He wanted to go to her but knew it was useless.

******

Carl and Fred returned in early afternoon. The fishing had been good again and they were showing John their catch. He showed little interest. Carl asked if something was bothering him.

"I guess I haven't been myself lately," he answered, realizing he owed them an apology. I don't know what it is. I really feel a need to get away by myself for awhile."

"I thought you were looking forward to this?" Fred interjected.

"Yes, I know. But it hasn't turned out like I expected."

"Is it the girl?"

"Partly."

Carl wasn't surprised. He looked at Fred. "Well, I guess we've had enough fishing anyway.

Fred shook his head in agreement.

Fishing had become boring without a third party. The two brothers had been together all their life. There was little to talk about now. If John had been more compatible it would have made things much more pleasant.

"Why don't we just break camp and head on back to Burnside," Fred suggested, then searched the faces of John and Carl to see how they felt about it. Both agreed it was best.

"Think we can make it before dark?"

"I believe we can," John replied. "We can hike over to that farmhouse we saw on the way over here. We'll pay someone to drive us the rest of the way."

"Yeah, maybe there's another Moose there," Fred said, smiling.

There was little response. Nothing seemed funny anymore.

"We'll have to travel light," John suggested. "We may as well leave the groceries and some of the other things here."

Nothing was said for a few moments then Fred agreed. "Yeah, I think that's best. Maybe somebody will find it, that needs it."

When they reached Burnside John told his companions he wasn't going back to Lexington. He explained he was going to catch a train for New Orleans. He hated to lie but didn't want his family to know he was going to Louisville. He wanted to be independent of them for the time being. He waited with Carl and Fred until they boarded their train. They exchanged farewells and soon the train pulled out of the station. He watched it as it pulled out on the tall, black, iron trestle that crossed over the picturesque river valley.

Puffs of black smoke forced its way out of the stack on the locomotive. Powerful jets of steam spurted from the cylinders and the big drivers picked up momentum. Powerfully and majestically the iron horse crossed the trestle and one by one the coaches trailed behind until the last coach disappeared where the tracks entered the countryside.

******

It was early morning when John's train backed into the Tenth and Broadway station in Louisville. After disembarking he walked along a platform and entered a rear door to the massive structure. Inside scores of people were crowded in the edifice. Some stood in long ticket lines; others sat on the long rows of benches extending back to back for the length of the building. Still others stood at the magazine counters while some hurried along lugging their baggage with their immediate destinations foremost in their minds.

Proceeding to the front John walked through one of the arched doors and down a flight of steps to a wide expanse of pavement and got his first glimpse of Louisville.

A long line of hacks was strung out along a curbing, and one by one their drivers walked their horses to the front of the station to pick up waiting fares. When it was John's turn a round-faced little man wearing a black stovepipe hat moved his carriage up and John climbed in the back seat.

"Where to, sir?" the driver asked.

"The Victoria Hotel." John had read an advertisement on the train and decided it might be a rather inexpensive place to stay.

The man's face took on a questioning look. "Where did you say?"

Thinking the man had a hearing problem John repeated in a loud voice, "The Victoria Hotel!"

The driver nodded as he slapped the reins across the horse's back, and they began bumping along the cobblestone street. John casually looked at the big brick homes lining each side of the street. Several street corners had beautiful tall steepled churches and rows of sycamore trees lined a plot of ground between the sidewalks and curbs. Turning north onto Fourth Street they passed St. Joseph's Infirmary and a number of small shops. The Customs House and Post Office Building with its clock tower came into view. There were more shops and several three and four storied buildings. Then they turned left and were on Main Street.

There was little doubt in John's mind this was the mainstream of Louisville's business district. The sidewalks were crowded with pedestrians; shop and office doorways could hardly accommodate the throngs of people entering and leaving. There was a maze of signs on building fronts and pennants were stretched across the street advertising products available in the individual stores.

John asked the driver if they would be passing the Galt House.

"No sir," he answered. "That's at First and Main. About three blocks up from here. Want me to turn around and take you there?"

John felt the urge to say yes but decided he had to be conservative with his money until he could find employment.

"No, I'll see it some other time. Just take me on to the Victoria." He was disappointed but there was plenty to see anyway.

After passing Sixth Street, the driver halted the horse and began pointing out some of the buildings. "Over there on the left is Seelbach's European Hotel." John looked over at a five-story building on the southwest corner and saw the Seelbach sign.

Pointing to an impressive looking building next door, the driver continued. "That's the Louisville Hotel." John saw the ten columns that rose from an iron railed promenade deck on a two-story high ornate porch.

An electric car was slowly working its way down the street and several carriages blocked its path. The motorman banged his heel against a floorboard lever, sounding out loud clangs of a warning bell.

Delivery wagons were parked along the curb taking up every space. Some were backed against the curb and teams of horses took up parts of the traffic area. John saw several automobiles parked along with the wagons. The sidewalks were filled with people going to work or taking care of business.

A stake body wagon loaded with eight hogsheads of tobacco and pulled by six stout draft horses was a menace to traffic. The driver looked as though he were used to being a nuisance and completely ignored the glaring looks and caustic remarks shouted by other drivers.

John's driver managed to get to Seventh Street. He pointed to a large building on the right. A large sign across the front read, Harbison and Gathright. "They make the finest harness and saddle that can be made," he said. "They use only the best leather."

"And right over there," the driver pointed to another building on the right, "is the Carter Dry Goods Building. Everybody around this part of the country buys things there. Course, they only sell wholesale to stores and the likes."

John noticed the building was much like others along Main Street in that its facade was a combination of ornate cast iron and stone.

At Eighth Street he could see a river packet moving along the Ohio. It looked to be less than two city blocks away. When they reached Tenth the driver turned left and they passed through a residential neighborhood.

They pulled up in front of the Victoria. The driver looked at his watch and announced the fare. For the first time he appeared to be in a hurry. John made little note of it. After paying and handing him a generous tip he stepped down to the brick sidewalk. The driver urged the horse into a fast trot and they sped away.

John looked at the hotel then glanced across the street to familiarize himself with the surroundings. He looked hard at a big stone building and realized he had been there before. It was the Union Station he walked out of earlier. He was directly across the street from the place where he hired the enterprising driver. He had been duped!

His first impulse was to run after the driver and pull him from the hack by the seat of his pants. Instead he walked into the Victoria lobby, amused at his gullibility.

******

In Lexington Mr. Broker's health continued to fail. He had great difficulty in breathing and the pains in his chest continued. The doctor permitted him to be moved to the Broker home with strict instructions that he would have to remain in bed and should relieve himself of all business responsibilities.

This was a great disappointment because he had hoped the Zenith would be a source of income for many generations of his family. Those aspirations vanished when John walked out on him. If John had not failed him things might be different, he thought to himself. But no longer did he feel any resentment towards him.

Instead he wondered if he were to blame for not taking time off from the business to be more of a companion to his son. How he wished he could live those days of his life over. It was too late for that now and he wished John would return home so he could make up for his misgivings.

Mr. Broker had never had so much time to reminisce. He realized how much John's mannerisms were like his. He remembered how he resented his own father's insistence that he study engineering and how he escaped all family ties to keep from doing so. The more he thought about John the more he wanted him back home so amends could be made.

Mr. and Mrs. Broker discussed the possibility of Frank's taking charge of the hotel but realized he was not adapted for hotel work. Mr. Broker did not want to force him into the business the way he had forced John. Mr. Hines was placed in full charge and was told he was not to consult Mr. Broker for even the smallest detail about operations. Fortunately Hines had been closely associated with Mr. Broker and was qualified temporarily to manage the hotel.

Mr. Broker asked Frank to talk with the Rint brothers to see if they might know where John had gone. At first the brothers were reluctant; but after learning how serious Mr. Broker's condition was they told Frank about John's experiences on the camping expedition. They told him about Ellen Boone and suggested he might have gone to her home to find a way to help her. They also mentioned John's saying he was going to New Orleans adding they doubted this story.

Frank did not tell his parents he was going to Burnside nor did he tell them about Ellen. Instead he said he was going to New Orleans to see if he could find John.

******

Ellen managed to keep busy just as she did each Friday before Jed came home for the weekend. This helped to keep her mind off the abuse she knew he would inflict on her.

Soon she heard the returning lumbermen shouting as their big chuck wagon came down the road leading to the village. Their work week was over and as usual they had spent a portion of their pay for whiskey and had been drinking freely on the way home. As the wagon drew closer Ellen could hear Jed's voice above the others. He was arguing with the other men and they were shouting back at him.

She heard the wagon creak to a stop and the harness chains rattle as they took up slack. Jed climbed out over the tailgate and clumsily dropped to the ground.

As he staggered up to the cabin Ellen realized how much she despised him and dreaded his coming home. Seeing her in the garden he motioned in an awkward gesture for her to follow him. When he reached the cabin, he used his boot to kick the door open. As she followed him inside she saw him pull a bottle from his pocket and place it on the kitchen table.

He ordered her to come to him. When she was within arm's reach he gripped her arms with his powerful hands and looked down at her. "What's this that Coy Therman's ole' lady is sayin' about you being down at the ole' mill with some city fellar?''

Ellen was terror stricken. She wondered what kind of lies had been told about her. She tried to answer as Jed's grip became tighter. The jaws of a vice could not have hurt more. She felt his body trembling as he continued. ''Who is he? Tell me so I can choke the livin' life out of him.'' He released his grip and shoved her backwards. Both fists were clenched as he waited for an answer.

Ellen turned to run from the room but Jed caught her and spun her around. ''Tell me who the bastard is 'fore I smash your head in!''

Ellen shook her head in disbelief at what was happening. She began sobbing hysterically. Jed drew back his arm and his fist was poised to strike her. ''Tell me!'' There was a wild look in his bloodshot eyes.

''His name is Broker! -- John Broker!'' Ellen spoke without realizing what she was saying. Before she could explain, Jed slapped her across the face and she fell to the floor. Her heart was pounding so hard she wondered if it would burst. Her face was aching with pain. Choked with fear she waited for him to come after her again.

She watched as he walked to the table and reached for the bottle. He turned it up to his lips and gulped until the last drop was gone then still clutching it he staggered into the bedroom. Ellen waited for him to order her to come into the room with him. Instead he fell across the bed in a senseless stupor.

Ellen rose and went to a washstand and looked into a wall mirror. When she saw her bruised and swelled face she closed her eyes in disbelief. She sat and laid her head across the table sobbing uncontrollably -- wondering why her life had to be so miserable.

That weekend was the worst Ellen had ever known. Jed berated and abused her unmercifully. He accused her of everything. Whenever she tried to explain he accused her of lying. Finally the weekend passed and he went back to work. Before leaving he ordered her not to leave the village. He told her she would be watched by neighbors and if he heard of her being around another man he would kill her.

******

Frank caught the early morning train and as he sat back in his coach seat he wondered about John. He greatly disliked the idea of having to go into backwoods country and felt resentful toward him for his own predicament. He was determined to get the search over as quickly as possible.

When he stepped down from the train at Burnside it was hot and the air was thick with dust stirred up from wagons traveling down the dirt street. He pulled off his coat and loosened his collar to become more comfortable.

Wondering where to begin he asked an elderly mountaineer sitting in the shade of a big oak tree where the courthouse was located. The man was more than helpful. He pointed to a two-story frame building where groups of men dressed in faded overalls and wide-rimmed crumpled straw hats were gathered.

"Hit's rite down thar," he said. "The circuit jedge is here and havin' court rite now."

Frank thanked him and walked to the building and entered an open door leading from the sidewalk. It was hot and musty inside. A middle-aged clerk saw him. "Kin I help ya', stranger?" he asked.

"Perhaps you can," Frank replied. "I want to go to a little village that's not too far from an abandoned lumber mill that's down the river from here."

The clerk scratched his head. "I reckon ya' mean the ole' lumber mill that Sam Emerson used to run."

"I wouldn't know who it belonged to," Frank answered politely.

"Well, thet's the onliest mill I know of. And you must be wantin' to go to Dry Holler, 'cause thet's the onliest village anywhars' near the mill."

"That must be it." Frank was pleased to find the location so quickly. He asked for directions and the clerk went into great detail to explain and drew a crude map to make it clearer.

After thanking him Frank ate lunch at a little restaurant then rented a saddle horse and began his search. The horse picked his way along a dirt road. After riding for a little more than an hour Frank spotted a log cabin where several people were sprawled on a crude front porch. He checked the horse and rode up to the porch steps. Two heavily bearded men were asleep, an overly plump woman was busy pushing a handle up and down in a butter churn and a boy who looked to be in his early teens was playing mournful tunes on a harmonica.

Frank asked if he was on the road leading to Dry Hollow. The woman walked over and poked one of the men and the boy removed the harmonica from his mouth to hear what was being said.

"This here man wants to know ifn' he's headin' fer Dry Holler."

The man sat up and leisurely rubbed the sleep from his eyes. After a lengthy discourse Frank finally learned he was on the right road and continued his journey.

After making a turn along a rather steep incline he caught sight of the village. He pulled the horse to a halt and studied the cabins. They looked so much alike it was difficult to distinguish one from the other.

Riding farther down the hill he stopped at the first cabin he came to. A frail looking woman was bent over a scrub board rubbing clothes against the corrugated surface. After asking her the location of Ellen Boone's cabin she pointed to a house on the far side of the valley. She barely raised her head. After Frank walked the horse away the woman dried her hands on her apron and scampered over to a neighboring cabin to spread the news.

******

Jed Boone was driving a team of horses hitched to a big log being dragged along the ground. As he neared a storage area at a riverside clearing he was aware he had never felt more uncomfortable. Sweat rolled down his face and his bushy hair and beard were a soggy mess of grimy dust and wood shavings. He cursed the horses as they faltered and whipped them unmercifully.

Jed had never been so sullen. He thought about Ellen constantly and the thought of her having been with another man provoked him to no end. His feelings about her were far different than before. He had felt he did her a great favor by marrying her. Never had he thought of her wanting to be with somebody else. The thought that she might want another man filled him with bitter rage.

Jed was oblivious to his surroundings. At times the horses would stop in their tracks and he would be so engrossed in thought he would stand in a daze and make vows he would see to it that Ellen would never want to be with another man again. In a few moments he would come to his senses and pick up clods of dirt and throw them at the horses startling them into a quick, jerky strain to put the log into motion again.

He was in one of these rages when he heard someone calling his name. Turning he saw Sarah Therman's boy and he was screaming.

"Mr. Boone! Mr. Boone! Stop! My maw sed fer me to tell ya sumpin'!"

Jed pulled back on the reins and halted the team. The boy continued.

"Mr. Boone, my maw sez to tell ya to come home rite away. Thar's a man ridin' rite down near your place and he's been askin' about Mrs. Boone. And my maw sez to tell ya thet he looks like the same man thet she wuz with the other time!"

Jed felt his stomach muscles churning and his mind became clouded with rage. He dropped the reins and half ran and half stumbled up to the lumber office and mounted a horse tied to a hitching post. Furiously he kicked his heels against the horse's sides and raced to the village.

******

Ellen was seated on the porch steps when she heard the hoofbeats of Frank's horse. She turned to see if it was someone she knew and couldn't believe her eyes. "It's John Broker!" she thought. She got up and ran for the cabin door, but Frank had dismounted and was calling to her. "Hold up a minute please. I must talk to you."

Realizing it wasn't John's voice she turned to study his face. She saw the close resemblance to John.

"What do you want?" she asked in a strained voice.

"I'm looking for a girl named Ellen Boone."

"What do you want?" Her voice was filled with fear.

"Are you Mrs. Boone?" he asked.

"Yes, but you got no business here," she answered nervously.

"I have some very important business," he said authoritatively. "I'm looking for my brother, John Broker."

Ellen turned pale. "Why are you lookin' here?"

"His fishing companions told me I might find him here."

She shook her head frantically. "They're wrong. He ain't here and ain't never been here."

"But you do know him?"

"I met him over at the mill, and that's all there wuz to it, but you better git away from here, rite now."

"Not until you tell me where John is."

"If my husband finds you here he'll kill you in a minute."

Frank wished he could leave. He didn't like the situation but knew he couldn't back down. He wondered if her insistence on wanting him to leave was due to John's being inside. It wasn't like John to hide from anything still there might be reasons. He decided to play a hunch.

"Is he in the cabin?"

This angered her. "No. And you better leave before you git yourself into some real trouble!"

"All right then," he said with finesse.

"You let me look through the house. If he isn't there, I'll leave right away. It's the only way I can be sure."

Ellen thought for a moment. It would be the quickest way to get rid of him. "All rite," she said desperately. "But you make it real fast, then git away from here as fast as you kin."

Frank was mildly disappointed. He doubted John was inside otherwise she would not permit him to enter. He would make the search quickly. He stepped inside as Ellen stood by the door then walked through the primitive kitchen and entered the bedroom. After opening a closet door he got down on his knees and looked under the double bed.

Ellen heard the commotion outside and looking out saw Jed pulling his startled horse to a halt. She was terrified! She ran to the bedroom calling for Frank to leave. She heard Jed barging through the kitchen. He clumsily bumped his leg against the kitchen table, knocking it to one side. When he entered the bedroom she buried her face in her hands.

Jed spun her around. "You're no good!" he shouted. His fists were clenched and he was breathing heavily. "You're just no damned good!"

He saw Frank on the floor and went after him. Ellen stepped between them.

"No, Jed! No!" she pleaded. "You're wrong!"

Jed brought his fist hard against her mouth, sending her backward against a wall and falling to the floor.

Frank wondered if Jed was insane. He didn't take time to notice his huge build nor would he have done differently if he had. Lunging at him he drove his fist to Jed's jaw. It didn't phase him. Instead he wrapped his hands around Frank's neck and drew them tightly. Vainly struggling to breathe Frank slumped to the floor and Jed went down with him and knelt across his prostrate body. Jed pushed this thumbs hard into the glands of Frank's throat.

Ellen got onto her feet. Her mouth was dripping blood. She grabbed Jed's shoulders and tried to pull him back. She couldn't budge his tense body.

In desperation she ran to the kitchen and removed a shotgun from a rack on the wall. In a second she was back in the bedroom pointing the end of the barrel against the back of Jed's head. She pulled the trigger. For a quick moment Jed didn't move. Then his huge shoulders began moving backwards, there was a dull thud and his twisted body sprawled grotesquely on the floor. A pool of fresh blood began forming around his head. The edges crept outward and irregularly and then it stopped.

Ellen managed to utilize the little strength left in her body. She crawled to Frank's side. Seeing the deep purplish marks on his throat and the ashen lifeless face she dropped her head on his chest and sobbed hysterically. There was little doubt in her mind. Both of them were dead.

*****

The tragic news of Frank's death was a severe blow to the Broker family. His body was laid out in the big reception hall at Fern Lea, where large gatherings of people came to pay their lasts respects. While most were relatives and friends, there were numerous strangers drawn to the wake by the publicity associated with the murder.

A newspaper had captioned a story: FRANK BROKER REPORTEDLY MURDERED WHILE COURTING HIS BROTHER'S SWEETHEART.

Strong resentment built up around Burnside and gossip and curiosity swept through Lexington circles. Fate could not have been more unkind to Ellen Boone nor the members of the Broker family.

During the days preceding the funeral Mrs. Broker managed to control her emotions remarkably well but when she was alone at night she became distraught and sleepless.

Margaret could not contain herself in public as well as her mother. She became hysterical often and cried constantly at the mention of her brother's death. While thinking about John she was filled with contempt. If she ever saw him again and she hoped she would she was determined to see he settled down in Lexington and make up for the sorrows he had brought to the family.

There was one happy consolation for Margaret, though. Neil Hathaway spent long hours with her during the wake and greatly helped out with things. Actually it was a needed outlet for him and afforded him a renewed interest in life.

The main interest was Margaret. When he was courting Brenlyn he seldom gave her much thought. But now he saw an attractiveness about her he had not observed before.

Whenever he noticed her becoming too tired to continue receiving visitors he would escort her to a sun porch where they could be alone. She greatly appreciated his attention and once when she was telling him so he put his arms around her and pressed his lips to hers. She wasn't surprised -- she knew how he felt and she loved him too.

******

Grief continued to engulf the family as Mr. Broker lapsed in and out of a coma. During the periods of consciousness he often asked if they had heard from John and expressed a strong desire to see him. Margaret and Mrs. Broker discussed this with Neil.

After learning Carl and Fred Rint had told Frank about Ellen Boone, Neil decided to ride out to see if they could shed any light on where John might have gone.

The day after this visit he was considering a trip to Burnside to continue searching. He was discussing this with Margaret at the Broker home when a butler told them Carl Rint was waiting in the parlor to see him.

Neil and Margaret went to the parlor and Carl handed Neil a letter. It was from a bank in Louisville stating John had applied for a loan there and had given Carl Rint's name for reference. It listed John's address as the Victoria Hotel.

******

Neil walked into the rather small lobby of the Victoria and spotted John sitting in a chair reading a newspaper. Walking up in front of him he gripped the top edge of the paper and slowly moved it upward.

Looking up John was surprised. "What in the world are you doing here, Neil?" It was the last person he expected.

"To see you," Neil said with a warm smile and at the same time extended his hand. "And it's sure good to see you again."

John shook Neil's hand. "How in the world did you know I was here?"

Neil didn't want to be too abrupt. "I'll tell you about that later. Right now I'm starved. Is there a restaurant nearby where we can get something to eat?"

"Sure, there's a place right across from the station. Just a few doors from here."

After ordering their meals Neil managed a light-hearted conversation about state politics. John realized he was stalling. "What's this all about, Neil? You didn't come down here to elect a governor."

Neil dreaded the task ahead of him but knew he could put it off no longer.

"I have some mighty unpleasant news to tell you."

"Does it concern my father?"

"Yes, John, it does," Neil nodded his head sadly, then added, "And it also concerns your brother, Frank."

"Frank?" John asked curiously. "Is he in some kind of trouble?"

Neil had to force himself to continue.

"I wish there was some way to spare you this."

"Sounds pretty serious."

"I'm afraid it is, John. You see, your brother Frank is dead."

"No!" John said, unbelievingly. "It can't be. Not Frank!"

"I'm sorry, but it's true, John. He was buried last week."

John looked down at the place mat. He still couldn't accept what he heard.

"Buried?" There was a moment of hesitation. "Surely you can't be serious?"

Neil bundled his napkin in his hand, unconsciously, then shook his head to acknowledge what he had said was true.

John leaned back in his chair. "What happened? Was he sick?"

Neil looked at him sympathetically. "No, John. You see, he was murdered by a lumberman named Jed Boone where you and the Rint boys went fishing."

John frowned in despair. "At the South Fork? What was he doing down there?"

"He was looking for you."

Neil went on to explain all that had taken place since he had left Lexington and told about his father's bad health and how he wanted so badly to see him.

They took a late train for Lexington and arrived at Fern Lea in the early hours of the morning. John stepped down from the carriage and hurried up the porch steps and tried the door. It was locked so he rapped the big brass knocker against its striker plate.

After a short delay, Carlos, the butler appeared. Carlos had been a family employee for many years and seemed a part of the family. Seeing it was John he swung the door open widely and greeted him with a warm handshake. "It's so good to have you back home," he said, happily.

John thanked him, then asked about his mother.

"She's sleeping now," he answered quietly. "She don't sleep much anymore, but she's sound asleep now."

"What time did she retire?" John wondered if he should wake her to let her know he was home.

"Oh, she's not really retired. She never does retire anymore. She just sits in that big rocking chair by your father's bed and watches over him, except when she falls asleep like she is doing right now. All of us keeps telling her she ought to go to bed and get some rest, but she don't pay no attention to us. Why, just the other day --" Carlos didn't get to finish. John ran up the stairway to his parents' bedroom.

The only light in the room came from a small incandescent lamp placed on a table at a far corner of the room. When John saw the dark shadows on his mother's face he was appalled.

Always she had seemed so young to him but now her face was drawn and her hair was no longer rolled up in a neat coiffure. Instead it hung loosely over her shoulders.

Walking to the bed John looked down and saw his father's head resting on a soft pillow with the covers rolled up over his shoulders. His eyes were closed and his breathing was heavy. His expression was lifeless. John looked at him unbelievingly. "Am I responsible for this?" he asked himself. The strain was too much. He dropped to his knees and buried his face in the covers and sobbed in deep despair.

The outburst startled Mrs. Broker. Instinctively she went to John's side and gently pulled him back urging him not to disturb his father. John stood and whispered his sorrow and hugged her tightly. Mrs. Broker ran her fingers through his hair and told him how glad she was to have him home. Both were crying and at the same time trying to compose themselves.

Mr. Broker heard John's voice and in a weak whisper called out to him. John clasped his covered hand.

Mr. Broker strained to speak. His voice was little more than a whisper. "Where have you been, son? Your mother and I have been worried about you."

"I just didn't know," John answered compassionately.

"I'm sorry about everything."

Mr. Broker struggled to pull his arms out from the covers. John pulled the covers back and held on to his hand.

"I'll make it up to you," he said. "Get well and I promise I'll be everything you want me to be."

A weak smile formed on his father's lips. He tried to speak but no words came out. John felt his grip tightening. Frantically he called to him. "Father, what is it? Are you all right?"

The grip tightened more then it loosened as his eyes closed.

Mrs. Broker ran to the hallway and summoned the doctor who was resting on a couch. Rushing to Mr. Broker's side he felt his wrist then raised an eyelid. Then he turned to Mrs. Broker and took her hand.

"It's all over now," he said in a sympathetic voice. "He's found rest from all the pain."

******

At the convent Brenlyn had been given the name of Sister Jude. The Mother Superior had excused her of all duties after giving her the message telling of her father's death. It was a great shock to her and the thought of never seeing him again grieved her terribly. She spent a good part of the day in the chapel but even there she found great difficulty in trying to concentrate on anything spiritual. Her mind was clouded with grief.

She had not completely recovered from the news of

Frank's death and now it was her father. She wondered if she could bear up under it all and for the first time since entering the convent had thoughts of leaving. She worried about her mother and wanted to be with her to help alleviate the sorrow she was sure to have. She remembered the promise she had made to return home if she ever became dissatisfied.

Kneeling in a front pew at the chapel she raised her head and stared at a life size statue of the Blessed Virgin. The statue was a great inspiration to her and she thought it truly reflected everything she had read about the Holy Mother. It had never seemed so beautiful as it did now. She prayed for help never taking her eyes from the statue. For a moment she forgot the image was stone. The downcast eyes stared sorrowfully and a soft glow of light seemed to form around the veiled head.

Sister Jude felt a tear running down her cheek but she didn't bother with it. Somehow her thoughts became engrossed in Christ's Crucifixion and the tremendous suffering He endured. Then she thought of the shortness of time in this world and the length of eternity. She remembered a prayer that had been framed and hung on a wall at Fern Lea and began reciting it to herself.

"Oh, God, please send down Thy blessing on this Thy family so that someday we may be united with Thee in heaven."

She remembered her father had brought it home from the hotel and had had it mounted on the wall. It comforted her to think of it now.

After reciting other prayers Sister Jude rose from the kneeling bench, stepped out into the aisle, genuflected and walked toward the rear of the chapel.

She was surprised to see the Mother Superior kneeling in a back pew. She thought she had been the only one in the chapel.

She was only a few steps outside in a hallway when the Mother Superior caught up with her.

"Sister Jude," she said, "I came to the chapel to see if you were all right and wanted to kneel beside you, then thought it best not to disturb you. I have never known such peace. I felt as though I was watching a beautiful ceremony of some kind yet I could not see anything except the sanctuary as it has always been."

Sister Jude thanked her for her interest and explained she was all right. After they talked awhile she went to her cell and felt greatly relieved of the anxiety she experienced earlier in the day.

******

The day following the funeral John tried to put together all that had taken place. There was a lot to think about. The hotel had to be sold. His father requested this after he was told by the doctor that he would be a bed patient for the rest of his life. It had already been put up for sale and Neil Hathaway was handling the details. Neil suggested John take over now that he was home. John refused. There were a number of reasons for this. He didn't want to remain in Lexington because he wanted to go to Burnside to see if he could help Ellen. Then too, public sentiment was strongly against him in Lexington. People in both the business and social circles blamed him for all the family troubles. John felt this resentment during the time of the funeral and was snubbed by many of the visitors who came to pay their last respects. He could have ignored this but realized it could be a bad influence in obtaining a top price for the business. His main reason for refusing to be involved was he wanted to go back to Burnside then to Louisville. He liked Louisville and felt there were many opportunities for him there.

John discussed these things with his mother and she tried to discourage his going back to Burnside but to no avail. After she learned how determined he was about going she gave him her blessings and check for five hundred dollars.

******

When John stepped down from the train at Burnside
he found a damp and gloomy sight. There was a driving
rain and sheets of water gushed across rooftops and
spilled over into the dirt streets making them a sea of
mud.The station platform was crowded with people.
Many had come from the streets to escape the rain while
others like himself had arrived on the train and waited
for the rain to let up.

He spotted a three storied weatherbeaten house
across the street with a "Rooms for Rent" sign and
decided to make a break for it. Splashing through the
mud in long strides he made it to the house and saw a
sleepy looking attendant sitting in a chair tilted against
the porch wall.

"Want a room, stranger?" the man asked with little
expression.

John acknowledged that he did.

"Gimmie two bits and take the second room down the
hall on your left."

Handing him a coin John went to the room and found it
more uninviting than expected.

After freshening up he went back to the porch and was
glad to see the rain had stopped. The landlord was still
there.

"Lookin' fer some place special?" he asked.

"Well, I'd like to find a dry piece of ground leading to
the court yard," John answered jokingly.

"Better start diggin' ya a tunnel then!" The landlord
slapped his leg, amused at his reply.

"No thanks," John said, then rolled up his pants legs
and struggled down the street through the mud.

John had seen the jail before but never paid much
attention to it. Now he noted it was a three storied structure made of rough stones with iron bars at the windows.
It was located in a courtyard with other buildings. A high
picket fence with spikes at the top isolated it grimly.

As he walked along a brick walkway in the courtyard he saw a gathering of people listening to a bearded man strumming a guitar. When he spotted John he broke out into a song directed to him.

"Young man from the city comin' down the walk,
No doubt he's goin' inside for some mighty important talk.
Maybe he'll stop by a moment and listen to my song,
And leave a shiny coin to help a fella' get along."

Although he was anxious to see Ellen John stopped and dropped several coins into the songster's hat. The musician thanked him and sang another tune that was filled with words of appreciation. Several of the other men shook John's hand. One of them remarked, "Poor ol' fella's got a bad back. Ain't been able to hit a lick of work fer a long time."

Entering the office John felt a little uneasy. He came to a door and saw several men with badges pinned to their open collar shirts. One of the men saw him and asked, "Kin I do sump'n fer ya?"

"Perhaps you can," John replied. "I want to see a prisoner you're holding."

"Which prisoner? The man eyed John suspiciously.

"Mrs. Boone. Mrs. Ellen Boone."

All three men turned their heads toward John. The sheriff's voice became more aggressive. "What ya wanta' see her fer?"

"I have some personal business to discuss with her."

"Are ya a lawyer?"

John shook his head to show that he wasn't.

"What's her name?"

"Broker. John Broker."

The man got up from his chair and walked over to where the other two were seated. They discussed the situation in a low voice. After they finished the sheriff walked over to John. "Are ya any kin to Frank

Broker whut wuz killed up on the South Fork?''

John lowered his head as he thought about Frank. "Yes, Frank Broker was my brother."

The sheriff walked back to the table and looked at the ceiling as though he were weighted with a great problem. John waited patiently.

"Ya kin see her fer ten minutes and that's all." He motioned for a skinny deputy to take him to Ellen's cell.

The deputy led him up a stairway to the second floor hallway. "We keep the wimmin' prisoners, what few we git, up here," he said contemptuously. Without answering John followed him to a doorway at the end of a dimly lit hallway. The deputy rapped on the door and called out, "There's a fella' out here whut wants to see ya." He unlocked the door and pushed it open.

When John saw Ellen standing at the doorway he couldn't believe it was she. She was ghostly pale and there was a lifeless expression in her eyes. She had on a plain, dirty looking gown and it hung loosely from her shoulders. Her eyes widened when she saw him and she gathered the cloth at her neck in embarrassment.

John was first to speak. "Oh Ellen, what have they done to you?" he asked. She dropped her head and didn't answer.

"Ellen honey, are you all right?"

She shook her head affirmatively.

John smiled. "Glad to see me?"

"Sure to goodness I am." Tears gathered in her eyes.

John held her hand and led her to a bench in the hallway where they sat down. He looked tenderly into her eyes.

"I'm terribly sorry about this and know I am much to blame."

"It wasn't your fault," she said, shaking her head.

John hated to ask but it was important to know about the events that led to Frank's and Jed's deaths. After inquiring Ellen explained about Frank's insistence on entering their cabin and the events that followed. She trembled in horror as she told him about it.

"You poor girl," he said, despairingly. "You've been through so much."

She lowered her eyes. "You're the only one that believes me."

"Have you talked to a lawyer?"

She told him she hadn't.

John squeezed her hand affectionately. "Well, don't worry. I'm going to Somerset and find the best lawyer in Pulaski County and get you away from here forever."

"You're so good," she said, looking up at him admiringly. "I just wish I could let you know my appreciation fer comin' to see me."

Visiting time went by quickly and the sheriff reminded them that their time was up. John walked her back to the cell, still holding her hand. His heart was nearly broken as he faced her and the sheriff reached for the door to close it. "Have confidence in me," he said with a warm smile. Then he let go of her hand and the sheriff pulled the door closed and locked it. John knew he must lose no time in getting an early trial date.

When he left the building John noticed the musician and his followers were again looking at him but there was no music. One of the men from the sheriff's office was standing with them. John nodded his head and smiled, but there was no smile on their faces. There was little doubt what the man had told them. John shrugged his shoulders realizing people are the same everywhere.

He went back to the boarding house and the landlord was still sitting in the same place. As John crossed the porch the man turned his head and asked in a slow drawl, "Done got all yer bizness takin' keer of?"

"Sure have," John answered, "and that's not all. I actually found a spot on one of the streets where water wasn't standing and someday I hope to erect a monument there to commemorate the occasion."

After John walked back into the hallway the landlord rubbed his chin in wonderment.

"Thet's a mighty strange thing to have a marker fer," he said to himself and spent the rest of the day wondering about it.

******

In Somerset John stopped in a barber shop for a haircut and drew the barber and several customers into conversation about the capabilities of Pulaski County lawyers. His mind was quickly made up. He wanted a man named Squire Benson to defend Ellen and located his office over a clothing store.

Walking into the office he saw a small wiry looking man sitting in a slouched position in a swivel chair that faced a roll top desk. His disarrayed white hair hung down over his face and he was breathing heavily, making strands of hair move alternately up and down with each breath. His unbuttoned shoes were on the floor beside his bare feet and two red socks hanging on a desk drawer were an obvious mismatch to the black serge trousers he wore. Drawing closer John saw the man's chin was resting on his chest and he was obviously sound asleep. Not knowing if it was advisable to disturb him John began walking toward the doorway and planned to return later but a gruff voice interrupted his departure.

"You came in my office. You're leaving without saying a word. How do you ever get anything done?"

John turned and saw the man was still slumped in a comfortable position but his bushy eyebrows were raised.

"Are you Squire Benson?" John asked politely.

"Born with the name Benson a little more than sixty-four years ago. Got the name Squire attached to it thirty-nine years back. Could have been a judge a dozen times but didn't want to be tied down to a bench every day. Ever do any fishing?" he asked.

"A little."

"Good pastime. Keeps your mind relaxed. By the way what's your name, young man?"

"John Broker."

"Are you in some kind of trouble?"

"No not exactly. You see, I want you to defend a girl that's been charged with murder."

You must be talkin' about Ellen Boone."

John was surprised. "How would you have known?"

"Your name is Broker. I figured you were kin to Frank Broker who was killed up at the South Fork."

"He was my brother."

The Squire slowly straightened up in his chair and began putting his socks and shoes on. Grunting from the ordeal he continued. "They got that Boone girl charged with murdering her husband. Too bad she didn't kill him before he got to your brother. Jed was a mean one all right."

"Then you know about it all?" John asked.

"Well, I've heard a lot of talk about it."

"Will you defend her?"

"Can you afford to pay a hundred dollars?"

"No problem at all."

"If I get her acquitted, that's what you'll pay me. If I lose the case, it'll cost you twenty-five."

John was happy with the arrangement, but wanted to make the incentive greater. "Make it two hundred if you get her acquitted."

The Squire smacked his lips as he pondered the situation. "If you were my age you'd not be so foolish as to make such an offer. If I were your age I would not be so foolish as to turn down such a bonus. But the price remains at a hundred or twenty-five. Now tell me all you know about Ellen Boone."

John went into great detail about his acquaintance with Ellen except that she had attempted to steal their food. He didn't want that to come out in the trial.

Squire Benson was satisfied. "I'll make arrangements

to have her transferred to the county jail here in Somerset and we'll have the trial here too.''

"How long do you think it'll take?"

We'll get her transferred tomorrow and hope for the trial to take place next week.''

"John felt that he had selected the right man. He reached out his hand and as Squire Boone extended his for a handshake he replied cautiously, ''Don't get your hopes too high. You never know how these things will turn out.''

******

The trial lasted two days. The prosecuting attorney subpoenaed Ellen's parents, Sarah Therman, and several of her neighbors, some of the men Jed worked with and John Broker.

He argued that Ellen had planned Jed's murder for a long time and that she had had affairs with both John and Frank in order to get them to assist in the killing. Ellen broke down several times during the questioning but the prosecutor was unable to get her to change her story. The fact that John was helping her was reassuring and gave her the courage to answer questions.

Squire Benson cross-examined each of the witnesses carefully. He managed to get Ellen's father to admit he abused her and forced her to marry Jed. Sarah Therman's testimony that she had seen both Frank and John making love to Ellen was proven false. He proved that Frank had been in the cabin for less than a minute when Jed entered and two of the villagers admitted under heavy cross-examination they heard Jed say he would kill Ellen if he ever caught her talking to another man.

The Squire re-enacted the crime before the jurors to show how Jed murdered Frank and how Ellen tried to save him. After deliberating for three hours the jury foreman delivered a verdict of not guilty and Ellen was acquitted.

Squire Benson lost no time in escorting John and Ellen out of the courthouse and took them to his office where they could talk in private. John and Ellen praised him and thanked him for the way he handled the trial. John handed him an envelope with the money for his services. The Squire told them that they both conducted themselves well during the proceedings then explained he had other things to look after and they could use his office to talk things over.

John took her hand and looked down into her face. "Well Ellen, it's all over now and at last you can look forward to a happier life." He had an assuring smile. She thanked him over and over for all he had done.

John had thought about Ellen's future while he sat in the courtroom. He felt confident she'd be acquitted and he knew he would have to get her away because resentment against her was strong. He began telling her his plans for her future. "Ellen honey, you know that both of us will have to get away from here as soon as possible." She said she understood. He looked into her eyes. "I don't think I ever told you but one of my sisters is a nun in a fine boarding school up in Ohio."

Ellen listened intently.

"I think it's best that you go there where you'll get the best of care and at the same time complete your education." John noted the change in her expression. All signs of happiness diminished. She began shaking her head back and forth unbelievingly. "I don't want to go to a place like that."

Ellen wanted to tell him she wanted to go away with him but was afraid to do so because she didn't know how he felt about her. During the trial she hoped it was not through sympathy alone that he was helping her. Somehow she hoped he might feel toward her as she did about him. Never before had anyone shown her the kindness and understanding he gave her and she was deeply in love with him.

She had thought of him constantly since the day they met but all along she knew she had little to offer him. She had read articles about herself in newspapers. Some described her as being frail homely and unwanted and she thought even worse of herself.

The answer to her hopes was evident. The one man she wanted to spend the rest of her life with was sending her away to a boarding school and a Catholic one at that. She had never been associated with Catholics before and had heard tales about them and believed them to be a clannish group that never associated with anyone outside their faith.

John was sorely disappointed.

"Ellen honey, I don't know where else you can go just now." He paused a moment to find the right words to make her understand. "You'll soon find out what a wonderful sister I have."

"Do they let people who ain't Catholic go there?" Ellen asked, hoping he had overlooked this point and would change his mind.

"Yes there's always a number of non-Catholic girls there. You won't feel out of place at all." He had no way of knowing this was true, but thought it was this way.

Ellen realized that it was useless to refuse any longer and resigned herself to her fate. She knew she should be used to surrendering her will to others but this time she had hoped it might be different. Her hopes that John would take her away with him were shattered.

"When would I have to leave?" she asked quietly.

"I think it best you catch the next train. It will be leaving an hour from now. You see, I have written my sister telling her you would be coming there and she will take good care of you."

Ellen bit her lips and tears filled her eyes. Not only was she disappointed, she was frightened at the thought of going to a place she knew nothing about.

John rubbed the back of her hand affectionately.

"Ellen, it's not as if you are going there for the rest of your life. And you don't have to stay there if you don't like it. As soon as I get situated I'll write and let you know my address and if you are unhappy all you have to do is write me and I'll come and get you."

Squire Benson returned to the office and John told him of his plans for Ellen.

"Well, that might be all right," Squire said, then added caustically, "I just hope you know what you're doing."

John looked at his watch then turned to Ellen. "We've just got enough time to get something to eat before your train leaves. I'll bet you are starved."

Ellen didn't answer. She could only think of being separated from him and going to the boarding school. She wondered if she could bear up under it all.

"Tell you what," Squire Benson interjected, "I'll walk along with you and treat you to a steak dinner. I'm hungrier than a woodchuck in a rock quarry." He wasn't that hungry but thought it best to accompany them to the station. Some of Jed's old friends might be in town.

While they were eating Ellen listened intently to everything John had to say hoping she might hear some word to let her know if he had helped her because of pity or if he shared the love she felt for him. Her hopes were in vain. He gave no indication of either.

Squire Benson waited in the station while John escorted Ellen to her coach seat. John sat down beside her. "This is your railroad ticket to Cincinnati," he said then gave her two envelopes. One contained money, the other a letter for her to give to Brenlyn when she arrived at the school.

John saw the conductor and asked him to walk to the rear of the coach. He asked him to look after Ellen and see that she got off at Cincinnati, and to help her catch the stage to St. Martin. John handed him a generous tip and the grateful conductor assured him that he would do as he wished. John walked back to the coach and sat with Ellen again. He dreaded telling her goodbye but felt sure she would be happier after she was in school. He couldn't let himself think of her being alone on the train and tried to be cheerful.

"Well Ellen, I guess it's almost time for the train to leave," he said squeezing her hand. "You've been very brave and I know this isn't easy for you." He felt her hand trembling. She looked at him with pleading eyes and hoped he would never let go of her. Leaning over he kissed her cheek. "I'll come to see you often and we'll write each other." He felt his eyes watering and fought back the desire to take her in his arms.

"You're going to be all right," he said.

She closed her eyes and pretended she was looking out the window. He kissed her again then let go of her hand and stood facing her. She couldn't look up. It took all of her strength to keep from breaking down. The conductor advised John the train would be pulling out in a few moments. He told her goodbye and quickly left the coach.

As the train started moving Ellen touched her cheek where he had kissed her then she moved the tip of her fingers to her lips. A new feeling of loneliness overcame her. She thought she should be used to disappointment by now but knew she would never get used to seeing all her hopes shattered. She couldn't hold back any longer. Covering her eyes with a handkerchief a flood of tears emerged and she broke down and sobbed openly. Her heart was broken.

Part II

"We must all be seasoned one way or another."

DICKENS - *Nicholas Nickelby*

John caught the night train for Louisville and arrived shortly after daybreak. He climbed in a waiting surrey and instructed the driver to take him to the Galt House. At Fourth Street he asked to be driven north so he could again see the activity there. The street was rather deserted except for a few early risers sitting on their front porches or standing at the iron gates that provided openings for the ornamental fences bordering the sidewalks.

Reaching Guthrie the activity increased as a large group of people stood in front of the magnificent Renaissance Revival Post Office building waiting for the doors to open. John looked at the big tower clock and checked the time against his watch.

At Walnut Street a custodian was busy sweeping the wide stone steps leading up to the doorways of the big Christian Church at the northwest corner of the intersection. The elaborate Macauley's Theatre building with its two candelabra lamp posts out front stood next door.

The traffic became heavier at Jefferson Street. John was amazed at the number of motor cars that moved along with the horse-drawn vehicles. An electric streetcar was stopped on Jefferson where passengers were getting off in front of the Masonic Temple.

They passed Market and the impressive Columbia Building on Main street came in view. John counted the windows upward to the tenth floor and was greatly impressed with the skyscraper's architecture. The archways and base columns were constructed of huge chipped red granite stones. The base stones were stepped to join the descending walkway that extended down Fourth Street to the river. John thought it the best looking skyscraper he had ever seen.

He was inwardly amused as his driver turned east on Main Street. He thought of the earlier trip when another enterprising driver took him on a long route from the Union Station to the Victoria Hotel. They bounced along the rough cobblestone street past Third Street and John looked toward First Street and saw the Galt House on the northeast corner.

It thrilled him to see it. How he remembered his father's telling about its wonder. He had described it as the finest hotel in the South often talking about the lobby and its beauty; he described the exquisite second floor parlors as "fit for kings and presidents." He would rave about the dining room and its myriad of incandescent lamps glowing from crystal chandeliers, and thought of it as the ultimate in accommodations.

When they reached the east end of the building the driver reigned the horse in a sharp "U" turn and pulled up in front of the arched entrance way. A uniformed doorman walked out to the curb and signaled a bellhop who came running out to the carriage. The bellhop lifted John's satchel and moved sharply up through the doorway. John paid the driver. After stepping down to the pavement he heard the doorman's "Right this way sir," and followed him up between the tall doric columns and entered the lobby. He was amazed at the vastness and splendor of the room and hesitated for a moment to look around but the bellhop motioned toward the desk and a waiting clerk so he went to the counter.

"Would you like a room sir?" a well dressed middle-aged clerk asked politely.

"Yes, I need a single room and would appreciate one with a good view."

"Yes sir," the clerk replied as he dipped a quilled pen in an inkwell then handed it to John. "Would you like one facing west? You'll be able to see both the river front and the city. There's usually a pleasant breeze blowing in during the evening hours."

"Sounds great," John answered then signed the book.

The clerk handed the bellhop a key and after picking up the satchel again asked John to follow along to the elevator.

The room was on the fourth floor. John gave the bellhop a liberal tip. After he was gone John went to the opened window and looked at the view.

The river was only a half block away and he had a commanding view of the activities at the wharf where more than a dozen sidewheelers and sternwheelers were tied up. Some were taking on passengers, some had people leaving, others were being loaded and unloaded with freight. A heavy purge of black smoke belched out of the twin stacks on a big packet as it pulled out into the current.

The cobblestone wharf was teeming with activity. Fine carriages were transporting travelers to and from the boats. Big draft wagons loaded with freight were being pulled up the incline by teams of straining horses.

Looking farther to the west John could see the outline of a waterfall that extended from the Indiana shore to the outer wall of the Portland Canal. The churning waters below the dam smoothed out as the river rounded a wide sweeping bend and the clear sky afforded a view of the Indiana Knobs. One hill overlooking the little town of New Albany was covered with trees whose leaves and limbs glared out silvery colorations. A closer look revealed the skyline of commercial buildings along Main Street and farther to the south the roof tops of the heavy residential area were evident.

John was infatuated with it all. He liked Louisville and looked forward to living here. Surmising that there were many opportunities for success he felt he would become a prosperous and important figure in the thriving city.

He walked back into the room and viewed the surroundings. A big walnut table was placed along one wall; the bed had a high walnut headboard with two turned posters at the foot. A matching dresser with glass drawer pulls was at another wall. Everything was extremely clean and the furniture had a high shine.

Sitting on a comfortable arm chair near a window John collected his thoughts. His immediate concern was money. He removed his wallet from a coat pocket and counted the currency. Forty-four dollars left from the money his mother had given him. Enough to last for at least two weeks he thought. The room would cost him ten dollars a week. He wanted to buy some new clothes and figured his meals would run about a dollar a day. By that time he would find a source of income. He wasn't anxious to look for a position because he wanted to look the city over before deciding what he wanted to do.

John washed his face and brushed his clothes and went back down to the lobby. With more time to look around he was amazed at the immense size of the room. The checkered tile floor was wide and long and two rows of cushioned chairs were placed back to back throughout its entire length. Beautiful potted ferns were placed along a back wall. Six large chandeliers hung majestically from the lofty ceiling.

The desk where he had registered was located along the west wall. It was enclosed in marble panels topped with delicate ornamental iron grill work. Three clerks were busy registering and checking out guests. A porter wheeling a cart filled with polished spittoons replaced soiled ones spotted throughout the lobby floor. A steady flow of guests paraded back and forth through the lobby, while others sat in chairs reading or chatting with friends. Bellhops, elevator men and doormen wearing colorful uniforms with brass buttons and gold braid were busy taking care of guests. Several men neatly dressed in black suits and wearing starched high collars with big bow ties stood at the cigar counter along a west wall.

John thought it to be the most elegant lobby he had ever seen. It was the ultimate in design and sophistication and he was thrilled at the thought of staying there and looked forward to seeing other parts of the building.

Wanting to see the river front he walked out on the sidewalk and headed down Second Street. The acid smell of the water filled his nostrils but it wasn't an unpleasant smell. There was a freshness about it that was invigorating.

The Louisville-Jeffersonville ferry boat, Columbia, was docked at the foot of the street and a steady flow of passengers walked down a gangplank, while others waited to go on board for the trip to Jeffersonville. Just below it a string of coal barges was being unloaded as lumps of coal were dumped into two-wheeled carts hitched in single file to two mules. When they reached the top, the lead mule was unhitched and walked back down to the water's edge to help pull other carts up the incline. As John walked along the shoreline he saw pieces of driftwood being washed up on the bank. Some had weird shapes and the four-inch waves lapping up on the shoreline made them appear as weird and comical animated objects as they bobbled up and down.

He walked past several packet boats that were tied up to big iron rings anchored in the wharf bed. The City of Louisville, a picturesque sidewheeler, was docked at the foot of Fourth Street unloading passengers from Cincinnati. John sat down on a bale of hay hear the gangplank to watch them disembark.

The first-class passengers were the first to leave and

most of them boarded fine carriages awaiting them. John eyed the pretty young ladies and if one happened to look his way he would flash a wink and a smile. Some were attracted to his gesture and seeing how handsome he was they would respond with a returning faint smile.

John felt sorry for many of the third-class passengers as they left the steamer. John thought the passengers looked weary from traveling under the poor accommodations provided for their low fare. Not being able to afford a carriage they were walking up the long hill to Main Street where they could get public transportation on one of the electric railcars.

Tiring of the wharf activities John walked up the steep inclined sidewalk on Fourth Street to the seemingly endless rows of business houses along Main Street.

He walked down the wide brick sidewalk toward Fifth Street and passed by harness shops, furniture stores, wholesale grocers, tobacco outlets, jewelry shops and haberdasheries.

Wagons were backed up to the curbing loading and unloading crates and boxes. Front wheels were turned at right angles as the horses and mules stood parallel to the sidewalk and out of the path of traffic. Bales of hemp were stacked on the sidewalk in front of a rope factory and hogsheads of tobacco were stacked along the curbing in front of a warehouse.

Sweaty workmen were handling freight and well dressed merchants wearing black derbys stood along the sidewalk. Ladies wearing long chiffon dresses and wide-brimmed hats were windowshopping. It made John feel good to see all the activity as he continued down to Sixth Street.

He stopped in front of the Burdorf Building and gazed across the street to get a good look at the Louisville Hotel. Deciding he wanted to see what it looked like inside he walked up the steps to the first floor lobby and stood there to inspect the surroundings. Marble stairways were placed at each side of the room. These led to a platform where the steps were reversed to provide easy access to a mezzanine floor. Huge mirrors framed in gold were mounted on the walls next to the platforms. It was impressive and John wanted to see more, but he was anxious to continue walking down Main Street.

He walked past the red sandstone and brick Bernheim Building and saw the cast iron facade on the corner building next door.

Stopping in front of a shop at 712 West Main he looked across the street at more buildings with cast iron fronts. The Carter Building took up nearly one-fourth of the block between Sixth and Seventh Streets. Its high Victorian-Italianate facade made it stand out from other fine buildings on the street. Several fine surreys were parked in front and John admired a well-groomed team of Hackney mares that were hitched to one of them. Their bay colored bodies and black legs gave them class. Each had a white star on its forehead and they stood proudly with their long arched necks and high carriaged tails. John envied their owner and hoped he would some day have a team like them.

He saw a group of men standing in front of the McKesson and Robbins Building on the corner at Seventh Street. They were having a friendly argument and John stood for a moment to listen. The Louisville Baseball Club franchise had been sold to a Pittsburg sportsman. The men were disgusted at the move blaming the loss of the club on the lack of support by local enthusiasts.

Their discussion was abruptly interrupted as a team of four black horses galloped down the street pulling a red fire department pumper. A trail of black smoke filled the air as it purged out of the stack from the boiler. One of the firemen clanged a brass bell and the noise startled many of the other horses standing along the curbs. The strength and speed of the stallions fascinated John and filled him with excitement. He watched them closely as they raced up Main Street, made a wide sweeping turn at Fifth Street, then disappeared from view. John had seen the same type of fire fighting apparatus in Lexington but he never tired of seeing the colorful equipment go by.

The next few days John had a lot to think about. There had to be a lot of opportunities in Louisville. How to find them he didn't know. He thought of getting involved in the tobacco industry but didn't know enough about that kind of business to know how to get started. He felt his best bet was to get work in one of the hotels. He could readily qualify as a desk clerk but wanted something better than that. Perhaps he could land a position as assistant manager or maybe even as a manager. But it would have to be one of the first class houses — no second class outfit would be suitable to him. John pictured himself sitting in the manager's office of the Louisville Hotel or even Seelbach's European Hotel. The thought of managing the Galt House made him wince. That would be asking too much. It was too big and too magnificent. But some day he thought to himself I want to be the Galt House manager. That would be the ultimate for anyone in the hotel business.

Then he thought of opening his own hotel. It would be the finest ever. The dining room would serve food of superlative quality; the lobby would be built like a castle; there would be elaborate parlors complete with a little bar and ice box so guests could have everything they needed for private parties. He would spare no expense in making it one of the best hotels in the Country. But that would have to wait for awhile.

John had not forgotten his early desire of becoming a trainer of fine thoroughbred race horses but a lot of that glamour had escaped his mind. "After all," he mused, "I haven't seen a race horse for months much less being around a stable. Maybe if I went out to Churchill Downs and talked to someone out there, but they would probably tell me I'd have to be a stable hand first.''

Somehow the desire to clean stalls, polish harnesses and walk hots had lost its appeal. Maybe he would wait until the Fall meeting at the Downs. He didn't know when the races would start. Sometime in October he thought. That would be in about six weeks. He would have to check into this then go out to the track and see if the sight and smell of horse flesh would stir up the interest like it used to. That's what he would do. Anyway, the Downs was a little hard to get to. It was located several miles beyond the city limits and he had heard that public transportation to the track was poor.

These were the things John thought about as he leisurely strolled around town visiting saloons or resting in his room at the Galt House. The one thing he had little concern about was money. He had never been without it completely and the thought that he might run out of funds didn't bother him. He would find a way to get more if he needed it. That would be simple enough he thought.

******

John dreaded Sundays in Louisville. After attending an early mass at the Cathedral of the Assumption he would have breakfast at one of the downtown restaurants. There was little activity around the business district on these mornings and seeing happy families together at church and eating places made him feel melancholic. It was the one day of the week he hated being alone. Sometimes he felt an urge to go back to Lexington but he knew things wouldn't be the same there.

One Sunday morning late in July he decided to visit the Portland area where many Irish people lived. He had heard about the joviality among these people and thought it would be an interesting place to visit. Taking a trolley car he got off in front of the Marine Hospital in the 2200 block of Portland Avenue. Looking through the iron picket fence surrounding the extensive grounds he saw a number of patients wearing blue robes and sitting under shade trees. He remembered someone telling him the hospital cared for sick and injured river boat employees.

Walking down the sidewalk he saw well kept brick and frame homes bordering each side of the street. Some were big three-storied structures with wide front porches and others were modest bungalows. Many of the residents were sitting on their porches and lawns enjoying the balmy morning air. Most of the men wore ties and vests and the ladies were dressed in colorful swiss and muslin dresses with wide full skirts and pretty sashes tied around their waists.

Flowers filled the borders around the homes and the air was filled with the scent of fragrant blossoms. Happy couples walked along the sidewalks exchanging pleasantries with neighbors. Spotless carriages pulled by well groomed horses traveled up and down the avenue. In one side yard children were romping on the lawn in a game of tag. John was delighted with it all and thought it to be the most fresh and relaxing neighborhood he had ever seen.

Strolling farther he came to a small business district and saw a group of men loafing in front of a drugstore. He struck up a conversation with one of them and learned they were waiting for a draft wagon to take them to a baseball game.

"Why don't you join us?" the man said in a heavy Irish accent. "You can ride both ways help us drink up a barrel of beer and see a double header for a quarter and you just can't get a better deal than that anywhere."

John thanked the man for the invitation but explained he wasn't much of a sports fan. He headed back past the hospital and the thought of a cold glass of beer was tempting. He remembered seeing a saloon a block above the hospital and this was his immediate destination. Passing a two-storied home he saw a group of young people gathered in a front yard. Picnic baskets were stacked near the front steps and kegs of beer and jars of lemonade were sitting on the sidewalk close to the front gate.

John envied them and wished he had lived in a neighborhood like this. Happiness seemed to prevail everywhere. Before he passed the gathering of picnickers he heard them burst out in laughter and somehow thought they might be directing their attention to him. Going a few more steps he heard a voice calling out, "Hold up for a moment, stranger."

Instinctively John turned his head and saw one of the men swinging open a picket gate and running to catch up with him.

John stopped to see what he wanted. The man had a friendly smile and John noted that he was probably close to his own age.

"Excuse me sir," the young man said in a thick Irish voice. "My name is Tim Connelly and I wonder if I could ask a favor of you?"

John was dubious but listened to what he had to say.

"We saw you walking along the sidewalk alone and thought you might like to join us on a boat trip up the river?"

Before John could answer Tim extended his hand and asked, "And what might your name be, sir?"

John acknowledged with a handshake as he replied, "John Broker."

"Mighty glad to know you, John," Tim said enthusiastically. "You see we are in a mighty desperate situation. A fellow was supposed to take one of my sisters on a boating expedition and got sick. Now she refuses to go along without an escort and none of us want to go without her. We thought you might favor us by going with her."

"Well, I don't know," John answered trying to collect his thoughts.

"I hope you're not married?" Tim asked solicitiously.

"No it's not that."

"Well come along then. You'll have a good time and it won't cost you a red cent. And my sister -- well she's a real beauty if I must say so myself."

John was intrigued by Tim's insistence and tried to make up his mind.

"How does your sister feel about going out with a total stranger?"

"Oh she's dead set against it. But don't bother about that because she is just a little on the shy side. She'll be all right after you two get acquainted."

Tim took John's arm and guided him through the gate and began introducing him to the men who were standing in front of the house. "This is my brother Mike. This is Tom, another brother. Still another, Marty, and here's the youngest, Pat." He introduced others as cousins of friends. John was confused and couldn't have called any of the new acquaintances by his name if his life depended on it.

Tim escorted him into the house where a group of young ladies were gathered in a big parlor. He began a second round of introductions. "This is my sister Catherine, better known as Katy. You've heard about her before you know..." He began acting like he was strumming a banjo and broke out singing. "Oh beautiful Katy."

Katy shook her head and smiled. "You're terrible," she said. This man will think you're crazy."

Tim continued the introductions. "This is another sister Michelle, and my other two sisters, Peggy and Sally." Then he introduced his brothers' girl friends and several other girls who were dates of friends.

"Aren't they all cute?" Tim asked teasingly.

John shook his head in agreement because they were all truly attractive girls.

"Which one of my sisters do you think is the

prettiest?'' Tim asked then raised his eyebrows and crossed his arms as he waited for an answer.

"Why I just don't know." John felt awkward at having to answer such a question. The girls showed their embarrassment at the question and there were blushes and squirms. Katy turned to her brother and began scolding. "You're embarrassing Mr. Broker and all of us too!''

Her objection had little effect on Tim and he continued the teasing. "Why Catherine I do believe you're trying to persuade our new friend to choose you as being the prettiest.''

Katy looked daggers at him then turned to John and managed an apology. "You'll have to overlook him. He never knows when to stop.''

John smiled to let her know he undestood but he was annoyed at the unusual situation. Tim prodded him further. "Come on. Choose the one you think is the prettiest and I'll bet you choose the one you're to be with.''

It was readily apparent that Tim would not let up until some sort of commitment was made, and John knew he must somehow comply to relieve both him and the girls from further embarrassment. Actually it would have been easy to make a choice. He was partial to brunettes and Michelle had beautiful dark brown hair and also was as beautiful as any girl he could think of at the moment. His pulse quickened at the thought that she might be the one.

Tim wouldn't let up. "You better make a choice or all of my sisters might get angry thinking you don't like any of their looks.''

John managed an answer. "Well you know that beauty is not a thing to be judged in such a short time. Right now I am so overwhelmed by your hospitality that I must ask for more time before making a decision. You see, all of your sisters are truly beautiful girls.''

Before Tim could answer his brother Pat rushed into the room and informed the group that the wagons were out front and everyone should get ready to leave.

Pandemonium broke out. Young people began running out the doors. Some clutched baskets others carried watermelons and cakes. Someone yelled for Tim to help carry a big wooden box then disappeared into a hallway. John stepped back to get out of the way. Someone else stuck their head in the door telling the girls to hurry. Katy grabbed John by the arm. John tried to hide his disappointment at her being his date but didn't have to hide his feelings very long because she led him to Michelle.

******

The morning after the boat ride John was happy. He stood in front of a mirror in his room and intermittently maneuvered a razor across the smooth lines of his face and hummed a tune as he thought of the events that had taken place the day before. Never had he remembered having a more delightful time. He couldn't get his mind off Michelle and thought of the way she laughed at his jokes and listened intently as he told her about his boyhood days in Lexington. He carefully refrained from telling her about the unpleasant things but did emphasize the role his family played in Lexington's social and business life. He couldn't resist telling her this but now he regretted doing so because he knew he was using this to make an impression on Michelle and her family.

He continually thought of her beauty and remembered how her dark almond-shaped eyes sparkled and her pretty smile radiated each time he spoke to her. Never before had any girl dominated his thoughts as Michelle did now. He was impressed with her family too. They were extremely congenial and carefree and he looked forward to being with them again.

John learned that Michelle's oldest brother Marty was

general manager of a tobacco rehandling factory that shipped loose leaf tobacco overseas. Tom was a foreman in the plant and Tim and Mike worked in the office.

Michelle's eyes were downcast when she told John about her mother. She explained that she had been ill for many years and was confined to bed. After the boat ride Michelle took him up to meet her and he was surprised how well she looked. John could see the resemblance between Michelle and her mother and thought she looked pretty as she lay with her head back against a soft pillow. He recalled what she said after Michelle introduced him to her. After raising her eyebrows she remarked that she had heard about the way Tim picked him up as he walked down the sidewalk past their home. John was pleased as he recalled what she said to Michelle. "I'll have to tell him to keep his eye peeled and fetch someone for me because he certainly can pick 'em handsome enough."

John found her to be a charming person and they talked for a long time. Once she asked about the kind of work he was engaged in. Wanting to make an impression he told her that he had come to Louisville to investigate the prospects of opening a hotel. He added that he was presently employed at the Galt House to better survey the prospects of a new hotel in the downtown area.

Wiping the lather from his face he shook his head in disgust and wondered why he had told such a fantastic lie. He wondered what they would think of him if they knew he was unemployed and actually had only enough money to keep him in Louisville for another week or so.

John couldn't allow himself to think about this. It made him feel too remorseful. Instead he thought of the last minutes of the day with Michelle. As they walked along a hallway Michelle told him he had made a good impression on her mother.

"I wonder if her daughter likes me too?" John asked.

"I'm afraid we all do," she answered, at the same

time looking up at him with a happy smile.

"Then that has to include you too," John replied.

John hummed as he dressed and reflected on the memories of the day before. Then he sat down on the edge of the bed and lifted his wallet from a bedside table. He removed the money, counted it then estimated the cost of living for one day. He mentally divided this into his worth. "Enough to last about ten days," he said to himself. "But I'll figure out a way to get more."

Leaving the Galt House he walked along the sidewalk until he came to a flower shop. He ordered a bouquet of deep red roses and made arrangements to have them delivered to Michelle enclosing a handwritten card, "For a lovely girl with a delightful family." After signing his name he thought about her mother. He looked around the shop again and saw a vase filled with cut flowers. Without asking the price he told the clerk to send it along with the roses and inscribed on another card. "Dear Mrs. Connelly: Nothing could have given me greater pleasure than meeting you. It's no wonder you have such a lovely family. They are all so much like you."

After signing it he paid the clerk and walked to a nearby restaurant and did some quick mental arithmetic along the way. "Not quite enough money to last for ten days." He was so happy he hummed a tune as he waited for service. He ordered a big breakfast and thought about Michelle and dismissed all signs of unpleasantness. That evening he wrote his mother for more money.

The next few weeks were busy ones for John. He visited Michelle every evening and there was usually some kind of revelry going on at the Connelly home. John soon learned it was a gathering place for all the young people in the neighborhood. The porch swing and chairs would be occupied and others would sit on the porch steps or find comfortable spots on the lawn.

John was over-generous in insisting on paying for the

many pitchers of beer and bottles of soda pop that were consumed during these evenings. There was a "hot tamale man" who stood in front of the saloon where the drinks were bought and John would have him come down in front of the Connelly home and serve everyone hot dogs and hot tamales.

With his funds dissipating so quickly John contacted the manager of the Galt House and applied for a position as room clerk. The manager was impressed with his background and personality and assigned him to the desk working the 7:00 a.m. to 7:00 p.m. shift. The manager explained he demanded the utmost in courtesy be extended to guests and any infraction of this rule would be cause for immediate dismissal.

He went on to explain the fringe benefits. Free room rent, two free meals a day. There were no holidays or vacations but each clerk was permitted one day off each month but this could not be taken during the busy seasons. Drinking was prohibited during working hours but each clerk would be permitted two free drinks at the hotel bar when he was off duty.

John was well pleased with the day off and realized he had not heard of this being done at any other hotel. He was disappointed at his starting salary of nine dollars a week but knew it would afford him enough spending money to enjoy himself. He felt embarrassment about working as a desk clerk after telling the Connellys he came to Louisville to start a hotel. Never-the-less he continued with the story that he was making a study of the local business situation. Marty and Tim agreed that was the best thing to do and were glad he was so solicitous before making an investment.

Michelle wished John wasn't so wealthy. When she thought of his having a large amount of money it made her feel inferior and uncomfortable around him. She liked him very much and realized he was fond of her but wondered if he would soon tire of her after awhile and return to the high society that he had been accustomed to.

With a new source of income John established credit at a clothing store and built up his wardrobe with the purchase of new suits, shirts, neckties and other articles. He not only wanted to look personable at the hotel but he also wanted to make an impression on Michelle, her family and friends.

It was during this time that he received a letter from Ellen and several from his mother. Ellen's letter was cheerful and apparently she was very happy at St. Martin's. She sent several of her completed test papers that had excellent grades and explained that Sister Jude had spent untold hours helping her with her studies so she could catch up with her classmates. She told him how kind his sister had been to her and that she was every bit the wonderful person he had told her about. She asked him to visit them and explained how much both she and Sister Jude wanted to see him. John was glad she was well satisfied but the letter troubled him because he remembered his promise to pay for her tuition and to look after her. He had not fulfilled this promise and knew this was unfair to both Brenlyn and Ellen. He felt worse when he realized he would not be able to fulfill either of the promises. He noticed that Ellen closed her letter by expressing her love for him. This troubled him too. He knew he couldn't be worried about this and crumpled the letter and tossed it into a waste basket. He was glad she was well cared for and let it go at that.

In her letters Mrs. Broker told John the Zenith had been sold and Neil and Margaret planned to be married in Lexington. The wedding was to take place in three weeks. She explained that after the wedding she was going to put Fern Lea up for sale because she had no desire to live there alone. She said that Neil was building a beautiful mansion on the outskirts of Lexington and he and Margaret wanted her to live with them. She explained she planned on living there and making frequent visits to the Brown County Inn at St. Martin so she could be near Brenlyn and visit her at the convent during the day.

John wrote a short note to Ellen complimenting her on her grades and explained that his work took up all of his time and he would not be able to visit until a much later date.

Then he wrote to his mother and explained he was working at the Galt House and would be unable to attend the wedding. He wrote a letter of apology to Margaret and Neil and sent a matched pair of decorated china vases for a wedding gift.

As the Winter months passed many activities brought added happiness to John's life. There were a number of weddings in the Portland area. Michelle's sister Katy was married in January of 1900 and Marty and Tom had a double wedding in March. All were followed by lavish receptions with much drinking, singing, dancing and an air of gaiety prevailing everywhere. John remembered how he had despised these affairs in Lexington and realized how much he enjoyed them in Louisville. He loved the Irish people and thought how different their parties were from the formal gatherings in Lexington's social circles.

John enjoyed his work at the Galt House too. He had met and seen many prominent people in the lobby and corridors. He was working at the desk when President McKinley and his party arrived for an overnight stay. The manager assigned him to look after all their needs.

When the party left McKinley thanked him for his services and gave him a gold plated souvenir coin commemorating the end of the Spanish American War.

In April of 1900 the Galt House served as official headquarters for the annual reunion of the United Confederate Association, and more than a thousand Civil War veterans registered at the desk. They gathered around the lobby reminiscing about the war that had been fought nearly forty years earlier. Some were ex-generals others had never been raised above the rank of buck private. They re-fought the battles at Bull Run, Shiloh, Gettysburg, Perryville, and Chickamauga. There was little doubt among most of them that the South would have won had the timing and strategy of the battles been slightly different. When John was near a group of veterans refighting the battles, he would mingle with them and join in the discussions.

Renowned Major General Simon Bolivar Buckner enjoyed John's company and invited him and Michelle to join him at his table for the gala closing reception in the main ballroom. The affair was to be the main social event of the convention and was to take place in the evening. John sent word to Michelle to be ready at eight.

John borrowed a fine surrey that was pulled by a pair of matched Hackneys to pick up Michelle on the night of the banquet. He dressed in a black suit and wore a derby hat and as he drove down to Portland he felt elated to have control of the team as they stepped along with their high bold knee action and elevated steps.

He parked in front of the Connelly home and as he waited for Michelle to get ready he answered questions about the horses as her brothers and a number of their neighbors stood on the sidewalk admiring the team.

When he went to the parlor and saw Michelle he was sure she would be the prettiest girl at the hotel and looked forward to a happy evening. She was dressed in a black satin dress with a long skirt and high collar.

When General Buckner saw them he stood up. John could see a glint in the aging soldier's eyes as he introduced Michelle. The General introduced them to his other guests then had them sit next to him and his wife.

Michelle was awed at the size and decor of the dining

room. She looked at the paintings on the walls and marveled at the colorful and realistic scenes depicting the Boston Harbor, Natural Bridge, Virginia, West Point Military Academy, the New York Harbor, and another of the Winnebago Indians preparing for battle.

A myriad of incandescent lights furnished a dazzling display on the decorated walls and ceilings. When it was time for the waiters to serve dinner they came into the dining room from doorways on each side and as they appeared held silver trays of food high above their heads and stood at attention until the orchestra started playing. Then they walked swiftly to the center aisle where they met in unison then spread out in perfect timing, serving all tables at the same time.

After dinner John and Michelle joined others in a cotillion and following the lively dance, each of the ladies was presented with a bracelet and a lace handkerchief as a remembrance of the gala occasion.

When the confederate convention was over and all the veterans were gone John felt a little depressed as he worked at the desk. He thought of the many fine people he had met and realized he would not likely see them again. It wouldn't be like so many of the other assemblies that came to the Galt House each year. The Civil War veterans were aging and in their waning years they would be meeting in other cities. As he looked out into the lobby there were only a few guests around and the memory of the assembly that had been there for the past week filled him with a feeling of loneliness. This was a feeling that often engulfed him after being around big groups of people he liked. While they were staying at the hotel they seemed as though they should be a part of the establishment and their leaving brought on a feeling of emptiness and abandonment.

But this feeling never lasted for long because the Galt House rooms would soon be filled with a new registry of guests as new conventions or other activities would take place. Then he would feel happy again as he became acquainted with other groups of people.

After the Confederate Convention the Galt House began to fill for the twenty-sixth running of the Kentucky Derby at nearby Churchill Downs. Derby fever ran high and the lobby and parlors were booked up for the many private parties that were scheduled during Derby week. John felt the excitement of it all and wished that he could take Michelle to the race but this was unlikely because all the employees were needed at the hotel. A horse named Lieutenant Gibson won the race and the owner received a grand purse of four thousand, eight hundred and fifty dollars for the victory.

The aftermath of the Derby caused John to do some serious thinking about the future. Although he liked working at the Galt House he became restless to have a hotel of his own. Not only did he want to be in a position to attend special events like the Derby he also wanted to acquire a substantial amount of money so that he and Michelle could get married and live in luxury. He wondered how he might acquire enough funds to get started and thought of getting another loan from his mother. He also thought of the many wealthy guests who had stayed at the Hotel. Many of them seemed to like him and he wondered if he called on them and told them his plans whether they would be interested in investing in such a venture. John considered these things in his spare time at the desk and late in the evenings as he lay in bed.

******

One evening John got off work a little earlier than usual and went to the Connelly home to visit Michelle. After arriving he learned that she had gone to visit Katy in her new home so he went upstairs to visit with Mrs. Connelly.

She was glad to see him and they laughed and talked until she surprised him with an abrupt and unusual question. She cocked an eyebrow and in her distinct Irish accent asked, "John, why in the world don't you and Michelle get married?"

John was too amazed to have an immediate answer. She continued, "You two have been going together for nearly a year now and I think it's time you get married or break up." John started to speak as she interrupted. "Of course I would much rather see you married. It would be a shame for Michelle to lose such a prize as you."

John was glad she thought of him as someone special but he felt compelled to tell her about his poor financial status. He walked to the window to collect his thoughts.

"I wonder if you would still think I was a prize if I told you I don't have a dime to my name?"

Mrs. Connelly raised her eyebrows. "Why I would say you were even a greater prize."

John was puzzled. "I'm afraid I don't understand."

"Well I never did like the idea of any daughter of mine marrying a man with a lot of money and you are much too young to have had time to have accumulated a fortune on your own. Money often spoils a man's ambition, makes him lazy and doesn't give him a goal in life. Give me a man who is hard up for money and he'll be a man that knows how to make every dollar count." She squinted her eyes as she continued. "If a man like that ever does get an opportunity to make something of himself the world better look out because he's going to cut a wide path that's going to make a mark that will make a lot of people sit up and take notice." She shook her head in an assuring manner. "Now what were you going to say before I delivered my epistle?"

John shook his head in amazement then felt ashamed as he replied, "Mrs. Connelly, it isn't easy to sit here and tell you that I lied about coming to Louisville to open a hotel. You see I came here looking for work and I was so impressed with you and Michelle and the others that I wanted you all to think I was a person of position and wealth. I don't know how I could have ever done such a foolish thing. It's really not like me to put up a false front. Nevertheless I have lied to you good people and now I know how I must disappoint you. I hope Michelle won't --"

He had more to say but Mrs. Connelly interrupted again. She sat up and braced herself with her elbows. "Look here," she said in a scolding tone, "if you think Michele took a shine to you just because she thought you were rich you have another think coming."

"Oh I didn't mean that. It's just that she may lose confidence in me for not telling her the truth."

"Josh!" Mrs. Connelly answered. "I can see you don't know much about love. Why if she don't love you enough to overlook a little fib like that you wouldn't want her love. Why I'll have you know when any of my daughters loves a man they are with him through thick and thin. That's the way it has always been with us Connellys. And that's the way it will always be!"

John patted her hand affectionately then leaned over and kissed her forehead. He felt his eyes watering and attempted to keep it from showing. "You're wonderful," he said, "just wonderful."

She let herself back down and as her head sunk into the pillow she spoke again. "Now about you two getting married. What do you think?"

"Well I can't help but wonder if it wouldn't be best to wait until I can accumulate a little money."

Mrs. Connelly shook her head in disagreement. "You know I don't approve of long engagements."

"I just don't feel that I can give Michelle the things she should have with the small amount of money I earn. I just don't see how we could have much of a home."

Mrs. Connelly showed her impatience. "If you love each other enough to marry go ahead with it and you'll find a way to make ends meet. I just know you will."

"I've accumulated a lot of debts. You know I like to

dress well." A smile formed on his lips as he continued, "And you know I like to put up a good front -- spend money like crazy."

"If you wait until your debts are paid off you'll be an old man and your insurance man will be the only disappointed one when you die. You won't have anyone around like I have to love you. You've just got to have a big family or you're going to be mighty lonesome in your old age."

They both laughed and John felt she was probably right since he owed a considerable amount of money.

John saw Michelle coming up the sidewalk and heard her come into the house. He apologized to Mrs. Connelly. "I better go down and meet her.

Mrs. Connelly nodded her approval. Before leaving he thanked her for her advice. "I'm a lucky guy." He added, "Not only am I going to get a wonderful wife but a wonderful mother-in-law to boot." He kissed her again and left the room.

******

John and Michelle were married in June. The wedding took place at St. Cecilia's Church and every seat was taken. John's mother, Neil and Margaret came down from Lexington and Mrs. Connelly was brought to the church in a wheelchair.

Following the wedding ceremony a gala reception was held at Mackin Council Hall. The hall was decorated from one end to the other with colorful trimmings and flowers. Long serving tables were filled with cuts of baked ham and cheese, bowls of potato salad, pickles, olives and pretzels. A large beautifully decorated seven-tiered wedding cake had its own place on a table at the end of the hall and several tables were stacked high with neatly wrapped wedding gifts. There was a bar at the opposite end of the building and five moustached bartenders wearing long white aprons were kept busy dispensing mugs of beer to the guests.

A brass band filled the room with lively tunes. A nattily dressed photographer, wearing a loose fitting white shirt and a matching scarf around his neck, carefully posed the bridal party for pictures.

With precise gestures and articulate instructions he directed those to be photographed to remain perfectly still and to be "as motionless as statues." When he was satisfied with everyone's stance he moved back of the tripod mounted camera and poked his head into a cloth hood attached to the camera. Then holding a "V" shaped bar filled with powder he squeezed a flexible rubber bulb. This actuated the camera shutter and ignited the powder into a momentary flash and sent a puff of bluish-white smoke into the air. Afterwards the girls showed embarrassment at being photographed while the men assumed an air of pride.

Mrs. Connelly felt the strain of sitting and after excusing herself asked Tom and Marty to take her home. She could see that John's mother was forcing herself to act as though she were enjoying the activities and asked her if she would like to spend the afternoon with her. Knowing she could not readily join in with the frivolous activities of the celebration Mrs. Broker accepted the invitation.

Margaret was greatly delighted with the happy atmosphere at the party and danced merrily with many of the young men as Neil took up a place near the bar and conversed with some of the older guests and joined them in rounds of drinks. He wasn't there long though. Margaret grabbed him by the arm and led him to the floor where they laughed and danced.

A young man cut in to dance with Margaret and his lively spouse automatically put herself in Neil's arms. As they danced Neil quickly got into the spirit of the occasion and soon was dancing with one girl after another pausing only briefly to enjoy another glass of cold beer.

The reception continued until late in the afternoon. Then John and Michelle boarded a carriage for the trip to the railroad station at Tenth and Broadway where they were to board a train for Niagara Falls.

The newlyweds' carriage was followed by a long procession of wagons filled with members of the wedding party. At the rear of the entourage a large draft wagon carried the band members and a barrel of beer. The group continued beating out noisy tunes along the way and there were many sour notes but no one cared because the effects of the beer had reached the point where everything was enjoyable no matter what was taking place.

As they passed neighboring houses along the way many of the wedding guests shouted to friends sitting on their porches who called out greetings to John and Michelle. Margaret and Neil rode in one of the crowded carriages and both were enjoying themselves immensely.

When the party reached the station the wagons were parked and everyone followed John and Michelle into the building. The usually somber interior became alive with the carefree antics of the wedding party and the loud band music reverberated in hollow tones back and forth against the bare walls.

John and Michelle boarded their coach and walked to the platform at the rear of the train to wave farewells to the happy celebrants. The train moved slowly along the tracks and soon disappeared from view. After waving their last goodbye John and Michelle went inside and relaxed in a world of happiness.

******

In not too far away Ohio, there were two girls who also were aware of the wedding but did not share in the happiness of those at the party. Sister Jude walked along a corridor leading to a dormitory and as she entered she saw Sheila Reider entertaining a group of girls. When they saw Sister Jude everyone spoke and one girl asked her to join in the fun. Sister was well liked by all the students and they were sincere in wanting her to be with them.

Sister Jude smiled as she asked, "What in the world are you girls up to anyway?" Sheila answered in her polite native South Carolina accent. "Sistah, weah havin' a contest to see who can impersonate Sistah Gabriel the best." Sister Gabriel was in charge of the kitchen and was as sweet as she was fat. Whenever she stood in front of one of the wood-fired ranges stirring the foodstuffs being cooked she would shake and roll with each movement of her arm and the loose flesh on her face would bounce up and down with each movement of her body.

Sister Jude was amused but instinctively suppressed her feelings. "Sister Gabriel might not appreciate your impersonations," she said in a soft voice.

"Oh she doesn't mind at all," Sheila answered. "She watched us one time an' she laughed hardah than any of us."

"Why don't you stay and tell us who you think is best," another girl asked as others showed their interest in wanting her to stay.

"Oh I can't just now," Sister Jude answered. "I'm trying to find Ellen Boone. Have any of you seen her lately?"

"She was heah just a little while ago," Sheila answered. "She tol' me she was goin' to make a visit in the chapel."

Sister Jude thanked her and told the girls to go ahead with their fun then walked to the chapel. Entering she blessed herself, genuflected and knelt in a pew at the rear of the church.

She saw Ellen kneeling at the communion rail in front of a side altar and looking toward a statue of the Blessed

Virgin. The peaceful silence inside the chapel was broken by the sound of a hushed sobbing. Sister Jude immediately walked down the aisle and knelt beside her. She saw the anguish in Ellen's face. Patting her hand Sister Jude asked in a solicitous whisper if she was all right.

Ellen bit her lips and wanted to answer that she was but the words wouldn't come out.

"Let's go out and get some fresh air." Sister blinked her eyes to hold back her tears. She pulled a linen handkerchief from the cuff of her sleeve and handed it to Ellen. "Don't be afraid to cry," she said sympathetically.

Ellen blotted her tears as Sister Jude asked her if she was ready to go outside. She nodded she was and the two walked out of the chapel and down the front steps of the building towards the picturesque lake on the convent grounds. As they walked under the branches of the big oak and sycamore trees, the air felt refreshing.

They neared the lake and two swans moved gracefully across the water looking for a handout. Seeing there was none, they turned and quietly moved to a shady area along the opposite shore.

The two girls talked for a long time and Ellen felt better after telling Sister Jude what she already knew. She was greatly disappointed she had lost John and the hopes of becoming his bride after her graduation. She realized how little reason she had to think he ever cared anything about her. She knew now it was either through compassion or a feeling that he was indirectly responsible for the tragedy at her home that he helped her. It nearly broke her heart to think about it.

Sister sympathized with her by saying she could look forward to a world of happiness after graduation. She explained that several parents of her classmates were very fond of her and wanted her to live with them. They talked as they had many times before, sharing their happiness and sorrows together. Sister Jude had taken a great personal interest in Ellen and tutored her into becoming a charming and lovely young lady.

Actually Sister also felt disappointed because she hoped he cared for Ellen and would marry her. Not only did she want him to do this so Ellen's hopes would be fulfilled but she also felt this would be the means of having her for a sister-in-law. This way she thought she would be sure to see her often.

As time moved on Ellen managed to hide her continued disappointment in losing John. It distressed her to think of his showing his love and kindness to another girl. She fought to keep from hating Michelle and hated herself for feeling resentful toward someone she had never met. She wondered what would happen next and instinctively looked back at the many disappointments that had taken place in her life and had only a pessimistic outlook for the future.

******

When John and Michelle returned from their honeymoon they moved into a comfortable little cottage on Western Parkway. The next five years passed by seemingly fast as many new developments took place. They were blessed with a baby girl in the Autumn of 1902 and a second child, a boy, arrived during the summer of 1904. There were marriages too. Michelle's two brothers, Tim and Mike, were married in a double wedding and a few months after their wedding Sally was married. That left Peggy the only unmarried one at home to look after her mother.

The street scene in Louisville changed greatly during these years. Automobiles began to appear in large numbers and were successfully competing with carriage and wagons. Motorists were complaining though. Many argued that only two roads were suitable for automotive traffic. Third Street Boulevard to Jacob's Park and the Shelbyville Pike were the only two paved with Macadam topping to provide smooth riding. They wanted all of the city's brick and planked streets Macadamized.

All horse-drawn railcars were replaced with electric trolley cars and new rails were being installed to provide service to other parts of the city. Other changes were taking place too. Overflow crowds were attending weekend baseball games at Eclipse Park at Seventh and Kentucky Streets. Theatres were playing to packed houses. Macauley's on Walnut Street was billing top plays from New York. In 1904 the Dreamland Theatre opened its doors to the public at Fifth and Market and it was advertised as the first movie house to be built in Kentucky and the third in the nation. Both sides of Main Street from First to Twelfth Street were lined with factories and commercial establishments and the sidewalks were usually crowded with businessmen and shoppers.

A little to the south of the business district many executives associated with business houses lived in elaborate homes. There was a combination of High Victorian, Gothic and Italianate, Second Empire, Queen Anne and Renaissance revival architecture. They stood in magnificent splendor and were kept in immaculate repair.

Louis Seelbach, general manager of Seelbach's European Hotel on Main Street, announced that he and his brother Otto were going to put their famous Main Street up for sale and would soon build a lavish million-dollar, two-hundred-forty-room hotel at Fourth and Walnut Streets.

A number of leading businessmen on Main Street were skeptical of this venture. They contended it was too distant from the river front. Louis Seelbach answered them saying the business houses would soon follow him and Fourth Street would become the main business district. "After all," he said, "it's only four blocks south of Main Street. Main is choked with buildings from First to Tenth and there's no more room for expansion. My only regret," he added, "is that those fine architectural masterpieces that adorn each side of Main Street might some day be demolished."

There were many pros and cons about Seelbach's enterprise. As John listened to people discussing it he began to think more and more about his own future. He felt there would be a good future for him at the Galt House. He was already classified as a senior clerk and had been given several increases in pay since starting to work there.

John surmised that he would one day become chief clerk at the Galt House and not only would be in that prestigious position but would be receiving a substantial amount of pay. He didn't doubt for a moment that the elaborate Galt House would continue to thrive forever. Its reputation alone would make people want to stay there more than any other house in the Midwest. After all many of the presidents of the United States and other dignitaries had been there. Anyone looking through the old registers would find signatures of great men like Charles Dickens, the famed English novelist, Grand duke Alexis, son of the Czar of Russia, Mark Twain, Presidents Grant, Taft and Teddy Roosevelt, and many others.

He loved the Galt House and was proud to be part of it but he had never forgotten his desire to be the owner of a fine hotel himself. The dilemma about the new hotel at Fourth and Walnut and the speculation that other business houses would be built along Fourth Street caused him to do some serious thinking. He made a rough sketch of Main Street and drew a line showing the river front. Then he added another line depicting Fourth Street running south to Broadway.

He dotted in some of the major buildings along the streets, the Galt House, the Bank of Louisville building, the hotels, the Columbia Building, the railroad station and the business houses along Main Street. On Fourth he showed the location of the soon-to-be-built hotel, the Post Office Building and St. Joseph's Infirmiry.

John studied the sketch and visualized a new hotel at various points along the way. After rejecting all but one he circled a spot between Third and Fourth on the north side of Main Street. "This," he said to himself, "is where I will open a hotel that will be one of the finest in Louisville. It won't be the biggest but it'll be so elaborate that guests will line up for reservations."

The building he had in mind was five storied. There were six columns with high arched windows between four of the columns. A brass double door with small panes of glass stood between the two center columns. It had a cast iron guild work facade that was backed by gray Indiana stone.

John remembered a "For Rent" sign on the front of the building and was anxious to see the interior. "I'll see the owner and find a way to lease it." He mused, feeling the excitement of the prospect of having his own hotel. "My hotel will be centered between the Galt House and the new Seelbach Hotel. It'll be closer and have a finer view of the wharf." He wondered if there was a room large enough to accommodate a lobby on the first floor. He wanted a fine lobby.

He looked at his watch went to the chief clerk and obtained permission to leave the desk for a few hours then went to the hotel barber shop and had his shoes shined and his clothes brushed. He wanted to look his best when he talked to the owner.

Walking briskly down Main he stopped across the street from "his" building and again admired the architecture. He crossed the street dodging the heavy traffic of carriages draft wagons automobiles and trolley cars. "Busiest section in the city," he said to himself. "What a spot for a hotel!" He was glad no one else had thought of the building for this use.

He saw the sign on the door and read the inscription. "Those interested in leasing this fine building may see the owner in his private offices in the nearby Columbia Building." The name Millard Monroe, owner, was printed in script at the bottom of the card. John tried the door and found it locked. He walked down the sidewalk to Fourth Street.

The Columbia Building was impressive looking with its big granite stone base and the matching stones bordering the six big arched windows along Fourth Street and the ones facing Main Street. John was elated at the thought of obtaining a lease for the building. He didn't know where he'd get the money but he felt confident that he'd find a way. He'd just have to play it cool and not let Monroe know that he didn't have the funds at the time.

He looked for Monroe's name on the first floor directory found it and rode an elevator to the first floor. There he located a door lettered in gold, "Millard Monroe, Real Estate and Insurance Agent." John combed his hair and straightened his tie, then entered the office.

A well dressed bookkeeper asked if he could help him.

"Yes, I would like to see Mr. Monroe," John replied in a businesslike manner.

"May I ask what you want to see him about?" the man asked politely.

After stating his business he was ushered into Monroe's office. Monroe was tall and slender, his thinning hair was parted neatly in the middle and he wore a pair of gold-rimmed glasses over his pointed nose. He looked up when he heard the bookkeeper enter. There was a quick introduction.

"You wanted to see me?" Monroe asked. His voice was stern and impressive.

"Yes sir," John replied. "I would like to talk to you about the office building you have up the street."

"I'll be happy to tell you anything you want to know about it," Monroe said without showing any signs of enthusiasm.

John explained his interest in the building and asked questions about the interior. He learned that the offices on the upper floors might be suitable for hotel rooms. They were enclosed with solid walls and doors and most had plumbing heating and electric facilities. There was a large storage area on the first floor that once served as a men's store and there was an elevator. But there were no facilities for cooking and John was disappointed at this. He wanted a fine dining room in his hotel.

Mr. Monroe was too busy to take John through the building so he assigned one of his clerks to the task. John liked what he saw but realized there would have to be a lot of work done. The rooms would have to be papered; there was a lot of painting needed; curtains and window shades would have to be installed. The corridors appeared to be in fairly good shape except for worn carpeting on some of the floors. The building smelled musty but John knew that a good airing would correct this. Many of the window screens were rusted and had holes in them. There was little doubt these would have to be replaced.

He went up to a fifth floor room at the rear of the building to look at the view of the river front. He pulled the window open and the fresh air blowing in from the river was chilly but refreshing. Although it was the last part of February the temperature was mild and many of the people along the wharf had shed their topcoats and wore only suit coats and sweaters.

The United States Coast Guard floating station was directly in line with the building and surrounding it was a conglomeration of packets, ferry boats, floating docks, tow boats and small pleasure craft. The twin stacks of the Louisville-Jeffersonville ferry "Columbia" were again puffing out clouds of black smoke as it pulled away from the wharf and the "City of Louisville" was boarding passengers for its scheduled trip to Cincinnati. Hogsheads filled with tobacco stood in rows in front of one of the floating docks and in front of other docks there were bales of hay, barrels of whiskey sacks of grain and stacks of lumber.

"A beautiful sight," John said to his clerk escort. "It's one that can't be equaled by any of the hotels on Main Street. It's the center of everything on the wharf." He was well pleased and anxious to secure a lease for the building. He closed the window and the clerk followed him down the stairway to the first floor. John asked to see the boilers and other parts of the heating plant and the clerk explained that steam for the building's radiators was supplied by a heating plant in an adjacent building. John liked this arrangement and was glad he wouldn't have to staff men to operate and maintain the equipment.

John's second meeting with Millard Monroe was brief. Monroe listened to the plans for renovating and remodeling the building then he explained his proposition for leasing it.

"Mr. Broker, I don't know what your financial circumstances are but I hope you realize it's going to take a large amount of money to adapt the building to suit your needs." John started to speak but Monroe continued. "This and the fact that I'm anxious to have the building occupied makes me want to be as liberal as I can with the lease agreement."

John was glad to hear this and waited anxiously to learn how much it would cost to rent the building. He was glad Monroe hadn't asked him to explain his financial status because he would have been forced to lie about it. He still didn't know where he would borrow the money but there was an endless list of names that crossed his mind. His mother, maybe Neil Hathaway or the manager of the Galt House. He even thought about some of the more wealthy guests he had met while working at the hotel. He'd find a way to get the money. He felt sure of that.

Monroe pulled a ledger from one of the pigeon holes in his desk opened it then began scratching figures with a pencil. He looked at John then rolled his lower lip against his upper and concluded his thoughts.

"I'll tell you what, Mr. Broker. I'll give you a three year lease on the building for four thousand dollars a year, payable one year in advance." He searched John's face to see if there was an outward sign of how he felt about the figure.

John didn't doubt for a minute that he could raise it. His face brightened. "That sounds fair enough to me," he replied, then started to ask for a day or two to make the first payment as Monroe spoke again.

"There's one more thing, Mr. Broker, I wouldn't want my building used for any immoral purposes. I hope you intend to run the hotel as a hotel only, without all the vices that many of the others have."

John surmised that Monroe didn't want it to be a lustrous house of prostitution and cringed at the thought that he would think he was planing to operate a hotel in this manner.

"I can assure you that I wouldn't tolerate anything like that," John replied.

"Well then, I suppose I've got a tenant and you've got a hotel. I'll have the papers drawn up by my lawyer. You come back tomorrow with the fee and we can sign the lease at that time." Monroe got up from his chair and the two men shook hands. Before leaving John asked if he could have the keys to the building so he could begin to formulate plans for the conversion. Monroe was agreeable and called the clerk to his office and had him turn them over to him.

John went back to the Galt House to finish his day's work and felt so elated that he found it difficult to think about anything except the building. Before leaving he handed in his resignation at the Galt House explaining that he was entering into a business venture and needed to get started at once.

Instead of going directly home that night John stopped by to see Michelle's mother. He had grown extremely fond of Mrs. Connelly and often stopped by to keep her posted on everything that was happening. Then too, he knew she liked to hear of anything amusing that went on at the Galt House and kept his eyes peeled for things of this nature to tell her.

Mrs. Connelly was reading when he entered the room and immediately put down the book when she saw him. John had brought her a box of chocolates and laid it on her bedside table then sat in a rocker facing the bed.

"Land sakes," she said, "you'd think I was an invalid or something the way you're always bringing me things." John was always amazed at the way she joked about her poor health.

"Well," he said, "everytime I look at you, you look ten times healthier than the last time I saw you and I'm just being nice so you'll visit Michelle and me every day as soon as you are well."

"Oh, I just wish I could get out of this bed. I'd be mighty hard to keep up with and that's for sure."

"You will, one of these days," John assured her.

Mrs. Connelly changed the subject. "Have you got a funny story to tell me tonight?"

"Yes, I guess I've got one but it's one you might not like to hear."

"Get on with it, then. You're not going to embarrass me," she said anxiously.

"It's not that kind of story," John assured her.

"Are you going to tell it to me?" she asked good naturedly. "I haven't had a good laugh since you told me the story about the backward racehorse."

"Well," John said with a rather serious look on his

face, "this one might not make you laugh."

"You let me be the judge of that. We Connellys have a knack for finding humor in most anything."

"Well, it's this simple," he said with a slightly hesitant voice. "I've rented a big building on Main Street and I'm planning to convert it into a hotel."

All the signs of amusement disappeared from Mrs. Connelly's face. She looked at him and knew he was waiting for her comments.

"Tell me about it," she said anxiously.

John went into detail explaining everything except how he planned to raise funds.

"Where will you get the money?"

"I guess that's the joke," he answered wistfully. "I really don't know for sure that I can get enough to do all the things I plan."

Mrs. Connelly didn't say anything for a few moments. She was trying to analyze the situation. She knew it would take an awful lot of money and didn't know if he could borrow it. She felt she could talk him out of going any further into the transaction yet hated to disappoint him. Then too, she was concerned about advising him wrongly.

"You must have felt that you could raise the money or you wouldn't have told Mr. Monroe you would sign the lease."

"I sure did, and I still do. I want that building so bad that I'm willing to sign anything or do anything to get the money."

Mrs. Connelly raised her head proudly. "That's the way I like to hear you talk. I've always said that if a person wants to do something bad enough they'll find a way to get it done. Perseverance is one of the greatest gifts a man can have. When a man thinks about something he wants to do and he thinks about it long and hard enough to make a plunge, then he's got to sink or swim to the other shore. If he turns back, he'll always wonder if he could have made it, and if he sinks, he's not a fighter. The plunge is the sign of self-assurance.'' She squinted an eye and pointed a finger. ''You've made your plunge. Now go to it with everything you've got. There'll be a lot of people besides me that'll be pulling for you.''

''And if I don't make it?''

''You're not that kind of a person. You'll make it all right.'' She shook her head assuredly. ''You've already got your first five thousand dollars.''

''First five thousand dollars?'' John was puzzled. ''Why, I haven't even got fifty dollars.''

''Well, you'll have it in a minute.'' She reached for her pocketbook.

John shook his head. ''If you think —'' She cut him off. ''I do what I want with my money and I'm going to make out this draft for five thousand so you can pay for the first year's rent and have enough left over to pay your household expenses.''

While she made out the check John continued his objections. ''Mrs. Connelly, I wouldn't have come here tonight if I had thought you were going to do anything like this. All I wanted was your confidence.''

She handed him the check. ''Well, you've got my confidence and you've got my money and if I could get up from this bed I'd go down to that building of yours and roll up my sleeves and help you get it ready for business.

John was embarrassed. He didn't know exactly what to do. The money was tempting. If he could deliver it to Millard Monroe the next day it would give him time to raise more. ''Are you sure you can spare this?''

''If I couldn't I wouldn't have given it to you but there's just one stipulation. You needn't mention this to anyone in the family and this includes Michelle. You know it's a funny thing, John. When Mr. Connelly died, God rest his soul, he left me a goodly amount of money and told me it was mine to spend as I saw fit. Well I've been careful with it. Very careful! The children haven't had to want for anything now they're all grown. So I think I'm pretty good at handling money. But you know what? All of them want to tell me what to do with it now. Buy a smaller home, take a pilgrimage, invest in railroads, go to Minnesota where a couple of skilled doctors have started up a clinic." Then she gestured amusingly with her hands. "Go here, buy this, go there. Of course they all mean well but after people have lived most of their lives they don't need anyone to tell them what to do. They've learned that life is what you make it and it's best not to make too many plans because things don't always turn out the way you expect. It's best to just kind of take it easy and sort of do the best you can to make yourself and others happy.

"You've seen an old dog lay in the shade while the younger ones run around in the sun wearing themselves out. Well, those old dogs are smart. They've experienced everything the younger ones are going through and they're happy if everyone just lets them be. But that don't mean young dogs should lay around while they can stand the heat. There's things to do and places to go. They can lay in the shade later on."

John smiled. "I could listen to you forever."

"Well, just don't get too busy to stop by and visit me when you're an important hotelman."

"I'll never be too busy to do that. Besides you're my partner now and I'll have to keep you posted on the business and bring you your share of the profits."

"I didn't say anything about investing in the business. That money is yours to do with what you like."

"If I thought for one moment that I couldn't repay you many times over, I could never accept it."

Mrs. Connelly looked at the clock. "If you don't get home to Michelle and the babies soon, she might think you're out with some beautiful woman." She squinted an eye. "I'm joking of course. I know you too well to think you would ever do a thing like that.''

"I'm doing that right now," John said.

Mrs. Connelly was skeptical. "You're doing what?" she said with a worried look on her face.

"I'm with a beautiful woman and that's for sure."

She closed her eyes and sighed in relief. "You better get on home before I get to believing you and crawl out of this bed and start looking for another John Broker."

John kissed her on the cheek. After he had gone, she closed her eyes again and began blinking them to allow the tears to escape. For a pensive moment she longed to be young and well again.

******

As John and Michelle were having breakfast the next morning, they felt the chill of the cold air that had penetrated the walls during the night. John banked the fires before going to bed and was glad to see that some of the embers were still glowing as he stoked chunks of coal in the stoves in each room.

He sipped his coffee and looked out the window and saw a flurry of snowflakes blowing against the window pane. Michelle was concerned about his having to go out in the weather. "I hope it lets up soon. It's going to be too cold for you to be out on the street."

John set his cup down. "You know what, Michelle? I feel so good this morning that I don't care what the weather is like."

"And you know what?" Michelle said, smiling. "I sure hope you'll always be this happy."

"What other way could I be with a wonderful wife like you?"

"It's nice of you to put it that way but you're happy this morning because you'll soon have a hotel of your own. Remember?"

"Yes, but if you hadn't shown your approval I wouldn't feel this way."

"You wouldn't expect me to do otherwise, would

you?''

"Well, it is a risk. We stand to lose everything we've worked for. That's not a whole lot but we've always been able to meet our expenses and have a little left over for a few luxuries. There's no reason to believe we wouldn't have improved our lot if I had stayed at the Galt House.''

"Yes, but you'd never be happy working for someone else. You know that. You need to have your own business. From what you've told me about your father you must have inherited this from him. Besides I know you wouldn't be going into this if you didn't feel sure you would make a success of it.''

John agreed. "That's for sure. I'm going to turn that building into a hotel that's fit for a king. Of course," he said with a laugh, "most of the rooms will be better suited for everyday people like the ones that stay in Louisville's other fine hotels.''

John finished his coffee then looked at his watch. "I've got seven minutes to catch the next trolley car for town so I better get moving.'' He put on his suitcoat then his overcoat. Michelle handed him his derby. He pulled the overcoat collar up around his neck, kissed her goodbye then pulled the derby down snugly over his neatly combed hair.

"I'll probably be back home before dark,'' he said as he opened the door to leave.

"I'll be waiting for you,'' Michelle replied with a smile. Then she watched as he walked down the sidewalk toward the car stop. "I'm a lucky girl,'' she said to herself, "To have such a wonderful husband.''

John got off the car at Third and Market and walked briskly against the cold wind down to the Bank of Louisville Building. He noted the address as he opened one of the polished brass doors. "Three Sixteen West Main.'' After he was inside he removed his hat and looked across the street at the building he was going to rent. It looked better than ever to him. He walked over to a teller's window and deposited Mrs. Connelly's check and soon was issued a check book.

Afterwards he went to the Columbia Building and up to Mr. Monroe's offices. The clerk that accompanied him the day before spotted him and informed him that Mr. Monroe had left town on business and he was authorized to handle the lease arrangement. The clerk removed some papers from a file and unfolded the contract. "Mr. Monroe told me to be sure you read the papers carefully before you sign them."

There were two typed pages of fine print and John scanned them rather quickly. The terms were the same as previously stated by Mr. Monroe. "Four thousand dollars a year, payable in advance." He saw the words, "three year lease," written in long hand. There was a lot of legal terminology. "Party of the first part — party of the second part." John skipped over most of this. He was satisfied and told the clerk so. He made out a check then signed the lease and after getting his copy of the agreement left the building feeling extremely happy. He had negotiated the first step in his process of opening a new hotel. A three year lease was secured in his inside coat pocket. He remembered the date and added three years. "March the eighth, nineteen and eight," he said to himself. "I'll renew it then— or build a hotel of my own.

******

The next week went by quickly for John. He made a trip to Lexington and talked to his mother about another loan. He explained about his plans to open a hotel and projected a bright outlook for its success. She reminded him that she had a limited income because his father had stipulated in his will that all the money in his estate was to be held in trust. Consequently, she received only a fixed monthly allotment.

It was a generous amount but not sufficient to make withdrawals such as the five thousand dollars he had asked for. She explained she would have to take this out of a savings fund she had built up from the allotments. It would take most of it but she was willing to do this because of his immediate need.

He went to see Neil Hathaway too. Neil was reluctant to let him have any money and confessed that Margaret had asked him not to ever let him have any money unless it was urgently needed for illness or something of that nature. After a long discussion Neil loaned him three thousand dollars with the stipulation that Margaret was not to know about it.

Before leaving Lexington John had dinner with Neil, Margaret and his mother and spent a wonderful evening with them. They sat in the Hathaways' parlor in front of a big fireplace kindled with seasoned logs. As the fire flashed and sputtered, they laughed and joked as John entertained them with his pleasant and charming personality. They had almost forgotten what a delightful person he could be.

Neil drove John to the station the next morning and as they exchanged farewells he pulled an envelope from his pocket and handed it to John.

"Here's another two thousand. I know you'll need it."

"You'll never know how much I appreciate your confidence," John said gratefully. "I hope to have your money back with interest, of course a few months after the hotel is opened."

"You have the option to put it in stock, if you want."

"Livestock?" John asked jokingly.

"You know what I mean," Neil replied, laughing.

"Well, I ought to. I'm a 'stock Broker', you know."

Neil shook his head. "Get on that train," he said facetiously, "before I change my mind."

John waved a quick parting gesture with his hand. "I'll look forward to seeing you and Margaret at the opening." Then he stepped up and entered the coach.

As John rode on the train he pulled a small notebook

from his shirt pocket and began checking dates. "May tenth — Kentucky Derby." "Just two months from now." He thought to himself, "Have to move fast to be open for business by that time."

The nerves in his stomach pulled tight as he thought of all there was to do. "I'll need more money of course but I have enough to get started with the remodeling. I'll get an office fixed up first and have a cot installed. I'll be there day and night during the remodeling.

He knew several competent builders who had done work on the Galt House. "Romney Company could do it; so could Otis Wiley. I'll call Otis first and see if he's in a position to get it done in time. He does architectural work and I'll need help planning the layout." He wished the train would move faster. He pulled his watch from a vest pocket. If the train arrived at 3:10 p.m. as scheduled he might have time to get in touch with Wiley. He felt the tension building up and went to the club car and had several drinks. This calmed him and he sat back in a lounge chair and rested his head against the back. "I'll get it all done and that's for sure." He fell asleep and didn't wake up until the train pulled into the Louisville station.

Wiley got the job. He worked with John and came up with a set of plans. His crew started work on March the 14th. John notified both the COURIER-JOURNAL and the HERALD POST newspapers of his plans. When a reporter asked what he was going to name the hotel he realized he'd been too busy to think of a name. He knew he'd have to come up with one quickly. He remembered that his father had often spoken of a luxurious hotel in Europe called the Rasineer. That would be it! He wasn't even sure how it was spelled but he spelled it like it sounded, "R-A-S-I-N-E-E-R." The reporter jotted it down and the editors of both newspapers gave the story front page coverage.

Word spread fast about the hotel and many local

merchants sent their salesmen to see "Mr. John Broker at the Rasineer." They offered their lines of furniture, linen, stationery, uniforms, carpeting, wallpaper and janitor's supplies. They waited in line to see him.

Job applicants came too. Clerks, bellhops, managers, janitors, maids, maintenance men, accountants and house detectives. Some were employed at other hotels, some were out of work. There was no way that John could see them all so he had a sign placed at the front of the building telling them to sign their name and address and the type position they wanted in a book that was placed on a table.

He needed someone to help with all the details and scanned through the book at night to find a likely candidate. He saw Randy Barnes' name. He and Randy had worked the same shift together at the Galt House. "Darned good man," John mused. "Hate to see him leave the Galt House though. They think a lot of him. But they're loaded with well-trained employees."

John sent word for him to come to see him, and Randy wanted to work at the Rasineer in the worst way. John hired him and was glad he did. He screened out the best applicants and had many come in for interviews. He talked to salesmen and advised John of the best buys.

One morning John was told that a well dressed lady had arrived in an electric automobile and insisted on seeing him. John had her brought to his office and she told him she came to inquire about his new enterprise. She had a special interest in Main Street as her husband had owned the foundry where many of the cast iron facades on the buildings along the street had been made. The building John leased was one of them. She was concerned about the new stores and shops that were being built along Fourth Street and was afraid the Main Street buildings might eventually be torn down if there was a mass exodus of Main Street merchants. She told John she thought his hotel would be an incentive for the merchants to stay and she was confident that his hotel would be a great success.

John thanked her for the confidence but before he could say more, she broke in.

"I don't have any idea how you're financing this venture but I'm sure it's going to take a great deal of money."

John nodded in agreement.

"To get to the point of my visit here I cannot help but feel that you'll be compelled to take some partners into the business and I would like to be one of the first to join you."

John became much more interested in her visit. He couldn't remember if she had introduced herself and asked her name.

"I am Mrs. Reymonte Patterson, and I live in St. James Court, just south of the DuPonts' estate on Fourth Street."

"Oh yes," John said enthusiastically. "A lovely neighborhood." He was anxious to find out how much she wanted to invest but didn't want to appear too eager for fear of losing her confidence.

"Yes, Mrs. Patterson there is a great deal of expense in opening a hotel and there is a need for additional capital. In fact there are others who have wanted to invest but I planned on being the sole owner from the beginning." John hoped his statement would not deter her interest.

"Mr. Broker, I think you would benefit from having a partner with my position in Louisville's social and civic circles."

"I'm sure of that," John agreed. "Just how much would you want to invest?"

Mrs. Patterson held her head high as she replied, "I am prepared to give you a check for fifty thousand dollars in exchange for a twenty-five percent interest in the business."

John was pleasantly astounded. "Mrs. Patterson," he said, "not only are you a charming person, you are a clever business woman and I'm fortunate to have you for a partner."

"You accept my offer then?"

"I not only accept it, I welcome it."

"All right then," she said as she removed a draft for fifty thousand dollars and gave it to him. "I'm counting on you to make a go of this place so don't you let me down."

You'll never regret this moment," he assured her.

John escorted her to her car. After he closed the door he watched as she drove away ever so quietly in her brand new "Electric."

"Unbelievable!" he said to himself.

With things going so smoothly John began to go home evenings. One evening he saw that Michelle's brothers, Marty and Tom, were in the living room. When John entered they stood and exchanged handshakes. He invited them to sit down and he sat in a chair facing them. Marty asked about the hotel. John explained that things were going well and construction was ahead of schedule.

"Then you'll be open for the Derby?"

"Yes, we've still got seven seeks to do."

Marty explained his reason for the visit. "You know, John, Tom, Mike, Tim and I are greatly disappointed you haven't invited us to invest in the hotel."

"I guess I've been too busy to give it any thought," John said apologetically.

"We hoped that might be the reason," Tom chimed in. He looked at Marty. "See, didn't I tell you?"

Marty acknowledged that he had. Then he turned to John again. "Then you'll let us in?"

"Sure if you want to but you must understand there's a risk involved. You men have worked hard for your money. I would hate to see you lose any of it."

"We fully understand the risks," Marty replied. "If the hotel succeeds we stand to gain. If it fails, we lose. It's that simple."

"I'll be glad to have you as partners," John answered, "as long as you understand that." He went on to explain about Mrs. Patterson's acquisition of twenty-five percent. Then he asked how much they wished to invest.

Marty made some fast mental calculations. "Let's see, based on what you said, Mrs. Patterson paid two thousand dollars per share." He hesitated for a moment then continued. "The four of us have a total of ten thousand dollars which would give us a five percent interest in the business."

John got out a notebook and checked the figures. "That's correct."

"Then you'll sell us the five percent?"

"Be glad to."

"When can we make the transaction official?"

"Anytime you like!"

"Tomorrow?" Marty asked hopefully.

"Sure, come up to the hotel and we'll make out the papers."

"We'll be there." Marty thanked him and John was happy to have them as investors.

Michelle asked them to stay for dinner but they explained they'd have dinner waiting for them at home. After much handshaking and well-wishing they parted company.

Michelle and John embraced each other. "Honey in a very short while we're going to be rolling in money," John said enthusiastically. "And you know what?" he added. "One of the first things I'm going to buy is the best automobile that is made and we'll drive up and down the streets in style. I want you to have the best of everything: clothes, fine home, servants --"

Before he could continue Michelle placed her fingers on his lips. "All that would be nice but for the time being

I like things just as they are."

She pulled away from him and took him by the hand and led him to the kitchen. After they finished eating John went back to the living room and sat in his favorite over-stuffed chair. He lit up a cigar and blew rings of smoke into the air and thought about the events of the day. He found them to be extremely comforting.

******

Several days after Michelle's brothers invested in the Rasineer there was an editorial in a local newspaper questioning the feasibility of an additional hotel on Main Street. While the article did point out that John appeared to be a very capable young man and seemed to have all the aspirations of his father as a successful businessman it also stated he might have had poor judgement in selecting Main Street for the site of his new business. It went on to say that the future business places in Louisville were most likely to continue moving farther south on Fourth Street and the modern structures would be more attractive for hotel guests. It stated that railroad travel was rapidly replacing the steamboat trade and Fourth Street business houses would be closer to the big Union Station on Broadway.

John laughed at the editorial after being questioned by some of his friends. "Why I intend to keep the street so much alive that the Union Station will no doubt move their entire operations, tracks and all, closer to Main Street," he advised them jokingly.

But it did make him do some serious thinking. He knew it was necessary to have something more than lodging accommodations to attract people to a hotel. He thought of a dining room but the building was not adequately arranged for this. He looked at a big room in the rear of the first floor lobby. It was nearly a hundred feet wide and extended a little more than that lengthwise. There were numerous columns spaced uniformly throughout the room to support the upper floors. It had a high ceiling that exposed rough planking.

John planned on using this as a storage area. But now that his financial status was greatly improved he looked at the room in a different perspective. He pictured it as an elaborate saloon with a long bar with an impressive mirrored back and many tables for the customers. He called in Frank Scherer, the owner of a local brewery, and asked his opinion. Scherer encouraged him to go ahead with the idea and suggested he use a German motif in the design.

He described a saloon he had seen in Austria. "They had an elevated platform where a brass band alternated with a string band playing for the customers. Sometimes there were lively tunes and other times soft serenades." Scherer gestured with his hands as he talked and jerked them vertically up and down quickly for the brass band and swept them with palms down in a graceful movement for the strings.

He went on describing the saloon's furnishings and other decor. Heavy but beautiful furniture. Red and gold wall coverings, ornamental trimmings, leather-covered bar, wooden clocks, polished earthenware and large paintings with heavy gold frames.

John liked the idea and later met with Wiley. His greatest concern was getting the work completed before the Derby and Wiley told him that the only way it could be done was by working men on two shifts around the clock.

"Then we'll do just that," John replied, satisfied it could be done. He noticed a worried look on Wiley's face. "Is something wrong, Otis?"

The contractor scratched his head. "Well, I hate to mention this, Mr. Broker, but I am running a little short on cash and wonder if it would be possible to get an advance?" Actually Wiley was not so much in need of the money but he had heard rumors that John was opening the hotel on a shoestring and would probably go broke before it even opened.

"No problem at all," John assured him. "How much do you want? Five, ten, or say — fifteen thousand?"

Wiley was embarrassed. "Five would be just fine, Mr. Broker."

John pulled a draft from his coat pocket and began filling it in for fifteen thousand. He showed it to Wiley. "I'll give you this on one condition."

"One condition?" The worried look returned to Wiley's face.

"That you buy me a drink."

Wiley shook his head in appreciation and smiled. "Oh, I'll be proud to do that. Mighty proud!"

John handed him the check.

Wiley reached for John's hand and shook it gratefully. They went to a river front bar at the foot of Third Street and had several rounds of drinks. As they discussed construction details for the saloon, the drinks began to take their toll on Wiley. His head waved as he started telling John how much he thought of him.

"You know what, Mr. Broker?" he said with a thick tongue. "Someone was telling me you were starting this hotel up on a shoestring and didn't have hardly any money at all, and I was really worried about it."

"Think nothing of it, Otis," John remarked, and gave him a friendly slap on the back.

Wiley was overcome with remorse. His eyes were watery and he was on the verge of crying. "Ya know what, Mr. Broker? You're jush the finesht man I've ever known and I feel awful for thinking you didn't have enough money to pay your bills."

"Glad you think so, Otis," John said cheerfully. Realizing the contractor had drunk more than he could handle, John helped him out of the saloon, hailed a carriage and instructed the driver to take him to his home.

The next few weeks were the busiest ever for John.

Work progressed rapidly and there were many last minute details to look after in order to have everything ready for the grand opening. A big vertical sign with thirty-inch simulated gold letters on a black background was installed in front of the building making the name "Rasineer" an "official" new establishment on Main Street. Furniture was ordered and delivered as were the linens, draperies, curtains, window shades, bedding, janitors' supplies, stationery and office supplies. Employees were hired and fitted with uniforms appropriately designed for their particular assignments. Cases of whiskey and barrels of beer were delivered to the saloon, and the furnishings for this area were delivered and put in place.

John was particularly pleased with the way the saloon turned out. The bar was seventy-eight feet long, the longest in all Kentucky. Wiley had built it, and the back bar too. Both were works of art. They were made from solid cherry and finished to perfection. Overhead fans were installed to provide maximum ventilation and cooling, and the platform for the musicians had a backdrop depicting a scene from a Bavarian village. Velvet drapes with matching valance were installed at the front of the platform and a row of stage lights had been installed behind a raised curbing at the front edge of the floor area. John spared no expense in making it one of the finest barrooms in the Country. He had little doubt this would entice travelers from all over the world to stay at the Rasineer whenever they visited Louisville.

John announced the opening of the hotel with full page ads and local newspapers told it all in bold print:

A Date To Remember In Louisville
Wednesday, May 3, 1905
IT'S THE OPENING OF THE NEW RASINEER HOTEL
Located On:
Main Street Between Third and Fourth

(North Side of Street)
You are welcome to inspect
the splended Hotel facilities,
the modern and unique Saloon
No Expense Has Been Spared
in Creating These Masterpieces
John Broker - Proprietor

John also sent out invitations to prominent citizens to visit the hotel on opening day. He received acknowledgements from Louisville's Mayor, Charles Brainger, and several aldermen. Governor J. C. W. Beckham sent a letter of apology saying he would not be able to attend but wished him the best of success. He closed the letter with: "I knew your father very well and I know he would be very proud if he were here today to see his son embarking on such an outstanding enterprise."

The Rasineer's opening was exactly one week prior to the 1905 Derby scheduled for Wednesday, May tenth. Three horses were expected to start. Agile was such a favorite that there was more speculation about how the other two horses, Layson and Rams Horn, would finish than there was of Agile's chance of winning.

John sent a letter to Agile's owner, S. S. Brown, and to the trainer, Bob Tucker, asking them to stay at the Rasineer but they replied they had previously made arrangements to stay at the Galt House. They did make reservations for Agile's jockey, Jack Martin, to stay at the Rasineer and assured John they would stop by to see the hotel before the race. This was greatly pleasing to John and he managed to have this information spread around town to get recognition for his establishment.

The day before the opening was the busiest ever for John. There were a thousand-and-one things to look after. Windows had to be washed, floors scrubbed, furniture arranged, beds made up, carpets swept, keys attached to numbered room tags. There seemed to be no end to all of the last minute details.

Finally at two o'clock on the morning of opening day John was satisfied that his hotel was ready. He went up to one of the rooms and managed to get several hours sleep before starting the most important day of his life. At five-thirty he walked down the main stairway into the lobby. A lone electric light bulb cast an eerie view throughout the otherwise darkened room. This and the silence was frightening as he thought about the hotel. "Will there be a crowd for the opening? Will all the rooms be occupied for the Derby? Will the guests like the facilities? Had he spent too much money in remodeling?"

He wondered what he would do if the hotel failed. It was the first time this had entered his mind. "It won't fail! Instead it will be one of the most successful hotels in the city," he said to himself over and over but the feeling of doubt was still there. There was no way to be sure. He went to the saloon and poured a small glass of bourbon and drank it down. This made him feel better and he became more optimistic about the Rasineer's future.

John had instructed most of the employees to arrive at the hotel at six thirty to get ready for the official opening at eight. Jim Fleming, the house detective, stood outside to see that no unauthorized persons got inside. John greeted the employees as they arrived and gave them last minute instructions on their assignments. Later he moved from place to place checking to see if things were being done to his satisfaction.

The head maid wanted to know where the wash cloths were stored, a desk clerk couldn't find the keys to the third floor rooms, a janitor wanted to know where the lobby spitoons were to be located, a bellhop reported a loose tile in the lobby floor and an elevator operator wanted instructions on what he was to do if an elevator got stuck between floors. There seemed to be no end to the questions but John didn't mind. He liked being busy. It helped ease the tension.

At seven thirty a crowd gathered on the front sidewalk waiting for the opening and John went to the door and let everyone in. The Rasineer was open for business! Each one congratulated him and wished him success for the hotel's future. John beamed with happiness and carefully noted that many were lining up at the desk registering for rooms. He was also pleased to see the bellhops efficiently escorting guests to their assigned rooms.

By nine o'clock the lobby and saloon were crowded with people and many were at the bar having an early morning drink. Others were moving about talking to friends and admiring furnishings as they got their first glimpse of Louisville's new hotel. John mingled in the crowd continuing to shake hands with everyone he met.

He saw Mrs. Patterson squeezing through the crowd and went to her aid.

"Don't you want to go to my office to escape all this commotion?" he asked.

"Why, I wouldn't miss this for anything," she said happily. "It's a wonderful sight." Then she added, "You've turned the trick, Mr. Broker. We're in business!"

John raised his head proudly. "Yes, it's a wonderful day, Mrs. Patterson. One we'll long remember."

The crowds continued throughout the day. Michelle and her brothers and sisters were there and marveled at the activity. Michelle was extremely proud of John and could see he was in his glory as he mingled with the crowd. John had a private hospitality bar and buffet set up in two adjoining rooms on the first floor. Michelle and the others made this their headquarters. Many of the prominent guests were invited to stop by for a visit.

John went up to the room occasionally and was glad to see everyone enjoying themselves. Tim Connelly never seemed to run out of funny stories to tell. John was there when he told about a cowboy who went into a drugstore complaining to a clerk about being galded from sitting in a saddle too long. Tim gestured artfully as he mimicked the cowboy walking stiff-legged and asking the clerk if he had a good ointment that would give him relief.

"Sure," the clerk said, "Walk this way and I'll show you something that will give you great relief."

"Hell," Tim quoted the cowboy as saying, "if I could walk that way I wouldn't need any ointment!"

John joined the others laughing as Tim continued with other stories. More than once he was admonished by Katy for telling borderline jokes but this didn't deter him. He knew they would leave the room if they were really offended.

Michelle remarked to John about a telegram Neil and Margaret had sent along with their regrets at not being able to attend the opening.

"Too bad they couldn't make it," Michelle said. "I know they would have enjoyed being here."

John's face took on a serious look. "Yes, but there is someone else who would enjoy it more."

Michelle became serious too. "You mean Mother, don't you?"

John shook his head in agreement. "You know, Michelle, I think about her a lot and I can hardly bear to think of her having to lie there in that one room all the time. She loves life so much and needs to be involved in things."

"She misses seeing you but she understands how busy you've been."

"Yes, and I'm going to do something about that. I'm going to have a corner room in the front of the building fixed up just for her and we're going to have her brought here so she can be a part of the hotel. We'll make the room bright and cheerful and put her bed where she can look out and see all the Main Street activity. Then I'll have her close to me. I can talk things over with her and get her advice. She's a smart woman, Michelle. Good logic, understands people. She'll be a real asset.''

"She would love that, John. It will be so good for her."

"I'll get Wiley to start on it right away. You tell her about it as soon as you can.''

"Oh, I will,'' Michelle replied happily. "I'll see her tonight.''

"Fine,'' John said to her with an assuring smile. He started to say more but Randy Barnes entered the room. He apologized for the intrusion then told John that Millard Monroe was waiting downstairs to see him.

"Millard Monroe,'' John replied eagerly. "To be sure. Show him to my office and tell him I'll be there shortly.''

He checked the buffet and saw that most of the hors d'oeuvres had been eaten. "I'll have more food sent up right away,'' he said as he prepared to leave. Tim tapped him on the shoulder. "Hey, John, did you hear what the little boy said to the preacher when he was asked if he always said his prayers before he ate?''

John stopped long enough to appease his happy-go-lucky brother-in-law. "No, what did he say?''

"No sir!'' Tim quoted the boy as saying. "My mother's one hellu'va good cook!''

John threw up his hands in a surrendering gesture then walked from the room. Voices from the downstairs crowd came in range as he walked down the stairs. He was nearing his office when Orion Irving, a renowned state legislator, stopped him and shook his hand. "Mr. Broker, I want to congratulate you on your taste. This is a mighty fine place you have here. Mighty fine!''

John thanked him. He knew the senator was one of the most prominent politicians in Kentucky and a strong candidate for the Lieutenant Governor's office. He hated to keep Millard Monroe waiting but it was important to give special attention to such a prized visitor.

"Have you seen the saloon?'' John asked.

"No, matter of fact, I haven't. You see, I arrived only a little while ago and have been busy talking."

"Let me show it to you," John said, placing his hand on the senator's arm and leading the way.

Doc Fisher, a pharmacist at one of the large downtown drugstores saw John and asked for a few minutes of his time. John apologized. "Can I see you a little later on, Doc? I have someone waiting to see me and I promised to show this gentleman the bar."

"Sure, Mr. Broker," Doc replied, showing his disappointment. "I'll be around for awhile."

There were other exchanges as John and the senator made their way through the crowded lobby. John enjoyed the recognition and compliments. When they opened one of the double doors to the saloon new sounds filled the air. The five piece German band was playing "Tales from Vienna Woods" and there were sounds of gaiety coming from happy customers who filled the room.

All seats at the tables were taken and customers were two deep along the bar. Smoke from lighted cigars, pipes and cigarettes swirled softly across the room as the overhead fan blades sliced through the thick air.

John pushed his way through the crowd and the senator followed close behind. Both laughed as well wishers slapped their backs, offering congratulations. To John for the opening day's activity and his success — to the senator for his nomination for Lieutenant Governor. When they reached the bar more well wishers greeted them and several men stepped aside to give them their place. Each had a double shot of bourbon. One bartender took time to tell John how he felt about the place. "I've been working hotel bars for many years and this is unbelievable. A seventy-eight foot bar with seven bartenders running their cans off trying to keep up." He paused momentarily as he poured a drink for another customer then added. "The customers love the place!''

John looked around at the crowd and waved cordially as some signaled him a greeting. There was a table surrounded by some of the top tobacco dealers in the city. Another had the owners of the famous ''Moving Rivers Packet Line.'' Other tables were occupied by executives from distilleries, tanneries, meat packing houses, railroad and the like. There were also a number of military officers, boat builders, racehorse people, politicians and downtown businessmen.

John was concerned about the senator. There was hardly room to stand and well wishers were crowding around him.

''Senator, there's a hospitality room upstairs where you can get away from the crowd.'' The senator objected, holding his hands up with the palms turned outward. ''No, indeed. I appreciate your interest but this is fine. Lots of nice people here. I'm going to need people like this to get elected. You go ahead, though. I know you have lots to do.'' Then grabbing John's hand and delivering a warm handshake, he added, ''I'll never forget your kindness.''

''Well, I do have someone waiting in my office.''

''Go ahead,'' he urged jovially. Then before John could leave the senator gave him a pat on the back. ''Just don't forget me on election day!''

John made his way back through the crowd and stopped by the desk to see if the register was filling up. Randy Barnes was there and showed his elation at the way things were going. ''All rooms on the second and third floors are taken and the ones on the fourth and fifth are filling up fast.''

''Fine,'' John replied. ''Hold at least a dozen rooms for prominent late comers. We don't want to turn down any dignitaries.''

''I'll be sure to take care of it, Mr. Broker.''

John thought how fortunate he was to have Randy for an assistant. His experience at the Galt House made him a valued employee. John was about to compliment him for his work but a soft, alluring voice distracted him.

"Hello, Mistah Broker."

Turning, John showed his surprise. "Harriett Metcalfe!"

She looked gorgeous as she gazed up at him mischievously. Her pretty brown eyes sparkled in happiness.

"It's awfully good to see you again, Mistah Broker," she said, cocking her head.

John wondered about the formality but didn't question it. "And it's good to see you, Harriett." Impulsively he made a movement to kiss her but she gestured gracefully with her hand. "This is my husband, Phillip Audubon. Phillip, this is John Broker from Lexington. You've heard me mention him before. We're former neighbors."

John felt somewhat awkward because he hadn't noticed him standing at her side.

"It's a real pleasure, Mr. Audubon," John said as the two shook hands.

"Mistah Audubon deals in furs," Harriett said, rolling her eyes devilishly and at the same time gracefully adjusting a mink stole covering her slim shoulders.

"Interesting work, I'm sure," John said, hating to take his eyes from Harriett. He wanted to mention old times but knew he shouldn't. It was frustrating.

"Are you planning on staying here with us?"

"Yes," Phillip answered. "I preferred the Galt House but Harriett insisted we stay here." His voice was cool and he held his chin high as he spoke. "An aristocratic slob," John thought to himself.

"I'll see that you have the best of everything," John said enthusiastically. He leaned against the counter top and told Randy to assign them to one of the bridal suites then he looked at Phillip again.

"I suppose you're here for the races?"

"Not entirely. You see, I will be calling on some of the more affluent business houses in Louisville."

John found this extremely interesting. Harriett could see this in his eyes and curled her lips in an inviting smile. Randy Barnes interrupted by reminding John about Millard Monroe's waiting to see him.

"Yes, I must see him right away." He looked again at Phillip and Harriett. "Please excuse me, I have someone waiting to see me."

Phillip motioned to the bellhop handling their baggage that they were ready to go to their room. The moment his head was turned, Harriett's and John's eyes met and he managed a quick wink. She smiled coyly.

Phillip took her hand and she followed along as John called out, "Don't hesitate to let me know if you need anything. I want you to have a pleasant visit."

Phillip nodded coldly as John straightened his tie. He watched them walk to the elevator. He addressed Randy again. "Have a bouquet of roses sent to their room with a card reading, 'May you have an unusually pleasant visit.' Put my name at the bottom."

"Take care of it right away," Randy replied in his usual efficient manner.

When John walked into his office Millard Monroe was talking to a heavy-set man seated next to him. Both men stood when they saw him. "It's good of you to come to the opening, Mr. Monroe," John said as they shook hands. "I hope I haven't kept you waiting too long."

"Waiting is never enjoyable," Monroe said coolly as though he did resent the delay.

John began explaining the reason but Monroe cut him off. "Never mind about that. I'm busy too."

He introduced his companion. "This is Belk Reegan, my attorney."

After acknowledging the introduction John was concerned that Monroe was unreasonably perturbed about having to wait. Wanting to get him in a better frame of mind he talked about the hotel.

"Did you ever expect to see so much activity in your building?"

"No, quite frankly, I didn't." Monroe was obviously tense and John wanted to put him at ease. "Can I get you anything? A drink? Cigar?"

Monroe shook his head negatively.

"How about you, Mr. Reegan?"

"No thanks, I never indulge in either."

"Well, let me show you around. There's some mighty fine people here. In fact, I just left Orion Irving. He's a front runner for the Lieutenant Governor's seat, you know. The place is full of people like him. Most are back in the saloon. I want you to see the place. I've had lots of compliments about it."

"This is what I came to see you about, Mr. Broker," Monroe said in a strained voice. "You have violated the terms of our lease by putting a saloon in this building."

"Terms of our lease? Saloon?" John looked at him unbelievingly. "I don't understand."

"You have every reason for understanding," Monroe shot back. "I not only mentioned this when we were discussing the transaction in my office but it is also plainly spelled out in the lease."

John had to sit. Frowning, he tried to think back. "Surely, surely," he said, "you don't object to a saloon! Why, a hotel without a saloon is like a wagon without wheels. You can't operate without either."

"I not only object to it," Monroe said bluntly, "I insist you close it down immediately."

John couldn't accept this. He was filled with anger. "That I will never do!" he said, looking up at Monroe in a challenging stare. Then he regretted his remark. An ugly confrontation wouldn't help things. He composed himself and beckoned with his hands. "Sit down, gentlemen," he said calmly. "Let's talk this over."

"We don't have time for that," Monroe said curtly. "Besides, there is nothing to discuss." He waited for John to react.

"You say this is spelled out in the lease?"

"Very definitely. In fact, we have it right here." Monroe motioned for Reegan to remove it from his brief case then took the papers from him. "Here it is, right here." He began reading, at the same time pointing with his finger so John could follow along.

"The party of the second part, that's you, Mr. Broker, agrees that the building shall not be used for the sale of intoxicating beverages of any kind, and further agrees that his lease will be forfeited if this agreement is violated in any content."

John's heart sank as he thought of the implications.

"Surely, you wouldn't hold me to this. I have a small fortune in this saloon."

"Then, you've made a terrible mistake, Mr. Broker. You see, both my late father and my brother have been ordained as ministers in our church and I, myself, am a deacon. There is no way I can condone the use of alcoholic beverages in any building of mine."

"And if I refuse?"

"You have no alternative. You must close the saloon at once."

"What happens if I don't?"

"Then, as much as I would dislike to do it, I would be compelled to have the entire building closed on a court order."

John looked at Belk Reegan. "He could have this done?"

"There's no doubt about it," Reegan said authoritatively. "The law is very clear about this sort of thing."

"But you must allow me to keep it open until Derby Day. It's necessary that I do that. Then maybe I can figure something out." John was pleading now.

Monroe shook his head. "I cannot condone horse

racing any more than I can condone the use of alcohol."

"Mr. Monroe, I just can't believe you'd do this to me. Why I've worked day and night to be open for the Derby and there is a great amount of money involved. Not only my money but others have invested heavily." John's voice became harsh again. "Do you realize this could result in the failure of the entire business? It would be a terrible setback. I'd be the laughing stock of Louisville. Opening a lavish saloon for one day of operation. No! You can't do this to me. You just can't!"

Monroe looked at his attorney again. "Mr. Reegan," he said in a firm voice, "if Mr. Broker does not stop the sale of alcoholic drinks in this building within fifteen minutes, I want you to take immediate steps to have the entire building vacated and the doors padlocked."

John couldn't believe all this was taking place. In desperation he offered to purchase the building. Monroe refused.

"This building was left to me by my father and to sell it to someone who would have a saloon in it would be sacrilege. No, Mr. Broker, the building is not for sale."

John searched for an immediate answer. The choice was his. The publicity would be detrimental and his prestige would be challenged. He couldn't bear to think of the criticism of his violation of a simple contract. He felt sure it would reflect on his ability to operate a hotel.

There was no alternative. He walked to the doorway and stood waiting for Monroe and Reegan to precede him. Monroe paused and shook John's hand coldly.

"Then you will close the saloon?"

"What else can I do?" John answered dejectedly.

Monroe's face was expressionless. "I'm sorry, Mr. Broker, but I don't have a choice either."

After they parted, John walked back to the desk and beckoned for Detective Fleming to accompany him. John went to the saloon and worked his way to the bar. Well wishers again slapped him on the back but he hardly noticed. The band music was nearly drowned out by the loud talking and laughter of the customers. The noise beating against John's ears was maddening as he thought of having to put an end to the happy atmosphere. He wondered if he could go through with it.

When they reached the bar, John climbed up and stood facing the customers. Then he helped Fleming up. "See if you can quiet the place down," he said, almost forcing the words.

"I'll do my best, but it won't be easy." The detective wondered what was important enough to take this kind of action. He signaled for the band to stop playing, then raised his hands, calling for quiet. The noise diminished to some extent but someone yelled out in a loud voice.

"You gonna' set the house up with free drinks, Mr. Broker?"

The noise picked up louder and several customers began singing:"Hooray for Broker!" Someone in the crowd was shouting:

"Hooray for Broker.
Ein, zwei, drei, vier,
Broker's gonna' buy the beer,
Hooray for John Broker,
He's a damned swell guy."

There was more laughing and the singers urged the crowd to sing along with them as they began a second verse. Fleming continued asking for quiet but the singing continued.

"It's hopeless," he said, shrugging his shoulders.

John stood quietly until the song was finished then one by one the customers took their seats and curiously waited for him to speak.

"Gentlemen, first of all, I do want each of one of you to have a drink on the house as soon as I finish here."

Someone called out, "You're the greatest, Mr. Broker." A spontaneous burst of cheers erupted. John thought how differently they would soon feel about him.

They wouldn't show it right away but it would come. Local newspapers would give the closing good coverage. It would be discussed in homes, factories, offices, everywhere. He would be laughed at, a fool who spent thousands of dollars on a saloon that couldn't operate one full day. He bit his lips. A few more words and the saloon's doors would be closed, perhaps forever.

The room became quiet again.

"I only wish," John said in a voice loud enough for all to hear, "the free drinks were cause for continued celebration but this is not the case." He looked at the ceiling momentarily thinking of the words to follow. "I have just received instructions from the owner of this building that the saloon will have to be closed within fifteen minutes."

There were groans coming from a number of customers but John didn't hesitate. "The owner is justified in ordering the closing. He has strong religious beliefs and cannot permit alcoholic drinks to be sold on his property."

A customer standing at the bar offered his objection. "One of these holy Joe's that's probably got a cellar full of booze." Someone else called out, "Don't listen to him. He can't stop you from selling drinks."

"The man is justified in ordering it closed," John said. "I overlooked a clause in the contract where it stated this very clearly."

John looked down at the bartenders. They stood silently in disbelief. "I want you to lock the cash registers and serve drinks for fifteen minutes. Then the room will have to be vacated. I'll be back to talk to you shortly and explain the situation."

He thanked the customers again for their patronage then jumped down from the bar and hurried back to his office avoiding all questions along the way. The office quickly filled. Michelle and her brothers were the first to enter then Randy Barnes and Mrs. Patterson came in.

The presence of reporters, friends, employees, Frederick Scherer and Jim Fleming over-crowded the room.

Randy took the initiative and asked everyone except members of the family and Mrs. Patterson to leave.

"Mr. Broker will see you later," he said tactfully. "Right now he wants to talk things over with his family." The outsiders left quietly.

Tim was the first to speak. "What in the world is going on, John? We heard that Millard Monroe ordered the saloon closed."

"That's right," John said, shaking his head, "and the worst part about it is that he's perfectly within his rights in doing so."

"I don't understand," Tim shot back. "What right does he have?"

"Look," John said, holding up his hands in disgust, "if everyone will just relax I'll explain everything."

He asked Michelle and Mrs. Patterson to be seated then explained all that had taken place between him and Monroe.

"Maybe we could raise enough money to buy the building," Marty suggested hopefully.

"Nope. I asked Monroe about that. He won't sell."

"What is this going to do to us?" Mrs. Patterson asked.

"Right now, I just don't know."

The discussion lasted for twenty minutes. John looked at Randy Barnes. "Will you and Jim Fleming see if the saloon is closed?"

Randy nodded and turned to leave. "Tell the employees back there I'll meet with them at nine in the morning."

"Sure, Mr. Broker. I'll do that," Randy replied understandingly.

"I'd like to be alone with Michelle for awhile," John explained and the others left the office.

"You look like you're exhausted," Michelle said. "Why don't you go up to your room and get some rest?"

"No, I couldn't relax just now. I've got to figure out a way to keep that saloon open."

They talked for a while and John asked to be alone. They walked to the door together and he kissed her.

"Don't you worry about this, sweetheart," he said with an assuring smile. "I'll find a way out of this mess."

"I know you will," she answered confidently. "But I want you to promise me you'll try to get a good night's sleep."

After she had gone John sat at his desk trying to think things out. He slowly tapped a pencil tip against the desk top and bit his lip. He could think of no way to barter with Monroe. He wondered if the saloon could be put to some other use. "A theatre, perhaps!" he thought to himself. The ceiling was too low and the columns would be in the way. He thought of other uses. None seemed logical.

He sighed and rubbed his chin then got up and took a bottle of bourbon from a cabinet and poured a generous drink. He took the bottle back to his desk and sat down intermittently drinking until the bottle was empty. He despaired at his predicament. His senses dulled and he folded his arms and rested them on the desk top. He lowered his head until his forehead came down on his arms. He felt a sense of comfort and things didn't seem so desperate.   He'd find a way in the morning. Sure, that's the way it would be. In the morning everything would be all right.   His head moved to the side but he wasn't aware of it. He was in deep sleep.

As John counted off each of the seven days before the Derby he became more dubious about the future of the Rasineer. Disappointingly, on Derby Eve only half of the rooms were occupied. Employees were skeptical too. To keep down operating costs John had to terminate the services of the employees who worked in the saloon.

Others working in the hotel wondered about their future. An editorial in one of the local newspapers didn't help matters. It pointed out the fallacy of John's spending such a large sum of money for a saloon without authority to operate it. "The blame," it read, "should rest entirely on John Broker's shoulders but Millard Monroe could have spared him the blunder. Monroe must have seen the early advertisements telling about the saloon and also must have heard about it from friends."

After reading the editorial Monroe made a prompt reply to the editor. He pointed out that he had been in Europe during the construction period and knew nothing about it and had returned, by coincidence, on the day of the opening.

Bad publicity wasn't the only problem. John was dismayed when his bookkeeper showed him an itemized breakdown of costs for constructing and furnishing the saloon and for each day's overhead for operating the hotel. The costs were more than doubled over what he had anticipated and daily receipts would cover less than half of the operational costs.

Resentment towards him was building up. All of Michelle's brothers with the exception of Tim were angry about the outcome. Tim told his brothers, "John didn't ask us for money. We went to him. We made a mistake and can blame only ourselves."

John went to the banks to get more money. They all refused him. In desperation he went to see Mrs. Patterson but she refused to see him. He called in an attorney for advice. After looking at the books he told John the words he expected but did not want to hear.

"Unless you can find a way to keep the rooms at least eighty percent occupied at once you cannot possibly operate another three weeks. Otherwise bankruptcy is your only alternative."

Derby day came. Agile won the race easily with Ram's Horn second. Layson, the third horse in the meet, finished last. Most of the guests checked out of the Rasineer the next day and it was a gloomy Thursday night as the register showed only twenty percent of the rooms occupied.

Things got worse. More employees had to be laid off. Creditors demanded payment for their goods and, not meeting with success, began reclaiming furnishings. Furniture, linens, drapes and other items were removed from the building. John worked hard to keep the hotel operating but in three weeks it was all over.

Bankruptcy papers were filed and processed. All remaining furnishings were sold at auction. After the sale was over John went back to the building to recover his personal items. He stood in the center of the deserted lobby. Trash was scattered over the bare floor. Everything was gone. Money, friends, employees and prestige.

He heard the front door open. The noise reverberated across the empty room. It was the sheriff and his deputy. The sheriff identified himself.

"I'm sorry, Mr. Broker, but I have orders to padlock the front doors. If you have anything to take care of in here you better take care of it now because only the owner and I will have keys to the lock."

John thanked him. "I have everything."

"Sure is a shame to see this place looking like this," the sheriff said, gazing around the place. "You sure had it fixed up great. I was here on opening day and never dreamed it would turn out this way."

"Yes, I know," John answered.

"Well, if you're ready to leave, I'll get on with my work."

John followed the men out on the sidewalk and waited until the sheriff snapped closed a heavy lock on the newly installed hasp.

John was filled with remorse. He couldn't bear the thought of facing anyone not even Michelle. Not until later. He wanted to get off to himself to try to think things out. He was sure he would eventually have to leave Louisville. He couldn't bear to stay and face all the people who had placed so much confidence in him. He thought of Michelle's mother. He owed her a hundred apologies but what could he say to her? Such a wonderful person. She would know he lost the hotel because of a stupid mistake. Yet she would be cheerful and offer him encouragement. He knew he wanted to see her but he thought of Michelle's brothers and sisters. Some of them would probably be there and he definitely didn't want to see them. He wished he hadn't accepted their money. This would have made a world of difference. If only he had read the lease agreement but he had been so intent on having a hotel of his own and there were so many things to think about at that time.

He thought of these things as he walked aimlessly past the Board of Trade building to Third and Market. A trolley car stopped at the intersection and a small group of passengers stood in line to board. John looked up. The car was marked "Fourth Street -- South to Churchill Downs and Jacobs Park." He wanted to get off the sidewalk. A moment of decision and he was the last to get on the car. A walk through the forest of trees at the park would give him the solitude he needed.

After passing Walnut Street the car was out of heavy traffic and picked up speed. They passed Central Park and there was nothing but open fields. The motorman was making good time and the wheels clattered rhythmically against the rails as the body of the car bounced and swayed on its springs.

John was oblivious to everything except the hotel. His mind could not escape the thought of his building being locked and the absence of any activity inside. He tried to think of a way he could reopen. If he could struggle along operating on a smaller scale maybe using only the rooms on the first and second floors.

He heard the motorman announce the Churchill Downs station and decided to get off there. He could go to Jacobs Park later. He looked up at the twin spires and saw the empty stands below. It would be several hours before race time and only the clean-up crew moved among the vacant seats.

He walked to the terrace area and leaned on the track rail. A number of horses were being exercised. Their hoofs beat hollow sounds against the track's loamy surface. Their bodies were soaked with perspiration, their mouths lathered with frothy saliva, their nostrils distended and they snorted and breathed heavily from the strained pace their riders were putting them through.

John was so intrigued he momentarily forgot about the hotel. He loved watching the horses. There were sorrels, chestnuts, bays and solid blacks. Their riders wore high-collared slipover sweaters to ward off the morning chill. Some of them looked as intent as if they had been actually racing in tough competition.

John walked over to the barns. Everyone was busy. Some walked horses in a wide circle cooling them down. Other horses were being washed and he could see several stable hands changing the straw in the wooden stalls. The pungent smells of alfalfa, polished leather and fresh manure filled the air. It brought back memories. "This is what I wanted in life," he said to himself. "If father would have consented to let me get into this kind of work, I might not be in the predicament I'm in now." He hated himself for allowing it to happen.

He doubted he could get into this work now. The starting pay was too meager for a man with a family. The future looked hopeless. He couldn't lower himself to look for hotel work in Louisville. Who would hire a failure that had to turn to bankruptcy? He would have to leave Louisville. He didn't know where he would go. He would go home and talk it over with Michelle. She'd be understanding. She always was. They would decide together what was best.

At home Michelle gave him a warm welcome then went about the chores of preparing dinner as if nothing had happened. She removed his shoes and placed his slippers on his feet. Then she placed the baby on his lap. She went back to the kitchen and John leaned back in the big easy chair and held the baby in front of him. She ran her soft, tiny fingers across his lips then up over his face. He talked to her, kissed her hand, pulled her close so their cheeks touched. Michelle brought him a glass of brandy. "This will make your dinner taste better," she said.

John looked up to her and took her hand. "I've made a real mess of things, haven't I?"

"Let's forget the past. Forget about Millard Monroe and everything. We've got lots to look forward to. Just wait and see. Everything will turn out all right." She leaned down and kissed him and the baby thought it was funny. She laughed and John and Michelle laughed with her.

John shook his head despairingly. "I don't see how either of you can look at me. I'm such a failure!"

Michelle placed her hands on her hips. "Look here," she said, "if I ever hear you talk like that again I'll make you drink warm milk before your meals."

"But it's the truth," he said.

"Now you just listen to me, John Broker. If you think you're a failure, I want you to keep it to yourself from now on because I think you're the smartest, finest man in the world and I don't care what you think because nothing will change my mind about that." She bent over and kissed him again.

"You sound just like your mother," John said in appreciation.

"Is there anything wrong with that?"

"Not in the least! You know how I feel about her."

"Yes, and I also know she wants to see you."

"First thing in the morning and that's for sure."

Michelle went to the kitchen and set the food on the table and told him that dinner was ready.

John stood and held the baby in his arms. "Maybe there's something left after all. Something to work for. After dinner Michelle and I can talk it over and decide what to do. Let's go see what mommy has fixed for us to eat," he said to the baby.

After dinner they made the decision. They would move to Cincinnati. John had enough money to pay the moving expenses and perhaps a month's subsistence. He would go to Cincinnati, find a place to live, come back and help Michelle pack and they would leave Louisville by boat.

******

It was Sunday morning and graduation day at St. Martin's. Forty-seven girls had completed their studies at the school and they walked along in columns of two through a hallway leading to the chapel. The girls were exquisitely dressed in long white satin dresses that were daintily trimmed in delicate lace and tailored to perfection. Many of the nuns were excellent seamstresses and they saw to it the girls looked their loveliest on these special occasions.

Following close behind the graduates were the undergraduates and after them, the faculty of nuns. There was almost complete silence. Only the swishing of the nuns' heavily starched veils and the occasional rattling of their long rosaries were audible.

Demurely they took their places in the aligned pews. It was a clear day and the bright sunshine lighted the vivid colors in the large stained glass windows. The main altar had six tall brass candelstick holders placed on its table and above them the lighted candles signified a solemn high mass was about to take place.

Six altar boys dressed in black cassocks and white

surplices emerged from the sacristy and were followed by the convent chaplain. Monsignor Caldwell was to say mass and two younger priests were to serve as the co-celebrants of deacon and subdeacon. Their white manicles blended with the marble altars and fine lacework trimmings.

The Monsignor took his opening place at the foot of the altar and bowed his head along with the others. Then he sang out in a trained voice: "In nomine, et fille, et Spiritus sancti. Amen. Introibo ad altare dei." The words echoed majestically throughout the hollow edifice.

Then from the choir loft came the response as the choir girls sang in unison to the accompaniment of the organ.

"Ad Deum, qui laetificat juventutem mean."

Their high pitched voices were sharp and clear and delightfully refreshing.

The mass progressed in its pomp and splendor but Ellen found it difficult to concentrate on the translations. She felt an inner sadness about having to leave the school. Instead of following the parts of the mass she fingered the beads on her rosary. Several of her classmates planned to return to the convent as postulants and Ellen wished she too could spend the rest of her life as part of the community.

Ellen and Sister Jude had discussed this several times with the Mother superior but it was thought, for Ellen's sake, it might not be the wise thing to do. Ellen's unfortunate background had remained a well-guarded secret at the convent and was known only to the Mother Superior, Sister Jude and Monsignor Caldwell. They felt if she were to become a nun her past would eventually be found out by some enterprising reporter and would be published and be a source of embarrassment to her. They didn't want to add more sorrow to her life so they discussed this with her. Ellen, too, realized it would be best to leave.

Sister Jude helped make arrangements for Ellen to live with a classmate, LaVerne Shelton and her family in New York City. LaVerne's mother was a former classmate of Sister Jude and had married a wealthy business man. Ellen had spent most of her vacations with the Sheltons and they were very fond of her and looked forward to having her. The Sheltons were told about Ellen's past and wanted to do all they could to make her happy. Ellen thought of these things as she knelt with her classmates.

A little farther back in the chapel Sister Jude also found it difficult to completely concentrate on the ceremony. She was filled with sadness as she thought of Ellen's leaving the community and how lonesome it would be without her. Ever since the day Ellen arrived at St. Martin's she had worked closely with her, helping her with her lessons, teaching her poise, sharing her problems and doing all she could do prepare her for the outside world. She thought of Ellen when she had arrived at the school, frail, ill at ease, homely. Then she thought of her transformation into a self-confident, charming and attractive young lady. She could not help but feel a sense of pride for the part she had played in the transformation but it was Ellen she was extremely proud of.

Delivering the sermon the Monsignor spoke of the good example the sisters at St. Martin's had shown the students and how fortunate the girls were to be educated at the school. He urged them to always give a generous portion of their lives to prayer and to live a life pleasing to God.

The mass progressed successively through the Creed, Offertory, Preface, Canon, Elevation, Communion, Last Gospel, Blessing and concluded with the prayers ordered in English by Pope Leo XIII. There was ample time for meditation during the mass, and each girl had much to think about. Those who were returning to the convent were happy at the thought of becoming nuns and looked forward to becoming a part of the community. The girls who were leaving felt a hint of sadness. They had looked forward to this day many times during their school years but now that it was here it brought back memories of many pleasant experiences. They looked forward to going home though and their remorse about leaving was only temporary.

After the mass the girls had their final breakfast together as classmates and they laughed and talked about everything they could remember about their days at the school. After breakfast they went to their dormitories and finished packing and refreshed themselves to prepare for the Commencement Exercises.

With their families seated in the auditorium the girls took their places in chairs at the front of the hall. The speeches and awarding of diplomas took little more than an hour and afterwards everyone went to a front lawn for a luncheon and reception. Most of the girls gathered around their families and happily introduced them to friends and former teachers.

Ellen and Sister Jude were side by side most of the time but neither wanted to talk about parting. They, too, moved about in the gathering, smiling, exchanging farewells and doing all they could to hide their feelings about no longer being able to see each other as residents of the community.

Ellen wanted to thank Sister for all she had done and the love and kindness she had shown her but she knew she would break down if she did. Sister Jude wanted to tell Ellen how she would miss her and praise her for the way she had conducted herself at the school. There were so many things they wanted to say to each other, each knowing there was no way they could talk with Ellen's leaving so imminent. They fought to keep from showing their pained feelings. They shared farewells with others, laughing at last minute small talk, recalling events that happened during school years. They saw Judy Miller, the cute little blonde from Milwaukee, crying. She had always looked forward to graduating so she could again live in the city. Now that it was time to leave she realized how much she loved the school. The thought of leaving filled her with sadness. She wasn't the only one. Others were crying as they prepared to leave.

When it was time for Ellen to leave, Sister Jude walked to the carriage with LaVerne and her parents. Sister forced a smile but didn't want Ellen to know her eyes were filled with tears. Mr. Shelton ushered LaVerne to a rear seat then helped his wife to the center of the black upholstered leather seat. He purposely waited to let Ellen and Sister have a moment together.

They looked at each other momentarily. "Write me to let me know you arrived safely," Sister Jude said. Her smile was as pretty as ever even though she was holding her lips together to keep them from trembling.

"You know I will," Ellen said. She took Brenlyn's hands and kissed her cheek. "I'll never forget you," she added and put her handkerchief over her lips to keep from crying openly. She didn't want to be remembered this way. Mr. Shelton took Ellen's arm and gently helped her into the carriage and she sat next to Mrs. Shelton. Mr. Shelton climbed into the front seat next to the driver.

The driver glanced down at Sister Jude for her approval to leave. She nodded and he released the brake and slapped the reins on the horses' backs and calling out for them to move on. The carriage jerked forward and moved noisily along the gravel roadway. Sister Jude saw Ellen bury her face in her hands and she wanted to run after the carriage and go away with her. She watched as the carriage made a rounding curve and entered a lane bordered by towering oak trees. She went to her cell to overcome her feelings and prepare for the vesper service.

Kneeling on the oak bench next to her cot, she asked God to look after Ellen and to spare her from enduring any more hardships. She stayed there until the bell rang for vespers. Wiping the tears from her eyes, she composed herself for the walk to the chapel. The hallways reeked with loneliness as she thought of Ellen no longer walking through them. When she knelt for vespers she looked at the pew that Ellen had occupied earlier in the day as if to find some consolation. The vespers started and she joined in the prayers and hymns.

After vespers, she opened a page in the same worn prayerbook she had brought from home and began reading. The particular page was titled "Models in Suffering." She knew the words from memory as she did many more in the book but she began reading anyway. The words were simple but meaningful to her.

"Little is it that thou sufferest in comparison with those who have suffered so much; who have been so strongly tempted, so grievously afflicted, so many ways tried and exercised. Thou oughtest, then, to call to mind the heavier sufferings of others, that thou mayest the easier bear the very little thou sufferest. And if to thee they seem not little, take heed lest this also procede from thine own impatience. But whether they be little or great, strive to bear them with all patience."

Part III

"More changes than you think for may happen."

DICKENS - *Cricket On The Hearth*

The trip to Cincinnati was pleasant. There had been little wind and the river was so calm the pointed keel of the "City of Cincinnati" sliced through the surface like a sharp knife splitting through a run of silk. It pushed up waves on each side of the boat extending all the way to the Indiana and Kentucky shorelines.

The big paddlewheel dug into the surface and left rolling waves trailing behind as far as the eye could see and the twin stacks belched out plumes of dense, black smoke that slowly paled above the line of rollers. Churned up by the boat, the river surface looked angered at its sudden transformation into a rough and choppy tributary.

John and Michelle enjoyed strolling along the decks with the children as the packet with her gleaming white hull wended its way upstream. Occasionally they would see a lone fisherman running his trotline. He'd pull the long line up across the bow of his skiff checking each of the numerous hooks for a fish. Once they saw a big perch being caught and watched his writhing struggle for survival before he was successfully landed on board. Sometimes they would sit in deck chairs looking out at the sandy banks along the shoreline and the heavy growth of green foliage along the upper banks. They waved to picnickers and swimmers at the beaches.

Another ten miles and they were looking at the docks and buildings in Carrollton. They squinted their eyes and held their hands over their ears whenever the pilot sounded the shrill steam whistle signalling an approaching vessel.

John was greatly relaxed and would not let himself think about the recent disappointments in Louisville. He was glad they were traveling by boat instead of train. It was like time standing still. No immediate problems and no place to go other than the limited confines of the packet.

Their furniture and belongings were stored on board. After they reached Cincinnati they would have them loaded into a wagon and taken to the cottage John had rented. He felt optimistic about obtaining a good position in Cincinnati. The future looked bright.

The big steamer pushed its way past Warsaw and maneuvered the turns and bends on its way up river. They passed Paint Lick Creek on the Kentucky shore and the series of creeks along Switzerland County on the Indiana shore. Soon they came to the outlet of the Great Miami River and in another fifteen miles they saw the steel work of the Cincinnati bridges to Kentucky.

As they neared the Cincinnati docks they could see large hills adjacent to the north side of the business district. A scattering of homes could be seen among the hills and Michelle wondered how the people managed to get to them. It looked as though every available docking space was occupied but the pilot slowly eased his way up past the other boats and pulled the "Cincinnati" along the wharf to an open area. A deck hand threw the coiled end of a thick hemp rope to a wharf tender on the shore and quickly secured the end by chocking his foot against it.

Given more slack he lifted the heavy rope over his shoulder and dragged it to a wharf ring pinned to the cobblestone undersurface. He skillfully lashed the rope with a seaman's knot and signaled for a deck hand to pull it taut. A white puff of exhaust steam spurted from a turbine and a capstan began revolving slowly drawing the rope around the spindle and securing the bow to the dock. A similar operation followed at the stern and the boat was fully berthed. The gangplank was lowered and the passengers filed along the walkway to the shore terminating their journey.

After their possessions were loaded on a draft wagon John gave the driver their home address then hailed a taxi and helped Michelle and the children into the back seat of the open touring car. They traveled north on Vine Street past the business houses. After passing Sixth Street they came to an elite residential area where prominent Cincinnatians lived in mansions surrounded by towering oak trees. They turned left onto Clifton and there were more fine homes. Soon John was pointing out the University of Cincinnati's buildings and campus on Clifton. They passed Burnet Woods and saw the forest of trees that beautified the park. Then they turned left on Ludlow and the driver pulled up to a little cottage. They were home.

John decided to spend the first week in Cincinnati with his family. He helped Michelle get the house in order and later took her and the children to the zoo and Ohio Grove Amusement Park.

They went on an all-day picnic at Eden Park, spent one day touring the city in trolley cars and thrilled at the experience of traveling up the steep inclined railway from Main to Mulberry Street. They attended an afternoon matinee at the beautiful new Music Hall on Elm Street. Michelle was infatuated with the building's array of turrets and towers, windows and steeples.

They strolled through picturesque streets in Clifton where the more affluent residents lived. They marvelled at the artistic French doors, heavy wrought iron grills, fluted stone columns, elaborate and inviting porticos, impressive turrets, steep gables and beautifully landscaped lawns.

John not only enjoyed all the activities but it also forestalled seeking employment. The thought of applying for a position was provoking because of all the unknowns. He wanted to continue working in some form of management and knew it would have to be hotel work since that was the only thing he knew. But he was dubious. Would anyone hire him as a manager? Would he be "blackballed" because of his hotel background in Louisville?

He had often heard there was a grapevine of communications among major hotel executives that ostracized undersirable prospective employees. Would he be in that category? His string of unpaid debts and the bankruptcy claim might have been circulated in print. There was only one way to know. Apply at the best hotels and hopefully become a responsible employee at one of them.

He went to the Burnet House at Third and Vine Streets first. It was listed in some quarters as the finest hotel in the world. John had heard about the lavish house when he worked at the Galt House. Albert Edward, Prince of Wales, had stayed there and on the way to his inauguration, President-elect Abraham Lincoln made a stop in Cincinnati and was driven from the railroad station to the Burnet House in an open Victoria carriage pulled by six spirited white horses. There was no end to the names of noted guests who stayed there.

John anxiously applied at the hotel and hoped he would be privileged to work there. The manager was very courteous. He listened intently as John explained his qualifications mentioning his failure at the Rasineer but elaborating on the work he had done to transform it from an office building to a fine hotel with an outstanding staff. He hoped these achievements would overshadow his failure.

Then he got his answer as the manager tactfully explained the situation. "Mr. Broker, if I had an opening here in the management field, I would be very tempted to give it to you but as much as I hate to tell you, your name has been circulated. He cleared his throat, then continued. "I hate to tell you this but you might find it difficult to get into hotel work, especially in a management position."

John felt the veins in his temples surging. "Then I have been blackballed?"

"I'm sure you don't deserve it, Mr. Broker, but like I said, if I had an opening --" The manager looked at his watch and apologized. "I'm sorry. There are some things I must look after."

John thanked him as he turned and walked away then stood for a moment and collected his thoughts. He thought about Michelle and the children and he knew he must find work soon. If he were not married it would be different. He could do anything.

He walked up Fifth Street to picturesque Fountain Square quaintly hemmed in on all sides by commercial establishments and sat on a bench facing the fountain. Water spewed from the hands of a statue on top and sprayed out over the circle of statues below. Other bronze figures in sitting positions were reaching out as if to feel the clear water overflowing from the four large urns above them. John sat for an hour trying to think things out. "I'll find a postion in a hotel if it's the last thing I do. I'll go to every hotel in the city if necessary."

He went to the Gibson House. There was no opening. He tried the Honing at Fourth and Vine. Same thing. After visiting the Sterling, the Alms and the Palace and meeting with no success, he gave up for the day.

He didn't let Michelle know how disappointed he was. Instead he told her the manager of the Burnet House was very encouraging and wanted him to come back the next day. Michelle was happy for him at first but by the time the evening was over she could see he was worried and had little to say. She tried to be cheerful and to encourage him but could see it did little good. She worried too. Not only because of John's depression but because their finances were low and would provide for only one more week of subsistence. Their moving costs had been more than they thought and they had spent a considerable amount enjoying their first week in Cincinnati.

The next morning John was turned down at other hotels. In the afternoon he went to the Hilliand. It reminded him of a hotel he had seen in Chicago. It was fourteen stories, faced with red brick, had arched windows on the first and third floors and a stained glass marquee over the front entrance.

He waited in the lobby for an hour before the manager could see him then repeated his story and enthusiastically begged for a position. He was that desperate. The manager shook his head. "We don't have any openings." John started to leave but asked if there was anything open in a lower pay bracket. "I'm in need of work and willing to do anything."

The manager shrugged his shoulders. "We've got a stock room helper's job open but I'm sure you don't want that."

He waited for John to leave. "Maybe something will turn up later." He started to walk away.

"But, I do want it," John called out impetuously.

The manager was dubious. "We don't need anyone with your qualifications for that kind of work."

But John wanted it. It surprised him he did but a lot of things crossed his mind. He felt too insecure with no income, he didn't like job hunting. He felt he could work into something better and being employed would remove the desperate need to find work. Then too, he would have time to think things out and decide what he might do later. These were fleeting thoughts but they were convincing.

"Yes sir, I really want that job bad."

He lied to sound more convincing. "I would enjoy doing something different."

"It's a low-paying job. A lot of lifting."

"I can handle it and the money's not important." He wouldn't give the manager a chance to back down.

"All right, then," the manager said, shrugging his shoulders. "Come with me."

John followed him to a lobby desk. The formalities were simple. "Name, address and age." The manager wrote them on a form and called a bellhop. "Take this man to the stockroom and tell the steward this is the new stock boy he asked for."

As he and the bellhop walked down the to the stockroom John asked the manager's name.

"His name is Langley. Meredith Langley. But you better call him Mr. Langley 'cause if he hears you call him Meredith you ain't gonna' be around here very long." The bellhop gestured with his hands making them appear as claws. "He's a bear. A real bear!"

"What's the steward's name?" John asked, realizing he might not be afforded the luxury of an introduction from him either.

"Don Fumer. You better call him Mr. Don. He don't like to be called by his last name." The bellhop laughed. "You know what his last name means in French?"

"No, I don't. What does it mean?"

"Well, I ain't no expert on French, but everyone says it means 'manure'." The bellhop laughed again. "Can you imagine a guy named 'manure' in charge of the food supply?"

"What kind of person is he?" John asked, amused.

"No good. Strictly no good. I wouldn't trust him for a minute." They took a few more steps and the bellhop added, "Now don't you go telling him what I said. I don't want no trouble with him.''

"You needn't worry," John assured him.

They reached the stockroom. The bellhop made the introduction and John extended his hand and clasped it around Fumer's in a cordial grasp. It felt like a cold, limp dish rag.

"Know anything about working in a hotel stockroom?" Fumer asked abruptly, ignoring any pleasantry.

"Not a whole lot but I'm willing to learn," John answered.

Fumer shook his head indifferently. "Follow me and I'll get you started."

They walked through an aisle between shelves that reached to the ceiling. At the bottom of a sidewalk elevator cases of food were stacked on top of each other.

"This stuff goes on the shelves. The shelves are marked to show what goes where and see that all labels face the front."

John looked at the boxes and cartons and noticed some of the markings. "Vinegar," "Sugar," "Coffee," "Flour," "Cocoa." He wasn't sure if the cases were to go on the shelves or the individual items were to be placed there. He asked.

"Hell, if a guy has to open the cases when he needs somethin' he may as well leave them down on the floor," Fumer said in a whining voice. Then he added, still whining, "If you'll take the time to look, you can see some of the individual items are already on the shelves."

"I understand," John assured him.

"I hope so," the steward answered, sarcastically.

John decided he wouldn't be asking too many questions. It was evident his new boss wanted as few problems as possible. He went to work arranging the stock and wondered if he were doing it right. He worked for little more than an hour when Fumer called out to him.

"Hey, Broker, bring me one of them fifty-pound cans

of lard.''

John remembered seeing the cans on a bottom shelf and checked the lable to see if they were the right size. He slid one out and lifted it by the side handles and awkwardly carried it to the front.

"Follow me," Fumer ordered.

Not being used to handling cans of that size and weight, John struggled with the load. The small wire handles dug into his hands and he wanted to set it down to rest but managed to continue on.

They finally reached the kitchen and the redolent smell of food filled the air. It was a blend of seasoned soups, roasts, salads, fruits and vegetables. It smelled deliciously fragrant and inviting.

"Put it over here," the steward ordered.

After setting the can near a big cooking stove John stood for a moment. There were six stoves, each with eight to ten burners and black chefs wearing white frocks and tall hats were doing the cooking. One was broiling a thick steak, another was stirring a big kettle of green beans as pans on other burners spewed out puffs of steam. One chef was dicing stalks of celery on a work table. All were busy preparing food as waiters moved in and out swinging doors leading to the dining room.

John was fascinated. It reminded him of the elaborate kitchens at the Galt House. He forgot his reason for being there and asked a chef how many meals they average each day.

"Dunno," the chef said without turning his head. "Go ask the cashier upstairs. I'm a chef, not an accountant."

John moved away from the hot stove. He looked around for Fumer but didn't see him so he headed back to the stockroom. Fumer called him to his desk.

"You know, Broker, you've only got one thing to be concerned about here and that's to keep the shelves stocked and wait on anyone in need of something."

John wondered if Fumer was born with the whining voice. He shook his head to acknowledge the steward's instructions.

"Well then, you ain't supposed to go around asking questions. Everyone is busy around here. The chefs, the porters, the butchers." He repeated the word, "Everyone" then continued. "If you have questions that pertain to your work, you ask me. Otherwise keep busy and keep your thoughts to yourself."

It took everything John had to control himself. He wanted to punch the steward and walk out but knew he couldn't jeopardize his reputation with hotel people any more than he already had. He bit his lip before telling Fumer he understood.

Several times during the day kitchen employees came to the stockroom counter to get food items. John was surprised there was no paper work. He handed the items out and that was all there was to it. On one of the trips back from the counter he stopped by Fumer's desk to ask him where the washroom was located. Fumer's feet were propped lazily on his desk top and he lowered a "Police Gazette" he was reading to answer.

"Back of this room there's a hallway. The last door on the left. If you use the toilet you have to jiggle the handle to make it work right."

After thanking him John walked back to the washroom. There were no windows and a single light bulb lighted the way. Curiously John looked at the name plates on each door as he passed. The first one read "Produce"; the next, "Meat Storage." The next one was underlined, "Don't open this door unnecessarily. Ice melts and costs money." Another door read "High Voltage - Keep Out."

Then he came ot an offset in the dark hallway and there was an unmarked door. He assumed this was the washroom and opened it. There was a nauseating odor. It was too dark inside to make out anything other than a light bulb and a porcelain socket hanging from the ceiling with a beaded chain draping below it. He removed his handkerchief and held it over his mouth and nose to repel the odor then stepped inside to turn on the light.

His foot bumped against something! There was a soft hiss! It startled him! Instinctively he pulled on the chain and a dim light came on. He looked down and saw an ugly pear-shaped head and a scaly protruding neck. A pair of beady eyes were set in a fixed stare. John gasped, "Snake!" and froze in his tracks. His heart pounded in fear. He mustered strength to move slowly back toward the door never taking his eyes off the repulsive looking head and wistful eyes.

Then he saw it wasn't a snake. It was a huge turtle! John stared, appalled. The shell looked to be at least four feet across and the leathery head and neck at least six to eight inches thick. It was an errie sight. John saw the eyes slowly go closed. And then open again. It was alive!

Then he saw something else! The four feet were nailed to a wooden pallet and were heavily caked with blood. John was filled with compassion for the helpless creature. "What in the name of hell have they done to you?" he uttered in disgust.

He wished he had never opened the door. He just couldn't stand the sight of anything being mistreated. He had an urge to pull the nails but knew how futile that would be. He even thought of getting a knife and ending the creature's misery but he could never kill anything. He shook his head in dismay.

As he continued stocking the shelves he couldn't free his thoughts from the turtle's plight. He wondered how long he had been nailed to the board and where he had come from. He wished there was some way he could return him to the outdoors but knew that was hopeless. Occasionally he would go back to the room and pour buckets of cool water over its head and shell, but he soon stopped this. The turtle would feebly raise his head and gasp in relief then struggle to free himself causing the pierced limbs to start bleeding again.

After completing his first week at the Hilliand stockroom John wondered if he could last another week. Working conditions had grown worse each day. He could not communicate with Don Fumer. Whenever he asked a question Fumer reprimanded him. They were often without food items needed in the kitchen and he would leave a note on Fumer's desk advising him of the shortage. The notes would pile up with no apparent action taken and John would be reprimanded by the chefs for not being able to supply the items. He wondered why there was no way of accounting for the amount of merchandise received and dispensed and asked Fumer about it.

"Look here, Broker," he answered angrily. "You let me worry about running the stockroom and you'll stay out of trouble that way."

John had to restrain himself to keep from telling Fumer what he thought of him. He decided he must put up with it until he could find another job.

John had never been more lonely in his life. The twelve-hour work days seemed like they would never end. He had very little contact with any of the other employees. When he waited on chefs and other kitchen help and tried to draw them into conversation they never replied with anything but an affirmative or negative answer. He learned from observation that Mr. Langley and Don Fumer were close friends. It was obvious they were handling the horse racing bets for the bellhops and a number of taxi drivers.

John had little concern about this other than feeling that they ought to give more time to looking after the stockroom supply. He worried about not being able to supply the kitchen and it bothered him to be blamed for not having the items needed.

Once John asked Fumer about the turtle. He just couldn't rid his mind of the cruel way it was being held captive. "How much longer do you plan to keep that turtle back there?" he asked tactfully.

"Well, if you can tell me how many people will be ordering turtle soup in the next few days, I'll be able to tell you when he'll be slaughtered."

There was no need for a reply. It was obvious that Fumer resented the question. John started to go back to the shelves.

"Why do you ask?"

"No particular reason." John knew it would be useless to try to explain.

"You worried about that turtle?"

John shrugged his shoulders indifferently. "I hate to see him nailed down like that."

Fumer broke out into an arrogant laugh. "Hell, he don't know what it's all about. Why, he could live for a year like that so he ain't in too bad a shape."

John could only think of the bloody limbs and the way the turtle tried to escape by pulling at the spikes and its natural instinct to return to his native habitat. He thought of the millions of organisms that were developed over the years to add life. Now they were restrained from functioning. He knew is was useless to continue the conversation so he nodded and went back to work.

John persevered week after week at the Hilliand because he had to. He began to develop an inferiority complex and lost much of the drive of his earlier years. For the first time in his life he found himself where he could not act with some degree of independence and think of a way to make some kind of move to help himself. Jobs were hard to find and he had to provide for Michelle and the children.

He thought how strange it was that he found enjoyment in such simple things in life. A chef giving him several well prepared steaks to take home. Going to a saloon and getting a bucket of beer to take home and drink. A concert in Burnett Woods. A walk along the Clifton Avenue hilltop and looking down at the array of smokestacks, steeples, water towers topping the buildings along Cincinnati's streets. Seeing the giant golden fist with a finger pointing upwards on the Evangelical Church steeple almost at eye level from a viewpoint on the hill. These things were a source of enjoyment and his form of recreation with the little time he had away from the Hilliand.

John and Michelle often talked about their problems during these times. The atmosphere was more pleasant and circumstances easier to discuss and resolve. He often talked about his predicament at the Hilliand. He wished there were a way he could at least improve the stock situation. It was aggravating to be unable to supply the kitchen with everything that was needed. The chefs continued complaining to John about it but they knew it was Fumer's fault and they also knew of the friendship and lucrative bookmaking business that he and the hotel manager were involved in. Fumer could do as he pleased at the hotel and was not interested in making changes even if it would improve the hotel's business.

Once, when John explained to Michelle how simple it would be to set up a system to maintain enough supplies she came up with a suggestion. "Why don't you write it out on paper and hand it to Mr. Fumer. Maybe that way he'll study it and think about it."

"I don't think that would make any difference," John replied.

"Maybe it would," Michelle said. "I know you should get credit for the plan but since it will make the work easier for you let him take credit for it."

"What do you mean?"

"Suggest that he rewrite your report in his own words and submit it to the manager."

"He doesn't need to make points with him. They're

already the best of friends.''

"There's an old saying that, 'true friends want to do anything possible to make things more perfect for each other.' He should want to do it to make things better for his boss.''

"And to make points," John added.

Michelle gave him more encouragement. "Why don't you try it?''

John followed her advice. He wrote out the simple suggestion. It provided a minimum-maximum tally sheet that would be kept in duplicate. The tallies would be turned over to Fumer and the original would be posted near the individual items on the shelves. John would keep Fumer's copies in two different files. One would contain the items that were in good supply. The other file would have the items listed that were in either low stock level or were completely exhausted. Fumer would have these sheets at his finger tips and could readily re-order from food vendors.

He showed the report to Michelle. "I'll bet he'll like it," she said encouragingly.

"Maybe you're right. Anyway, we'll know soon," John replied dubiously.

At the hotel the next day, John waited for the right moment to talk to Fumer. He heard Meredith Langley enter the stockroom and soon he and Fumer were laughing and congratulating each other. Fumer was extremely jovial. He told Langley that most of the favorite horses had lost their races the preceding day and their "take" was heavy. They continued talking for a while. After the manager was gone John decided to present his proposal.

He went to Fumer's desk. "Could I speak to you for a few minutes?" he asked.

"Sure. What kind of nonsense are you up to now?"

The words stung but John managed to keep from showing his resentment.

"In the interest of keeping us from running out of stock I have written up a report which I feel will work and I would appreciate it if you would read it. Then if you approve it I will work out the details and put it into effect."

Without looking up from his desk Fumer asked, "What's wrong with the system we've got now?"

"Well I think you'll have to agree that we do run out of stock often."

"Is that your problem or mine?" The steward shot back.

"Well it's both of ours but in reality it's everybody's when the dining room guests can't get what they order."

The steward looked at John. His eyes and lips showed his anger. "Were you able to give the customers what they wanted at your short-lived hotel in Louisville?"

This was the first time John had been confronted by anyone at the Hilliand about his failure at the Rasineer. The remark hurt deeply but his continued need for discipline at the hotel afforded him the ability to maintain his composure.

"No sir I wasn't able to do that. I guess that leaves me no right to make suggestions here." He had his arm extended to hand the report to Fumer but dropped his arm to his side.

"Thanks anyway for your time," he said, then turned to leave.

Fumer dropped his eyes again. "Leave it on my desk. I'll take a look at it."

John handed it to him and waited until he read it through. When Fumer was finished he shoved the paper across his desk.

"It stinks. It just plain stinks and involves too much paper work. We didn't hire you to do accounting. We hired you to keep the shelves filled."

John couldn't control his feelings any longer. "It's better than the system we use now!" His voice was strong and filled with challenge. "In fact we haven't got a system!" He checked himself. It was an ugly confrontation and he was sure to come out on the short end. He started to apologize for losing his temper but Fumer didn't give him time.

He stood and looked John in the eye. "Look here, Broker," he whined authoritatively, "if you're not satisfied with the way things are run here you're free to leave any time!"

John wished it could be that simple. He would have to continue working there until he could find something else. The loss of just one week's pay would mean no money for rent and food and he could not let that happen.

"I understand. I'm sorry I lost control."

"We'll get along much better if you tend to your work and not concern yourself with my responsibilities."

John shook his head to acknowledge he would. Then went back to work.

After that incident he was determined to find another job. Until then he would have to tolerate things as they were. He knew he could never advance beyond the job he had as long as he stayed there. But somehow the prospects of finding other work seemed dimmer than ever. Many times before he had tried to think of a way to better himself and always was faced with the stark predicament that without a little capital his situation was hopeless.

He was greatly changed from the dashing and debonair man-about-town of his former years. He no longer had a fine wardrobe of clothes. Instead he wore clothes no longer in style and had become shabby. The boredom of doing work that was so unpleasant to him had contributed greatly to the change.

There was another problem that gave John cause to worry. It wasn't a big problem but it was something to annoy him. He had received a letter from his mother telling him that the Brown County Ursulines had purchased a piece of property at Oak and May Streets and planned to build an academy for girls there. She stated that Brenlyn might teach there. John felt it would be embarrassing for her to have a brother in the same city who was a stockroom employee. The Ursulines ran a rather prestigious school and John didn't like to think of her coming to Cincinnati.

But it wasn't just the possibility of Brenlyn's teaching in Cincinnati that caused John to make plans for moving to another city. He realized that living so close to Louisville was a handicap towards getting a hotel management position. He wondered where he might go. If only he had some extra money! He could make a trip to Detroit or Cleveland to see what the possibilities were. But he not only needed money for travel expenses, he needed funds for Michelle to live on. He felt it was almost impossible to better himself. He needed other things too. Clothes were something he would have to purchase in order to make an impression. The situation looked hopeless and the thought of continuing to work for Don Fumer was too horrible to think about.

He made up his mind. He would try to get into some other field of work and made a list of Cincinnati firms where he would apply. He headed the list with Proctor & Gamble Company. They manufactured soap, candles and glycerine, and employed nearly eight hundred and fifty people. Surely he would find work there. He added other names to the list: Rockwood Pottery, on top of Mount Adams; the Brighton Buggy Company, where thousands of carriages and wagons were made each year, and there were rumors that they were going into the new and exciting automobile business. He would try these places first. If he didn't meet with success, he would make another list. He was sure he would find employment somewhere.

******

John was dusting shelves as he thought about getting

away from the Hilliand. He would find a way to leave work for a couple of hours so that he could apply at the various industries during regular working hours. He heard someone at the stockroom counter and went to see if there was need for merchandise. Harry Clark, the jack-of-all-trades around the hotel, was there for his once a day visit.

"Hello, Harry. What are you tearing up today?" John asked jokingly. He liked for Harry to come around because he was better than a daily newspaper at spreading news. He knew all the hotel gossip and liked to be the first to spread it around to all the employees. It gave him a great feeling of importance.

Clark removed a pair of pliers from his hip pocket and used the blunt end of one of the handles as a back scratcher. He stretched an arm over an opposite shoulder and squinted in relief after reaching the itchy spot. After he finished, he rubbed his other shoulder in a nonchalant manner. "The old man has sold out," he said then glanced at John to see his reaction.

"Sold out?" John was surprised.

"Yep! Sold out to an Easterner. They say the new owner is loaded with money. Haven't heard his name but no doubt he's some kind of blueblood."

"Say, that is news!" John answered.

"The new manager is upstairs now." Clark was still acting unconcerned but looked at John again to see if this statement surprised him more.

"You mean --"

"Yep, ole' knothead Langley is on his way out and we're getting a brand new manager."

"You must be kidding?" John said in disbelief.

"Nope. He's leaving today."

"Today?"

John was anxious to hear more but the repairman excused himself saying he had some things to look after. John knew he had told everything he knew about the change in ownership and management and was on his way to tell other employees. He was having a field day.

The next day rumors were spreading around the hotel like wildfire. Some of the employees were saying there was to be a big layoff. Others said a cut in pay was imminent and there were also rumors that heavier work loads could be expected by all. John did not take any of the rumors seriously because he doubted the new manager would make any policy changes until he had time to learn what was going on around the hotel.

John did decide to forestall looking for other employment. He wanted to be around to see if any changes would be made. He wondered how Don Fumer would make out with his sidekick Langley no longer the hotel manager. He doubted the change would have any effect on his own problems but thought it unlikely things could get much worse.

It wasn't long until Fumer called John to his desk and it was apparent that the changes upset him. He was extremely nervous.

"I guess you've heard about the changes around here."

John told him he had.

"Well the new manager is making a tour of the hotel and will be coming down here this afternoon."

This pleased John. He was anxious to see what he was like.

"That's good," he replied without without thinking.

"What's good about it? This place is in a helluva' shape."

John wondered what he was talking about. The place was spotless and all the stock was put up. "It doesn't look too bad to me. I dusted the shelves and swept the floors."

"The shelves." Fumer pointed to them. "We need more stock. They're half empty."

"There's nothing else to put up," John answered. He

wished the steward had shown all this interest when Langley was manager.

"Well get over to one of the wholesale houses right away and have them rush a delivery." The steward walked through the aisles and checked the shelves. "We need more sugar, flour, corn syrup." He rattled off a dozen more items and John made a list of them. After he finished he asked Fumer about Mr. Langley.

"He's gone. Everything's in a mess. This new guy is a fanatic. Expects everything to be perfect. We have to get this stock in here right away."

"I doubt if we'll have time to get everything on the shelves."

"I'll help you get them stocked. Just get the stuff over here. If it's necessary hire a driver to bring it."

John had never seen the steward so nervous. He talked so fast he almost lost his twang.

John got the items delivered and he and Fumer worked feverishly to get them on the shelves. It was none too soon as the new manager walked in the stockroom escorted by the office manager.

He was tall, athletic looking, gray-haired, handsome and looked to be about forty-five.

Fumer greeted him, "Glad to see you, sir." He tried to hide his apprehension.

John wondered about the manager's name. He looked impressive to him. He thought it best to continue working and checked various items on the shelves to see if they were stacked neatly.

The manager began his tour of the stockroom and was closely followed by Fumer and the office manager. They came to the shelf area. "Looks like you have a sufficient number of items in stock," the manager said to Fumer approvingly.

"Yes sir," the steward replied. "We can't keep our dining room customers happy unless we're able to give them what they order." The statement had a familiar ring to John. He had made the remark to Fumer earlier.

The manager asked a number of questions. "What kind of a system do you use to maintain stock levels?"

"We use a minimum-maximum system," the steward replied. "We used to make inventories as time permitted but we changed over to the minimum-maximum system a few weeks ago and it works out much better." He explained the system in detail.

John laughed to himself. It was the same system he had made in writing and submitted to Fumer.

The manager seemed satisfied. He continued walking through the aisles and saw John.

"What's your name?" he asked.

"Broker, John Broker, sir."

"And what do you do here?"

John explained his duties. They were so simple he felt embarrassed.

"Been here long?"

"A little over four years, sir."

"The same job?"

"Yes sir."

"Well you ought to know your job pretty well."

John laughed. "There's not that much to it. You see --"

The manager interrupted. "I guess my escorts forgot to make an introduction. My name is Rodney Sinclair. No doubt you heard that I'm the new manager here."

John acknowledged he had, and extended his hand. "Certainly glad to meet you, sir."

Mr. Sinclair shook hands smiling. "Keep up the good work, Broker," he said then led his two escorts back to the kitchen area.

That evening John told Michelle about the day's events and explained about the manager. "He's a big man and handles himself well. No doubt he knows the hotel business from 'A' to 'Z'."

"Let's just hope he knows it well enough to recognize

your capabilities," Michelle said hopefully.

"You mean you're not satisfied with a husband who has done such an outstanding job of keeping shelves stocked with food?"

"Oh John, you know it's for your sake that I said that. You know you're capable of managing the biggest hotel in the country."

"Sure, like the way I managed the Rasineer."

"If I ever hear you say anything like that again, I'll never speak to you," she teased back.

They talked for a long time about the hotel. John said he would wait awhile before looking for another position. "But, I do plan to ask for an increase in pay," he said determinedly.

"And I bet you'll get it now that Mr. Langley is gone," she said.

"I hope you're right, Michelle."

When they retired for the night they both agreed there was more hope for better working conditions than they had ever dreamed of but John still felt he would soon be working in another type of business.

******

Five days later John was opening a box of canned goods when Fumer called him to his desk. "Mr. Sinclair wants to see you in his office." His voice was contemptuous.

"Wants to see me?" John wondered if the steward knew what Mr. Sinclair wanted to see him about.

"Yeah he's interviewing most of the employees. Don't get your hopes built up because he ain't looking for a stockroom clerk to take charge of anything."

John had had enough of Fumer's remarks. "Or a steward, either," he replied.

"Look here, Broker," Fumer shot back. "If I ever hear another crack like that out of you, your ass is fired. I mean, F-I-R-E-D!" He spelled it out in almost a shout.

John had to smile. Maybe that would be the best

thing, after all. Then he would have to find another job.
He left the stockroom and headed for the manager's
office. He felt good that he had shook up Fumer.

Mr. Sinclair beckoned for John to sit in a chair next to
his desk. He offered him a cigar but John refused it
saying he seldom smoked. Sinclair looked extremely
sharp. Confidence was evident in every move he made.

"I was just thinking as I waited for you to come to see
me that it's quite an honor to be working in the city
where the President of our Country, President Taft,
lives," Mr. Sinclair said jovially.

"Yes sir it is."

"They say he's the biggest man ever to run the
Country."

John agreed but really wasn't aware of it.

Mr. Sinclair chuckled. "Yes they say he weighs nearly
four hundred pounds."

John laughed. "I guess he is biggest then," he said,
feeling more relaxed.

"I guess he's doing a pretty good job up there," Mr.
Sinclair said terminating the subject of Taft. "I
understand you're from Louisville."

John was proud to acknowledge it. "Well I was born
and raised in Lexington, Kentucky, but moved to
Louisville when I was eighteen."

"Nice town. Lots of fine hotels. Ever been in the Galt
House?"

"Yes sir. I worked there as a desk clerk for several
years."

Mr. Sinclair appeared surprised. "You did?" he
asked, as if it were an honor to be employed there.

"Yes sir. I enjoyed working there. It was a wonderful
experience."

Mr. Sinclair made John feel so comfortable that he
momentarily forgot he was a stockroom employee.

"Tell me more about yourself," Mr. Sinclair added as
though he were anxious to know all about his past.

John was sure the manager used the same delightful method of making all employees feel at ease but he was glad for the opportunity to relate his experiences.

He told him about his father's operating the Zenith in Lexington. He skipped the experiences at Burnside and Ellen's ordeal. He talked briefly about meeting Michelle and their marriage; about his work at the Galt House; and, reluctantly, told about his opening of the Rasineer and its ultimate failure. He was glad when he finished and was anxious to hear Sinclair's remarks.

"And you've been a stock attendant ever since," Mr. Sinclair said as though he were finishing the story for him.

John lowered his head. "That's right, sir."

"Blackballed?"

John nodded his head in agreement.

Mr. Sinclair curled his lower lip over his upper in deep thought, then leaned back in his chair. "No doubt you would have made it all right if it hadn't been for the closing of the saloon."

"But it didn't work out that way. I not only lost the hotel. It seemed I lost every friend I had. I still can't realize it happened. It was all over so fast."

"You know John, there's a very strange thing about some of the people we call friends. They pat us on our backs and follow us around as long as we are standing firmly on solid ground. But, just let one good stumble come along, and there's a hard fall to the ground. They'll wait a little while. But, if they see the ground is soggy and you can't get to your feet you're not going to get much help. They'll leave you in a minute and you might even expect a few hard kicks before they leave."

John shook his head in agreement as Sinclair continued. "I know how it is with friends. I've been there."

"Yes, I've thought about that many times over the past few years," John said wondering why it had to be like that.

"I sincerely believe," Mr. Sinclair continued, "that the only real friends a man has are his parents, his wife and children, and sometimes his brothers and sisters. They're the only ones who will stick by him through thick or thin. You disgrace yourself or them. You go to prison. Commit a criminal act, go broke, get sick. They're the only ones who will share your problems and stick by you. No matter what."

"I don't know why it has to be that way," John said.

Sinclair smiled. "Well maybe it's not all that bad."

"It sometimes seems that way though," John replied.

"Yes you took a pretty hard punch and you did the best thing that could be done under the circumstances. You got away to get some peace of mind and to make a new start."

"Well it's nice of you to put it that way. "But I guess if I really had anything to offer I surely could have overcome my mistakes in Louisville." No sooner had he said this than he realized he was telling the new manager that he wasn't qualified to do better. "But, of course— "

Sinclair interrupted. "I'm going to be making some changes in the near future. Perhaps I can move you up to the desk as a room clerk. You have the kind of personality and the background needed there."

John closed his eyes in disbelief. For a moment he felt his lips tremble in appreciation. He bit his lips and fought back any signs of weakness. His eyes opened as he waited to hear more.

Mr. Sinclair turned in his swivel chair and pulled a ledger from a cabinet. Then he turned again towards John but his eyes remained downcast as he opened the book. He laid it on the desk top and ran his finger down a list of names and stopped when he came to "John Broker."

Mr. Sinclair noted the amount of John's weekly salary. He wrote it on a slip of paper and added twenty-five percent. This changed his salary from twelve dollars to fifteen dollars. He noted the salaries of the other clerks and saw that the new figure was comparable to theirs.

He handed the slip of paper to John. "How does this figure sound to you?"

John looked at it unbelievingly. "Fine sir, just fine. I don't know how to thank you."

Sinclair walked him to the door. "I want you to take a couple of days off and report for your desk job Monday. You'll be paid for the time off at your new rate."

John thanked him again. "Shall I go down and tell Mr. Fumer I won't be in?"

Mr. Sinclair told him he would take care of that.

"He'll need someone to take my place."

"No I'll talk to him about it. He can handle the stockroom by himself until I get a replacement." Mr. Sinclair excused himself saying that he had some things to look after.

John left the hotel and anxiously hurried home to tell Michelle the good news. The next day he bought a new suit of clothes, a pair of shoes, shirts, ties, and he felt like a new man.

It didn't take him long to adjust to his new position. After reporting for work in the early hours of a hot August morning the chief clerk took him in hand. He briefed him on the arrangement of racked keys, the numbering system, the neat pigeonholed cabinet on a back wall, the cost of various rooms and the accounting methods for receipts. Then he was taken on a tour of the hotel; through the corridors, into the dining room, parlors, ballrooms and many of the unoccupied guest rooms.

After being assigned to the desk for duty he was meticulously careful in his actions. He checked with fellow room clerks before assignment of rooms and double-checked rates before accepting payments.

Each day he became more efficient in handling the

desk position. A week after his new assignment he had acquired the confidence of his earlier years. He greeted guests cordially and handled their requests with poise and efficiency. Hotel hermits liked to talk to him as they loafed at the desk, fellow employees liked working with him, pretty girls still flirted, old ladies marveled at his flattery, businessmen appreciated his dexterity.

Six weeks after his desk assignment Mr. Sinclair called John to his office to review his work. He had only a few minor complaints, otherwise he was pleased with his performance. Then they talked. The manager explained about some major modifications that were going to be made at the hotel and the business outlook for future months. "Nineteen and ten should be a good year in Cincinnati. Automobile manufacturers are coming for a convention. Carriage and wagon manufacturers are planning a week-long conference to discuss what they might do about their dwindling business. The city is becoming a major center for machine and tool manufacturing and engineers and industrialists are filling railroad coaches as they travel to the city to purchase equipment."

Cincinnati was already a heavy trade center for soaps and candles, pottery, tobacco products, coal, lumber, pumps, valves, furniture, pianos and organs, and the T. G. Tapp Company at Twelfth and Main Streets was doing a brisk business in ladies' and gentlemen's wigs. They manufactured toupees, half-wigs and hair dyes and were prospering at the increasing demand for their products. The city had a bright economic outlook.

John asked Mr. Sinclair about the owner of the Hilliand. He learned that it was owned by a wealthy Pennsylvanian by the name of Chester S. Paulson. "He owns large holdings of real estate throughout the Eastern states. Office buildings and hotels are his specialty but he also owns vast acres of farmland in the New England countryside."

John was impressed. "I'm glad he bought the Hilliand."

"Yes,"Sinclair added, "he is buying up hotels in other areas and plans to consolidate them into a single corporation. A sort of chain enterprise."

"Sounds wonderful," John said and selfishly thought of the opportunities it might afford him.

Before leaving Sinclair's office John learned he was getting another increase in pay. "We're giving a blanket five percent increase to all the employees and of course that includes you."

John was delighted.

"Of course we expect a full day's work from everyone. If everyone gives his best the hotel's business will grow and this will mean advancements for those who deserve it."

"You can count on me."

"Glad to hear it," Sinclair said, then explained he had several other employees coming in for an interview.

******

By the fall of 1911 many of Sinclair's preditions had come true and the Hilliand had been enlarged. The original sections had been redecorated and new furniture installed. Telephones were placed in each room and most of the rooms were equipped with modern bathroom facilities. The hotel had superb accommodations.

The hotel became part of the new chain Sinclair had talked about and he had been made vice-president of the syndicate. Mr. Sinclair continued living in Cincinnati and had his headquarters in the Hilliand although he spent most of his time traveling to the other hotels.

A series of promotions had been made locally and John was moved from the desk appointment to the assistant manager's spot but with Mr. Sinclair's being away much of the time John was often left to run the hotel. Mr. Sinclair continued to keep a close watch on the

Hilliand's activities and instructed John not to make major decisions without first reviewing them with him. He had a tremendous respect for Mr. Sinclair and carefully looked after every detail to keep the hotel running as efficiently and smoothly as possible.

With their income greatly improved John and Michelle purchased a comfortable two-story frame house on Middleton Avenue in Clifton. They methodically budgeted their money and allotted payments on their debts in Louisville. John wanted to do this although he realized he was not legally responsible for the debts since they were included in the bankruptcy suit. He particularly wanted to repay the members of Michelle's family. He doubted he would be able to fully repay all of his debts but would do what he could.

In October, 1911, John celebrated his thirtieth birthday by giving a private party at the Hilliand. Most of Michelle's family came from Louisville to attend. Neil and Margaret were there. Some of their former neighbors on Ludlow as well as their new neighbors on Middleton came too. John invited some of the hotel employees. Mr. Sinclair was there and John invited Don Fumer and all the other supervisory employees.

The party was held in the lavish Loreli reception room which was of high German design. Red velvet curtains, lavish crystal chandeliers, dark walnut chairs and tables, Brissel carpeting, large polished mirrors with heavy gold frames, and colorful earthenware beer steins. A huge painting of Kaiser Wilhelm in full military dress hung majestically above a white marble fireplace giving the room an added German setting.

John explained to the Connellys that he thought they might enjoy the German atmosphere and taste of their savory dishes. They were grateful for the opportunity.

The party began with a buffet of crisp garden salads, cordon bleu, beef roulade, weinerschnitzel, sauerbraten, potato pancakes, dumplings, dishes of savory green vegetables, liederkranz cheese, pumpernickel and Vienna rolls. For drinks there was a choice of Bavarian beer, schnapps and kirchwasser. For those who had room for dessert there were trays of strudels and Black Forest cherry tarts.

After they finished eating the men patted their stomachs, loosened their belts, laughed and joked and felt the stimulating effect of the drinks. The ladies had eaten more sparingly, cautiously sipped their drinks, and were much more comfortable as they sat in amusement at the sight of the men. There was an atmosphere of frivolity and relaxation everywhere.

Mr. Sinclair stood up and asked for everyone's attention. He apologized for interrupting and explained how much he would enjoy remaining at the party but that he had to leave early to catch an evening train to Baltimore. He expressed his delight in meeting the members of John and Michelle's family and asked them to come back to the Hilliand often. He joked about the Connellys' having to dine on a German bill of fare and said he hoped St. Patrick wouldn't disown them. He spoke highly of the Ludlow and Middleton Avenue guests who were there and remarked how he enjoyed seeing the employees doing something besides working around the hotel.

Then he directed his remarks to John. He wished him a happy birthday then told him how much he enjoyed working with him and thanked him for his cooperation in helping oversee the hotel's operation. He pulled a small box from his coat pocket and asked John to stand beside him.

He addressed the guests again. "I don't know how many of you are aware of the fact that the new owner of the hotel, Mr. Paulson, has bought a number of hotels in other cities and plans to operate them as a single enterprise. I am extremely flattered that he has appointed me as President of the corporation and only hope I can live up to his expectations of running the organization. But I'm not here to talk about myself and only mentioned my appointment as a prelude to another announcement I think will please you all."

He held the package up for everyone to see. "Mr. Paulson has traditionally presented a diamond stick pin to the managers of any of his organizations and it is my pleasure tonight to act in his behalf in announcing that John Broker is now the manager of the Hilliand and to present him with this token that goes with it."

He smiled and handed the package to John then congratulated him with a warm handshake.

John was greatly surprised. He looked at Mr. Sinclair. "I hardly know how to tell you how much I appreciate this. Tears gathered in his eyes.

"Well don't tell me then," Mr. Sinclair said goodnaturedly. Just open the package instead."

John slipped the ribbon off and carefully removed the wrapping from the small black velvet container. He raised the hinged lid and saw the pin. The stone sparkled under the bright lights and he shook his head in disbelief. Tim Connelly called out for him to hold it up for all to see.

John raised it higher and turned the box at different angles so everyone could see the contents. He gestured to Michelle knowing how happy she would be about the promotion.

Mr. Sinclair took the box and removed the pin then carefully slipped it on John's tie. Everyone applauded and Marty began singing, "For he's a jolly good fellow," and everyone joined in the singing.

When they finished John again shook his head in disbelief. Tim called out to him, "Tell us how it feels to be made manager of the best hotel in Ohio!"

"Yeah, tell us," others shouted.

The party quieted as he spoke. He expressed his gratitude to Mr. Sinclair and thanked the employees for their good work which he said had to be a contributing factor in his promotion. Then he expressed his gratitude to Mr. Paulson and asked Mr. Sinclair to tell him how much he appreciated the pin and his approval for the management position.

Each took their turn congratulating John on his promotion. Don Fumer was having difficulty maintaining his balance as he spoke to John.

"You know what, Broker?" he said too accustomed to calling him by his last name and too drunk to realize it was out of place now. "I never dreamed you would ever — " He lost his train of thought for a moment and his head shook back and forth, uncontrolled. John knew Fumer was too drunk to be interesting and he didn't like to be tied down and have to listen to him but waited to let him finish. Fumer remembered what he wanted to say.

"No sir, Broker. I never dreamed you would ever be manager of this hotel.

"I'm sure you didn't," John said assuredly.

"I didn't treat you very good down in the stockroom did I?" he added in a thick tongue.

"It was all knothead Langley's fault. He didn't --''

"Sure, sure I understand," John said excusing himself. "I have to get back with the others."

"I know you do," Fumer said, then he held his finger up and moved it in uncontrolled jerks. "Bu—bu'—bu'—but," he stammered. His finger was only a few inches from John's nose. But, he repeated, "I bet I know one of the first things you'll do now that you are the man'--man'--er uh--manager." His head was bobbling more than ever.

John wondered what he was leading up to. "What's the first thing I'll do?" he asked to appease him.

"Quit sa'—ser'—serving turtle soup!"

John had to laugh although there was some truth in what he said. Wanting to get back with the other guests, John concluded the discussion. "I'll see you later,

Don."

"It's—Mr. Don—and don' you ever forget it!" Fumer was too drunk to know what he was saying. His legs suddenly buckled and he slumped to the floor. John summoned one of the waiters to look after him. Soon he had another waiter escort Fumer from the room.

The party lasted until after midnight and everyone enjoyed the evening. The Connellys were overwhelmed at the hospitality and all signs of ill-feeling toward John were gone. Neil and Margaret had a wonderful time too. They all stayed overnight at the Hilliand and expressed their appreciation to John and Michelle before retiring.

After John and Michelle went home they were discussing the new appointment.

"If Mr. Sinclair hadn't been sent here to be manager I might not have gotten the opportunity to get the promotion," John said. "I might have been a stockroom employee for the rest of my life."

Michelle looked up at him. "Yes, but you know who sent Mr. Sinclair here, don't you?"

"Sure. Mr. Paulson, of course."

"Maybe so and maybe not."

"Who else then?" John asked curiously.

Michelle walked over towards a wall shelf and pointed to a statue. "I give her most of the credit." Before John could question this she continued. "If you only knew how often I prayed to St. Anne that you would someday get the opportunity to make good at the hotel, you would know she was the one who brought him here."

John was skeptical. "It must be wonderful to have all that faith but I still have to give the credit to Mr. Paulson."

Not wanting to be outdone Michelle answered cleverly. "St. Anne has directed more important men than Mr. Paulson. I'm sure she helped him make the decision."

"Maybe you're right but shouldn't I get a little credit

for the success of John Broker?'' John wanted to change the subject and used this for diversion.

Michelle laughed. ''Of course. In fact I feel sure that if you weren't such a handsome and clever individual St. Anne would not have done this for us at all.''

John held her in his arms. And you know what?'' he asked. ''I wouldn't trade all of the hotels in the world for you.''

Michelle placed her arms around his waist. ''You might make a good hotelman but I can see you would make a mighty poor trader.''

They both laughed and decided it was time to retire.

******

During the first three years following John's appointment as manager of the Hilliand a great many changes had taken place in Cincinnati and many outlying farms and villages were annexed and made part of the city. Hyde Park, Evanston, Bond Hill, Winton Place, Cumminsville, Fernbank, Hartwell and Pleasant Ridge were included in the Queen City's boundaries.

New factories and commercial establishments sprang up along the river front and the business district surrounding the Hilliand was an ever-changing scene. Cobblestone streets were replaced with smooth asphalt to eliminate the bouncy jolts in automobiles and carriages and an extensive trolley car system provided efficient transportation from outlying areas to the business district. The Cincinnati Reds built a modern two-tiered stadium between Walnut Hills and Liberty Streets. New office buildings and hotels sprang up along the business district and towering structures like the twelve-story Ingall's building and the Gwinn office building brought on a new look to the city's skyline.

But Cincinnati had its disappointments too. Woodrow Wilson defeated President Taft and the city no longer had a native son in the White House. A major strike was staged by streetcar company employees and this crippled the transportation system. Then to add to the city's woes politics were said to be corrupted by powerful organizations and many citizens demanded a complete investigation. The city was also badly in need of one central railroad station to consolidate the seven stations that were spread out at inconvenient locations.

Cincinnati survived its set-backs and the city progressed as one of the major metropolitan areas in the country. John Broker shared in the growth and prospered as one of the city's outstanding citizens.

******

On a cold February morning in 1914 John received word that his mother had died. He and Michelle boarded a train for Lexington. They stayed with Margaret and Neil in their colonial mansion where Mrs. Broker was laid out in a large reception hall. An air of sadness prevailed as many visitors came to pay their last respects.

John was annoyed that Brenlyn had not come to the wake. "Surely she will be here for the funeral?" he asked Margaret.

"No John, the Ursulines' rules will not permit the nuns to enter a home."

"Are you saying she won't be here at all?"

"She would be here if she could." Margaret wanted him to understand.

Not wanting to see an unpleasant confrontation Michelle came up with a suggestion. "Maybe we can all go up and visit her at the convent after the funeral?"

Neil explained that he didn't think Margaret should go at this time. "She hasn't been feeling well, and I'm afraid the long ride in this cold weather would not do her any good. Maybe we can all go in the spring."

"Yes I guess you're right," John said. "It would be a cold ride for the girls. I'll make arrangements to go there as soon as I get back to Cincinnati."

"Do you want me to go with you?" Neil asked.

"No that won't be necessary. Like you said, maybe we can all go together when the weather breaks."

Margaret expressed her appreciation to John for planning to visit Brenlyn. "I know how sad she must be and she'll be so relieved to have someone in the family to talk to. I wrote and told her the details of Mother's death and will write again telling her we will soon visit her.

After the funeral John and Michelle spent another night with Margaret and Neil. They talked about many things and discussed the disposition of their mother's estate. All agreed it should be donated to various charities in her memory.

During their discussions Margaret insisted that Michelle should have many of the fine linens, china, silverware, furniture and other articles that belonged to her mother. Michelle expressed her appreciation but accepted only a few of the items saying she felt the rest should belong to Margaret.

As John and Michelle traveled back to Cincinnati they looked out the train window and saw a flurry of snowflakes change into a great snowstorm. They marveled at the change in scenery. Everything on the surface had turned white. Rooftops, tree limbs, fence rails, pastures and farmlands. It was like a Winter Wonderland.

When they arrived in Cincinnati they saw the snow was much deeper and the city was temporarily crippled by the storm. Transportation was almost at a standstill and trolley cars were stalled in their tracks on the hilly streets. Some of the rough shod horses managed to pull wagons up the less inclined streets but a number of them had slipped and fallen to the ground and were rescued after their owners relayed the cry of, "Horse Down!" to nearby pedestrians.

John was delayed several days before the snow melted and he could travel on to St. Martin. He made arrangements to take a carriage destined for Hillsboro

and Chillicothe and to get off at the Fayetteville stop
which was only five miles from the convent. He had been
told that he could make arrangements at a country store
for transportation to the Inn at St. Martin where he could
be lodged.

The coachman provided each of the passengers with
heavy wool blankets to cover their laps to ward off the
cold. The four-horse team broke into a swinging trot as
they began their journey and traveled along Eastern
Avenue toward Milford. When they reached open
country at Woodlawn the driver gave the horses their
reins and quickened their pace. They made a quick stop
at Milford to take on another passenger. An enterprising
vendor came to the carriage and asked if anyone wanted
a hot "Tom and Jerry, or a steaming cup of tea" to warm
their bodies. John bought one and tastefully sipped the
drink and felt the hot fluid warming his insides.

John and his fellow passengers didn't want for
conversation for the rest of the trip. The new passenger
was a dedicated pessimist and added gloom to the
lackluster journey as he discussed his philosophy to the
captive audience.

He began his discourse by saying that Cincinnati's
political boss, Gerald Mead, was leading the city into a
calamity that would result in complete destruction of
everything. He was dead sure that everyone would have
to move out of Cincinnati and all the buildings and
streets would be deserted.

To make matters worse he continually gestured with
his hands as he talked. Pointing a finger in the air he
continued to forewarn the passengers. "Don't you know
that Cincinnati's water works cost more than three times
as much as Cleveland's water plant? And it ain't half as
good or half as big as Cleveland's and I can prove that
down to the last penny!"

He didn't wait for an acknowledgement. "And that
assistant of his, Randy Hicks, do you know he keeps a

card file on all of Cincinnati's voters, and 'woe-be-tied' if anyone has been listed as an enemy of Mead.'' Then with great emphasis he added, ''That Mead machine would ruin him! And I do mean -- completely ruin him!''

The tirade on Mead and Hicks ended and then the man started in on President Wilson. ''That man ought to be impeached. Why he's leading this country into a war that will destroy this country.'' He repeated his favorite phrase as he continued. ''Don't you know,'' his finger was fanning the cold air again, ''That those Germans have a mustard gas that will kill their enemies in less than a minute?''

He looked at each of the passengers individually as he continued. ''And that means you, and you, and you, and you.'' Then he pointed to himself as he added, ''And me, too!''

John was glad he included himself and was sure the man would go down talking. He didn't give his listeners time to meditate over the gassing. ''And I want you to know something else. This new law that was just passed. You know the one that will allow only one saloon for every five hundred citizens. Well it ain't worth a hoot! Why more than seven hundred saloons have been closed up already! And what good does that do? It just gives more business to the ones that stays open.''

John tried to change the subject by pointing out a picturesque cluster of icicles hanging from a low jagged cliff. But the man didn't hear him. He continued his tirade never giving his finger a rest. ''If they keep on closing the saloons down do you know the next thing that's going to happen? They'll pass a law making it illegal to sell a man a drink. That's what'll happen next but I can tell you it won't work. If a man wants a drink bad enough he'll get it somewhere law or no law. He'll buy it from some bootlegger.''

The man was still talking when the carriage made its Fayetteville stop. When John stepped down to the roadway he felt relieved to escape the continued chatter. There was a cold wind blowing and he headed for the country store that he had been told about earlier. It looked deserted but he hurried there hoping to get relief from the weather. He was glad the door was unlocked and stepping inside he saw a tall, skinny, raw-boned clerk standing behind a counter. A coal oil lantern cast flickering shadows on a disarrayed assortment of merchandise surrounding him.

Seeing John, the man squinted over his horn-rimmed glasses hanging half way down his nose. Then he pulled a corn cob pipe from his mouth.

"Well," he said in a cheerful voice, "what brings you out on such a cold and gloomy evening?"

John had moved close to a pot bellied stove to warm himself. "I'm on my way to the convent at St. Martin's and need transportation to the Brown County Inn where I plan to stay overnight. I was wondering if you could help me out?"

"Won't do you no good to go to the convent," the clerk said with a troubled look on his face.

"Is something wrong there?" John asked wondering if he had made the trip in vain.

"Ain't nothin' wrong at the convent but there's something wrong with you."

"Me?" John asked solicitiously.

"Yeah! You see they only let women folks become nuns!"

The clerk smiled and cocked an eye as he looked at John to see if he recognized the humor.

John had all he could take for the day -- the cynic in the carriage and now this. He shook his head in dismay.

Seeing that John had not found humor in his clowning, the clerk apoligized. "Didn't mean no harm. Jest wanted to have a little fun."

John smiled, letting him know he understood.

"I kin get you a ride in an open chuck wagon in about

an hour. A feller's gonna deliver a stove to a farmhouse right across the street from the Inn. Or if'n you like I can put you up here fer the night and you can catch a ride in the mornin'. It won't be as cold then.''

The thought of staying at the store wasn't very appealing but neither was the prospect of riding the five miles in an open wagon. Knowing it was not likely to be much warmer in the morning he decided it best to make the trip that evening.

"I appreciate your offer but I think it best I go on tonight.''

"Suit yourself,'' the clerk said. "I kin loan you a horse blanket to wrap up in.''

The cold wind whistled around the wagon and John wondered if he would freeze. The driver had his head and body covered with blankets and he gripped the reins with hands protected by heavy woolen gloves. The big draft horse pulled the wagon along in a slow trot and there were white vapors spurting from his nostrils. Now and then he snorted objecting to the cold. John was glad Michelle had not come with him and thought she would have frozen for sure.

Fortunate for John too the driver was as chilled as he was and made several stops at farmhouses along the way. Fortunately also the farmers offered them drinks of corn whiskey to warm their bodies.

A little after eight the driver nudged John and pointed to a spiraling steeple that stood out under a frosty sky. "That's the convent," he said and John was relieved to know that their bone-chilling trip was almost over.

As the driver drove the horse along a winding driveway leading to the Inn John wondered if he would be able to walk. His toes felt numb and any bit of movement made him rack with pain.

Moving cautiously he managed to get down from the carriage and walk up the front steps leading to the Inn. He rapped the door knocker and a middle-aged lady with graying hair opened the door and graciously ushered him inside. John explained that he wanted to stay there overnight so he might visit his sister at the convent the next day. The landlady acknowledged she had a vacancy and led him to a big fireplace where several burning logs flickered hot flames and radiated their heat in the room.

After asking him to be seated in a big leather chair facing the fire she went to the kitchen and brought in a pan of warm water and put it on the floor for him to warm his feet. Then she brought him a cup of hot tea. With all this attention John felt much better and expressed his gratitude for the service.

He was assigned to a room on the second floor and after freshening up crawled in bed and pulled a layer of blankets and an eider down comfort over his body. He closed his eyes and felt happy that he was near the convent and would soon be seeing Brenlyn again. He fell asleep and never slept more soundly in his life.

The next morning he joined the other guests at a long table covered with a heavy linen cloth and enjoyed a hearty breakfast of fresh orange juice, cooked oats smothered in cream, thick slices of fried country ham, scrambled eggs, hot biscuits, marmalade and hot tea. Afterwards he dressed warmly and followed a tree-lined path marked ''Solomon's Run'' and walked to the convent.

The Innkeeper sent word that John was on his way and a young postulant opened the door as he walked up on the convent porch. She smiled prettily. ''You came to see Sister Jude?''

''Yes, sister,'' John answered politely. ''I'm her brother, John Broker.''

She led him to a well furnished parlor and asked him to be seated. ''I'll tell her you're here,'' she said in a cheerful voice.

As John waited in the visiting room he almost forgot the main reason for his being there was to console

Brenlyn about the details of their mother's death. He thought about her when she was home and remembered her beauty and popularity in Lexington. He had never been able to understand why she had become a nun and it made him feel sad to think about it now. He wondered how she could ever be happy in such remote and quiet surroundings.

He thought about Ellen Boone and felt remorseful that he had sent her to such a lonely place. He wondered where she was now and if she were happy. He couldn't bear to think how neglectful he had been. That seemed so long ago. "Maybe there is some way that Michelle and I can help her now," he thought to himself. "I'll ask Brenlyn where she is and get Michelle to write her and see if she is in need of anything."

His thoughts were quickly interrupted as Brenlyn walked into the room. John immediately stood. Brenlyn was beaming with delight. "Oh, John," she said happily. "It's so good to see you."

John wanted to hug her. The black and white habit she wore made him hesitate. He was filled with joy at seeing her. "I just have to kiss you," he said beaming. He held her hands and reached over and kissed her soft cheek.

She blushed. "I thought you would never come to see me," she said still smiling.

"Let me look at you," he replied. "Your smile is as pretty as ever." He didn't like to see her in the habit with only her face showing. He remembered her golden hair and beautiful neckline. It angered him to see her dressed this way but he knew he must hide his feelings.

"How have you been?" she asked. "And your wife, Michelle, and the children? I wish you would have brought them along. But I guess with the weather like it is, it's best they didn't come."

John assured her they were well and happy and agreed about the weather.

She asked him to be seated and she turned a chair to

the side so they sat facing each other. After exchanging pleasantries John told of the events leading to their mother's death and the details of the funeral. Brenlyn had a pained look on her face as she listened intently. She fought to hold back the tears and John was deeply moved. He knew how close the two had been and how much she would miss her mothers visits. He hardly knew what to say. "Why don't you have a good cry, Brenlyn. It will make it easier."

He removed a handkerchief from his pocket and handed it to her. She wiped her eyes and bit her lips. Then quickly composed herself. She changed the subject. "Tell me about your family and about yourself. Margaret told me about the nice position you have." She was smiling again.

John explained about everything except the unpleasant period when he worked in the stockroom. He realized their mother had probably told Brenlyn about it so there was no need to mention it further.

"I heard you were supposed to come to a school in Cincinnati to teach and I was looking forward to visiting you there.

"There was a change in plans but I might possibly be sent there for a conference next Summer."

John was glad to hear this and told her to be sure to let him know so he could bring Michelle and the children to see her. They talked about other things. John learned that she taught music to the high school students attending the school. During the summer months she was overseer of the convent farm. She laughed as she told about the herd of dairy cattle they had and the many crops that were grown.

There was little doubt in John's mind that Brenlyn was happy. Her every expression radiated this and she told him she wouldn't change her life for anything in the world.

"You haven't asked about Ellen," she said as though

she wished he had.

"No. I haven't," John replied apologetically. "But I certainly want to hear about her."

Brenlyn told him how well she had done in school and about her other accomplishments. Then she told him about her being adopted by the family of one of her classmates.

"Then she's happy?"

"Very, very happy. In fact she is married to a wonderful man. He's quite wealthy too."

"That's wonderful," John said relieved to know that she was all right. "I'm glad things have worked out so well for her. By the way," he added, "what does her husband do?"

"He's involved in real estate. Mostly business property. Incidentally he owns several hotels. I thought you might be interested in that."

John was mildly interested. Hotel owners were not unique. There were hundreds of them. "What's his name?" he asked casually.

"Chester Paulson." Brenlyn seemed proud to announce his name. She was grateful he was so good to Ellen.

"Chester Paulson?" John questioned the name as he recalled his memory of it. His face took on a stunned expression.

Brenlyn noticed the change. "Is something wrong?" she asked.

John was deep in thought. "It couldn't be," he said in almost a whisper.

"What is it, John?" she asked.

He looked at her with a questioning expression. "A Chester Paulson owns the Hilliand Hotel."

"Owns the hotel you manage?"

John nodded his head. "Surely it can't be the same man?" he replied as if he were asking himself the question.

"Is he tall and rather handsome?" Brenlyn asked anxiously.

"I have never seen the man. He's never been to the hotel."

Brenlyn thought deeply trying to recall something significant. "I remember getting a card from Ellen and Mr. Paulson at Christmas time. It was personalized. It had a picture of the New York Harbor and a lonely sailor standing guard on a ship and looking at the city's skyline and the Christmas decorations there. I remember Ellen's saying they had several hundred printed. Do you remember getting one like that?"

John shook his head. "I'm afraid not. I never look at Christmas cards."

"Don't you remember ever hearing anything about him?"

"I have never given him much thought. Mr. Sinclair is the only one I know who has ever met him and he has seldom mentioned him."

Who is Mr. Sinclair?" Brenlyn asked.

"He's the former manager of the Hilliand who promoted me. He's president ot the entire hotel chain now."

John and Brenlyn continued trying to find something significant that might reveal whether or not Ellen's husband owned the Hilliand but it was evident that they couldn't think of anything.

"Did you know anything about this before today?" John asked suspiciously.

Brenlyn assured him that she didn't.

"Do you think its possible he does own the Hilliand and maneuvered things so they would turn out the way they have for me?"

"I would have no way of knowing that."

"Do you ever remember telling her about my being a stock clerk at the hotel?"

"I'm sure I mentioned it. She was always asking about

you.''

It was maddening to John but he thought it useless to discuss it any further. He knew he must forget about it for the time being. He didn't want to spoil the reunion. He changed the subject.

He and Brenlyn reminisced about their youthful days in Lexington and laughed as they recalled amusing things that had taken place. They recalled memories of their neighbors and friends and there were many remembrances of individuals who were so much a part of their lives at that time.

Then John led up to a question about Brenlyn's life at the convent and asked if she ever regretted giving up her worldly life.

"No," she replied smiling. "I'm very happy here. I have never wanted to change my life in any way."

"Well if you ever do want to change it you know you will always be welcome in our home. We've got plenty of room and we would love to have you."

"That's awfully kind of you but I couldn't be happier." She looked at her watch. "The bell for vespers will be ringing before long."

"And what does that mean?"

"It will soon be time for one of our community prayer services in the chapel."

"You'll have to attend?"

"Yes, and then I will be busy with other assignments until after lunch. I'll arrange for one of the farm hands to drive you back to the Inn but I want you to come back this afternoon for a visit."

John explained that he had to catch the afternoon stage to Cincinnati. "But I promise you that Michelle and I will visit you very soon."

Brenlyn was disappointed but she knew he was anxious to get back home. "I want you to see our chapel before you leave. We'll have to hurry to get there before vespers."

As they walked through the hallway leading to the chapel they met other nuns. Brenlyn proudly introduced John to each one. Then inside the chapel, they knelt side by side in a pew near the main altar. The winter sky had brightened and a stained glass window over the altar was brilliantly colored.

It was peaceful and quiet and John felt more reverent than he had for a long time. He said a few prayers then meditated. For a moment he thought he might have been happy living a peaceful life in a monastery somewhere. Then he thought of Michelle and his work at the Hilliand and knew he would never be happy without either one.

Brenlyn walked him to the door. They exchanged farewells. John wanted to kiss her goodbye but knew it wouldn't be proper at the doorway. He held her hand. "I'm so proud of you," he said, "We all love you so much."

She thanked him just as the bell rang again. He stepped outside and looked at her. Her eyes were filled with tears, but she radiated happiness. He squeezed her hand. "Pray for me," he said.

"You bet," she said happily, "and you give Michelle and the children my love."

He let her go and walked down and got into the waiting carriage.

******

The stage pulled into Fountain Square late that afternoon and John stopped by the Hilliand to see if everything was all right. Afterwards he hired a taxi driver to take him home.

Michelle met him at the door after hearing the engine rumbling in the driveway. After a warm embrace John pulled off his gloves, removed his hat and overcoat and he and Michelle walked over near the parlor fireplace.

John tossed a fresh log into the fire and kindled the ashes with a poker. Then they sat down and he told her about the trip. He explained about Ellen's being married to a man named Chester Paulson and they tried to think of something that might enlighten them as to whether he might be the same person who owned the Hilliand. They talked about it for a long time but there was no immediate way to resolve it.

"Someday we'll know," Michelle said.

"It's a funny thing," John replied, "but I'm not sure I ever want to know."

"St. Anne sometimes works things out in mighty strange ways," Michelle said with an enlightening smile.

Unmindfully, John ran his fingers through the long strands of his wavy hair. "It's been a long day and there are just too many loose ends to try to put together tonight." He placed a screen in front of the fireplace. "Let's get some sleep and maybe things will seem more clear tomorrow."

Michelle walked to the foot of the stairway and waited until he switched off the lights. Then they went up the stairs to their room.